Praise for the works of

LINDA LAEL MILLER

"Strong characterization and a vivid western setting make for a fine historical romance."
—*Publishers Weekly* on *McKettrick's Choice*

"Miller's name is synonymous with the finest in western romance. From the hard realities of life in an untamed land to the passionate people who bring the colorful history to life, she brings the best of the West to readers, never failing to deliver a great read!"
—*Romantic Times BOOKclub* on *McKettrick's Choice*

"Intrigue, danger, and greed are up against integrity, kindness, and love in this engrossing western romance. Miller has created unforgettable characters and woven a many-faceted yet coherent and lovingly told tale."
—*Booklist,* starred review of *McKettrick's Choice*

"Miller's prose is smart, and her tough Eastwoodian cowboy cuts a sharp, unexpectedly funny figure in a classroom full of rambunctious frontier kids."
—*Publishers Weekly* on *The Man from Stone Creek*

LINDA LAEL MILLER

DEADLY GAMBLE

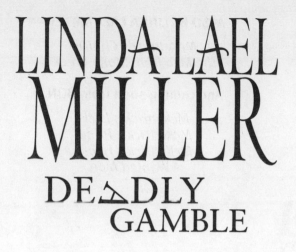

HQN™

HQN™

ISBN-13: 978-0-373-77141-7
ISBN-10:   0-373-77141-X

DEADLY GAMBLE

www.HQNBooks.com

Printed in U.S.A.

My Dear Friends,

I am delighted to bring you the first book in my brand-new romantic suspense series starring accidental detective Mojo Sheepshanks, her dead ex-husband, Nick, a ghost cat, a hunky undercover cop named Tucker Darroch and Mojo's foster sisters, Jolie and Greer. Of all the characters I've created, Mojo is one of my very favorites. She's funny, brave, inventive and smart.

In December of 2006 I hope you'll look for *Sierra's Homecoming,* a Silhouette Special Edition novel. Sierra is a long-lost member of the modern McKettrick family, a direct descendant of Holt and Lorelei from *McKettrick's Choice.* Like *Deadly Gamble,* the story has a paranormal element: Sierra discovers that she's sharing the family house with one of her ancestors, a woman who lived and loved in 1919.

Early in 2007 HQN will release three new contemporary stories: *McKettrick's Luck, McKettrick's Pride* and *McKettrick's Heart.* In these books you'll meet Jesse and Cheyenne, Rance and Echo, and Keegan and Molly, respectively. They're fun, sexy books, and those of you who read the historical series—*High Country Bride, Shotgun Bride* and *Secondhand Bride*—will see certain parallels between Jeb and Chloe, Rafe and Emmeline, and Kade and Mandy.

The Man from Stone Creek, my most recent historical romance, a June 2006 release, is available in hardcover from HQN. Sam O'Ballivan, an Arizona Ranger posing as a schoolmaster, strikes sparks with Maddie Chancelor, an independent and modern woman of 1903. These are two stubborn people, determined *not* to fall in love. (We'll just see about that!)

Thank you for joining me on the most wonderful journey of all—into the pages of a book.

For Joan Marlow Golan
with love, admiration and appreciation.
Thanks

DEADLY
GAMBLE

CHAPTER

1

Cave Creek, Arizona

At first, the chill was a drowsy nibble at the distant and ragged edges of my awareness, raising goose-bumps on the parts of my flesh bared to that spring night. The sensation was vaguely disturbing, but not troublesome enough to stir me from the fitful shallows of sleep. I remember rolling onto my side, pulling the comforter up to my right earlobe and murmuring some insensible protest.

That was when I heard Nick's voice. Or *thought* I heard it.

Impossible, I told myself, nestling groggily into my polyester burrow. He's *dead.*

Just then, a hand came to rest on my hip, and the chill sprouted teeth and bit right through cotton nightshirt, skin and tissue to seize the marrow of my bones.

I choked out a hoarse cry, too raw and guttural to qual-

ify as a scream, and shimmied off the mattress to land hard
on both feet. In the space of an instant, my senses shifted
from dial-up to broadband, and I pressed one hand to
my chest, in case my heart tried to flail its way out of my
chest. My brains pulsed, Cuisinart-style, then scrambled. I
couldn't seem to drag a breath past my esophagus, though
my lungs clawed for air like a pair of miners trapped beneath
tons of rubble.

I felt that way once on a stair-climber at the gym after
sucking in a pack and a half of nicotine in a bar the night
before, and subsequently swore off exercise forever. Hell,
somebody has to serve as the bad example.

But I digress. Get used to it.

My eyes must have bugged out, cartoonlike. Nick—
Nick—lay on top of the covers, dressed in his snappy gray
burial suit, with his hands cupping the back of his head. Except for a peculiar greenish glimmer emanating from his
skin, he looked pretty much the way he had before he collided with a semi on the 101 North and was thrown through
the windshield of his BMW. Along with Tiffany, Nick's lover
du jour, who was scarred for life and for some insane reason
blamed *me* for her Frankenstein face and deflated implants.

One of the many things I don't like about dead people is
that a lot of them glow in the dark. Not that I'd seen any
before my late ex-husband turned up that momentous night,
a full two years after his funeral. *Since* then, unfortunately,
I've become something of an authority.

"Hey," Nick said companionably, as though the situation

were entirely normal, and not something out of an old segment of *Unsolved Mysteries*.

My stomach quivered. Like my heart, it was threatening to leap out of my throat and make a run for it.

"You're dead," I pointed out—quite reasonably, I thought, given the circumstances. *I* knew he'd croaked, but I wasn't sure he'd been notified. He looked so calm and matter-of-fact, as though turning up in his ex-wife's bed in the middle of the night was a perfectly ordinary thing to do.

Nick sighed, slipped his hands from behind his head and hoisted himself as far as his elbows. "Sort of," he admitted, with a rueful note.

I managed a step backward, ready to hot-foot it out of there, jerk open the outside door, and dash down the fire-escape style stairway to Bad-Ass Bert's Biker Saloon. Normally, I didn't seek out the company of Bert's clientele, especially when I was naked except for a slip of cotton jersey that barely covered my thighs, but given the situation, I was game for just about anything. Trouble was, once I'd retreated half a stride, I couldn't seem to move again.

"How can you be 'sort of' dead?" I asked.

"It's complicated," Nick replied. "In some ways, I'm more alive than you are." With that, he swung his legs over the side of the mattress and stood up, turning to face me across the expanse of tangled bedding. The glow surrounding his lean frame flickered a little, as if somebody had turned a celestial dimmer switch.

"Relax," he said. "It's okay."

Sure. No problem. Pay no attention to the walking, talking corpse.

"You're *dead,*" I repeated stubbornly.

"Yeah," he agreed wryly. "I've noticed. So maybe we could get past that?"

"Don't come near me," I ordered. Pure bravado, of course. I'd read *The Damn Fool's Guide to Self-Defense for Women* and practiced all the moves on Bert, who was a genuine bad-ass, but if there was a chapter on phosphorescent assailants, I must have missed it.

Nick tilted his dark head to one side and looked pathetic, though still damnably handsome. Apparently, being deceased was neither messy nor strenuous; his suit was wrinkle-free, if slightly out of fashion, his hair sleek, and there was no sign of his hallmark five o'clock shadow. No tire marks, either, thank God, and no blood, guts or jutting bone fragments.

He must have read my mind. With a sad grin, he looked down at himself, before meeting my gaze again. "Hell of a patch job, though. You should have seen me before the mortician did his thing." He shuddered. "You haven't lived—so to speak—until you've seen yourself lying in pieces on a slab. Definitely not a pretty sight."

I winced. "Thanks for sharing," I said. At least we were on the same page with the dead-thing. I had a lot of questions, naturally, but I couldn't seem to articulate any of them. Shock does that to a person.

Another fetching grin. "You cried at my funeral," he reminded me, with pleased modesty.

I stiffened. My heartbeat had slowed somewhat, and I was

managing a full breath every few seconds, but my knees felt about as substantial as foam on a mug of draft beer. When the last few bubbles popped, I'd be on the floor in a quivering heap.

"So what?" I asked. "We were married once. You were only thirty-two, and you didn't deserve to die like that, even if you *were* an asshole. Too bad about Tiffany, too. Did you know her boobs popped and she had to have three surgeries just to look human?"

He ignored the reference to girlfriend #62. At least she was *post*-divorce; the first thirty-seven could probably be slotted neatly between "I do" and "Go-to-hell-you-bastard-I'm-taking-back-my-maiden-name."

"Black isn't your color," he observed gently, starting around the end of the bed, heading in my general direction.

I backpedaled. "Stay away from me."

He stopped, and once again that slight, familiar grin hitched up one corner of his mouth. "You looked for all the world like the classic grieving widow that day," he reiterated. "Divorce or no divorce, you weren't over me."

"The hell I wasn't," I shot back, and shoved a hand through my shoulder-length tangle of curly red hair. I did a quick mental review of *The Damn Fool's Guide to Lucid Dreaming* and wondered if I was experiencing some random version of the phenomenon. I pinched myself, blinked a couple of times and sighed.

Nick remained still there, which meant I was awake. The jury was still out on whether or not I was lucid.

"I'm sorry about the other women," he said sweetly.

"Too little, too late," I answered, stunned by the sharp, sudden pang of sorrow at the verbal reminder. It was like a rubber band snapping around my soul. "What are you doing here?"

He cocked one perfectly shaped eyebrow. In life, Nick had been a real estate developer, eating up the Arizona desert with tract houses, convenience stores and strip malls. I half expected his cell phone to ring. He was one of those people who go around with an earphone plugged into their heads, apparently talking to themselves. "I wondered when you'd get to that question," he said.

"Now you know."

Nick fiddled with his tie again. His mother chose that tie— red, with tiny silver stripes. I hated it, and I hated her. More on that later. "It's hard to get your attention," he said. Then, with a wistful look, he added, "Some things never change."

"Pul-eeze," I said. "We're not going to play the poor, mis-understood Nick game, okay?" I was *so* not in love with him, dead or alive, and I didn't want him hanging around. How do you get a restraining order against a ghost?

He held up a hand, palm out. "All right, all right," he said. "Let's not go there."

"Wise choice, Bucko. And you still haven't told me what you're doing in my bedroom in the middle of the night."

"It's a long story." He looked around the bedroom, with its linoleum floor, fading wallpaper and garage-sale furni-ture. "Still living over the biker bar," he observed. "When are you going to get a decent place?"

Thanks to Nick and his mother, Margery DeLuca, soci-ety scion and barracuda divorce lawyer, I'd gotten F-all in the settlement, except for a pile of credit card bills I was still paying off. I couldn't *afford* anything but what I had, and sometimes even that much was a stretch, but there didn't seem to be much point in going down *that* winding and treacherous road. "Did you come here to talk real estate? If so, kindly go haunt somebody else—your mother, for instance. I'm not in the market."

Nick looked hurt. That was my second cue to feel guilty. Not.

He sighed once more, philosophically this time, like some holy martyr, angling for his own prayer card. No sale there, either. Nick DeLuca was a lot of things, but a saint wasn't one of them.

"Damn it," he said, looking down at himself again. "I'm fading."

Sure enough, the glow indicated low batteries, and I could see through his left shoulder and part of his mid-section.

"Wait," I said. The word scraped my throat.

Nick's brown eyes connected briefly with mine, then he vanished.

I blinked, hugging myself now, ready to collapse but afraid to go near the bed, where I could expect to make a soft landing. "Nick?" I whispered, gripping the dresser for support.

No answer.

He was really gone, except for a faint reverberation in the air.

If he'd been there in the first place.

I stood still for a long time, staring at the space where Nick had been standing, then groped my way out of the bedroom, along the dark hall and into the kitchen, flipping on the light switch with numb fingers as I passed it. I sank into a chair at the round oak table, laid my head down on my folded arms and sat out the rest of the night.

AT DAWN, I made a pot of coffee, and as soon as I heard Bert's Harley roll up outside, I forced myself to go back into the haunted bedroom. There, I quickly pulled on a pair of jeans, stuffed my feet into the Sponge Bob slippers my foster sister, Greer, had given me for Christmas in one of her rare moments of whimsy, and finger-combed my hair. In the adjoining bathroom, I brushed my teeth and splashed my face with cold water. Gazing into the mirror over the cracked pedestal sink, I gave myself a brief lecture.

"Suck it up, Mojo Sheepshanks," I said. "You're probably not the first woman to wake up and find her dead husband in bed with her."

Despite the speech, I wasn't consoled. My face was so pale, my freckles looked three-dimensional, and my eyes, which vary from blue to green, depending on what I'm wearing, were colorless. I had the raccoon thing going, too—an effect that can usually only be achieved by cheap mascara and a crying jag.

Having made this grim but accurate assessment, I turned from the mirror, traversed the kitchen again and opened the door. I stood for a moment on the landing, looking down on the gravel parking lot. Bert, a brawny guy with a shaved head and both arms tattooed with road maps, bent over the sidecar attached to his bike, unbuckling Russell's helmet.

Russell was his basset hound, and the mutt gave a happy yip when he spotted me.

Bert Wenchal—Bert being short for Bertrand—turned and favored me with a broad smile. For all that he could have been an attraction in one of those road-side freak shows advertised on billboards—See the Amazing Human Map, 5 Miles Ahead—Bert had perfect teeth, never mind that they were the size of piano keys, and baby blue eyes.

"Hey, Mojo," he called, setting the dog's head gear on the seat of the Harley. Russell leaped out of the sidecar and trundled toward me as I descended the wooden stairs. Most days Russell sat on a stool at the end of the bar, and scored too many pepperoni sticks from the customers.

I bent to ruffle the dog's floppy ears. "You're too fat," I told him affectionately.

He tried to lick my face.

Bert's keys jingled as he shoved one into the lock on the service door. The bar wouldn't open until ten, but he liked to come in early, put the coffee on to brew, fire up the hot dog roaster, rake the peanut shells, cigarette butts and spit-lumps out of the sawdust on the floor and balance the till. As landlords went, Bert was unconventional, but the rent was right and he had a great dog, so we got along okay.

"You look like hell this morning," he told me brightly, washing his hands at the sink behind the bar. Bert was proud of his saloon, especially the bar. It was nothing but splintery boards, nailed across the top of six huge wooden barrels, bought at a junk sale in Tombstone, but according to Bert, the thing was a true historical artifact. Allegedly, in its heyday, the likes of Wyatt Earp and Doc Holliday had bellied up to it.

"Thanks," I said bleakly. Russell climbed onto the old mounting block next to his bar stool, then made the leap to the vinyl seat. I perched on the next one over.

Bert started the coffee. Despite his size and the fact that Route 66 coursed in a green line up his left arm, presumably across his chest, and down his right, complete with side roads, highway numbers and place names beside little red circles, he was a sensitive guy.

"Something happen to Lillian?" he asked.

My eyes burned, and my throat tightened. I ran a hand down Russell's broad back for a distraction. Lillian Travers was the closest thing I had to a mother, and she would have been my first choice to confide in, but she'd suffered a devastating stroke six months before. Now, she sat staring into space in a Phoenix nursing home, and I made the forty-five minute trip to visit her three times a week.

Sometimes Lillian seemed to know me, sometimes she didn't. Except for isolated, garbled words, she never spoke.

Bert paused in his coffee-making, waiting.

I finally shook my head. "She's the same," I got out.

"Then what?" Bert persisted, but gently. With the coffee-maker chortling and belching out fragrant steam, he flipped on the hot dog machine, opened the fridge tucked behind the bar and took out a package of frankfurters. I watched as he laid them carefully, one by one, on the gleaming steel bars rolling behind the glass.

"Something really weird happened last night," I said, with

understandable difficulty and no little reluctance. Russell laid his muzzle on my left forearm, mesmerized by the spinning wieners.

Bert arched his eyebrows, tossed the frankfurter package into the trash and washed his hands again. Time to rake the sawdust. I took comfort in Bert's unvarying rituals, maybe because I had so few of my own. Most of the time, I felt as insubstantial as Nick's ghost; I'd been living a lie for so long, I couldn't recall the truth, if I'd ever known it in the first place. "Like what?" he prompted.

I turned on the bar stool as he reached for the rake leaning against the weathered board wall. "Like I saw my dead ex-husband last night," I stumbled. There was no graceful way to say it.

Bert paused, rake in hand and gave a low whistle. "Dude," he said.

Since some people would have tested my forehead for a fever, I was mildly encouraged. "Maybe I'm going crazy." That was the thought that had kept me awake, too agitated to engage in my usual insomnia cure, which was to sit at my computer and work my way through one of the piles of medical billings that paid my bills. That and the fear that Nick would get a recharge and show up again if I lay down on the bed.

Bert began to rake noxious things into a pile between two massive pool tables. Anybody might think they were losing their mind if they'd seen what I had, but I had more reason than most. My parents were shot to death in our rented doublewide, down in Cactus Bend, when I was five years old. I knew I must have witnessed the murders, since I was found hiding in the clothes dryer off the kitchen, covered with their blood, but I had no memory of the incident, or of the next few months, for that matter. The first thing I could recall was waking up in a cheap motel, and Lillian dabbing at my face with a cold washcloth.

"I seen you do some strange things," Bert said. "Like the way you can make a slot machine pay off pretty much whenever you want. You come by your name honestly, but you ain't crazy, Mojo. Not you."

My heart warmed. Actually, I *didn't* come by my name honestly—or much of anything else, either. Like Lillian, I'd been using an alias for years—one I'd chosen myself, out of a library book—and some dead child's social security number. As close as Bert and I were, though, I'd never told him the whole story. Even Nick hadn't known, though maybe he did now. He'd seen his battered body after the accident, and he knew I'd cried at his funeral, so maybe being dead gave him a broader perspective.

Now *there* was a disturbing thought.

"He looked—real," I went on. "Except that he glowed in the dark."

Bert raked a little faster, and I hoped he wasn't revising his opinion about my sanity. "Was there a reason for this visit?" he asked, without looking at me.

"We never got that far," I said.

Bert glanced in my direction.

"Nothing happened," I told him firmly, and without delay.

He grinned. "I never said it did," he replied. "Give Russell one of them frankfurters, will you? He missed his breakfast."

I slid off the stool and went around behind the bar, glad to have something physical to do, however mundane. "You shouldn't let him eat stuff like that," I said. "One of these days, he's going to blow an artery."

Bert got out the dustpan and leaned down to rake the pile into it. "Poor dog gets nothin' but diet kibble at home," he said. Bert's girlfriend, Sheila, ran a tight ship. "One sausage ain't gonna hurt him."

I opened the door, speared a frank and plopped it onto a paper plate.

Russell watched, salivating, as I cut it into bite-sized pieces with a plastic knife. "Like you don't give him one every morning of his life," I chided, but I set the plate down in front of Russell and smiled as he snarfed up the grub.

"My aunt Nellie saw a ghost once," Bert ruminated, raking again. "It was her dog, Fleagel the beagle. He lived for seventeen years, and Nell swore she found crap on the same old place on the stairs for ten days after he croaked. She said that was how she knew she was going to die. When the beagle came back, I mean. Sure enough, a few weeks after the sighting, she bit the dirt, right in the middle of a game of blackout bingo."

I gazed across the bar at him, hands resting on my hips. With anybody else, I would have felt self-conscious in my jeans, rumpled nightshirt and Sponge Bobs, but Bert was different. Like a brother. "That was a pretty insensitive remark," I said.

"Aunt Nellie was a pretty insensitive woman," Bert an-swered, without missing a beat. "If Uncle Dutch hadn't been too embarrassed to call the cops on her, she'd have been run in on a domestic violence charge. The only thing she ever loved, far as I could tell, was that dog of hers."

I returned to my stool but sat facing Bert, with my back to the bar. "We both come from dysfunctional families," I reflected. "Maybe that's why we get along so well."

Bert chuckled, shook his bald head. "You know what worries me, Mojo? I can follow your logic, back-asswards as it is. Your brother went to prison for killing your folks. I was raised by two drunks and a pack of Labrador retriev-ers. We're a pair to draw to, you and me."

I nodded glumly. Bert's knowledge of my background was limited to the bare facts, but I'd told him more than I'd told just about anybody else in my life, including Nick or the men I'd dated since the divorce. "By psychological standards, we ought to be in padded rooms by now."

"If you mention seeing a ghost to the wrong person," Bert mused, pausing to lean on the rake handle and regard me with concern, "you might end up in one anyhow."

By then, my thoughts had shifted to Lillian. Maybe she was having one of her good days. Even if she was, she wouldn't be able to carry on a coherent conversation, but she could lis-ten, and she always seemed to enjoy a surprise visit. I decided to shower, dress and motor down the 101 to see her.

"You're a real comfort, Bert," I teased, already on my way to the side door, which stood propped open to the still cool mid-April air. In another month, it would be so hot the asphalt on the highways would buckle.

"You didn't have your coffee," Bert called after me.

I doubled back, filled a disposable cup, stirred in sugar and powdered creamer and raised the brew in a toast as I went by. "Put it on my tab," I said.

Bert grinned and nodded, and I stepped out into the sunny parking lot just as another Harley roared up, flinging gravel, and came to a noisy stop beside Bert's bike.

Tucker Darroch, my most recent bad romantic choice.

He shut off the bike and gave a salutelike wave. Clad in jeans, scuffed black boots and a blue muscle shirt, which showed off his biceps to distinct advantage, Tucker was the complete opposite of Nick, at least when it came to appearance. He was six feet tall, square jawed, and his honey-colored hair was too long, falling in his eyes and curling at the nape of his neck, while Nick was of average height, compactly built and born to the boardroom.

Tucker looked like a Hell's Angel. In actuality, he was an undercover cop.

We'd done a little undercover work ourselves, Tucker and I. That was the best part of our relationship. The rest of it sucked, unfortunately, and we'd agreed, three and a half weeks before, to cool it for a while. Tucker was just wrapping up a nasty divorce, and he and the little woman were still duking it out over custody of their seven-year-old twins, Danny and Daisy.

Just watching Tucker swing a blue-jeaned leg over the seat of that bike made my nerves twitch. I wanted to nod a noncommittal greeting, climb the stairs to my apartment and go on about my business, but I might as well have been wearing cement shoes.

Tucker approached, his hips rolling in that easy, death-to-women walk of his. He shoved his hair back from his face and looked straight down into my eyes. "Nice getup," he said, hooking his thumbs in the back pockets of his Levi's.

It took me a moment to realize he was talking about my clothes. "It's a fashion statement," I heard myself say. "Care for a translation?"

He grinned. "I'll pass," he said lightly, but his green eyes were watchful, and slightly narrowed. "You okay? You've got dark circles under your eyes."

Between Bert and Tucker, I was pretty clear that the current look wasn't working for me. "I'm *fine*," I said, a little too quickly.

Tucker pretended to dodge a blow. "Excuse me for asking," he said.

I finally got my legs working again, and made for the stairs. "Things to do, people to see," I explained airily over one shoulder, concentrating on 1—putting one foot in front of the other, then repeating the process, 2—not spilling my coffee, and 3—not running back to Tucker and jumping his bones in the parking lot. "Nice seeing you again."

He didn't answer, but I felt his gaze on me as I mounted the steps.

LILLIAN WAS NOT having one of her good days, as it turned out.

She sat in her wheelchair, in front of the one window in

her fusty little room, a shrunken and fragile figure, arthritic hands knotted in her lap. A worn but colorful afghan covered her bony knees, and a lump rose in my throat as I remembered the woman she used to be. Her stepdaughter, Jolie, had crocheted that afghan for her long ago, as a Christmas present. Lillian had been luminous with delight that day, her laughter rich and vibrant, her brain and body in working order. Those painfully curled fingers had been busy, competent, glistening with shopping-channel rings.

Lillian was my babysitter, before my parents were murdered. Shortly after the killings, she'd been my kidnapper.

I swallowed the lump, blinked back tears and crossed the room to stand next to her, bending to kiss her lightly on top of the head.

"Hello," I said gently.

She looked up at me, and for a moment recognition sparked in her sunken eyes. She grasped my hand, squeezed it with a strange urgency and made a soft sound that I chose to interpret as a greeting.

I dragged up a chair to sit knee to knee with her, opened the bag of doughnuts I'd picked up on the way down from Cave Creek and offered her favorite, a double-frosted maple bar.

She shook her wobbly head, like one of those bobble-figures they give away at baseball games, but her watery eyes were full of longing. Lillian had been an off-the-rack size 16 ever since I could remember, but now she looked almost skeletal, with big dents at her temples and under her cheekbones. It was as though her skull were eating its way to the surface.

I broke off a piece of the maple bar and held it to her lips.

She took a nibble, like a baby bird being fed in the nest. My heart twisted.

Laboriously, Lillian gummed the morsel and swallowed.

"You look good," I lied.

"Cods," Lillian said.

I frowned. "Cods?" She wanted fish?

"Cods," Lillian insisted.

"She's talking about these," a female voice put in, nearly scaring me out of my skin.

I turned to see a pudgy nurse's aide standing by Lillian's neatly made bed, holding up a familiar deck of cards. Of course, I thought. The Tarot cards.

I didn't recognize the aide. The turnover was huge at Sunset Villa.

Lillian began to squirm in her chair, reaching with what seemed a desperate eagerness. "Cods!" she croaked.

"They're the devil's work," the nurse's aide said, with a self-righteous little sniff. She was overweight and looked like she might attend one of those churches where they drink antifreeze and juggle snakes. "Only thing worse is them Ouija boards, if you ask me."

"I *didn't* ask you," I pointed out, crisply polite as I dropped the maple bar back into the bakery bag and went to claim Lillian's deck. They were her most treasured possession, those creased and battered cards. When we were on the run, after my folks were killed, she'd sometimes given readings to pay for a tank of gas or a meal in some diner. They'd warned us, those cards, Lillian claimed, when somebody recognized my picture from the back of a milk carton, and the Tarot had predicted disaster if I married Nick.

I should have listened.

I took the cards and stared at the nurse's aide, bristling in her flowered scrubs, until, in a minor snit, she turned around and left the room.

"Give," Lillian demanded.

I handed her the cards, bracing myself to watch the inevitable struggle. Once, Lillian had plied that deck with the skill of a riverboat poker sharp, but that was when her fingers were straight and strong, with a hotline to her brain.

She gripped the cards in both hands, and I saw a tremor pass through her as she closed her eyes to concentrate. I wondered, not for the first time, if large portions of her mind were dark and boarded up, as the doctors said, or if the old Lillian crouched in there someplace, smart as ever.

I didn't know what to hope for. For a woman as bright and full of life as Lillian had been, it would be hell if the wires were down between her mind and her body. On the other hand, being a vegetable was no fun, either.

It tortured me, wondering how it was for her.

I watched bleakly as the woman who'd saved me from so many things fumbled with a pack of tattered playing cards.

She turned the deck over, thumbed them until she settled on one. The Queen of Pentacles, a colorful card, showing a medieval woman seated on a throne. That one dropped into her lap, followed, after more excruciating selection, by the Page of Cups. A young man in tights, holding up a chalice with a fish, presumably dead, flopping over the rim.

I waited tensely, resisting the urge to help her.

Lillian still had her pride. I had to believe that.

When it came to interpretation, I was useless. The deck was a familiar fixture, since Lillian had carried it in her pocket or purse for as long as I could remember, but I knew next to nothing about the images, even though I'd seen them many times.

It was almost an anticlimax when she settled on the third and apparently final card—Death. It showed a skeleton, wearing black armor and mounted on a fierce-looking horse, bodies littering the ground beneath. I drew in my breath.

Lillian's hands relaxed suddenly, and she looked up at me, her contorted face imploring me to understand.

"Take," she ground out.

I plucked the three cards from where they'd fallen onto the pilled afghan covering her thin legs. My palms sweated as I examined the pictures, one by one. I knew there was a message, but the circuits were blocked.

I tried to hand them back.

"Take," Lillian repeated, and shrank back in her wheel-chair, the remaining cards bending in her grasp.

I bit my lower lip, nodded and tucked the Queen, the Page and Death gently into the side-flap of my purse. I'd stop at a bookstore on the way back to Cave Creek, I decided. Pick up a *Damn Fool's Guide to Tarot*. I wasn't ready to leave Lillian, but she was clearly overwrought, and staying too long might plunge her into an even steeper decline.

"Want some more of the maple bar?" I asked, and prac-tically choked on the words. If she'd been in her usual staring mode, I might have told her about last night's visit from Nick, just to have a sounding board, but she was too agitated to listen to a ghost story. Besides, even if she understood, what could she do?

"No," she said clearly, and at first I thought she was answering my question about the maple bar. Instead, her gaze was fixed on the doorway.

A tall man stood on the threshold, a finger hooked in the suit jacket hanging behind his right shoulder. He had a full head of gray hair and one of those benignly handsome faces that inspire instant confidence. I felt a spike of recognition and reached out to close my fingers over Lillian's hands. They were clenched.

My uncle, Clive Larimer, smiled.

"Hello, Mary Josephine," he greeted me. "Long time no see."

Lillian began a soft, gurgling murmur.

Larimer stepped into the room, momentarily distracted when the nurse's aide pushed past him and rushed over to Lillian.

"What's the matter, Mrs. Travers?" she asked anxiously.

I peeped at her name tag. *Felicia*.

A tear slipped down Lillian's right cheek.

"You'll have to leave, both of you," Felicia decreed.

Larimer backed into the corridor, out of sight. I forgot all about him, in my concern for Lillian.

"It's those damn devil-cards," Felicia declared, but she was patting Lillian's shoulder, and Lillian seemed to be calming down a little. "Time for your medicine anyway, isn't it, Mrs. Travers? And after that, you can take a nice nap."

Felicia paused to glare at me. "That's what Mrs. Travers needs. Medicine and a nap. You'd better go now."

I didn't protest. I'd already made the decision to split, after all. Lillian had drifted back into herself, and the cards lay forgotten between her palms. I might have been transparent, the way she stared through me.

I nodded, certain I'd break down and cry if I tried to say anything. I picked up my purse, leaving the bakery bag on the window sill, where I'd set it earlier, and dashed for the door.

I ran smack into Uncle Clive in the corridor, and he steadied me by placing avuncular hands on my shoulders.

"Mary Josephine," he said, as if he couldn't believe it was really me.

I bit my lower lip, speechless. I hadn't seen the man since I was five, and I probably wouldn't have recognized him at all if he hadn't been a state senator, making regular appearances on TV and in every major newspaper in Arizona. He looked harmless, even friendly, but he was one of the people Lillian had wanted to avoid, all those years ago. She'd been scared to death, for herself and me, which was why she'd snatched me from the front yard of my foster home. At least, that was her account of what happened—I didn't remember any of it.

"Let's have some coffee and talk," Uncle Clive said quietly.

I was twenty-eight years old, a self-supporting adult, not a kid. I'd been married and divorced. I'd read *The Damn Fool's Guide to Self-Defense for Women*.

There was nothing to be afraid of.

And, besides, I was curious as hell.

Uncle Clive was my mother's older brother. He'd been around when the killings took place, and he could fill in a lot of gaps in my memory, bring me up to speed on my half brother, Geoff, who'd gone to prison at sixteen for second-degree murder.

"Okay," I said.

The cafeteria at Sunset Villa wasn't much, so we walked, my long-lost uncle and I, to a nearby Starbucks, with outside tables and misters to cool the customers. Even in April, it's warm in Phoenix.

I didn't think I could choke down anything—the whole scenario was an excuse to talk, after all—but Clive bought us both a cup of classic roast. Except for a few university students bent over textbooks and one doughy guy with piercings and vampire teeth—a poet or a serial killer or both—we had the place to ourselves.

"I can't believe it's you," Clive said, as he joined me under the shade of a green-and-white striped umbrella, setting down our cups. His black metal chair, which matched the black metal table, scraped on the patio stones as he drew it back to sit.

I didn't answer. After twenty-three years, I didn't know where to start.

It wasn't that there was too much to say. It was that there wasn't too much.

Tentatively, my mother's big brother and only living sibling touched the back of my hand. "It's okay," he said, and his voice was so gentle that tears smarted, like acid, behind my eyeballs. "I used to carry you on my shoulders. Help you find Easter eggs. Do you remember?"

I shook my head. Nebulous memories *were* teasing the far borders of my mind, but I couldn't seem to corner any of them long enough to take hold.

"We looked everywhere for you." He spoke quietly, but a muscle bunched in his jaw as he took a sip of his coffee. "My God, it was bad enough, what happened to Evie and Ron, but when you went missing on top of it—"

Evie and Ron Mayhugh. My parents. My work-frazzled, distracted, waitress mother. My moody, chronically unemployed father. For a moment, I could see them clearly in my mind's eye. It was an image I'd longed for, wracked my brains for, during many a sleepless night, and now, suddenly, there it was, a vivid little tableau branded on the inside of my forehead.

"How did you find Lillian?" I asked. The air seemed to pulse around both of us, as though charged, and there was a slow, dull thudding in my ears.

For a nanosecond, Clive looked confused. Of course, I thought. He'd known Lillian as Doris Blanchard. He made the leap quickly, though, and something eased in his face.

"By accident," Clive Larimer answered. "Just a fluke, really." He gave a sigh of benevolent resignation, and his eyes were warm and kind as he looked at me, studying my features, maybe searching for a resemblance to his murdered sister. "It's ironic, really. The day you disappeared, the police put out an all-points bulletin. After a few weeks, the FBI got involved. The case was featured on *60 Minutes*. Beyond an occasional sighting, nothing. And then a friend of mine happens to recognize Doris—Lillian—while visiting her sister at the nursing home. I walk in, thinking I'm crazy to still be hoping after all these years that I'll find out anything, and there you are."

"How did you know who I was?"

He smiled. "You look like your mother," he said.

Well, that answered one question. I found it curiously comforting, even though I had no aspirations to be anything like the woman I barely remembered.

"What happened, Mary Jo?" he asked, after a long pause.

Mary Jo. It was odd, hearing the name. Familiar as it was, like the words of a ditty learned in childhood, it made me feel like an impostor, or maybe an eavesdropper. Anybody but Mary Jo.

"What happened?" I echoed. Was he asking about the murder or the years afterward, when Lillian and I and, later, Greer, lived like the proverbial gypsies?

"You were there, and then you were gone."

I wondered how much to tell him. On the one hand, he was my uncle. He might have given me away at my wedding to Nick, ill-advised as it was to marry the jerk, if Lillian hadn't snatched me. I might have had a father figure in my life. On the other hand, Lillian must not have trusted him, back in the day, or she wouldn't have grabbed me up and hit the road. And she'd seemed startled, even scared, when he appeared in the doorway of her room at Sunset Villa.

I shrugged, picked up my coffee, set it down again, untasted. Some of it sloshed over the rim of the cup and burned my fingers. I almost welcomed the pain, because it jarred me out of the muddle of surprise that had fogged my thinking and limited my vocabulary from the moment the thought formed in my mind: *This is my uncle.*

"It wasn't a bad life," I said. "Lillian took good care of me. We...traveled a lot, but I thought it was fun." Except, of course, for the times when I'd just settled into a new school, made some friends, gotten myself another library card and then had to go on the run again, usually in the middle of the night.

"Catch me up," Clive urged, after another extended silence. "What do you do for a living? Are you married? Do you have kids?"

I bit my lower lip. Clive Larimer was a state senator, with a socially connected wife named Barbara and four big-toothed, impossibly blond, Harvard-educated children. I'd Googled him whenever I got into one of my Norman Rockwellian moods and turned nostalgic. I figured when I answered his questions, he'd think the apple didn't fall far from the tree, that I was as shiftless as my dad and as codependent as my mom, and I wished I could whip out pictures of two-point-two munchkins, a dog and a successful husband, and refer circumspectly to my part-time job as a rocket scientist.

"I work at home," I said instead. "Medical billing and coding. Doctors like to outsource that stuff these days." Feeling stupid, I blushed, but then plunged on. *Telling the truth is good for you,* Tucker had taunted me, not so long ago, during one of our screaming fights. *You ought to give it a try sometime.* "No kids. I was married for a couple of years, then divorced."

The truth, I told Tucker silently, *is overrated.*

My uncle's face reflected a calm, intense interest as he listened.

I left out the part about seeing Nick's ghost, of course, and I didn't get around to mentioning that I lived in a rented apartment over a biker bar in Cave Creek, either. I'd save that for when I really wanted to make a major impression. Show him my stack of dog-eared, highlighted *Damn Fool's Guides,* too, and tell him how I'd educated myself on every subject from psychic pet communication to private investigation. Who needed Harvard?

"So that's about it," I said, letting the words dwindle to a sigh.

Uncle Clive settled back in his chair, tented his fingers together over his chest. "You must have a few questions yourself," he remarked.

Hell, yes, I had questions.

The first one, which I didn't voice, was: *What ever happened to that no-good, scum-sucking, parent-murdering brother of mine?* Correction, Geoff was a *half* brother—but the whole topic congealed in my throat, like some gelatinous mass, and the words my brain framed were slithering along, flattened against the side walls, trying to squeeze past it.

I'd run a hundred Googles on Geoff if I'd run one, after finding his last name in the newspaper archives. I didn't remember it, for reasons already stated, and Lillian had always clammed up whenever I raised the subject. Geoff Waters, born to my mother by her first husband, had gone to a juvenile detention facility in California after confessing to shooting Dad in the back of the head and Mom through the throat. At twenty-one, he'd been released and his record expunged. It galled me a little—and scared me a lot—to know that he was out there somewhere, lily-white as far as the law was concerned. Going on just as if nothing had happened.

"Geoff," I finally managed. "Where do you suppose he is now?"

I hadn't realized Clive was tense until he visibly relaxed. "Who knows?" he replied, followed by an unspoken, *Who cares?*

"He killed my cat," I said. The words just came out, without my consciously forming them.

What cat?

Clive leaned forward slightly in his metal chair. His bushy brows lowered a little, and his eyes narrowed.

I blushed again, rubbed my right temple with my fingertips. "I don't know why I said that," I admitted, flustered. "I don't remember owning a cat."

My uncle bent a little further at the waist and laid a hand on my shoulder. "This is too much, too fast," he said. "I'm sorry for springing myself on you out of the blue, Mary Jo.

It's just that I've wondered for so long, what was happening to you—if you were all right. When I saw you, I..."

I wasn't used to that kind of concern, and I've got to admit, it felt damn good. After I married Nick, Lillian and I weren't exactly estranged, but we weren't as close, either. She flat-out didn't like him, and she didn't mince words about it. Around the same time, Ham, Lillian's husband and Jolie's father, had been diagnosed with liver cancer, with all the attendant sorrows for all of them. And Greer had been too involved in stealing her rich doctor husband away from his former wife to care much what was going on in *my* life, so I'd coped as best I could.

I swiped away a tear with the back of one hand.

Clive took out his wallet, produced a card, and laid it beside my coffee cup. It was official, with raised print and the Arizona State Seal in the upper right-hand corner. "When you're ready, Mary Jo," he said, "give us a call." He pushed back his chair, soundlessly this time, and stood. Collected his jacket from the armrest of the seat next to his. Waited.

I finally realized I was supposed to reciprocate with my own information. I took the pen he offered and wrote my cell number on one of the napkins that came with the coffee. I guess I should have added the address in Cave Creek, but I was afraid he'd MapQuest it when he got the chance, and find out I lived over Bad-Ass Bert's. Maybe before the next mini family reunion, I could swing a decent place.

"Thanks," my uncle said. He took the napkin, folded it

carefully and tucked it into the pocket of his coat, now draped over one arm. "It's so good to know you're all right, Mary Jo," he added gruffly. "I used to worry that Geoff might have found you…"

I swallowed, felt the soft fur of a cat brush against the underside of my chin. A cat I didn't remember owning.

Chester, whispered one of innumerable wraiths haunting the depths of my subconscious mind.

Clive, who had been about to turn and walk away, paused and frowned. "Are you all right, Mary Jo?"

"Mojo," I corrected. "Nobody calls me Mary Jo."

He registered this information with a half nod, his eyes still narrowed with concern. "Just then, you looked—"

"I'm fine," I insisted. Like I'd wanted to tell Tucker, the truth is not what it's cracked up to be.

Still, he hesitated. "You've had quite a shock. Maybe I should walk you at least as far as your car."

I shook my head. "I need a few moments to work through all this," I said.

Score one for the truth.

"The memories must be tough to deal with," Clive ventured.

I favored him with a thin, wobbly smile. "That's the problem. There aren't any memories."

Uncle Clive looked taken aback, and sympathetic. "No memories?"

"Zip," I said.

He surprised me then. He leaned down and kissed the top of my head, just lightly, the way I'd kissed Lillian at Sunset Villa. Something in my heart locked onto the feeling, like a heat-seeking missile, and launched itself into unknown territory.

WHEN I GOT HOME an hour later, still shaken, but with a copy of *The Damn Fool's Guide to Tarot* under my arm and a spanking-new deck in my purse, the parking lot was full of Harleys and pickup trucks, and Bad-Ass Bert's was jumping, even though it was still early afternoon. I probably should have rescued Russell from the steady flow of pepperoni and hot dog scraps, but I was already upstairs before I really focused on the idea.

I would take a shower, I decided, fall into bed—Nick or no Nick—and sleep until I could face the world again. After that, a couple of hours at the computer, coding and billing, and I could meet my quota, hold on to my various jobs and reasonably expect to pay next month's rent when the first rolled around.

I fumbled for my keys, dropped one of the Tarot cards Lillian had pressed on me in the process, and watched as it slipped between the boards of the landing and fluttered to the ground beneath.

With a groan, I unlocked the door, tossed my purse and the book inside, and went back down the steps to retrieve the card.

The skeleton on horseback stared up at me.

Death. Of course it would be that card.

I picked it up, hiked back up the stairs and got a fresh shock.

No, Nick hadn't come back.

But the cat had. He was fat and white and fluffy, with china-blue eyes, and he sat on the cheap rug just inside the door, switching his lush tail back and forth.

"Chester?"

"Meow," he replied.

I dropped to my knees, reached for him, drew back my hand. If it went through him, I was going to lose it. I couldn't deal with another ghost.

"Chester?" Okay, so I was repeating myself. I'd automatically called him by name, so I must have recognized him.

Another meow, this one a little less patient than the last.

Tentatively, I touched his head. Warm. Solid. Soft.

I saw a flash of crimson in my mind. The cat—*this* cat, lying on his side, dead, shot through with an arrow. I swallowed a rush of bile and sat back on my haunches, still on the landing, still clutching the Death card in my left hand. I had to take four or five deep breaths before I could be sure I wouldn't either faint or vomit.

"How did you get in here?" I asked.

Like he was going to answer.

The way things had been going, he might have. I had definitely tumbled down the rabbit hole at some point. Let's just say, if I saw a bottle marked Drink Me, I wasn't planning to take a swig.

Chester gave his bushy tail another twitch, turned and strolled regally back into the apartment.

I heard the side door open downstairs and, afraid somebody would see me kneeling on the landing and ask a lot of questions I didn't want to answer, I scrabbled inside, with considerably less grace than the cat had exhibited, and hoisted myself to my feet.

My mind was racing.

I remembered what Bert had said earlier, about how his aunt Nellie had seen her dog, gone to Bingo and died.

I peered at the Death card again, then made my way into the living room. Chester was perched on the back of the couch, delicately washing his right forepaw with a pink tongue.

"Nick?" I demanded. "Is this your idea of a joke?"

No answer, of course.

Chester paused in his ablutions and regarded me with pity.

"This is not funny," I told him.

"Meow," he agreed.

I looked around the apartment. No one had a key except Bert; I'd had the locks changed after Tucker and I called it quits—not because I was afraid of him, but as a statement, as much to myself as to him—and besides, he'd never have pulled a mean trick like this. Even if he'd been so inclined, he couldn't have known about Chester.

"Get a hold of yourself, Sheepshanks," I said aloud. "This *can't* be the same cat."

"Meow," said Chester, sounding almost indignant.

I saw the blood again. The arrow sticking out of the animal's side.

I ran into the bathroom and dry heaved until my empty stomach finally shriveled up into a tight little ball and stopped convulsing.

"I thought you'd like him," a familiar voice said mildly, from the doorway.

I whirled from the sink, my face still dripping water from the frantic splashing, and there was Nick, in his funeral suit, leaning casually against the doorjamb.

"Y-you—"

Nick's mouth quirked at one corner, and he nodded his head. "It's me, all right." He wasn't glowing, I noticed fitfully. Must be a nighttime phenom.

"This cat—where—?"

"I found him wandering in the train station," Nick said.

I stared at him, goggle-eyed. My stomach threatened more mayhem.

"*What* train station? What the *hell* are you talking about?"

Chester arrived on the scene, wound himself, purring, around Nick's ankles.

"It's a kind of cosmic clearinghouse," Nick explained. "On the other side."

"Right," I agreed. "You just head for Platform 9 and 3/4 and catch the Hogwarts Express."

Nick looked blank. He'd never been much of a reader.

"Forget it," I said. I pushed past Nick, noting that he was neither cold nor nebulous. Maybe the bone-freeze was a night thing, too.

Maybe I was out of my freaking mind.

"He was your cat when you were a little girl," Nick wheedled, following me. "I thought—"

I made it to the kitchen, wrenched open a cupboard door and ferreted around until I found a can of tuna with a fairly recent expiration date. "Do dead cats eat?" I asked, furious with confusion.

"I don't know," Nick said uncertainly. I jumped when I realized he was standing directly behind me, peering over my shoulder into the cupboard. "Are those Oreos?"

I grabbed the package of cookies off the shelf and thrust them at him. "Yes. They're old, but what the hell. It's not like you could be poisoned."

"You could be a little kinder," Nick pointed out, affronted. But he took the cookies.

"*Excuse* me," I snapped.

He stuck his nose into the Oreos, sniffed with decadent appreciation. His eyes rolled closed in ecstasy, the way they used to do when we had serious sex.

"Delicious," he said.

The can opener whirred jarringly as I opened the tuna. I dumped the contents onto a saucer, crumbled them with a fork and set the whole shooting match down on the floor.

Chester nosed the food with interest, but didn't eat.

I looked up at Nick.

He was holding a cookie in one hand and staring at it as though it had just tried to bite him.

"Damn," he muttered.

I glanced at the cat again, partly to make sure he was still there and partly to see if he would eat.

"Problem?" I asked, shifting my attention back to Nick.

"I bit into the thing, and nothing happened."

"I'd like to see that," I said. "Do it again, while I'm watching."

Nick did his ironic look. "This is not a performance designed for your amusement," he told me.

"Duh," I shot back. "I am definitely not amused."

Just then, a familiar knock sounded at the outside door.

Nick arched an eyebrow. "Company?"

"Disappear or something," I whispered. "It's Tucker!"

Nick folded his arms. "Oh, *well,* if it's *Tucker*—"

"I mean it, Nick. Go back to the train station or whatever it is."

He didn't move.

"Boogie!" I ordered, and made for the hallway.

Tucker let himself in, since I'd forgotten to lock the door when I encountered Chester on the mat, and we practically collided. By that time, I was wishing I hadn't told Nick to get lost. I would feel a lot less crazy if somebody else witnessed the dead-husband demo.

"Come in," I said cordially. "I was just about to whip up a grilled cheese sandwich." The last thing I wanted to do was eat, but I knew if I didn't, I'd get sick. My stomach needed something to digest besides its lining.

Tuck looked surprised by my reception. He'd clearly expected a rebuff, given our agreement to take a step back, not to mention the bristly meeting downstairs, and he'd probably had some speech all prepared, like Ten Reasons Why We Should Have Sex.

No way was I doing the deed with the Great Decease-o watching.

Sometimes I wish I were a little less principled.

The biker-cop followed me into the living room, and I waited for him to acknowledge Nick, who was standing in the middle of the room, his arms still folded, grinning like an idiot.

Tucker didn't react. Not to Nick, not to the cat.

They might as well have been invisible.

"He can't see us," Nick said.

"Shit," I said.

Tucker gave me a wounded look. "I didn't expect you to be glad to see me," he said, "but you don't have to swear."

This from a guy who hung out in a biker bar when he wasn't on duty.

"He's right," Nick said smugly. "It's very unladylike to curse."

"Shut up!" I snapped.

Tucker squinted. *"What?"*

I felt heat sting my cheekbones. "Never mind." I glanced at Chester, who was grooming himself again. I won't go into the details. After all, I wouldn't want to come off as *unlady-like* or anything.

"Never mind?" Tucker retorted. "First you ask me in for a grilled cheese, then you—"

"Just never mind," I said, rubbing my temples. "You didn't drop off a cat earlier today, did you?"

"Drop off a cat?"

I was losing patience, and possibly hemorrhaging brain cells at the same time. "Can we just stop doing the echo thing?"

"It's very annoying," Nick submitted.

I bit back another "Shut up." Said nothing, because that seemed safest.

"Mojo, what the *hell* are you talking about?" Tucker demanded.

"You haven't—well—seen a cat around? A white one, with blue eyes and a fluffy tail?"

Tucker crossed to me, took me gently but resolutely by one arm and squired me to the couch. "Sit down," he said, somewhat after the fact. "Put your head between your knees or something."

Nick chuckled.

I glared at him. Tucker caught me and followed my gaze. And saw nothing, of course.

"What's going on, Mojo?"

"It's been a difficult day." More truth. My God, I was getting good at it.

"I'll get you some water," Tucker decided. He looked pretty worried, and that pleased me. When he went into the kitchen, I waved at Nick to get out.

He must have been running on alkaloid. Not even a flicker.

I heard the refrigerator door open, close again.

A pause followed.

"Mojo?"

I tried to sound normal. "Yes?"

"How come there's a plate of tuna on the floor?"

Nick gave me a pointed, how-will-you-get-out-of-this-one look.

"Go screw yourself," I told him.

Tucker appeared in the kitchen doorway, with a bottle of water in one hand. "Did you say something?"

I smiled endearingly. "No," I lied. Hell, it's just easier to do what comes naturally.

"So what's with the fish?" Tucker pressed.

"I was sort of hoping to get a cat," I said.

Chester nestled against my side, purring. I just barely caught myself before I would have stroked his back.

"O—*kay*," Tucker said.

I went for perky. "Do you still want that grilled cheese?"

Tucker looked around the room and, for a second or so, I thought he might have sensed something. "No," he decided. "I think you need to get out for a while. How about a steak and some vino at my place?"

I wanted to go home with Tuck. I *really* wanted to go. He was a great cook and an even better lover, but there were solid reasons for the decision we'd made. He was still entangled with his ex-wife, and I didn't want to be Transition Woman. Hot sex, easy promises, and then either back to the old setup or on to a new one. And here's me, in the middle, trampled.

With most guys, that experience would have been a mere bummer. With Tucker, it might mean checking into Heartbreak Hotel and never checking out again.

"Bad idea," I said. "Steak, vino and your place, I mean. For reasons previously stated."

"Bad idea for a *lot* of reasons," Nick interjected.

Shut the frick up, I thought fiercely, smiling tenderly at Tucker, and I think Decease-o picked up on the brain waves, because he looked insulted and tugged at his shirt cuffs, the way he always did when he was miffed.

Tucker sighed. His broad shoulders sloped slightly. "Listen, Mojo, I know we agreed—"

"To be friends," I finished for him.

"Friends," Nick scoffed.

I ignored him. I'd tell him off later, if his batteries didn't run down before Tucker left.

Chester nudged me again. It was harder to ignore him.

"This is no good," Tucker lamented quietly. "Our being apart, that is. And it's not as if I'm married. Allison and I are legally divorced."

"Go home, Tucker. Go catch a bad guy. I've got nothing to offer you but grilled cheese."

Nick rolled his eyes.

Tucker brought me the water. He hesitated, then said, "You're sure you're all right?"

"I'm *fine,* Tucker."

I set the water bottle aside on the end table, stood, and sort of steered him to the door. There, he laid his hands on my shoulders and brushed a kiss across my forehead, beneath my bangs.

I hoped he didn't feel the tremor that went through me.

"Call me if you need anything," he said.

"'Call me if you need anything,'" Nick mimicked, from about a foot behind me. "Gag me with a kickstand." If he'd been breathing, I probably would have felt it on my nape.

Tucker left. Reluctantly.

I closed the door and turned on Nick, ready to rip a strip off him.

But he was gone.

I looked around. "Chester?"

My cat was gone, too.

For a long time, I just stood there, trying to make sense of it all. Then, disconsolately, I went into the kitchen, picked up the plate I'd put out for Chester and dumped the tuna down the disposal.

I didn't miss Nick. If he never came back, it would be too soon.

But I sure as hell missed the cat.

I slept in the living room, on the couch, figuring I'd be less likely to wake up and find Nick lying beside me, since he wouldn't fit. I guess it worked, because he wasn't there when I opened my eyes, but Chester was.

He sat on the coffee table next to Lillian's three Tarot cards, which were standing in an ominous little row, propped against the big Mexican fruit bowl I'd bought at the flea market a couple of years before.

I swung my feet over the side of the couch, sat upright and rubbed my face with both hands. When I looked again, Chester was still there.

"Meow," he said.

Okay, this was a major sign of my mental instability, but I was glad to see him just the same—sans the arrow from Geoff's bow. I had mostly visceral memories of the cat, nothing very specific, but his bloody end was vivid in my mind.

I knew I'd found him in the backyard of our place in Cactus Bend, behind the storage shed where my dad kept all the stuff he was constantly swapping. He'd called it "horse-trading." I recalled that, too, all of a sudden, but there were never any horses.

That was Dad for you. All dreams and wishes, no substance.

"Hey, Buddy," I said to the cat. After the briefest hesitation, I reached out to pat his head. Silky soft, solid and warm. No glow, either.

I was heartened. Glad I'd taken the risk of touching him.

He meowed again, and knocked down all three Tarot cards with one swipe of his tail.

I left the Queen, the Page and Death where they lay. I'd studied them half the night, along with their corresponding chapters in *The Damn Fool's Guide to the Tarot,* with a sensation of dread in the pit of my stomach the whole time. I was still in the dark. I didn't know much about the symbology, but I *did* know that Lillian always read them intuitively, without recourse to books. She'd told me once that Tarot cards were like little windows into the psyche; you just had to learn the language of the subconscious mind.

Since the day was already underway, whether I wanted to go along for the ride or not, I decided I'd better jump aboard. Do something constructive, like eat and make coffee.

The phone rang as I entered the kitchen, Chester prancing twitchy-tailed behind me, and I picked up the cordless receiver and opened the refrigerator door simultaneously. It's a mobile age, all about multitasking.

"Yo," I said.

"Yo," Greer mocked, with a peaky smile in her voice. "That's a fine way to answer the telephone. What if I'd been one of your doctor clients? You certainly would have made a businesslike impression."

Greer cared a lot about impressions. Interesting, since Lillian and I had found her in a bus station in Boise, Idaho, when I was nine and Greer was barely thirteen, working the waiting room in an effort to cadge enough money to buy a meal at the seedy lunch counter. She'd been wearing tight hip-hugger jeans that cold winter day, I recalled, along with a fitted black leather jacket, a blue Mohawk, a fat lip and an attitude.

Now, she was married to a famous plastic surgeon; she'd become the classic Snottsdale wife, with a tasteful blond pageboy, winsomely brushing her gym-fit shoulders, an Escalade and enough jewelry to add ten pounds to her weight on any given day.

"Thanks for the timely vocational pointer," I said, reaching for the milk carton standing lonely on the top shelf of the fridge and taking a cautious sniff. I flinched, dumped the stuff in giant curds into the sink and tossed the carton. The water made a decisive whooshing sound as I washed the works down the drain. "If Alex told you to call about his Medicare billings, you can tell *him* I already e-mailed them to the office. And I'm not altering the codes."

Alexander Pennington, M.D., was Greer's husband. He was twenty years older than she was, with a very bitter exwife and a creative bent for diagnosis. As in, if the medical facts didn't jibe with Medicare's payment schedules, he whittled them to fit.

A chill wafted into my sphere, coming from Greer's direction. "Alex didn't ask me to call," she said stiffly. "Nor did he say *anything* about the billings. We're trying to *help* you, Mojo. Throw a little business your way, since you seem determined never to get a *real job*."

I could have pointed out that at least I worked for my money, instead of drawing an allowance from a rich husband, but I didn't. Greer really pissed me off sometimes, but I considered her my sister, and I loved her. That day in the bus station, Lillian had bought her a meal and a seat next to us on the Greyhound to Las Vegas. Our latest car had just died alongside the highway, but not to worry. When we got to Vegas, Lillian put twenty dollars into a slot machine and won a spiffy subcompact. Greer was as much a part of our strange little family as if she'd been born into it.

I'd been too young to get the big picture, back then. Greer was a runaway and, thus, pimp bait. She'd already done some hooking by the time Lillian took her in, but afterward, she'd been a straight-A student and an all-around good kid.

"Are you still seeing that cop?" Greer asked, when I went too long without saying anything. Greer was uncomfortable with silence. If I didn't chatter like a magpie, she thought I was mad at her.

"No," I said, examining the fridge again. There was nothing for it. I was going to have to tap my bank account and spring for a few provisions.

"Good," she answered. "He might as well still be married."

No way was I walking into *that* one. Alex Pennington, M.D., had been married when Greer met him at a country club mixer, where she'd gone to network, hoping to line up some jobs for her interior design firm. Yes, Pennington's wife had been a raging drunk, but that didn't excuse the fact that he and Greer had started an affair the same night. Systematically, they'd eased the first Mrs. Pennington right out of the picture, and within a year, Greer took over the title.

"Tucker," I said, "is not married. He's divorced."

"Emotionally, he's married," Greer insisted. She sounded so damn self-righteous that I had to bite my lip and remind myself that she'd taken to the big sister role like a pro from the moment we cruised away from that bus station in Idaho. She was devoted to Lillian, too. It was Greer's signature on the checks covering the nursing home.

Yes, I had a problem with people who cheat on their spouses, obviously because of Nick, but it was *my* problem, not Greer's.

"Okay, whatever," I said, shutting the fridge with a little slam. I hate grocery shopping. Nothing ever looks good, and when I get it home, I have to cook it. "Is there a point to this call, Greer, or did you just want to needle me about my unconventional lifestyle?"

"'Unconventional lifestyle,'" Greer repeated. "Now why would I suggest anything like that—just because you live over a bar with a nasty name, do only enough work to survive and play the slot machines every chance you get?"

"Greer," I said patiently, "don't *make* me fight back. It isn't as if the arsenal's empty, you know."

She sighed. "I didn't call to fight," she said wistfully, and I wondered if she was really talking to me or to herself. "Alex is out of town for a medical convention. I would have gone along, but it's always so boring, with him in meetings the whole time. Besides, I haven't been feeling my best—if there's a God, I'm pregnant—so I decided to stay home. I was hoping you might come over tonight, keep me company for a while. We could have dinner by the pool."

I looked down at Chester. I liked him, and I was glad he was around, but, hey, he was a ghost, likely to fade away at any moment. Tucker and I were on the outs, so I couldn't expect any companionship from that quarter. And maybe if Greer and I spent a little time together, we might get back some tiny part of the old sisterly camaraderie we'd lost since she moved uptown, metaphorically speaking.

"Sure," I said. "I'd like that. What time, and what can I bring?"

We agreed on six o'clock, she pleaded with me not to attempt anything culinary and we hung up.

Chester made the leap to the countertop and sat next to the coffeemaker. I elbowed him gently aside to get a pot brewing.

"So," I said, "do dead cats need litter boxes?"

JUST MY LUCK to run into Psycho Bitch in the supermarket.

I was minding my own business, making the Lean Cuisine selections for the week in the freezer aisle, when all of a sudden, she rams my cart with hers and practically sends me headfirst into the stacked boxes of Sesame Chicken, New England Pot Roast and French Bread Pizza.

I whirled on her. "God *damn* it, Heather," I cried, "I'm about one inch off filing a restraining order against your crazy ass!"

Heather Dillard, ex-wife of a guy I dated precisely twice, three years ago, gripped the handle of her cart and prepared for another assault. I didn't see her for long periods of time—then, with no warning, she'd pop up out of nowhere, bent on avenging a whole slew of imagined wrongs. I'd caught her letting the air out of my tires once, and another time she'd waltzed into the bar and told Bert she was an old friend of mine, planning a surprise birthday party, and would he please, pretty-please, give her the key to my apartment?

Fortunately, he'd refused, but here's the creepy part. It *was* my birthday, so she'd taken the trouble to find that out, along with God knew what other personal details.

And she'd sent me a present, too.

Three dead birds in a shoebox, tied up with a bow.

"You're seeing Brian again," she accused, knuckles whitening on the cart handle. Her nostrils flared, and her spiky hair—blond that week—stuck out all over her head, as if she'd gotten drunk and cut it herself, with a dull razor blade. Her pupils had white all around, like that bride in the news a couple of years ago, the one who skipped out on her wedding, stirred up a media frenzy and had a conglomeration of local, state and federal agencies frantically searching for her.

I sighed. "I'm not seeing Brian," I said. My dead ex-husband and my murdered cat, yes. Brian, no.

"Of course you'd deny it," Heather challenged, but she looked uncertain, and that gave me a moment's hope that she might actually be reasonable. Which begged the question—who was crazy here, her or me?

"When something isn't true, I deny it. Go figure." I threw a couple of Yankee Pot Roast dinners into my cart, just to let her know I wasn't scared.

"We have *four children*," she said.

Two old ladies shopping for Stouffer's backed off, and a manager appeared at the far end of the aisle, looking worried. I might have been reassured, if he hadn't been about sixteen and roughly the same weight as Chester.

"I'm happy for you," I replied, "and sorry for them. You need help, Heather. And you need to get away from me—and *stay* away from me—before I have you arrested."

Her lower lip wobbled. It looked cracked and dry, as though she'd bitten it a lot. I felt a twinge of pity, but it passed quickly when her cart clanged against mine and one of the wheels ran over my toe.

"Bitch!" she screeched. "Homewrecker! Tramp!"

That did it.

I went after her. Right for her throat. I probably would have strangled her if two box boys and one of the old ladies hadn't intervened. She must have been up on her Fosomax, that ancient shopper, because she dived straight into the fray, with no evident concern for broken bones.

"Somebody get security!" one of the box boys yelled.

A rent-a-cop appeared, overweight, his uniform shirt speckled with white powder, most likely doughnut residue.

"Did anybody see what happened?" he huffed.

"I did," said the old lady, stepping between Heather and me.

I shook free of box boy #1.

Heather struggled in the grasp of #2.

"What?" asked the security guard—Marvin, according to his name tag—dusting off his shirt with one hand.

"This one," answered the geriatric she-hero, pointing to Heather, "was harassing *that* one." The arthritic finger moved to me.

"You've got that right," I said huffily, tugging at the hem of my Be a Bad-Ass at Bert's T-shirt. "It's a fine thing when a person can't even shop for frozen dinners without being attacked by some maniac. I've got a good mind to take my business elsewhere after this."

Marvin and the box boys looked hopeful.

Heather started to cry. "She stole my *husband*," she said, with more lip wobbling.

Marvin, the box boys and the old lady studied me thoughtfully.

"She's nuts," I said. "Certifiable. Over the edge. And furthermore, her *husband* is a jerk."

"One of these days," Heather said, "I am going to kill you."

Public opinion swung in my direction.

"I rest my case," I said.

"*Did* you steal her husband?" the old lady wanted to know.

"No," I replied, ready to wheel into the sunset with my frozen dinners and what was left of my dignity. "And if I had, I'd have given him back."

With that, I pushed my shopping cart between them and headed for the checkout stand. I didn't start shaking until I was safe in my secondhand Volvo, with the windows rolled up and the doors locked.

Back at Bad-Ass Bert's, I carried my groceries inside. Eight frozen dinners, a litter box and a bag of absorbent pellets.

"I wasn't sure," I told Chester, who was waiting for me when I lugged the stuff through the door. "About the litter, I mean."

Chester sniffed the bag curiously.

"Of course," I reasoned, because I needed to hear a voice, even if it was my own, "if you don't eat, it follows that you don't poop, either."

"Meow," Chester said.

"Thanks for hanging out," I answered.

"I wish you felt that way about me," Nick said.

I swung around to see him standing next to my bookshelf, which was beside the computer, where I kept my sizeable collection of *Damn Fool's Guides*. Unfortunately, there wasn't one dealing with dead people—trust me, I'd looked the day before, when I stopped to get the Tarot tome, but Near Death Experiences was the closest thing—or crazy female stalkers, either.

"*Now* what?" I demanded, letting the kitty litter and the plastic box topple to the floor. I clutched the bag full of Lean Cuisines to my chest, like a shield.

Nick was perusing titles. "*The Damn Fool's Guide to Dating,*" he mused, running a finger along the spines. "Tantric Sex. Raising Ferrets." He paused, looked me over closely, and with compassionate concern. "Ferrets?"

"It was a passing fancy," I said, and started for the kitchen.

He followed, of course, and so did the cat.

"Tantric Sex?" Nick pressed.

"I'm single and over twenty-one," I reminded him, jerking open the freezer section of the refrigerator and tossing in the week's meals, bag and all. "And what are you doing here, if you don't mind my asking?"

"Just a friendly visit," he said. Then he opened the cupboard, took out the Oreos and sniffed them. A look of pathetic longing crossed his face.

"Here's an idea," I said, whacking the freezer door shut with the flat of one hand. "Go 'visit' your mother."

"Your attitude is very unbecoming, you know," Nick said. With a sigh, he put the Oreos back in the cupboard. "What did my mother ever do to deserve this…rancor?"

"Well, first of all," I replied, ticking number one off on my finger, "she gave birth to you. Second, she stuck her nose into our business every chance she got. And *third,* she saw to it that I got *bupkis* in the divorce." I paused. "Oh, and then there's the way her head sprouts snakes at the most unexpected moments."

"You don't like her," Nick said, sad and surprised.

"Don't take it too hard, but I don't like you very much, either."

"If you knew the trouble I have to go to, to keep a charge," he replied, quietly stricken, "you wouldn't be so rude."

I grabbed the coffee carafe, poured out the stale stuff I'd never gotten around to drinking earlier and cranked on the faucet. The pipes rattled. "If that little illusion gives you consolation, Nick," I said, "you just go with it. And while you're at it, why don't you tell me what the hell you want? As long as it isn't sex, I'll give it to you, and you can move on to the next plane of existence, or whatever it is you dead people do."

Any self-respecting spook would have been insulted enough to vanish, but not Nick. He grinned, pulled back a chair at the table and sat down. "No sex, huh?"

"Not on your—life," I said.

"Bummer," he sighed.

"Don't you have something to do? In the train station or whatever it is?"

Another sigh. "I'm stuck in the depot until I deal with you," Nick said, and he looked just earnest enough to be telling the truth.

A clear indication that he was lying through his perfect teeth.

"Are you sleeping with that biker?" he asked.

"That comes under the heading of None of Your Damn Business." I sloshed the water into the top of the coffee-maker, spooned some Starbucks into the basket and jammed the carafe onto the burner.

"A *biker,* for Christ's sake?"

"Tucker's not a biker. He's a cop. Narcotics division."

"At least his name rhymes with my opinion of him."

"Gee, and your opinion matters so much."

"You didn't used to be so hard."

"Well, *you* haven't changed at all." I leaned against the counter, folding my arms. Chester wound his silky way around my ankles. "You're still an arrogant, self-centered ass."

"I *have* changed, Mojo."

"Right," I agreed tartly. "You're dead."

"That was a low blow."

"It's true, isn't it?"

"I'm trying to help you."

"How? By scaring me out of my wits? By undermining my sanity?"

"I brought back your cat."

I looked down at Chester and, on impulse, scooped him up. He felt so real, and pretty chunky. Whatever they were feeding him on the other side, it was sticking to his ribs.

Suddenly, I wanted to cry. I knew I'd loved Chester once, and I was dangerously close to loving him again.

"You never got to say goodbye to him," Nick said.

I buried my face in white, warm fur. "He can't stay," I mourned.

"No," Nick agreed gently. "It's a frequency thing. These appearances are pretty tough to sustain. But he's not dead, Mojo. He's alive, but in a whole different way. That's the point."

Chester's fur was damp, where I'd cried on him. "It's the same with you." Statement, but it had the tone of a question.

Nick nodded. "The difference is, when he goes back, he'll be able to get onto a train and go on to whatever his idea of heaven happens to be. I'll still be stuck at the station."

I was grudgingly intrigued, if not necessarily sympathetic. I'd loved Nick completely, and he might as well have torn my heart out of my body and backed over it with a UPS truck. "Why?"

"Unresolved issues," he said, with yet another sigh.

I studied him, still holding Chester as close as I could without squashing him. "What kind of unresolved issues?" I asked suspiciously.

"You trusted me. You loved me. And I betrayed you. I have to earn your forgiveness."

"Is that all?" I sniffed, reluctantly set Chester down on the floor, straightened again. "Okay. That's easy. You're forgiven. Now, kindly hop on the Starlight Express and stop showing up in my apartment."

If I hadn't known better, I would have sworn Nick was being sincere. He actually looked remorseful. "Sorry," he said. "It *isn't* that easy. You can't just toss off a platitude. You have to really mean it."

"Shit," I said.

He looked like a kicked puppy. "Was it that bad? I remember some really good times together."

"Do you?" I grabbed a mug down off the shelf. No sense getting two; if Nick couldn't eat Oreos, he probably couldn't drink coffee, either. "Maybe you're confusing me with your secretary—excuse me, *executive assistant*. I caught you boinking her in a construction trailer once, remember? Or maybe it's that sweet young thing in the condo down the hall from ours. The one who always wanted you to fix something. Or—"

Nick put up a hand, rose wearily to his feet. "I'm sorry, Mojo. What else can I say? I can't change the past."

Tears stung my eyes. "Get out, Nick."

He was gone in a blink.

And Chester went with him.

"YOU'VE BEEN CRYING," Greer accused, when I showed up at her mansion outside of Scottsdale at five to six that night, bringing along a bottle of Chardonnay donated by Bert. A glorious Arizona sunset blazed crimson and pink and apricot on the western horizon.

"No, I haven't," I said. It was a partial truth, anyway. I'd spent the afternoon at my computer, coding and billing, and the May rent was a sure thing. I'd also gone through a whole box of tissues.

Greer looked rich—and skeptical—in her floaty flowered skirt and pink matching top. Her blond hair was in a French braid, and I wondered how she stood so straight, with Dr. Pennington's diamond weighing down her left hand. I figure the jewelry alone keeps Scottsdale chiropractors operating in the black.

"Your eyes are red," she said.

Once, I would have spilled it all. Told Greer about Nick and Chester. But Greer was different now that she was married. The change was subtle, but I wasn't imagining it.

I had to tell her something, so I went with Lillian, the three Tarot cards, and my chat with Uncle Clive. Maybe, I thought, after a glass of wine I might even get as far as Crazy Heather and the supermarket caper.

Listening intently, Greer led the way across the brick-paved portico and through the open doors at the top of the steps. The house alone covered more than ten thousand square feet of prime desert, and the art inside was museum quality stuff. The furniture was tastefully expensive, and I could see the back patio in the distance, through a set of glass doors. Nothing but the best for Greer Pennington, world-class trophy wife.

Okay, so maybe I sound a little mean-spirited. I loved Greer, but she could have been a lot more than some old fart's pampered wife, and that bugged the hell out of me. Before Alex, she'd put herself through art school, worked for other people for a while to learn the ropes, then gone on to start and run her own design firm. She'd been successful, too, after a rocky start.

When Alex snapped his fingers, though, she'd sold the company without even a mild protest. In fact, she'd seemed relieved. And that was what bothered me. Not that Greer was set for life, at least financially. I was happy for her. No, it was the way she'd given up on her own dreams. Put on a costume, learned the lines and played the second wife as if she'd never done all that hard work to make something of herself.

We settled ourselves in cushioned patio chairs, under a sloping tiled roof, near the sparkling pool. Greer checked out the wine label, smiled charitably and carried the bottle into the kitchen by way of yet another door.

When she returned with two crystal glasses, I figured she'd pulled a switcheroo, probably dumping Bert's Chardonnay down the sink and filling the goblets with something French or Napa and ridiculously expensive.

"Should you be drinking if there's a chance you might be pregnant?" I inquired.

Greer looked away for a moment, then looked back. "Not

to worry," she said, reaching for her glass. "I am definitely *not* pregnant."

I knew she wanted a baby, to make her happy home with Dr. Pennington complete, and I felt a pinching sorrow behind my heart. "I'm sorry," I said, and I meant it.

Greer downed a couple of sips—more like gulps—of her wine, and gave a gurgling, disjointed little laugh. Nothing was funny, and we both knew it, but Greer liked to pretend. Maybe it was a survival mechanism.

"You told me on the phone this morning that you didn't feel well," I said. "Have you been to a doctor?"

"I'm *married* to a doctor."

Didn't I know it? "You have shadows under your eyes, and I think you've lost weight. What's going on, Greer?"

She sucked up some more wine before answering, and when she did, she ignored my question entirely and presented one of her own. "Do you think it's because of—well—things I did when I was young?"

I scrambled to catch up. "You mean your not being pregnant?"

Greer looked around nervously, as though the editor of the country club newsletter might be crouching behind the cabana, taking notes, or lurking on the other side of the towering stucco wall enclosing at least an acre of backyard. The windows of the guesthouse, opposite the pool, caught the colors of the sunset and turned opaque. "Yes," she said, and it seemed to me that she'd gone to a lot of trouble, scoping out the landscape, just to say one word.

"Lillian had you checked out at a free clinic in Vegas,

remember? You were fine. No STD's, no residual effects whatsoever. It wasn't the hooking, Greer."

She tensed, and what little color she'd had drained from her cheeks. "Keep your voice down!"

"Sorry," I said, chagrined. I always felt out of place at Greer's, and I tended to put my foot in my mouth. "You're alone here, aren't you? Carmen is gone for the day?"

Carmen was her housekeeper—a very nice woman, but not much for overtime.

Greer nodded miserably. "I didn't mean to snap," she said.

I patted her hand. "It's okay."

She fortified herself with more wine. I decided it was probably cramps that made her look so woebegone and beaten. "Nothing in my life," she said, "is 'okay.'"

CHAPTER

I'd love to report that Greer and I got right to the heart of things, over our dinner of thinly sliced smoked salmon, gourmet bagels and cream cheese with capers, and settled all our collective and individual problems, but we didn't. Greer drank wine—first hers, then mine. She shook her head when I told her about Heather and the supermarket incident, and said I ought to move to a civilized neighborhood.

What one had to do with the other was beyond me then, and I still don't exactly get it.

I tried to communicate. I really did. I told her about Lillian and the Tarot cards, and running into Uncle Clive at the nursing home.

She recalled that he was a state senator and wondered aloud if he and his wife would ever make the trip up from Cactus Bend to attend one of her gala parties. It wasn't so much that Greer was uncaring; she just couldn't seem to get any kind of grip on the conversational thread.

I would have been better off talking to Chester, and I don't think the evening did much for Greer, either, except perhaps to provide some brief respite from whatever was weighing on her mind.

At eight-thirty, I thanked my sister for her hospitality, said my goodbyes and left. Greer was a lonely, shrinking figure in my rearview mirror, standing in her brick-paved driveway, watching me out of sight.

I was too restless to go straight home. I knew the cat was gone, and if he'd come back, the chances were all too good that Nick was with him. I wasn't up to another dead-husband fest, so I headed for one of my favorite places—the casino at 101 and Indian Bend.

Talking Stick was doing a lively business that night, its domed, tent-shaped roofs giving it a circus-type appeal. I parked the Volvo at the far end of the eastern lot and trekked back to the nearest entrance, my ATM card already smoking in my wallet.

Inside, I pulled some money at the handy-dandy cash machine next to the guest services desk. A security guard gave me a welcoming wave; I won a lot, though I was usually careful to keep the jackpots small, so I wouldn't attract too much notice, and it had gotten to the point where everybody knew my name.

"Cheers," I told the guard as I breezed by, weaving my way between banks of whirring slot machines beckoning with bright, inviting lights. I passed the Wheel of Fortunes, with their colorful spinners up top, and the ever popular Double Diamonds, which were always occupied. I used to play them a lot, but then the powers-that-be cranked the progressive jackpot down by a thousand bucks, and it became a matter of principle.

I passed the gift shop and the bar and came to the blackjack tables, lining either side of the wide aisle. A shifting layer of cigarette smoke hung over everything like a cloud. I'm not a smoker, but hey, the poor bastards have to have *somewhere* to hang out.

Brian Dillard, one of the blackjack dealers, stood idle. My jerk o meter went off like a slot machine on tilt, but I stopped anyway. Discretion may be the better part of valor, but discretion, like truth, sometimes gets more hype than it really warrants.

Brian checked out my jean jacket and cotton sun-shift, as if there were a dress code and he got to decide whether I met it or not.

"I saw your ex-wife at the supermarket today," I told him.

Brian made a visible shift from lascivious to nervous. "Heather?" he asked weakly, keeping his voice down lest a pit boss overhear. Personal exchanges are not encouraged in any casino I've ever been to, especially if they have dramatic potential. If you want to get the bum's rush, just make a scene.

"Unless you've been married and divorced again since last time I saw you, yes. If she's not on medication, you might suggest it."

He looked anxiously around, then met my gaze again. "What happened?"

I don't think Brian was concerned about my personal
safety. He just wanted me to spit out whatever I was going
to say and get away from his table.

I told him about the cart ramming, and the death threat.

He paled.

I wondered what I ever saw in the guy.

"You have four kids, Brian," I said, bringing it on home.
"They're living with a crazy woman. You might want to re-
visit the custody agreement."

The pallor gave way to a flush. "I can't take care of four
kids," he shot back in a hissing whisper. "Hell, two of them
aren't even mine."

Double what-did-I-see-in-this-guy. "Okay. Then maybe
some concerned citizen—like me, for instance—ought to
call CPS and get a social worker to look into the situation."
I got out my cell phone.

"Wait," Brian rasped, as a pit boss glanced our way. I
could have played a hand or two, for cover, but blackjack
isn't my game.

I raised an eyebrow. Didn't put the cell phone away.

"I'll talk to Heather, okay?" Brian blurted. "I'll tell her to
leave you alone."

I must not have looked satisfied.

"And I'll make sure the kids are all right."

"You're a shoo-in for Father of the Year," I said dryly, but
I dropped my weapon. I was by no means reassured that the
innocent offspring were out of the parental woods, but I
wasn't Lillian, and I couldn't snatch the mini-Dillards and
take to the road. I had a life.

Well, a semblance of one, anyway. I hadn't completely given up.

I left Brian to his dealing and headed for the "car bank," a group of slot machines just inside the main entrance. There's always a gleaming new vehicle parked on a high platform in the middle; you have to hit three of something, on the pay-line, to win it.

I've seen it happen, so it's legit. Sometimes, the same rig sits there for weeks on end, and sometimes they give away two of them in a day. I'd have worked my mojo and snagged one for myself, but I liked my Volvo well enough and, besides, I didn't want to pay the taxes and license fees.

I sat down at my favorite, a certain twenty-five-cent Ten Times Pay machine, shoved in my comps card—hey, I could eat free for months on the points I've racked up, and you never know when you're going to get poor all of the sudden—fed a fifty dollar bill in to buy two hundred credits.

I drew a deep breath, let it out slowly, and tried to align myself with the Cosmic Flow. Even the best casinos are energetic garbage dumps, with all that greed and desperation floating around, and it's important to get Zen. Lillian taught me the trick, and when I play, I usually win.

If I get the mindset right, that is. I had to shake off the Brian influence.

That night, I'd burned through seventy-five credits before I got a hit. Ten Times Triple Bar, nine hundred virtual quarters. I rubbed my hands together.

"Come to mama," I said.

I didn't focus on the guy who dropped into the seat at the

machine next to mine right away, though I got a glimpse of him in my peripheral vision as soon as he sat down.

He was good-looking, probably in his late thirties, with a head of sleek, light brown hair and the kind of body you have to sweat for, often and hard. I wanted to ignore him, but I could tell by the way he kept shifting around and glancing my way that he wanted to talk.

Shit, I thought.

"I'm just waiting for a spot to open at one of the poker tables," he said.

"Mmm-hmm," I replied, hoping he'd take the hint and leave me alone. Watching the reels spin is a form of meditation for me, and I like to focus. It unscrambles my brain in a way nothing else does, except maybe really good sex, and even on a generous gambling budget, it's a lot cheaper than therapy.

Come to think of it, it's cheaper than really good sex, too, from an emotional standpoint.

"I think I've seen you somewhere before." Mr. Smooth.

I suppressed an eye-roll and pushed the spin button with a little more force than necessary. He wasn't even pretending to play his slot machine anymore; just leaning against the supporting woodwork, with his arms folded.

"I get that all the time," I said tersely. "I must be a type."

He chuckled. It was a rich, confident sound, low in timbre, and it struck some previously unknown chord deep inside me. It could have been fear, it could have been annoyance. All I knew was, it wasn't anything sexual; I'm a one-man woman, even when the man in question is thoroughly unavailable. "And not a very friendly one, either," he observed.

I gave him a brief look. Ever since the first Nick episode, I hadn't trusted my own eyeballs. "You're not dead, are you?"

He shrank back, but with a grin, and extended one hand. "What a question," he said. "Do you run into a lot of dead people?"

I ignored the hand, took in his boyish face, his wide-set, earnest gray eyes, his strong jaw. In the next moment, I leaped out of my chair and backed up a couple of steps. I know my eyes were wide, and my voice came out as a squeak.

"Geoff!"

My parent-murdering, cat-killing half brother contrived to look affably mystified, and threw my own line back in my face. "I must be a type," he said. "My name isn't Geoff. It's Steve. Steve Roberts." He actually fished for his wallet then, as though prepared to show me his driver's license or something, and prove his identity.

"Maybe *now* it is," I retorted, snatching up my purse so I could get out of there. I didn't even push the "cash out" button to get a ticket for my credits, that's how rattled I was. Still, I couldn't resist asking, "When did you get out of prison, Geoff?"

He sighed. He had one of those give-your-heart-to-Jesus faces, good skin, good teeth, neat hair. And there was a cold knowing in his eyes that bit into my entrails like a bear trap.

"You must be mistaking me for somebody else," Geoff said sadly.

I turned on my heel and bolted.

Midway through the casino, I turned to see if he was following me, but the place was crowded, and even though I didn't catch a glimpse of him, I couldn't be sure. I found a security guard, told him I'd won a major cash jackpot, and asked him to walk me to my car.

Even then I didn't feel safe.

I locked the doors as soon as I was in the Volvo, and my hand shook so hard as I tried to put the keys in the ignition that it took three tries before I got it right. I screeched out of the parking lot, checking my rearview for a tail every couple of seconds, and laid rubber for the 101, hauling north.

My heart felt as though it had swelled to fill my whole torso, and my blood thundered in my ears like a steady thump on some huge drum.

Geoff.

Parent killer.

Cat murderer.

He hadn't turned up at the casino by accident, that was too great a coincidence, so he must have deliberately followed me there. How long had he been watching me, keeping track of my movements? Did he know where I lived?

Was I on his hit list? And if so, why? He'd already done his time. What did he have to fear from me?

He killed Chester. The reminder boiled up out of my subconscious mind. *What other reason could he have had, except pure meanness?*

My dinner scalded its way up into the back of my throat. I swallowed hard. I might have been scared shitless, but I wasn't about to vomit in the Volvo. You can't get the smell out.

I got back to Cave Creek without incident, and for once, I was glad to see Tucker's distinctive bike parked in the lot. I sat there in my car, with the engine running and the doors locked, and felt frantically around in the depths of my purse for my cell phone.

It eluded me, so I upended the whole bag on the passenger seat, scrabbled through the usual purse detritus until I closed my hand over high-tech salvation, and speed-dialed Tucker's number.

"Mojo?" he said, after three rings. I heard the sound of pool balls clicking, and the twang of some mournful tune playing on the jukebox.

Thank God, I thought.

I tilted my head back and closed my eyes, hyperventilating.

Tucker tried again, this time with a note of urgency in his voice. "Mojo? Is that you? Where—? Damn it, *say* something."

"I saw him," I ground out. Then I had to slap a hand over my mouth for a moment, because I was either going to puke or start screaming.

"You saw *who*?"

According to the *Damn Fool's Guide to English Grammar,* he should have said "whom," but this was no time to split hairs. The man was an ASU graduate, for God's sake. If he hadn't mastered the language by now, there was no point in correcting him.

I spoke through parted fingers. "My b-brother."

"I didn't know you *had* a brother," Tucker mused. "Where are you?"

I uncovered my mouth, but screaming and puking were still viable options. "In the parking lot," I squeaked.

"You're calling from the parking lot?"

Screaming squeezed out puking and took a solid lead. "No, damn it! I'm calling from the freakin' roof!"

"Chill," Tucker said. "I'll be right out."

I watched, still clutching the phone to my ear, as the side door swung open and Tucker ambled out of Bad-Ass Bert's. He scanned the lot, got a fix on the Volvo, and sprinted in my direction.

I rolled down the driver's side window about an inch.

"He might have followed me," I whispered.

Tucker braced his hands on the side of the Volvo and peered in at me. "Open the door, Mojo," he said.

"He killed my cat," I said. *Not to mention my parents.*

"Christ," Tucker snapped, and pulled at the door handle.

I popped the locks, and he almost fell on his very attractive ass in the gravel.

"I need help," I told him.

"That's for damn sure," Tucker agreed. He sounded testy, but I could tell he was concerned by the way he kept sweeping the lot with his gaze. He reached into the car, unfastened the seat belt and tugged me out, onto my feet.

I landed hard against his chest, and I'll admit it, I clung for a couple of seconds.

"I saw him," I repeated.

Tucker held me up with one arm, reached inside for my purse and car keys with the other. "Come on," he said.

"Let's get you upstairs. Can you make it on your own, or should I carry you?"

The offer was tempting, but I had a thing about standing on my own two feet whenever possible, literally and figuratively. Besides, Tucker and I were officially Not Dating, and I was just scared enough to go from being carried to being laid without passing Go and certainly without collecting $200.

I gave a moment's forlorn thought to the credits I'd left in the Ten Times Pay machine when I fled the casino. I could have made my car payment with that money.

"I can walk," I said, though it was still pretty much a theory.

Tuck squired me up the stairs, unlocked the door and swung it open.

Chester sat waiting in the hallway. There was a faint, greenish glow around him.

I burst into tears.

Tucker muttered something, steered me to the couch and bent over me to look deep into my weepy eyes.

"Booze," I said.

"You've been drinking booze?"

"No. I *want* to drink booze. Now."

Tucker nodded, probably relieved that he wouldn't have to bust me for drinking and driving, went into the kitchen, rifled the cupboards and came back with a double shot of Christian Brothers in a jelly glass. I hadn't touched that bottle since the last bad bout of cramps, but if things kept going the way they'd *been* going, I'd be hitting the sauce on an hourly basis.

I took a few sips, holding the jelly glass with both hands. Chester jumped onto the back of the couch and nestled behind my neck, purring. Tucker dragged over an ottoman and sat down, his knees touching mine.

"Start at the beginning and take it slow," he said.

I knocked back the rest of the brandy and set the glass aside. My nerves, all trying to break through my skin only seconds before, collapsed with dizzying suddenness.

"When I was five years old," I said shakily, "my half brother shot my mom and dad to death."

Tucker's face tightened. "Jesus *Christ*," he muttered.

I drew another deep breath. Let it out.

"Go on," Tucker urged.

"I was there, but if I saw what happened, I don't remember. A neighbor found me hiding in the clothes dryer. I was d-drenched in blood. *Their* blood—"

I gagged a couple of times.

"Easy," Tucker said, and took both my hands in his.

His strong grasp felt so treacherously good that I immediately pulled free.

"My half brother—his name is Geoff—was arrested that night, according to the newspaper accounts I read a lot later. He confessed, so there wasn't a trial, and they sent him to a youthful offenders' program in California."

Tucker nodded in solemn encouragement when my voice faltered again, but he didn't say anything. He might have looked like a biker, but he was in cop mode now.

"I saw *him* tonight, Tuck. At Talking Stick. He sat down at the slot machine next to mine—" I swallowed, pushed my hair back with the palm of my right hand. "It was the Sizzling Sevens."

A faint grin flickered at one corner of Tucker's mouth, gone as quickly as it appeared. His eyes were dead serious.

"Are you sure it was him? Not just somebody who *looked* like your brother?"

"My *half* brother," I said. I didn't want to claim even that much of Geoff, but we had the same mother. The thought made me want to check into a hospital, have all my blood drained out and replaced with somebody else's. "And *yes,* Tucker, it was Geoff. He tried to pass himself off as Steve Roberts, but I know who he was."

Tucker took a notepad from his hip pocket and scrawled the name on a page, but I knew what he was thinking. There were probably a dozen Steve Robertses in Phoenix alone, never mind all the once-separate cities butting up against its sprawling borders—Scottsdale, Mesa, Tempe, Chandler, Glendale.

"Google," I said, catching sight of the computer across the room, and started to get off the couch.

Tucker pressed me gently back onto the cushion. "Take a few minutes to catch your breath," he said. "You look like you've seen a ghost."

An hysterical laugh bubbled out of my throat at the irony of that statement. Then I started to shiver.

Tucker got off the ottoman, disappeared into the bedroom and returned with an afghan, which he wrapped tightly around my shoulders. I snuggled in.

"Did he threaten you?" Tucker asked.

"Not exactly," I answered, huddling inside a field of yarn

daisies. Jolie had made the afghan for Nick and me, years before, as a wedding gift. God, I wished I could talk to Jolie, but she was a workaholic and probably busy in her Tucson lab, sorting bones.

"How come you never told me what happened to your parents?" Tucker asked. At the same time, he went to the computer, perched on the edge of the desk chair, and logged onto my Internet account. The password was stored, so there was no delay.

"The time never seemed right."

"Uh-huh," Tucker said tightly.

I bristled. "We were only together for six weeks," I reminded him. "What was I supposed to say? 'Oh, by the way, when I was five, my half brother slaughtered our parents, and a neighbor kidnapped me, and I've been living under an alias ever since'?"

Too late, I realized that I'd given away a lot more than I'd intended.

Tucker spun around in the desk chair. "*What?*"

"I don't want to talk about this right now."

"You've been living under an alias?"

"Not *now,* Tucker."

He glared at me for a long moment, then spun back to the computer and started punching keys. On TV, cops usually use the hunt-and-peck method, but Tucker knew his keyboard, and all ten fingers tapped at a steady clip.

"Don't think for one damn second," he warned, without turning around, "that I'm going to pretend we didn't have this conversation."

He paused after a while, and peered at the screen.

"Is this him?"

I got off the couch, letting Chester roll unceremoniously to the cushions, and padded over to look at the monitor.

Sure enough, there was Geoff, smiling out of a Web page. I sucked in a breath.

"I'll take that for a yes," Tucker said, and printed the page.

I leaned over his shoulder, studying the site.

"Steve Roberts" worked as a private nurse, an RN, no less. He sold vitamins for some network marketing outfit, too, and was available for consultations. Consultations! *Have you been thinking of murdering your parents? I can tell you how to do it and get away with a slap on the wrist. Why, in no time at all, you'll be back on the streets, looking for your next victim!*

I shivered.

"I don't think you should be alone tonight," Tucker said.

"I'm not going to your place."

"Then I'll stay here."

"On the couch."

He sighed.

"On the couch," he agreed, but belatedly, and with reluctance.

SOMETHING LANDED heavily on my chest. Sprawled in the middle of my bed, I opened one eye to sunlight and a purring white cat. I felt the familiar mingling of delight and sadness as I looked into Chester's fuzzy face.

"I'm so sorry he killed you," I whispered, stroking his back.

I heard the shower running and for a moment I was jarred, until I remembered that Tucker had spent the night. I'd no more than formed the thought when the pipes stopped rattling. I eased Chester off my breasts and rolled onto my side; I didn't want to be caught petting empty air when Tucker put in an appearance.

He did just that, a minute or so later, standing naked in the doorway, except for a towel around his waist. I put down an unseemly urge to 1—summon Tucker to my bed and 2—lick the little droplets of standing water off every muscled inch of his flesh.

"Coffee's on," he said.

Chester hopped onto the broad window sill and sat looking down at the main street of Cave Creek, tail slowly sweeping the warm morning air.

I was grappling with my libido. In short, I wanted some nookie.

What harm would it do? said libido inquired.

I thought of Tucker's kids. The custody battle. His beautiful ex-wife. Sure, they were divorced, but Allison still had a powerful hold on him. He visited regularly, despite their conflict; he'd been up front about that from the first. I couldn't be sure all the emotional ties had been broken, and I knew it would kill me if they were still sleeping together.

The best orgasm I ever had with Nick happened an hour after we left the courtroom, with the ink still wet on our decree.

I don't need another broken heart, I replied.

"I'll be with you in a few minutes," I said, quelling the need to stretch because it might be misinterpreted as a sensual invitation, and I was barely holding on to my resolve as it was.

Tucker looked disappointed but resigned. "I've got to get to work anyway," he said. "You'll be all right alone?"

For some reason, those innocuous words blew through my soul like an icy wind. *You'll be all right alone?*

It wasn't just Tucker talking. It was the whole universe.

I blinked a couple of times. "Sure. I was just a little freaked out last night, that's all. Thanks for staying. I really appreciate it."

After a beat, Tucker nodded. "If you don't mind, I'd like to take that printout from your brother's Web site. Do some follow-up."

"I'd appreciate that," I said.

Tucker made the slightest move, a sort of gathering of his forces, as though he might take a step toward me. Then he stopped himself, turned and went back into the bathroom to put on yesterday's clothes. I wondered if a shower violated his job description, since he usually looked like he'd been living in a shelter for at least a week.

It occurred to me, as I was lying there feeling sorry for myself, that I didn't know much more about Tucker than he did about me. I knew he was a detective with Scottsdale PD, and that he worked Narcotics. I knew he had an ex-wife and two beautiful kids.

Oh, yes. And I knew he could drive me crazy in bed.

That was about the sum of it, though.

I felt a little better, having thus justified keeping my own secrets, but not much.

When I heard the outside door close and Tucker's boots on the stairs, I got out of bed. After nipping down the hall to turn the dead bolt, I wandered into the kitchen and poured myself a cup of coffee.

It was when I went to the refrigerator, hoping a carton of eggs might have materialized while I slept, that I saw the sticky note he'd left on the freezer door.

"We've got a lot more to talk about. Like why you own a litter box and no cat. See you tonight. Tucker."

"That's what I get," I told Chester, now watching me with interest from the floor, "for getting involved with a detective."

Chester wound himself around my ankles, his fur tickling my bare feet.

"Ree-ooow," he said earnestly.

I bent, my eyes stinging, and gathered him in my arms. "How am I going to explain the cat litter?" I asked.

He snuggled close, humming like a lawn mower at full throttle.

"Don't go," I whispered. "Don't leave me."

He did.

It wasn't a poof—nothing as dramatic as that.

He just dissolved in my arms, between one moment and the next.

One of these days, I knew, Chester was going to pull his vanishing act for good, and I would never see him again.

I was standing there in my kitchen, wondering what to do with the rest of my life, never mind the remains of the day, when the telephone rang. It's funny how fate answers questions like that, even when I don't consciously ask them.

I checked the caller ID in the wild hope of heading off a conversation with either Heather the Stalker or Geoff the Parent/Cat Killer, and saw Clive Larimer's name and number in the little window. With only slight trepidation, I pressed the talk button. "Mojo Sheepshanks," I said.

My uncle responded with his name, in a businesslike tone, and then a smile sneaked into his voice. "Mojo Sheepshanks, is it? I guess I'll have to get used to that, but you'll always be Mary Jo to me."

I didn't know what to say to that, so I didn't say anything. If things fell out right, though, I decided I *might* get around to telling him about last night's casino encounter with the mad killer. I was used to playing my cards close to my vest, and it would be a hard habit to break.

"We have a lot of catching up to do," my uncle went on. I liked the warm, confident timbre of his voice. "Barbara— that's my wife—and I are hoping you'll drive down to Cactus Bend for a visit today or tomorrow, if it's not too short notice. We have a guesthouse, so you'd have a little privacy. We don't want this to be too much, all at once."

I knew Larimer's voting record in the state senate, and his surface stats—married to Barbara, four beautiful offspring, gracious mansion just outside of Cactus Bend. He was considered a contender in the upcoming governor's race, too. Beyond those public-consumption details, though, he was merely a misty figure from a past plunged into oblivion one horrible night in 1983.

I hadn't been back to Cactus Bend since the day Lillian and I went on the lam. I couldn't help passing it whenever I went to see Jolie in Tucson, but I always whizzed by the freeway exit with my jaw clenched and my gaze fixed straight ahead.

An old, nameless fear gripped me, all of a sudden; Jolie and six or eight different therapists had suggested, more than once, that I had deliberately chosen *not* to remember the murders. Now, scared as I was, I was also curious, and I needed some answers. Maybe it was time to bite the bullet and wade in.

"Okay," I heard myself say. It was Thursday; the weekend was coming up. I could check out Clive and Barbara, in their native habitat, ask a few questions and answer a few of theirs. In case of cataclysmic anxiety, I could always either speed back north to Cave Creek or pay Jolie a visit in Tucson. Come to think of it, the latter wasn't a bad idea. I hadn't seen my foster sister in two months.

"Will I be meeting the children?" I heard myself ask. I hadn't given the Larimer sibs a conscious thought, but my shadow side wasn't up for the inevitable comparisons between their lives and mine. They were professionals, no doubt. I, on the other hand, lived over a bar, read *Damn Fool's Guides,* and did billing and coding for half a dozen doctors to scrape out a living.

Greer could be right, I conceded silently. There was a good chance that I needed to get a real job.

Hell, I needed to get a *life.*

Uncle Clive chuckled warmly. "The 'children' are thirty-two, twenty-nine, twenty-six and twenty-four respectively, and scattered all over the country. We'll show you their pictures and tell you all about them—probably more than you want to know. Anyway, it's better if you just have Barbara and me to contend with on this first trip." He paused, waiting for me to agree.

"You're right," I said.

"You'll join us, then?"

"Yes," I decided, in that moment. It would be good to get out of town for a few days. I was caught up on my work, Tucker and I were on hold, and here was an opportunity to put some miles between myself and my half brother.

Unless, of course, he decided to follow me.

Don't be paranoid, I told myself.

"When should we expect you?"

I glanced at the clock on the stove. It was barely eight-thirty, but I was running low on clean clothes, so a trip to the Laundromat was critical. I needed some cash, too, and I wanted to stop and look in on Lillian before I left the area. "Four o'clock?" I ventured.

"Just in time for cocktails," Uncle Clive said, and gave me unnecessary directions. I hadn't been to Cactus Bend in a lot of years, it was true, but I still knew the general layout of the town. Guess it was sort of like riding a bike—one of those things you don't forget, no matter how traumatized you are.

After Clive and I hung up, I immediately put a call through to Jolie.

"Travers," she answered. Evidently, her assistant, who usually screened calls, either hadn't come in yet or was otherwise occupied.

Sweet memories washed over me at the sound of Jolie's no-nonsense voice. My life changed for the better when I was thirteen, and Jolie was a major factor in the turnaround. Lillian met Jolie's dad, Michael "Ham" Hamilton, a recently widowed security guard, in Ventura Beach, California. They'd fallen madly in love, and Lillian had finally settled down. There was never a wedding, as far as I know, but Lillian took Ham's last name, and it was definitely a good match. Jolie hadn't accepted Lillian, Greer and me right away, but in time we'd melded into a family.

Lillian had loved Ham so much that, when he'd decided to take a job in Phoenix, she'd willingly followed him. Jolie, Greer and I had all come along, of course, though Lillian had insisted on home schooling Greer and me. I don't know if she ever told Ham the whole truth, or any part of it. I *do* know that she was happy with him, and when he died nearly a decade into their relationship, she went on the emotional skids.

"Hell-ooo," Jolie prompted.

I laughed. "Don't hang up," I said. "It's Mojo."

"Give me one good reason why I shouldn't *slam* this phone down in your ear," Jolie shot back. "I haven't had so much as an e-mail from you in three weeks."

"I'm heading down that way, and I'd like to see you."

"Really?" Jolie sounded pleased. "You wouldn't jerk a girl around, would you?"

"It's for real. I'm sorry about the e-mails—I've just been…well…distracted."

"By what?" Jolie demanded suspiciously.

"Things," I said evasively. "I'll tell all when I get there, I promise."

"Freakin' A," said Jolie.

"I have some business to attend to tonight, and you've got work in the morning. How about tomorrow night?"

"I'll even change the sheets on the hide-a-bed," Jolie said, with one of her rich laughs. Jolie's voice matched her dark-chocolate skin. She was smart as hell and beautiful enough to be a model or a TV star. If she hadn't worked an average of eighteen hours a day, she'd have had men making pilgrimages to her door on their knees.

"Anybody sharing *your* bed these days?" I ventured hopefully.

Jolie's sigh was telling. "No. How about you?"

"Tucker and I are on hiatus."

"Mmm-hmm," she agreed skeptically.

I let that one pass. "It's really okay for me to crash at your place? I wouldn't want to impose."

Jolie gave a snort. "Just don't sneak off in the middle of the night, like you did last time. I swear, Mojo, sometimes I think you turn into a she-wolf at the full moon, or something."

"What is that supposed to mean?" I retorted, hedging. I knew exactly what Jolie was talking about. It hadn't happened in a while, but occasionally I had nightmares, full of faceless characters in black hooded robes, grabbing at me with skeletal fingers. My own personal crew of Dementors. On the referenced occasion, I was staying at Jolie's place. I'd gotten out of bed at roughly 1:30 a.m., pulled on my clothes, left a hasty note, and booked it back to Cave Creek.

"Let's not get into an argument before you even get here, all right? You may be white, and you may be crazy, but except for Sweet Lillian and Greer, you're all I've got. How *is* Lady Bountiful these days, anyway? Still livin' the high life in Scottsdale? And before you answer—how's Lillian?"

"I'll bring you up to speed on Lillian when I get to your place. I'm planning on stopping by Sunset Villa on my way south to make sure she's all right." I paused. "As for Greer— well, she's Greer." There was something off about Mrs. Pennington, but mentioning that could wait until Jolie and I met in person.

"I'll be looking for you Friday night, then," Jolie said. "Call my cell if I'm not at the apartment when you get there."

I promised I would and hung up.

Breakfast was a Lean Cuisine. I kept hoping, as I went through my wardrobe for clean and presentable items of clothing, that Chester would pop in—it would even have been worth another round with Nick to see my cat—but he didn't show. Maybe he'd hopped one of those trains out of the heavenly depot, bound for feline glory.

I had mixed feelings about that. On the one hand, Chester deserved Cat Paradise. On the other, I'd have to start missing him all over again.

I packed my toothbrush and cosmetics, stuffed what I intended to wear into a black garbage bag, and left the apartment. Next stop, Maggie's Spin-N-Dry.

Bert's bike wasn't in the lot, and I could see the padlock gleaming on the side door, still fastened tight. I wanted to let him know I was going to be away for a few days, both so he wouldn't worry and as an incentive to keep an eye on my apartment. I decided to stop by after my laundry was done.

A chill tiptoed up my spine and did a moon-walk at my nape.

I looked around again. Nobody in sight, but I would have sworn I was being watched. Seriously creepy feeling.

I opened the rear door of the Volvo, on the driver's side, and tossed in my trash bag. Something drew my gaze upward, to the apartment, and I saw Nick's face, framed in the kitchen window. I couldn't read his expression from that distance, but I knew he was trying to push my buttons.

I'm a poor lonely ghost. How can you leave me like this?

I actually considered going back upstairs to keep the dead ex company for a little while—and maybe Chester was with him—but I wasn't going to get my laundry done and make

Cactus Bend by four o'clock if I tarried. So I smiled and did a waggly-fingered wave, then got into the Volvo and sped away.

I felt only mildly guilty.

Things went okay at Maggie's. I folded my blue sundress, clean jeans, fresh underwear and T-shirts, put them back in the garbage bag and made for the Volvo. One of these days, I was going to have to invest in a suitcase.

The lot was full at Bert's when I got back, and the kitchen window was empty.

I decided not to go upstairs and conduct a paranormal investigation. If Nick's business, whatever it was, suddenly became urgent, he could probably haunt me even if I was on the move.

Bert was busy behind the bar as I entered, so I stopped to pet Russell, who was on his bar stool, licking his chops after a pepperoni donation. A few scraps remained, but I predicted he'd make short work of those, and I was right.

"Hey, Mojo," Bert said. "Trying to score a free coffee?"

"I wouldn't mind one for the road," I answered, and zeroed in on the coffeemaker.

"You goin' somewhere?" Bert asked.

I lowered my voice, although the jukebox and the steady click of pool balls were so loud, the risk of being overheard was minimal. "Cactus Bend," I said. "Then a day or two in Tucson, with my sister. I ought to be back by Monday afternoon. Would you mind trying my apartment door a couple of times, just to make sure it hasn't been kicked in or jimmied open?"

"Sure," he said, and the old baby blues twinkled. "Sheila's

after me to shut down the bar for a few days next week, so we can go camping up at Oak Creek Canyon. You mind dog-sitting while we're gone? Russell isn't much for sleeping under the stars."

I grinned, touched Bert's shoulder as I passed with a large coffee to go. "I'll bet he doesn't mind camp food, though." In my opinion, Sheila was right—Bert needed some time off. In the two years I'd lived over the saloon, he'd never turned away a day's business. In fact, last Christmas morning, he and Sheila had thrown a party for their customers, right there on the premises. I stopped to ruffle Russell's ears. "I'd be happy to look after the fur-face."

Bert's smile broadened with gratitude. "He farts," he said, in farewell.

"Great," I said, in mock horror. "I'll lay in some air freshener. See you Monday."

Bert nodded, and I ducked out.

I gave the parking lot a quick sweep of the eyeballs, but I was basically over yesterday's fright. Anyway, if Geoff appeared, all I'd have to do was yell for help and half the bikers in Maricopa County would spill out of the saloon and be all over him like liberals on a budget cut. As for Heather—well, I could handle her myself.

Maybe I'd gotten through to Brian at the casino the day before, I thought. And maybe *he'd* gotten through to Heather. Between the two of them, they might have one good brain, and use it to figure out what they were doing to their kids.

I was almost to Sunset Villa when I remembered Tucker's

note on the refrigerator door that morning. He planned to stop by my place to chat about why I had a litter box and no cat, among other things.

I knew I wasn't obligated to keep him updated on my changing schedule, especially since we weren't an item and I hadn't agreed to the rendezvous in the first place. Still, Tucker had been a good friend to me the night before, sleeping on my couch so I wouldn't have to spend the night alone, jumping at every little sound.

Once I got off the freeway and onto a regular street, I pulled into the parking lot of a convenience store, dug out my cell phone, speed-dialed him and waited.

"Darroch," he said. Very clipped.

"It's Mojo," I told him.

"Busy," he replied.

Yeesh. I'd caught him in the middle of some sting, or even an actual drug bust. "I'm on my way out of town," I ventured.

"Check," he said.

So much for that.

I pushed the end button, tossed the phone in the general direction of my purse, which was plunked on the passenger seat and pulled back onto the road. Next stop, Sunset Villa.

I met Felicia in the hallway outside Lillian's door. She was wearing hot-pink scrubs and a glare.

"No more of them cards," Felicia ordered. "Mrs. Travers ain't havin' a very good day."

I could have been pissed off, but I knew Felicia's main concern was her patient's welfare, so I didn't go for her jugular. Anyway, I was too worried to bother with drama. I held up both hands to show I wasn't trying to smuggle in a Tarot deck, Ouija board, or Magic 8-Ball. "What's the matter with Lillian?"

"Starin' at the ceiling," Felicia said stormily. "Won't take a bite of food. Don't you go in there and upset her, now."

I hurried past Nurse Ratchet and into Lillian's room.

My self-appointed mother lay utterly still in her bed, small under the thin white blanket, and she'd aged a year since I'd seen her the day before yesterday. Her hair looked straggly and thin, and her skin was papery.

My heart lurched. I went to her bedside, took one of her hands gently in both of mine. "Hey, there, Diamond Lil," I said, using the nickname Ham had given her soon after they got together. "How ya doin'?"

Lillian looked up at me with an expression of helpless, befuddled fear. Her mouth moved, but no sound came out.

I held her hand a little more tightly. Blinked back tears.

"I'm still trying to figure out those Tarot cards you gave me," I said.

Felicia crepe-footed it up beside me. "Mrs. Travers's been like this since I started my shift this morning," she fretted.

"I want to see her doctor," I answered.

Lillian's eyes drifted closed, as though the lids were just too heavy to manage.

"She's down the hall," Felicia answered. "I'll get her."

Lillian began to snore.

I tucked the blanket around her, leaned down to rest my forehead against hers for a few moments, then straightened, sucking up all my angst. Falling apart wouldn't help.

Dr. Alice Bilbin was standing in the doorway when I

turned from Lillian's bed. Bilbin was small, with plain features and a severe hair-style, and she had that jumpy look typical of the permanently harried.

I approached and offered my hand. Bilbin took it, her grasp firm, and let it go just as quickly.

"Your mother's vital signs are good," the physician informed me. I guess she didn't have either the time or the energy for preliminaries. "I'm convinced she just needs to rest."

"Rest?" I echoed. The word came out high and thin. I cleared my throat, took a steadying breath, and tried again. "Doctor, it isn't as if Lillian's been running marathons. She does nothing *but* rest."

"The vital signs are good," Bilbin insisted, in the same monotone as before. "According to the night staff, she hasn't been sleeping well for the past two or three days. I plan to administer a sedative before I leave the facility this afternoon. I'm sure she'll be right as rain by tomorrow."

"What if she isn't? What if she's taking a turn for the worse?"

The doctor tried to smile, but she must have been out of practice, because it didn't quite fly. "Try not to worry," she said. "The elderly are fragile."

I looked back at Lillian, ignoring Bilbin's convoluted statement. I wanted to protest that Lillian wasn't "elderly"—until the stroke, she'd been active, if a little depressed. Now, she didn't even seem like the same person. "I was planning on leaving town for a few days," I said, "but now…"

"You go ahead," Dr. Bilbin told me, when my voice fell away. "We have your contact information. If there's anything to report, we'll notify you immediately."

I bit my lower lip, turned to study Lillian again, lying there in that spartan bed. "Maybe I should sit with her for a while," I said.

"She won't know the difference," Bilbin assured me. I supposed her words were intended to be comforting, but they weren't.

What broke my internal stalemate was knowing what Lillian would say if she *were* in full command of her body and mind. *You go and spend some time with Jolie. It wouldn't do for the two of you to grow apart.*

Grimly, I nodded. I went back to the bed, kissed Lillian's forehead, and forced myself to walk away. After making absolutely sure my cell number was on file at the desk, and that it was correct, I left Sunset Villa, got into my car and followed the signs to the 10 East.

An hour later, the Cactus Bend exit came in sight.

My foot automatically pressed down on the gas pedal. *Keep going*, I thought. *Just keep going!*

I let up on the petrol, determined not to wimp out, and merged onto the off-ramp. By the clock on my dashboard, which was right, give or take twenty minutes, I wasn't due at Uncle Clive's for over half an hour.

I decided to drive around a little. Acclimate myself.

My cell phone played its ditty-of-the-week just as I made a right turn onto Center Street. Certain that something dire was going on with Lillian, I dived for it. The trucker behind me leaned on his air horn, and I swerved to the side of the road, parked.

"Hello?" I cried breathlessly.

"It's Tucker."

I closed my eyes, dizzy with relief. No bad news about Lillian. At least, not yet. "Tucker," I repeated numbly.

"Are you all right?"

"I'm fine," I said. He was always asking me that, and I always gave him the same answer, whether it was true or not. This time, I *was* fine, or I would be, anyway, once the echo of that eighteen-wheeler's air horn stopped reverberating through my nervous system.

"Sorry about cutting you off earlier," Tucker said. "I was in the middle of something."

At the time, I'd thought he was working. Now, I wondered if he'd been with the ex. "If you're busy, you're busy," I said coolly.

"You're going out of town?"

"I'm *already* out of town. I'm on my way to Tucson to see my sister."

Long silence. "Probably a good idea," he said, though he didn't sound thrilled about it. "What's with the litter box?"

For a moment, I was stumped. Then I remembered the sticky note on the fridge door, back there in my kitchen in Cave Creek. "I already told you—I'm thinking of getting a cat."

He absorbed that, but didn't make a comment one way or the other. "We need to talk when you get back," he said.

A sick feeling settled in the pit of my stomach. This was it. He was going back to the wife and kids. Maybe he and the missus would renew their wedding vows, then they'd all go to Disneyland. The wife would graciously forgive Tucker everything he'd done since their divorce, including me, and Tucker would forget I'd ever existed.

"Mojo?" It was a verbal nudge.

"I'm here," I said.

"I'm going to be undercover for a few days. Don't call me unless it's really important."

My eyes burned. He *was* moving home, or at least planning on spending some time there. I blinked rapidly and sucked in a deep breath, so my voice wouldn't sound shaky when I answered. "You've gotta do what you've gotta do," I told him.

"You sound weird. Are you sure you're all right?"

Oh, I'm just terrific. "I told you—I'm fine."

"I'll call you if I get the chance."

That was big of him. *Don't call me, I'll call you.* That way, he could make sure the kids and the little woman didn't get the wrong idea. Naturally, he'd lie to them, too.

"Don't knock yourself out," I said, and hung up.

The ditty started up again almost instantly.

I peered at the little screen. Tucker, all right.

I ignored the cheerful tune until it stopped, and pulled back onto the road. The car seemed to be driving itself, and it went straight for the local cemetery. Since it was still light outside, I let the vehicle have its way.

I didn't have a lot of time, but Cactus Bend is a small place, so I had enough. I stopped at the cemetery office, a small, stucco cottage, and went inside. The keeper-of-the-plots was a man of indeterminate age, as wide as he was tall, and dressed more like a mechanic than a graveyard official. Maybe, I reflected, he did some of the digging.

"I'm looking for the Mayhugh graves. Evelyn and Ronald."

The mechanic didn't bring out a dusty tome, or tap into the computer at the end of the counter. He merely stared at me, as though I'd just wafted up out of the nearest buried coffin.

"You kin of theirs?"

I checked my watch. Cocktails in ten. Why had I thought I could make this detour and still get to the mansion on time?

"I'm doing some research," I said. "And I'm in kind of a hurry, so if you'd just give me a map—"

"Horrible thing," Cemetery Man broke in. "I remember it like it was yesterday. Ron and Evie were both hometown kids. Grew up right in Cactus Bend. Evie had that boy out of wedlock, and we all knew he was a bad seed." He plucked a sheaf of papers from a stack, flipped through until he came to the page he wanted, and drew X's on two small squares, amid dozens of anonymous others. "Killed them in cold blood, he did. And they sent him to one of those country club jails out in California. Ask me, they should have fried him."

I shuddered, though it was warm in the office, and my hand shook a little as I took the map. Deciding to dig into my past was one thing, and actually discussing my parents' grisly fate with one of the locals was another.

"Thanks for your help." I'd come back to the cemetery, I decided, after I'd checked in at Casa Larimer, and perhaps ask a few questions.

"I didn't get your name," Cemetery Man said, tagging

alongside me all the way to the car. He walked with a funny little hopping trot.

"Mojo Sheepshanks," I answered. I even managed a smile.

"Boomer Harrison," he supplied. I supposed watching over a cemetery was solitary work, and a person had to take his conversations wherever he found them. "You say you're doing research? You writing a book or something? I know a lot about that case, if you are. They had a daughter, those folks. Prettiest little girl you ever saw. Somebody found her hidin' in her mama's dryer after the murders. Blood from head to foot. She wasn't right in the head after that—well, you can just imagine—then darned if she didn't go and get herself *abducted*! My wife and me, we always thought there must have been a curse on that whole Mayhugh outfit."

"I'm not writing a book, Mr. Harrison. Just checking facts for a friend's genealogy project. I'd like to come back and talk to you again, if you wouldn't mind. Say, tomorrow?"

Boomer's whole face lit up. "Well, that would be fine, Miss Sheepshanks. It would be *just* fine. I'll be watchin' for you."

As I got into the Volvo, I was thinking that Boomer was smarter than he looked. He'd heard "Sheepshanks" once, and he'd used it, several minutes later, without stumbling. Usually, when I met a stranger, I had to go into my spiel about how it was English, spelled just like it sounded, and weren't those British names quaint?

The Volvo knew its way to the Larimer place, as it happened, as well as the cemetery. At five minutes after four, I drove up a circular driveway and under a portico that made Greer's seem downright miniature by comparison.

The house itself looked antebellum, and therefore wildly out of place in a shit-heel town in the belly button of Arizona. I must have been there often, as a child, but I couldn't work up a memory to save my life. Maybe, I speculated, my folks and the Larimers hadn't been close. The disparities between their lifestyles would surely have made things awkward.

I left the cemetery map on the seat, grabbed my purse, and headed for the massive front door, with its lion's-head knocker. If there was a butler, I could send him to fetch my garbage-bag suitcase.

As if. My real plan was to wait until it got dark, sneak out, and carry my stuff into the guesthouse by the back door. If guesthouses *had* back doors.

Before my hand came to rest on the gleaming lion's head, the great portal opened, and Clive stood in the gap, flanked by marble floors, a grand, curving staircase and a very beautiful woman seated in a wheelchair.

"You came," he said fondly.

I smiled, though my stomach was quivering. I hadn't even stepped into the house yet, and already I felt like an impostor, up to no good. God, why hadn't I bought a suitcase, or better yet, borrowed one of Greer's gold Halliburtons?

"Sorry I'm late," I said. "Traffic."

"Come in," my uncle commanded good-naturedly. "We've been waiting for you." He turned, looked down at the aging goddess in the wheelchair. Blond hair perfectly coiffed. Makeup artful. Pearls at the neckline of her black St. John suit. "Barbara, look who's here. It's Mary Jo."

I didn't correct him. In a place like that, "Mary Jo" sounded a lot better than "Mojo." I met Barbara's blue eyes, nodded and waited. She went over me like a CAT scan, but I supposed it was natural, after all that had happened.

"Welcome home, Mary Jo," she finally said. I don't think I imagined the faint note of reserve in her voice.

The Larimer mansion was about as likely to be my home as the White House, but I figured it would have been rude to say so. The woman had problems enough, stuck in that wheelchair, without some long-lost relative giving her back-talk in her own foyer.

"Thank you," I said. The author of the *Damn Fool's Guide to Proper Etiquette* would have been proud.

A young man in jeans and a green polo shirt appeared from the periphery of my vision. I figured him for the senator's bodyguard, or maybe a traveling massage therapist. He didn't look like any butler I'd ever seen.

Not that I'd ever actually seen one, except in the movies.

"Joseph will move your car, if that's all right," Clive said diplomatically.

Right. No good having my battered Volvo hunkered in the middle of the drive when the next limo rolled in. Besides, the neighbors might see it, and by now, they probably had their binoculars out. I handed over the keys.

Joseph looked me over like he thought Clive and Barbara ought to check my pockets before I left, but he had the good grace not to say anything.

Barbara wheeled into a cavernous parlor, to the right of the entryway, and since Clive followed, so did I. My mind was on Joseph, however. He was about to get an eyeful of my luggage, and I wouldn't put it past him to go through my glove box, either.

Cocktails were served by a maid in an honest-to-God uniform, complete with ruffled apron and one of those little white hats. They must have paid her extra to wear it.

After the elegant and costly booze, there were little quiches and things wrapped in bacon, and after *that,* an eight-course dinner.

I kept waiting for the probing questions, but it seemed none were forthcoming. The Larimers talked about their wonderful children—a doctor, a lawyer and a couple of Indian chiefs.

"Mary Jo is in the medical field," Clive told Barbara, at one point. The way he made it sound, I was doing neurosurgery at Johns Hopkins instead of punching in Medicare codes.

"Isn't that nice?" Barbara said sunnily, but every once in a while, I caught her looking at me the same way Joseph had.

When dessert was served, Mrs. Larimer announced that she was feeling a little ill.

Clive excused himself, as well as his wife, and wheeled Barbara out of the dining room. I sat there, staring down at my Bananas Whatever, and wondered whether I was expected to wait until Clive came back to get lost or just go ahead and make myself scarce right away.

I heard a whirring sound in the near distance and decided it was an elevator.

I was about to get out of my chair and go looking for the guesthouse—or just hightail it for Jolie's place in Tucson—when Joseph came through the door that probably led to the kitchen.

He fixed me with a glare and snapped, "Who are you and what the hell are you trying to pull?"

Who are you and what the hell are you trying to pull?

Joseph's question pulsed between us. It was merely rude on the surface, but I sensed a more disturbing undercurrent, and my body was sending subtle, visceral read-outs from some database deep in the subterranean regions of my brain.

I pushed back from the Larimers' dining room table and stood to face the militant massage therapist. No need for him to know that my knees were a little unsteady.

I *was* intimidated; Joseph was maybe thirty and very fit, and even though I'd practiced on Bert, I hadn't mastered the techniques from *The Damn Fool's Guide to Self-Defense for Women* to the degree that I could fend off anybody who really wanted to hurt me.

My m.o. in situations like that was simple and to the point: bluff to the big dogs.

"*Who are you?*" I retorted. "And what gives you the right to talk to me like that?"

Joseph flushed, not with embarrassment, but with rage. He had a buzz cut, and the skin underneath turned pink. "I'm the senator's personal assistant," he answered, "and bodyguard."

"And you perceive me as a threat?" I asked, with a lightness I didn't feel.

"I've worked for Senator and Mrs. Larimer for five years," Joseph replied, "and in all that time, he's never mentioned having a niece. Now, all of a sudden, when he's about to declare his candidacy for governor, *you* turn up, out of nowhere."

"Either you're not a local, or you didn't do your homework," I said mildly, but with an edge.

Joseph cast a glance toward the great arched doorway leading into the entryway and lowered his voice a notch. "I know about the Mayhugh murders, if that's what you're talking about. Senator Larimer's sister and her husband were killed. I also know that you—if you really are his niece, that is—disappeared twenty-three years ago. My question is, what brings you back now, after all this time?"

"My answer is, it's really none of your damn business, and if you want to pursue the subject further, you'd better ask my uncle."

Joseph glared at me.

The faint mechanical sound came again, and it was a good bet Clive was riding the elevator back down to the main floor.

I smiled a little. I could see that Joseph had no intention of asking his employer about me in the immediate future; he turned, without another word, and disappeared into the kitchen.

I'd won the skirmish, but I hadn't seen the last of the senator's personal assistant and bodyguard. That was a given.

I had just sat down again when my uncle walked in, looking rattled and slightly wan. "I've called Barbara's physician," he said, shoving a hand through his heretofore tidy gray hair. "She's suffered some kind of setback, it would seem. She asked me to apologize for deserting you on your first evening here."

I stood. I wasn't Barbara's new best friend, and she wasn't mine, but the woman *was* in a wheelchair, and I was not unsympathetic. "It would probably be better if I left," I said.

"Please, don't," my uncle responded, and he sounded sincere, though of course there was always the possibility that he was just trying to be polite. "There are so many things I want to ask you about. And Barbara is bound to feel better in the morning. The doctor will give her something, and she'll rest. That's what she needs—rest."

I nodded, though in truth I had no way of knowing what Barbara needed. "I'm sorry she's ill. And of course you need to be with her. I was planning to visit my sister in Tucson anyway, so—"

The senator interrupted, frowning. "You have a sister?"

Naturally he'd be confused. We were almost total strangers to each other, but he knew Geoff and I were our parents' only children, and with both of them dead, the chances of family expansion were nil.

I leaned down to collect my purse from the floor next to my chair, straightened again. "Jolie's an honorary sibling," I said. "I'll explain later. In the meantime, I'll get out of your way so you can concentrate on taking care of Mrs. Larimer."

He looked relieved, but regretful, too. "You will stay the night, won't you? I'll have Joseph show you to the guesthouse, and in the morning, we can have breakfast on the patio. Make up for lost time." He paused. "It's important to me, Mary Jo. When you get to my age, you realize that nothing matters as much as family."

As *if* I wanted to be alone with Joseph. "I'll find the guesthouse on my own," I said. "Is there anything I can do for Mrs.—"

"Barbara," Clive corrected gently. "Please, call her Barbara."

I would have been more comfortable if the injunction had come from *Barbara* herself, but I conceded with a nod. Since Joseph had departed through the kitchen, I decided to take the long way around, through the front door, even if I had to stumble around in the dark to find the appointed sleeping quarters.

I waited, and when my uncle looked blank, I reiterated, "If I can help in any way, just let me know."

Clive shook his head. "No. I appreciate your understanding, Mary Jo. I'll have Joseph walk you out—"

"That's okay," I said, hoping I didn't sound as nervous as I felt. After all, just because I'd refused Joseph as an escort, that didn't mean he wouldn't jump out at me from behind a shrub between there and the backyard, presumably where I'd find the guesthouse.

"Nonsense," my uncle argued. "Joseph!"

The troll stuck his head in from the kitchen. "Yes, sir?"

"If you'd see Miss Sheepshanks to the casita, I'd appreciate it. Mrs. Larimer is ill, and I'd like to get back upstairs and sit with her until the doctor arrives. You'll watch for him and let him in when he gets here?"

Joseph almost saluted. "Of course, Senator," he said.

Shit, I thought.

"I really don't want to impose," I said, but my uncle had already turned his back, and he was walking away. If he heard me, he gave no sign of it.

"No imposition," Joseph told me, with a little grin of triumph.

Besides bolting, my choices were limited. And, I remembered, the redoubtable assistant/bodyguard had driven my car around back when I arrived anyway. Since I couldn't leave without the Volvo, I sighed and reluctantly followed Joseph through a kitchen large enough to serve a mid size hotel, toward a rear door.

"Don't get any ideas about ingratiating yourself with Senator and Mrs. Larimer and moving into the casita on a permanent basis," Joseph warned quietly, once we were outside.

Every cicada in the state must have been in that yard, singing backup.

"I have a job, an apartment and a life," I answered evenly. What I *wanted* to say was considerably less polite, but I was alone in the dark with the man, and if I yelled for help, nobody would hear me over the bug chorus. Assuming there was anyone around in the first place.

"Keep it that way," Joseph said, leading the way along a broad flagstone path. I noted towering topiary on either side, and heard a waterfall somewhere nearby.

"How do you know I'm not a nice person?" I challenged.

Joseph didn't answer.

We must have triggered a motion light somewhere, because suddenly the "casita" sprang into sharp relief against the night sky. It was about the size of the three-bedroom tract houses in one of Nick's better developments, with its own modified courtyard and burbling fountain. Lamps behind the wooden blinds in the windows came on automatically, issuing an uncertain welcome.

"I put your…stuff inside," Joseph informed me, swinging open the front door. So he'd seen my garbage-bag luggage. I'd been hoping, foolishly, I know, that he'd overlooked it somehow. "Don't get too comfortable, and if you need anything, call somebody else."

Mentally, I threw patience into the same category as truth and discretion. "Bite me, Buckaroo," I said sweetly. "This is a here-today-gone-tomorrow kind of thing, and frankly, I'd rather be homeless than live within five miles of you."

At this, Joseph turned to look at me, and I thought I glimpsed a grudging respect in his eyes. It was gone quickly. "I guess we understand each other," he said.

"Only partially correct," I said, moving past him and through the open doorway into a spacious, tiled front room. "I understand *you*. The reverse, unfortunately, is not true."

"Whatever," Joseph said.

I shut the door in his face and turned the dead bolt. He probably had a key, but I doubted he'd sneak in and murder me in my bed while I slept—assuming, of course, that I *would* sleep, which was doubtful. The senator would surely notice my absence when he showed up for that patio breakfast in the morning, and it went without saying that wholesale slaughter would make a mess in *ye auld* casita.

Putting Joseph out of my mind as best I could, I took the grand tour. There were three bedrooms, each with its own bath, a kitchen half the size of my entire apartment and a master suite with a Jacuzzi tub and flat-screen plasma TV that came down out of the ceiling at the push of a button in a little console on the bedside table. Looking at that place, I almost reconsidered my stance on mooching.

My one-bedroom digs over Bad-Ass Bert's suffered by comparison.

My cell phone launched into a muffled tune as I was emptying the trash bag in the middle of the bed. I rummaged, checked the caller ID and debated answering. The number on the panel was Tucker's.

I'm a sucker for punishment. I thumbed the talk button and snapped, "What?"

"I guess I deserve that," Tucker said.

"I guess you do," I answered, fishing my nightgown out of the pile of semifolded clothes I'd laundered that morning.

He chuckled. "If I knew where you were," he cajoled, "maybe I'd send flowers."

"Is there a point to this call?"

"Yeah." All rumbly and gruff, followed by a note of boyish mischief. "I'm trying to find out where you are."

"Why don't you just ask me?"

"I did. In a roundabout sort of way."

"I'm in Senator and Mrs. Clive Larimer's guesthouse," I said. "Cactus Bend, off Highway 10 east. Do you want the zip code?"

"Are you premenstrual or something?"

I sighed. "Just tired." *And scared to death you're getting it on with your ex-wife.*

"Isn't Cactus Bend where—?"

Obviously, Tucker had been doing some research.

"Where my folks were murdered?" I finished for him. "Yes." I paused. "I thought you were undercover."

"I'm on a break. Look, Moje—"

I plunked down on the edge of the bed and squeezed my eyes shut. *Here it comes,* I thought, and tried to brace myself. "Just say it, will you?"

He hesitated. He was a cop; he picked up nuances. "What exactly are you *expecting* me to say?"

My peepers popped open. "I don't have the faintest idea," I said.

"Liar," Tucker countered. "Give it up, Moje. You've on the peck about something, I can tell by your tone, and you've obviously written a script for this particular conversation, so how about feeding me my lines?"

Heat surged into my face. "If you want to go back to your wife and kids, it's your business," I blurted.

"Go back to—?"

A wonderful/horrible possibility dawned on me. Wonderful because I might be wrong, and horrible for the same reason. The chances seemed good that I'd just made an ass out of myself.

I tried to brave it through. "Isn't that what you were going to tell me?"

"No," he said. He sounded terse and, at the same time, as though he might be trying not to laugh. "It isn't. If you're thinking of picking up some extra bucks as a phone psychic, forget it. You don't have the goods."

I rocked back and forth on the edge of the bed, feeling like the mother of all fools. Maybe if I pulled the garbage bag over my head and cinched the pull-ties at my waist, I could end it all. It would save Joseph the trouble, along with that pesky stretch in prison.

"Are you still there?" Tucker pressed.

"Yeah," I squeaked.

"I'm not going back to Allison," he said, "so put that out of your head."

I reached for the garbage bag. Pondered the cons of self-suffocation. There weren't any pros, as it turned out. "Then what?" Very small voice.

"It's job-related. As in, I'm going to disappear for a couple of days, minimum. If you see my face on the evening news, or on the front page, don't panic. Right now, that's all I can say."

"Okay," I said uncertainly.

Tucker was a man of his word. He hung up without even saying goodbye.

I stared at the phone. *If you see my face on the evening news, or on the front page, don't panic.* What the hell did *that* mean?

I dug out the charger and plugged the cell in to power up, then pushed a few buttons on the bedside console. The plasma TV came on, and I used the remote to scroll for the Phoenix stations.

Everybody Loves Raymond was wrapping up the second or third rerun of the evening.

I waited it out, watched the news.

Nothing about Tucker's face or any other part of his anatomy.

I left the bedroom, double-checked the locks on both doors, and backtracked as far as the big tub in the master bath. I took a long soak, followed the trail of disparate thoughts that wandered through my head—Lillian and the Tarot cards she'd given me, which were still a puzzle, the Nick-and-Chester ghost team, Greer's odd behavior, Heather and the supermarket incident, Geoff turning up at the casino, Joseph, Uncle Senator and the little wife and, last but certainly not least, Tucker.

I was almost afraid to go to sleep.

Nevertheless, I got out of the tub eventually, drained it, dried off and put on my nightgown. It was wrinkled—nothing I sleep in gets ironed, and neither does most of what I *don't* sleep in—but comfortably soft, and definitely clean. I brushed my teeth, checked all the locks again and tumbled into bed.

The next thing I knew, sunlight was streaming into the room and I could hear a lawn crew outside, chattering in Spanish, with an accompaniment of lively Latin tunes.

No night visits from Nick.

No bad dreams.

I figured I was on a roll, and the rest of the day would go well.

Yeah, right.

I put on jeans and a T-shirt with no logo—for dressup— and walked almost all the way around the main house before I found the patio. My uncle was already there, reading a newspaper. A china coffee service graced the table, and there was no sign of Aunt Barbara.

Oh, *well*.

"There you are." Uncle Clive smiled. He seemed relieved, as though he'd been afraid I might have been misplaced, like a cufflink or a nine-iron.

"I hope I'm not late," I said, stifling a yawn. I'd slept deeply, and my brain wasn't up to speed, or I would have asked about Barbara first. After the senator assured me that I was right on time, I corrected the oversight.

"She's a little fragile this morning," Clive said fondly. "Dr. Blythe gave her a shot and ordered her to spend the day in bed."

I wondered, a mite uncharitably, if Barbara would be an asset or a liability on the campaign trail. I'm not as bad as I sound. I just like to consider as many perspectives as possible.

"I hope she feels better soon," I said, as my uncle drew back a chair at the patio table so I could sit.

The moment my butt connected with the cushion, a maid bustled through a pair of French doors, beaming and carrying a tray. Efficiently, she set places for both of us, with china I could practically see through, and sterling polished to such a high shine that a hiker lost in the desert could have used it to signal for help. Orange juice followed, and buttery croissants.

I figured that was it and waited for the signal to dig in, but Uncle Clive was perusing the newspaper again.

"Awful what happened to that Scottsdale narcotics detective," he said. He shook his head. "Sometimes I wonder what this world is coming to."

I sat up as straight as if my backbone had been electrified, tried to eyeball the front page.

Clive passed me the newspaper, and I almost dropped the orange juice I was holding in my other hand.

There was an old shot of Tucker in a patrol uniform. His hair was still short, his eyes innocent of the things he'd probably seen since the day he graduated from the academy. He was even smiling a little.

The headline would have stopped my heart if he hadn't called the night before, and given me that cryptic warning.

Family, Fellow Officers Mourn Fallen Comrade

I blinked. *Don't panic*, Tucker had said. I almost did, just the same; the thing looked so real. According to the article—which I skimmed three times because my brain kept balking at taking in more than a glaring phrase here and there—Detective Tucker Darroch, 32, had perished when his car exploded in the parking lot of a convenience store. Darroch was survived, the reporter went on, by his former wife, Allison Darroch, and seven-year-old twins, Danny and Daisy Darroch.

I felt sick, and I must have looked pretty bad, too, because

Clive put a firm hand on my arm and spoke with concern. "Mary Jo? Was this someone you knew?"

If you see my face on the evening news...don't panic.

But this *wasn't* the evening news, it was the *Arizona Republic,* the biggest daily in the state. Did that mean...?

I shook myself inwardly. *No. It doesn't. Tucker mentioned the front page.*

But it was damn convincing.

Uncle Clive sent the maid back to the kitchen for water.

"Mary Jo?" he repeated.

I finally realized he was talking to me. "I've met him," I said, because I knew Larimer wouldn't believe me if I denied it. People don't react the way I did to the death of a stranger, no matter how tragic.

I wondered if Allison and the kids were in on the secret, or if Daisy and Danny really believed their father had been killed.

"It's a shame," Uncle Clive said.

I put the paper aside with a shaking hand. "Yes," I agreed, hoping to God this was what Tucker had meant when we talked the night before. What if, by some horrible coincidence, he'd really died in that explosion?

I was saved from meaningful conversation when Uncle Clive's personal communication device began to beep. He picked it up off the table, used a stylus to bring up the menu.

"I'd better take care of this," he said, with a frown. He got up and hurried into the house.

For the second time since I'd arrived at Casa Larimer the night before, I found myself sitting alone at a table.

I knew better, I really did, but I got out my own cell phone and speed-dialed Tucker.

"Hello?" It was a woman's voice, and she sounded as if she'd been crying. Allison Darroch. "Hello?" she repeated. "Who is this?"

I hung up without answering.

Because I didn't know what to say.

Because I couldn't have spoken if I had.

"PITY YOU CAN'T stay longer," Joseph said, with merciless good humor, half an hour later, as he jingled my car keys under my nose. I'd packed my trash bag, after Uncle Clive came back to the patio long enough to tell me he'd been called into the Phoenix office on an emergency, scribbled a thank-you note on a piece of paper from the desk in the living room of the guest house and asked the maid to give it to Mrs. Larimer.

"If you're the senator's assistant and bodyguard," I challenged, "how come you didn't leave with him?"

"I have things to do here," he replied.

"Sucks to be you," I said. I got into the Volvo, fired up the engine and got out of there.

I hoped I'd never have to go back.

I hoped Tucker wasn't dead.

Oh, *God,* how I hoped Tucker wasn't dead.

I wanted to go straight back to Cave Creek and try to find out for sure, but I knew it wasn't a good idea, and for once, I listened to my own advice.

It was too early to head for Jolie's. She'd be at work, and

totally focused on whatever bone or tissue sample she was decoding. If I showed up, I'd either blow her concentration, which she would not appreciate, or be ignored, which *I* would not appreciate.

I set out for the cemetery outside of town, planning to grill Boomer about the murders, since he seemed to be an authority on the subject, but my car went into override again.

I soon found myself sitting, with the Volvo idling, in front of the house Lillian had lived in, back in the day.

I hadn't remembered the address. I'd simply driven to it on autopilot.

We'd lived across the street, Mom, Dad, Geoff and I. Just to look in that direction was one of the hardest things I'd ever done.

I don't know what I expected, but it wasn't a vacant lot with a weathered For Sale sign sticking up from the dry, yellow weeds.

In my mind's eye, I saw a double-wide mobile home.

I saw blood-spattered walls.

I saw the little vent holes inside the dryer.

I shuddered violently, and for a moment, I actually thought I'd have to shove open the car door and throw up in the gutter.

I drew deep breaths until the images receded, then popped the Volvo into gear and sped away.

I'd barely covered a block when my cell phone started its merry little song.

Tucker.

I scrabbled for it. Peered at the screen.

Tucker Darroch.

I jabbed at the talk button. "Hello?"

"Who is this?" demanded Allison. "You called earlier and, damn it, *I want to know who you are.*"

"J-Just a friend of Tucker's," I said lamely.

"A friend," she echoed, plainly suspicious.

"I'm sorry," I whispered.

"Were you sleeping with him?"

I nearly took out a row of rural mailboxes, pulling off onto the side of the road, and I guess I took too long to answer, because Allison picked up the verbal ball and sprinted for the goal posts.

"Tucker's *children* and I are in mourning," she said. "Kindly have the decency to leave us alone."

It wasn't the best time to point out that she'd been the one to initiate this call, not me. Or to ask how she'd gotten hold of Tucker's personal cell phone.

"I wasn't—"

"You weren't *what?* Sleeping with my husband?"

I pressed the end button.

Then I laid my head on the steering wheel and did some more deep breathing. Just when I was starting to think I wouldn't faint, my cell made another noise.

Hope dies hard.

I checked it.

Text message.

I frowned, pressed the appropriate buttons to access it.

U-WLL-DY.

I squinted. "You—will—die," I translated out loud.

Then I flung the phone down.

Allison Darroch, overreacting?

Or someone else?

I jumped out of the car, walked around it three times in my own personal version of a Chinese fire drill, and got back behind the wheel again. I'd had a purpose in mind—to release the sudden and terrible energy that surged through me—but it hadn't worked.

I picked up the phone again. Hit the button for Tucker's number.

"Hello?" Allison rasped.

"I know you've had a bad shock," I told her evenly, "but sending me a threatening text message was over the line."

"I don't know what you're talking about."

The hell of it was, I believed her.

She clicked off before I could speak again.

I thumbed my way back to the text message. No name, no number.

Joseph?

Geoff?

Heather?

The list of people who wanted to harass me, if not kill me outright, was getting longer every day.

I shut the phone off, in desperate need of a technology break, and sat there at the side of the road until I thought I could drive without risking life and limb. Then I drove aimlessly for at least forty-five minutes, up and down the streets of Cactus Bend, trying to remember.

Trying *not* to remember.

Imagine my surprise when I pulled through the gate of the town cemetery.

I wondered if cars could be haunted, as well as apartments. Mine seemed to need an exorcist.

I got out of it, the map Boomer had given me the day before clenched in one sweaty hand. I consulted the map, and started off on foot for my parents' graves.

My subconscious didn't kick in, as it had with Lillian's old house and the vacant lot across the street. I took at least three wrong turns before I finally found the plots I was looking for, on a little grassy knoll in the shade of a tall cottonwood tree.

The monuments were impressive, made of smooth granite and polished to a shine. Clive and Barbara must have sprung for those, I thought. As little as I remembered about Mom and Dad, I knew their budget hadn't extended to things like cemetery plots and expensive headstones.

I stood there, a soft breeze drying my perspiration-glazed flesh, and tried to recall the funeral.

Nothing.

I took a step closer, read the chiseled letters on the first marker.

Evelyn Larimer Mayhugh
died, August 18, 1983

My throat constricted.

I closed my eyes.

Blood, warm and slippery, on my hands, my T-shirt, my shorts, my bare legs. *Mama.*

I backed away from the memory mentally, time-warped back to the present moment a dizzying rush that left me swaying on my feet. I forced myself to read the other stone.

Ronald Charles Mayhugh
b. June, 1957, d. August, 1983

Bile scalded the back of my throat.
"You came back."
I almost jumped out of my shoes.

CHAPTER

Boomer Harrison, the groundskeeper, stood grinning at me from the path snaking by on my right. Leaning on a shovel handle, he repeated himself.

"You came back."

My right hand had flown, fingers splayed, to my chest, in an unconscious effort to calm my startled heart. I made a fist before lowering said hand to my side. "You scared me," I told him, and though I spoke calmly, there was a note of accusation in my voice.

"Sorry," Boomer retorted, with no trace of regret.

I took in the shovel and wondered if he'd been digging a fresh grave. Whimsical thinking, I decided. They probably used heavy equipment for that, these days. Boomer was a groundskeeper. He could have been planting flowers or moving a shrub from one place to another or any one of a dozen other things.

"You're the daughter, aren't you?" he inquired companionably. "Ron and Evie's girl. I should have figured it out in the first place, with you so interested in finding their graves and all. I ain't never claimed to be the smartest dog hitched to the sled." Boomer paused. "Yes, sir, you're the spittin' image of Evie, with that red hair and those freckles."

For an instant, I went inside myself, and the vision I saw was more vividly real than Boomer or the surrounding cemetery, the sky overhead or the earth under my feet. I became two people; one small, kneeling on a cheaply carpeted floor, sick with terror and desperation, one grown, sprawled on my back, strangling on my own blood. There was no physical pain, but I knew I was dying. An image began to form in my mind...

Someone grabbed my arm. "Miss Sheepshanks? Are you all right?"

I blinked. Boomer came into sharp focus, and the rest of the environment assembled itself around him in a dizzying, chock-a-block way.

I was on my knees in the dry, sparse grass, hugging myself hard with both arms, as if I might splinter into fragments if I didn't hold on tight. Bile seared the back of my throat, and I couldn't speak for that, and for the knowledge that I'd just been inside my mother's dying body, with the face of her killer about to do a fade-in on the screen of her mind.

A mind we'd temporarily shared.

A horrible thought blindsided me just then, and nearly sent me plunging face down into the rough dirt of that cemetery.

Was I *the killer?*

Was that the real reason Lillian had whisked me away and cobbled together whole new identities, for me and for herself? Because she thought *I'd* been the one to pull the trigger and wanted to spare me the consequences?

"Take a swig of this," Boomer ordered, shoving a water bottle into my hand.

I unscrewed the lid and gulped. Even in that distracted state, it occurred to me to wonder if Boomer and I were swapping germs, but I made a split-second decision to consider the backwash issue later.

Presently, Boomer helped me to my feet and led me to a nearby bench, in the shade of the same cottonwood overarching my parents' graves.

"You stay right here," Boomer said. "I'm going back to the office to call 911."

I caught at his hand, work-roughened and bull-strong, and held on. "No," I rasped. "I'm—I'm fine. Please…just let me…sit here for a moment…."

Boomer eyed me with concern, obviously conducting an internal debate, then sat his bulk down beside me on the bench, giving a huffing sigh as he did so. I realized I was still gripping his hand and let go.

"It must be an awful thing to remember," he said hoarsely.

I nodded. Shoved my fingers through my hair. I'd shampooed it that morning, in the guesthouse shower at Casa Larimer, but now it felt sticky and tangled. The malaise seemed to affect me on every level of my being: full-body bedhead, on a universal scale.

"The problem is," I croaked, "there's too much I *don't* remember."

I fought off a ferocious urge to jump in my car, shoot back up to Phoenix, and slam into Sunset Villa like a one-woman army in invasion mode. The desire to take Lillian by the shoulders and shake the truth out of her was visceral, as well as insane.

Did I do it? I would scream at her. *Did I get hold of a gun somehow, and shoot my parents? Did I?*

I gulped. "Do you think I could have killed them, Boomer?" I couldn't bring myself to look at him—my gaze was fixed on the pair of headstones marking the final resting places of two people who hadn't deserved to die—but I felt him stiffen beside me, on the bench.

"It was Geoff that done it," he said. "Everybody knows that."

"Do they?" I mused. I remembered the blood, warm and already congealing. So *much* blood. I *didn't* remember Geoff, or any sense of his presence in that room, on that night.

"Your brother was found wanderin' the streets, with blood all over him," Boomer reasoned quietly. "*And* he confessed."

"Immediately?" I asked.

Boomer paused, probably to recollect the general shape of the incident and its aftermath. A double murder. It must have been the biggest thing that ever happened in otherwise unremarkable Cactus Bend, Arizona. "As I recall, the police took him in for questioning right away. I reckon a day or two went by before he said anything at all. My brother-in-law was a dispatcher, back then, with the sheriff's office, so

I might have heard it from him. Could have read it in the papers, too. It was all over the news."

"Nobody questioned me?"

Boomer made an executive decision and reached out to pat my hand tentatively. "They tried, but you was in shock. And you was real little, too, don't forget. What do they call it when somebody just stares into space and won't say nothin'?"

"Catatonic," I supplied dismally. My first conscious memory, after curling up inside the dryer after the murders, was finding myself in that motel room, with Lillian. I remembered the cool, soothing feel of that washcloth on my face, and the worried tenderness in her eyes. I'd been confused, and frightened.

"You're safe now, baby," Lillian had said, though I'd still thought of her as Doris then. Doris, my trusted babysitter. Doris, the woman across the street. My mother's friend, and mine. "I won't let anybody hurt you, ever."

She'd kept that promise, too. Until Nick came along, anyway—he'd been a different kind of threat. Even then, she'd tried to warn me.

And now the memories were beginning to force their way to the surface. I didn't have Lillian to protect me. I didn't really have anyone but myself.

I drew a deep breath.

I would have to do.

I gathered myself to stand.

Boomer stopped me. "Your brother," he said miserably. "He'd done stuff before he killed your mama and daddy. Bad stuff. Don't you go thinkin' it was really you that done it. You was just a little kid, no bigger'n a minute."

I thought of Chester, lying dead in the deep grass behind the storage shed in back of our double-wide. "What kind of bad stuff?" I asked quietly, dreading the answer.

"Tearin' things up, mostly," Boomer said. "Bullying, too. There was a rumor goin' around that Evie was fixin' to put him in some kind of institution for a while. That she thought he was dangerous." His sigh was telling, and for the first time, I linked up with the obvious. Both my parents would have been around Boomer's age, if they'd lived. Cactus Bend was a very small town, where everyone knew everyone else. Most likely, Boomer, Evie and Ron had grown up together. "I liked Evie," he went on sadly. "Never thought she got a fair shake, between your no-account daddy—if you'll excuse me for sayin' it—and the way things turned out for her in general. She was the prettiest girl in school. Prom queen. Had a scholarship to ASU, too. But she never got to use it. She just seemed to meet with bad luck wherever she turned."

Bad luck, I wondered, or bad choices?

"Tell me about my dad. I don't remember much."

Boomer sighed again, gazing at the headstones as if he could see Ron and Evie's ghosts standing in their places. "He wasn't one for hard work, your daddy. Always lookin' to make an easy buck. Get on the dole someway. I always said, if Ron Mayhugh had put half as much effort into a job as he did into tryin' to catch himself a free ride, he'd have been a millionaire five times over."

I felt uncomfortable. I wasn't afraid of hard work, but there was no denying that I had a certain aversion to the 9-to-5 life myself, as Greer so often pointed out. Was I like my dad?

And, come to think of it, where the hell did Greer come off saying stuff like that, anyway? Since when did selling a business she'd slaved to build and then throwing herself into the role of trophy wife qualify her to criticize my career choices?

"Go on," I said on a breath, reconnecting with the present moment, in which Boomer figured prominently.

"Clive Larimer had a truckin' company back then. Built it up himself, pretty much from nothin'. He was doing real well. Barbara's family owned a chain of tire stores, so when he married her, his bank account fattened up even bigger. I always thought he could have helped Evie out a little more than he did, but there was bad blood between her and Barbara right from the first. Evie was proud, too, so that was part of it I guess. Anyways, your daddy worked some for Larimer Trucking, and some at the tire store on Center Street, but he was usually in between. He managed to get sick or hurt, often as he could."

I closed my eyes, opened them again. "Mom supported us, then?"

"Mostly," Boomer said. "She sure deserved better than she got." He hoisted himself to his feet. "Best I get back to work," he told me. "The city ain't payin' me to yammer on about the old days. You just sit there, now, till you feel right."

If I'd sat there *that* long, I'd have become part of the landscape.

Besides, after what I'd seen in my personal flashback,

what I'd sensed, and all that Boomer had told me, I wasn't sure I'd ever "feel right" again.

I thanked him.

He'd left his shovel leaning against the trunk of the cotton-wood tree. He retrieved it and headed back down the path.

I stayed put on the bench for fifteen minutes or so, then made my way slowly to my car.

It was still early, and I knew Jolie would be in her lab, up to her eyeballs in the detritus of death. I wasn't about to go back to the Larimers' place and hang out, or do a hairpin turn for Phoenix and upset Lillian with a bunch of questions she couldn't answer.

My options were getting narrower by the second.

As soon as I was behind the wheel of the Volvo, with the doors locked and the motor running, I put a call through to the nursing home. A nurse reported that Lillian was resting comfortably; other than that, there had been no change.

Next, I drove around Cactus Bend aimlessly, for perhaps half an hour, getting the lay of the land. I cruised past the high school, the tiny library, the office of the weekly newspaper, the tire franchise where my dad had worked, when he couldn't get out of it.

The text message I'd received the day before niggled at the back of my mind, but the truth is, I was on overload. There were so many things to think about, I couldn't really settle on anything too specific. My mind kept swooping from one subject to another, like a bird far from shore, circling a shipwreck, trying to find something to light on that wasn't about to sink.

In time, I realized the Volvo and I were both low on fuel.

It probably means something that I hit the gas pump first, before forcing myself inside the Happy Trails Truck Stop. One of these days, I'll check out the *Damn Fool's Guide to Freudian Psychology,* if there is one.

I had no memory whatsoever of the diner. Nothing stirred as I walked in, took one of the stools at the counter, reached for a plastic-covered menu. Just the same, I knew my mother had run her feet off waiting tables there, doing her best to make ends meet and always falling just a few dollars short.

My stomach closed like a fist, but I was light-headed and shaky, which meant I needed to eat, whether I wanted to or not. The Volvo wouldn't run on empty, and neither would my brain.

I consulted the listed offerings.

A waitress in blue jeans and a tank top appeared across the narrow expanse of Formica, with its metal napkin holders, plastic ketchup bottles and salt and pepper shakers. "Help ya?" she asked.

I looked at her over the top of the menu. She could have been any age between nineteen and thirty. Her skin bore the traces of an old case of acne, and I counted seven piercings in her right ear. Her brown hair was thin, the kind that falls into roller shapes no matter how much you tease and spray. I wondered what her life was like—if there were kids at home, if she worked to support some loser boyfriend or undermotivated husband, the way my mother had.

I ordered coffee, orange juice and poached eggs on toast.

Was I like my mother?

Was I like my dad?

Who the hell was I, anyway?

Right then, I felt about as real as Nick.

I forced myself to eat most of the food, paid the bill and left.

Still too early to leave for Tucson, and my cell phone was silent.

I scrolled back to the text message, fortified by breakfast.

U-WLL-DY.

Catchy.

Also chickenshit. Up there with sending nasty e-mails and then blocking the reply, so the flamed can't fight back.

I tossed the cell back into my purse and headed for the high school. In these post-Columbine days, a person can't just walk into the nearest institute of lower learning and snoop around, so I followed presumed protocol and stopped off at the office. The secretary had probably been around since the Reagan administration, if not longer, and she went pale when I introduced myself and added that I was Evie Larimer's daughter.

Right then, I wasn't up to claiming Ron.

"Mary Josephine?" the woman trilled, looking up from the driver's license I'd given her as ID. She had blue hair, four chins, and wore a vintage polyester pantsuit. Either she shopped on eBay, or she didn't shop at all.

"I go by Mojo," I said. I'm not sure why I wanted to get that straight, up front, but I did. Mary Josephine Mayhugh was a stranger to me. Mojo Sheepshanks might have been a fraud, but I could recall every day of her existence.

The woman rose halfway out of her chair and promptly sank into it again. Her hand trembled as she handed back my license. "I'm sorry," she said, with a flustered attempt at a smile. "It's something of a shock."

I leaned on the counter. A bell rang shrilly in the background, and I was vaguely aware of kids stampeding through the halls behind me. Geoff had probably attended this school, I thought, with a jolt, at least until he was sent up for murder. I would have been a student there, too, most likely, if it hadn't been for the events of August 18, 1983.

I drew a deep breath and released it slowly. Tried to remem ber what I'd learned from *The Damn Fool's Guide to Zen*.

Not much, apparently.

My nerves were jumping, and the present moment sucked.

"It was awful, what happened," the woman said. I glanced belatedly at the little sign on the countertop; it was a day for afterthoughts. Her name was Mavis Rogers, unless she was filling in for somebody. "Geoff seemed like such a nice boy."

I didn't comment. Anything I said would have been ironic, if not scathing, and Mavis didn't deserve that. It wasn't her fault I came from a family that made the Mansons look like the cast of a holiday mayonnaise commercial.

"I was hoping I could look at some yearbooks," I said. I hadn't been aware, until the words came out of my mouth, that I was hoping any such thing, but there you are. My subconscious mind seemed to be elbowing its way to the foreground lately. "From when my parents were in school."

Mavis swallowed. "Well, dear," she said, "I can certainly show you the ones with Evie's pictures in them, but Ron

Mayhugh—" she lowered her voice, looked from side-to-side "—*dropped out.*"

I wasn't surprised that dear old Dad never got a diploma. Clearly, he hadn't been big on focused effort toward a goal. Some of my thoughts splintered off from the main bunch and hot-trotted it for the nearest employment agency.

Give me a real job. Any *real job.*

"We were all just *sick* when Evie married him," Mavis confided. She got out of her chair again, but this time, she followed through and actually stayed on her feet. "I'll be right back," she said. "Wait here."

I leaned against the counter and studied a schedule of PTA meetings.

Then it came to me that leaning was something an undisciplined person without a real job would do, somebody with Ron Mayhugh's blood flowing through their veins, for instance, and I stood up straight.

Mavis returned, after a considerable interval of good posture on my part, and handed me four dusty yearbooks from the 1960s. Back then, evidently, students went through eight grades, at least in Cactus Bend, and then made the leap to high school.

I thanked Mavis, took the books and sat down in one of the plastic chairs nearby. Another bell rang, and the shuffle of kids moving through the halls receded to blessed silence.

My hands trembled a little as I opened the cover of the first book, a thin volume with 1963 and the school logo embossed on the cover. I found Evie Larimer, geeky-haired and grinning, with the other freshmen. Her eyes were bright with innocence—she probably hadn't gotten involved with Geoff's father yet, or mine. She hadn't given up her scholarship, and her dreams, whatever they might have been, to work rotating shifts at the Happy Trails Truck Stop. I wished she'd start moving around within the picture, Harry Potter-style, and speak to me. Explain everything.

I could have warned her then. *Take another road, Mom. Write yourself another script, because this one ends badly.*

A tear plopped on the page before I realized I was crying.

I wiped it away with the tip of an index finger and studied the faces of the other students. No one looked familiar, and I didn't recognize any of the names beneath the photos.

When I turned to the sophomore class, though, my gaze went straight to one particular shot. Rod Waters. Class president. Captain of the football team.

His resemblance to Geoff was beyond uncanny.

Here he was, then. Nemesis #1. The guy who got my mother pregnant, the bearer of the Bad Seed.

The poached eggs I'd had for breakfast roiled in my stomach.

I closed the book and opened the second in the four-year sequence of my mother's high school career. All the career she was ever going to have, as it turned out.

I sniffled.

Mom made the honor society as a sophomore. She went to Girl's State, whatever that was, and made the varsity cheerleading squad. Her hair looked a little better, too. I felt an aching tenderness, flipping through those pages. It was a kind of reverse fortune-telling, like peering into a crystal ball focused on the past instead of the future. Evelyn Larimer didn't look like the kind of girl who would end up dead of a gunshot wound on the living room floor of a rented doublewide, but, then, what did that kind of girl look like?

I soldiered my way through my mother's junior and senior years. By the time her graduation picture was taken, the light had gone out of her eyes. She looked resigned. Maybe she was already carrying Geoff. She knew college was down the drain, I could see that in her face.

I wondered if anyone else had seen it.

Like my grandparents.

It came to me suddenly that I didn't know thing one about the Larimers, or the Mayhughs, for that matter.

I hadn't even thought to ask Uncle Clive for the genealogical particulars, or Boomer, either.

I'd Googled the senator and Barbara, and their progeny to boot.

And I'd stopped there, as if there had been no previous generations. As if Mom and Dad and all of the rest of them had simply sprung into being one day, fully grown.

"Holy crap," I muttered, stunned at the scope of my oversight, slamming the last yearbook shut.

Mavis started a little, behind her counter.

I took the four volumes back to her in a stack, thanked her and left.

I drove to the library next. It was about the size of Greer's closet, but there was a computer allotted to public use. I waited, none too patiently, until the matron cruising for

God-knows-what went offline and wandered away, then I grabbed the chair, bellied up to the keyboard and logged on.

There were a few newspaper pieces on the murders tucked away in various archives, and several chronicling my abduction. I'd seen them before, but I scanned them again. No mention of either Mom's parents or Dad's. I tried the senator's site and read his biography, but he too seemed to have skipped childhood and simply appeared on the planet as an adult with a political agenda.

I printed out the whole batch, paid the librarian for the copies and got back in my car.

Boomer was in the cottage at the cemetery when I walked in. He was just opening one of those old-fashioned black lunch boxes, the kind with a thermos in the lid. He paused in the act of removing the wax paper wrapping from what looked like a ham and cheese on rye and studied me with polite uncertainty.

He started to rise, and I gestured for him to stay seated.

"Did you know the Larimers and the Mayhughs?" I asked, right out. "My grandparents, I mean?"

Boomer sagged a little. He'd been a fount of information all along, but now, all of a sudden, he'd dried up.

I waited.

Boomer finally relented, but with obvious reluctance.

"Evie and Clive, they was orphaned real young," he said. "Come from Tucson or Phoenix originally, I think. Some folks named Wilkerson took them in as foster children, brought them here to Cactus Bend. The Wilkersons is gone now, of course. Been gone a long while."

A bleak shadow fell over my heart. "What about the Mayhughs?"

Boomer wanted to look away, I could see that, but he held my gaze. I braced myself for yet another non-Hallmark moment.

"Ron came here with his mama, when he was a little kid. She was no better than she should be, if you know what I'm sayin'. She worked at the old Bootstrap Saloon. Place burned down in 1962, along with the movie theatre. Her old man got out of jail around that time, and she lit out with him. Ron stayed behind, lived with whoever'd take him in, for however long. Dropped out of school after the eighth grade." Boomer found a bright spot in my dismal family history. "He got his GED, though. Did it to please Evie. He might have been good with computers, too, if he'd lived. Had an old TRS-80 he picked up someplace. Used to fiddle with it all the time."

I almost wished I hadn't asked about my grandparents.

The more I learned, the worse I felt.

I thanked Boomer, went back to my car and headed for Tucson.

Jolie wouldn't be off work for hours yet, but I needed a hole to crawl into.

I drove to her place, a garden apartment in the university district, extracted the key from the fake rock on the back patio, and let myself in through the kitchen door. I was peering into the refrigerator when a low growl sounded behind me.

The hairs on my nape went rigid.

Big dog, in deadly earnest.

When had Jolie gotten a dog?

More importantly, why hadn't she told me?

The growl deepened to a ferocious rumble.

"Don't move," I said, talking to both myself and the dog.

Slowly, *very* slowly, I straightened and turned my head just far enough to see the fiend half-crouched in the doorway between Jolie's kitchen and living room. He looked like a cloning experiment gone terribly wrong, with his coarse brindled coat and his laid-back ears. I swear to God his eyes were yellow as candle flames, and he didn't have teeth, he had fangs.

He lunged.

I scrambled up the shelves of Jolie's refrigerator with a clatter and huddled on top, as close to the wall as I could get.

The hell-hound reared up on his hind legs and did his level best to get me, but I was maybe three inches out from his snarling, slobbering maw. When he finally exhausted himself, trying to tear off a chunk of any old part of my anatomy, he curled up in a big, quivering ball in front of the fridge.

My legs were going to sleep, so I shifted, sat Indian-style, like some kind of human cookie jar, and waited for my sister to come home.

My cell phone rang at least three separate times.

It might have been Tucker.

It might have been the nursing home, calling about Lillian.

It might have been another text-message, threatening me with death.

If I got down off that refrigerator, I thought, I would never know, because the Beast would tear me to bloody shreds before I got to my purse.

The dog snoozed, snoring like a dull buzz saw.

I considered getting down, grabbing my bag and making a dive for the back door, but it was just a fantasy to pass the time. I didn't have a chance in hell of actually making it.

I cupped my chin in one hand and waited.

The dog woke up, snuffled around in the fridge for a while, since the door was still hanging open, and helped himself to a package of bologna. Devoured it in three bites—wrapper, UPC code and all.

I tried to communicate with Jolie by telepathy. I'd never done it before, but I didn't have much to lose, and the rest of my lifespan to gain.

Nothing happened, of course.

I could muster a dead ex and a ghost cat.

I could make a slot machine pay, if the energy was right.

Evidently, that was the extent of my psychic power.

White Fang dozed again, busy digesting the lunch meat and the plastic, and I got the bright idea to lean over, pull something out of the freezer compartment, and throw it across the room. While he was gnawing at a rock-hard pot roast, I'd make a break for it.

I leaned.

He sprang.

I felt his hot breath against my forearm as I jerked back, just in time to avoid the fate I'd planned for the pot roast.

I yelled for help. As I said, it was a day for afterthoughts.

No response.

Everybody in Jolie's building, it seemed, had a real job.

I decided to examine the contents of the cupboards on

either side of the refrigerator. Maybe I could bean the dog with a soup can and book it before he regained consciousness.

I found two boxes of outdated cereal, a package of stale crackers and the owner's manual for the microwave. I read it from cover to cover. Taught myself rudimentary Dutch, French, Spanish and Japanese by comparing the translation paragraphs to the English version. I figured I was a cinch for a bright future in appliance repair when, at long last, Jolie appeared in the back door window, shoving her key in the lock.

The Hound of Tucson rolled to his feet, yawned and gave a welcoming whimper.

Jolie paused to pet him, and her dark eyes danced as she looked up at me, perched on the top of her refrigerator. "I see you made yourself at home," she said, plunking her briefcase and purse on the counter next to the door. She'd had a weave since I saw her last, and she looked sleekly professional in her tailored black slacks and crisp white blouse. No blood, gore or bone dust in evidence. The wonder of lab coats.

"You didn't mention the dog when we talked on the phone," I pointed out. I had to pee like a cow on a flat rock, but I wasn't getting down until she either put the demon outside or shot him with a tranquilizer dart. Even then, he'd have to twitch for five minutes before the coast could be considered clear.

"Oops," Jolie said, with a crooked, twinkly little smile. She gave Brutus a dog biscuit, closed the refrigerator with dispatch and looked up at me. "You can get down now."

"No way," I said. "That thing is vicious. He'll rip my throat out."

"He's a pussycat," Jolie assured me, and bent to pat his head. Her plentitude of tiny braids shimmered as she moved. "I got him at the pound last week. Another day and a half, and they'd have put him to sleep."

"Timing is everything."

Jolie laughed. "*Get down*, Moje. Sweetnik isn't going to hurt you."

"*Sweetnik?*" I peered over the edge, sizing him up. The name didn't fit; he looked as big and mean as ever.

"Sweetie for short," Jolie said, eyeing him affectionately and scrabbling in the box for another Milk Bone. "We've had some robberies and home invasions in the neighborhood lately, so I thought it made sense to get a dog."

I eased one foot down as far as the countertop. Sweetie didn't lunge. He was too busy mauling the second biscuit. I risked the other foot.

Sweetie raised his head and growled.

"Sweetie, shush," Jolie cooed.

Sweetie shushed.

I got down.

Stretched my cramped muscles with some shoulder rolling and some careful leg shaking. "I don't think you have to worry about home invasions," I said.

"I don't have to worry about you sneaking out of here in the middle of the night without telling me, either," Jolie quipped. "Sister's on the move, I'm gonna know it." She laid her hands on my shoulders and looked me over from head to foot and back again. "When was the last time you had a decent haircut?" she asked.

I sighed. "It's good to be back in the bosom of my family," I said.

Jolie grinned. "I'll pour us some wine, and we'll have some good ole girl talk," she responded.

I took a cautious side step in the direction of the hallway. "I've been on top of your refrigerator for three and a half hours," I reminded her. "I need to use the bathroom."

Sweetie looked up, gave a companionable little snarl.

"You do, too, don't you, fella?" Jolie asked the dog, taking a leash from a drawer and hooking it to his collar. She met my gaze. "You do your thing, Sweetie will do his, and then we'll have that wine."

I nodded.

Dog and woman went out the back door.

I clamped my knees together and hop-sprinted for the john.

Like me, Jolie wasn't into premeditated cooking, so once Sweetie and I had both relieved ourselves—*I,* at least, washed my paws afterward—my sister and I piled into her black Pathfinder and headed for the nearest restaurant.

The place was Italian, a fragrant link in a national chain. The red-and-white checkered tablecloths, plank floors and Chianti-bottle candleholders provided atmosphere. We ordered iced tea, after sighing over the wine list, and the waiter brought warm bread and poured olive oil into a saucer, adding a squiggle of balsamic vinegar for yum.

While I pigged out, Jolie sat with her fingers curved into a graceful tent under her chin. Her dark eyes were large and luminous as she pondered me, and for a moment, I saw her dad in them and missed him sorely. Ham had made room in his life for Greer and me, and I would always appreciate that.

Jolie was perceptive, and she leaned in a little, prodded, "What are you thinking about right now?"

"Your dad." I tore off another chunk of bread and dipped it in the dregs of the olive oil and vinegar. "He was a good guy."

Jolie smiled softly. "Yeah," she said. "He's been gone all this time, and there are still days when I think of something I want to tell him and dial half his phone number before I realize he won't pick up on the other end."

My throat tightened.

Jolie reached across the table and patted my hand. "How's by you, Sister Girl?"

I replenished the olive oil and balsamic vinegar from the bottles the waiter had left behind. "I'm doing okay." *If you don't count the ghosts, and the flashbacks, and how the harder I try to figure out who I am, the more confused I get.*

"Your mouth is tellin' me one story," Jolie observed, with wry good humor, "but your eyes say something else. What's really going on, Moje?"

I swallowed. Should I tell her about Nick and Chester? I'd told Bert, but he was a bartender, used to wild tales, and more of an acquaintance than a friend. Jolie was a sister-by-choice, and she was a scientist. It mattered to me whether she thought I was crazy or not.

The waiter returned, exhibiting the lousy timing that seems to be endemic to the species and stalwartly accepted our decision to split a plate of spaghetti and meatballs. Jolie waited until he was gone, and then prodded me again.

"Moje? What's the deal? You look like you've been over some rocky roads lately."

"I'm not crazy," I said, as a preface.

Jolie grinned. "Debatable," she said. "Spill it, Mojo. Something's definitely going on with you."

I let out a long breath, and almost choked because I'd neglected to take one in first.

"Are you smoking again?" Jolie demanded, narrowing her eyes.

I drank a few sips of my recently arrived iced tea to quell the coughing. "Of course not," I said. It was the safe answer, and mostly true, since I never had a cigarette unless I'd had good—make that *great*—sex first. Three weeks and counting since Tucker and I had gotten it on, so I was nicotine-free.

"Is it Lillian?"

"Partly," I hedged, interlacing my fingers so I wouldn't go after the bread and olive oil again. I didn't exercise, and I wasn't overweight, but a person never knows when their metabolism is going to turn on them. I've seen it happen.

"Tell me," Jolie urged.

I described the Lillian situation as clearly as I could, without getting maudlin.

Jolie frowned at the mention of the Tarot cards Lillian had given me.

"Death, the Queen of Pentacles and the Page of Cups," she reflected thoughtfully, when I was finished. "What do they mean?"

"I don't exactly know," I admitted. Sure, I'd looked them up in the *Damn Fool's Guide,* but the descriptions had seemed superficial to me. I had the feeling that I was trying too hard to understand the images, and anyway, there was always the chance that Lillian hadn't deliberately chosen them.

I said as much to Jolie, and then remembered the urgent way Lillian had urged those cards on me. "Take!" she'd said. "Take!"

Tears welled in my eyes. I longed for the old Lillian, the strong woman I used to know.

Jolie patted me again.

The spaghetti arrived.

The conversation stalled until we'd divided the meatballs.

"Maybe Lillian's mind is gone," Jolie ventured, cutting delicately at her share of the protein. I speared my meatball with a fork and nibbled at it like a Popsicle. If anybody's written *The Damn Fool's Guide to Table Manners*, I have yet to come across a copy.

"It's possible," I said. We both knew it was a tad *more* than possible, but the agreement was tacit.

"What else?" Jolie asked. She'd have made a great detective, but I guess when you get right down to it, forensic science isn't all that different. Both involve gathering clues and putting the pieces together.

I put down the meatball Popsicle. I'd been starving when we came in, but now my appetite was subsiding. Maybe it was the loaf of bread I'd consumed while we were waiting for the main course.

"Do you believe in ghosts?" I ventured.

"No," Jolie said, without hesitation, but she looked intrigued. "Why?"

"Because Nick popped in the other night."

Jolie leaned back, studying me pensively. Probably wondering what I was on. "Shut *up*," she said.

"It happened. You don't have to believe me."

"Don't get your panties in a wad," Jolie retorted. "I didn't say I didn't believe you."

"The cat was real, too," I insisted. When I get into a hole, I start digging like mad.

"*What* cat?"

"Chester. My half brother killed him during my birthday party. I was four."

In the next moment, a vacuum opened, sucked all the air out of the restaurant, and reduced everybody but Jolie to black-and-white still-shots shimmering at the periphery of my vision.

"You remember that?" Jolie asked, almost whispering.

I caught my breath. Pulled myself back out of the vortex. Our surroundings solidified, and the noise, returning suddenly, seemed so loud I wanted to clamp both hands over my ears.

"Yes," I said, as surprised as Jolie was. I blinked a couple of times. Mom had bought one of those doll cakes for the party, the kind with a frosted skirt. I could see the wax 4 pressed into the front as clearly as the platter of spaghetti on the table between us. There had been presents, and even guests—kids from the neighborhood, all in faded sunsuits.

Jolie's eyes were huge. "Oh. My. God."

I started to cry. "I went looking for Chester, after the party. I'd saved him a piece of cake." I paused, drew a tremulous breath. "I found him behind the storage shed in the backyard, Jolie. He'd been shot with one of the arrows from the archery set some idiot—probably my dad—gave Geoff for Christmas."

Jolie handed me a red-and-white checked napkin so I could wipe my eyes. I stopped short of blowing my nose.

"I'm sorry, Moje," she said. "That must have been beyond awful. But you're *remembering*, and that's a *good* thing, isn't it?"

"I don't know," I said. I felt things gathering around me, unseen things, dangerous things. They pressed in so hard, I could barely breathe. *"I don't know."*

"Let's get out of here," Jolie said. She signaled for the check, turned down the standard dessert pitch from the waiter and paid up.

Five minutes later, we were back in the Pathfinder.

I rolled the window down, even though the AC was on. I couldn't get enough air.

We went back to the apartment, and Sweetie didn't even growl when we came in.

Jolie pressed me into a chair at the kitchen table and rummaged for wineglasses and a bottle of red. Poured us each a double dose. We hadn't said a word all the way back from the restaurant, but now it was nitty-gritty time.

"What *else* do you remember?" Jolie asked.

I shook my head. "Nothing."

"But it's a start."

I wondered why that would be considered good news. When it comes to double homicide and the victims happen to be your parents, ignorance could be bliss.

"It means you're getting better," Jolie persisted.

"I wasn't sick in the first place," I pointed out, testy now that I was receiving an adequate oxygen supply.

Jolie topped off my wineglass, even though I hadn't taken a sip. "Okay," she said, with cheerful resolve. "Let's talk about something else. The cop. What's his name again? Or what brings you down here. Or—"

"The ghosts?" I rested my elbows on the table and shoved the fingers of both hands into my hair.

"Or the ghosts," Jolie said slowly.

"Do-over," I said. "There weren't any ghosts. I made it up."

"You saw something."

"I was hallucinating. That's what you think, isn't it?"

Jolie lowered her eyes, licked her lips, took a taste of her wine.

"Isn't it?"

Probably sensing conflict, Sweetie snarled halfheartedly from his bed, which blocked the hallway.

Great, I thought. *If I get up to use the bathroom during the night, I'll have to get past Dogzilla.*

The glad tidings just kept on coming.

"All right," Jolie agreed, with hasty diplomacy, raising both hands and holding them palms out. "Forget the ghosts. Forget Lillian and your fourth birthday. Tell me about the cop."

"There's a poor-to-fair chance he blew up in a car explosion night before last," I said, and even though the thought that it might be true, by some horrible coincidence, wrenched my gut, I admit I enjoyed watching Jolie's expression.

When she found her voice, she said, "Girl, your life is a full-scale terrorist alert. Level Orange."

I considered describing my brief sojourn in Cactus Bend, but that would bring us back to the murders, and even though I wanted to know what had really happened the night my folks died, I needed to step back from it. It was like a psychological black hole, and if I didn't get some kind of grip, I was going to be sucked in and swallowed.

The whole subject could wait until breakfast. Things always looked better in the morning.

Didn't they?

I was inspired. "Let's talk about you," I said. "How's the job? How's your love life?"

"I'm thinking of leaving the university and working as a crime-scene tech," Jolie said. Which only went to prove I wasn't the only bomb-dropper in the family.

"Why would you do that?" I asked. I finally resorted to the wine; downed a couple of gulps while I waited for Jolie's answer.

She shrugged. I think you really have to be a black woman to pull that kind of shoulder action off with any style. "I'm tired of being stuck in a lab all the time," she said. "I'm always one step removed from the action. What I do is so— well—after the fact."

I couldn't believe what I was hearing. Jolie had a master's degree in forensic science, and she was working on a Ph.D. She'd waited tables and sold shoes to get through school, and still maintained a four point, throughout. Plus, she really knew her bones.

"Excuse me," I said, after clearing my throat, "but if

there's *anything* that can be described as 'after the fact,' it's a crime scene."

"I want to be on the front lines," she said. "I'm tired of weighing stomachs and counting bone fragments."

The meatball I'd eaten earlier did a line-drive up my esophagus and slammed into the back of my throat. I felt the blood drain from my face, and Jolie noticed immediately.

"Sorry," she said, with a little wince.

It was my turn to do the narrow-eyed stare. "What's really going on here?" Revelation struck, and I snapped my fingers. "I've got it. You're dating a homicide cop, and this is your misguided idea of togetherness."

"You should write fiction," Jolie replied. "I'm not dating *anybody*. This is about doing something different."

"Weighing stomachs and scraping up samples of somebody's brains are not all that 'different,' Jolie," I pointed out.

She got that stubborn look I remembered from when Lillian and Ham first got together, over in Ventura Beach. Let's just say if Jolie had written a letter to Santa Claus that year, Lillian, Greer and I wouldn't have been on her list of requests.

"At least it's a *job*," she said.

I'm not stupid. I know when to take offense. "I *have* a job," I retorted. "I do medical billings. Not just any idiot can remember all those codes, damn it."

"You live over a biker bar, Moje." She nodded toward my trash-bag luggage, slumped in the third chair. "You don't even own a suitcase."

"Have you been talking to Greer?"

"I don't have to talk to Greer," Jolie argued coolly. "I'm not blind. You're flying under the radar, Moje. You have so many secrets that there's nothing true in your life. Ever since you and Nick split up, you've been dodging emotional bullets. You're always darting from one thing to another, like some kind of moving target."

The truth hurts.

I sat back, feeling as if she'd slapped me.

Jolie sighed. "*That* went well."

I stood up, reached for my purse, then the garbage bag. I hadn't touched my wine since those first few sips, and I must have bumped the table, because the stuff trembled in the glass.

"Moje," Jolie pleaded. "Please—don't go."

I couldn't stay.

I couldn't even speak.

I took my purse and garbage bag and left.

Two and a half hours later, I pulled into Bert's lot, grabbed my stuff, and locked up the Volvo. There were a couple of bikes and half a dozen cars parked close to the side door, but plenty of noise spilled out into the warm night. I climbed the stairs and let myself into my apartment.

"Chester?" I called. My hand was on the light switch by the front door, but I wasn't ready to flip it and throw the whole place into stark relief.

"Re-oooow," Chester answered.

My spirits lifted. I turned on the lights.

Chester was there, all right. He hopped down off my desk chair—maybe he'd been surfing the Web—and trotted toward me.

At the same time, Nick meandered out of the kitchen, sniffing an Oreo.

"I'm getting really tired of this," I said, but secretly I was glad of the company. Well, I was glad of *Chester's* company, anyway, and I could put up with Nick.

I set the trash bag down, along with my purse, so I could hoist Chester up for a cuddle.

"Most people," Nick observed, "carry garbage *out,* not in."

"Don't start," I said.

"You look awful."

"Batting a thousand, as usual. You need to sign up for a course in Remedial Tact as soon as you bust out of the train station. And what's with the Oreo-sniffing?"

Nick cocked his handsome ghost head to one side. "Touchy," he said.

Chester butted the underside of my chin with his head, purring like crazy. My arms tightened around him, just a little. I wanted more than anything to cry, so I didn't.

"Your voice mail is probably full," Nick informed me. "The phone's been ringing ever since you left here yesterday."

Was it only yesterday that I'd packed my trash bag and hit the road?

God, it seemed as if I'd been gone a week.

"I'm surprised you didn't take messages," I said. I dropped into the easy chair, still holding Chester. "That way, you could have butted into my business in a really focused way." I glanced at the computer. Wondered if he'd been reading my e-mail.

Nick sighed and perched elegantly on the arm of the sofa. Tugged irritably at his cuffs. "I have better things to do than listen in on telephone calls," he said, with icy dignity. "*Or* read e-mail."

I stiffened. Did a little mental backtracking. *No.* I definitely had *not* mentioned the e-mail out loud.

Nick grinned.

"You can read my mind?" I snapped.

"Only some of the time," he said, and did the cuff-tugging thing again. This time, it wasn't a sign of irritation. It was him being smug.

"That *really* bites!" I considered protective noggin gear. All I had on hand was a roll of Reynold's wrap, so I discarded the idea.

Nick chuckled. "You wouldn't actually swath your head in tin foil, would you? It's an amusing image, though."

"Shut up."

He softened visibly. "Tough times, huh?"

"Stop trespassing in my brain. It's a restricted area."

"Sorry," Nick said. He examined the Oreo, sniffed it once more, and set it on the coffee table, albeit reluctantly. "Forgive me yet?"

"Not a chance," I replied.

Nick sighed.

"Tell me what it's like." Chester gave up the head-butting routine and curled up in my lap for a snooze. I watched Nick with interest, awaiting his answer.

"Tell you what *what's* like?"

"Don't be obtuse. If you can read my thoughts, then you know exactly what I'm talking about. Dead City. Toes-up-ville. What's it like?"

Nick looked away, looked back. "I couldn't tell you," he said. "I'm stuck in the train depot, remember?"

"Right," I said. "So tell me about the depot."

A slow smile settled on his lips. "You don't want me to leave."

"You're company. I'd settle for just about any warm body at the moment—not that you really qualify."

"That hurts."

"Good."

Nick's smile faded. "I'm sorry, Mojo. About the times you waited up for me, and the times you cried. If I could do it over again—"

"Get out of my head," I interrupted, shoving the ragtag, disintegrating-marriage memories back into the appropriate mental closet. "I want to know about the train station. And how you happened to hook up with Chester."

"It's just—a train station. Like something you might see in one of those black-and-white movies from the forties. All kinds of people, milling around, confused. Others standing in line for tickets."

"It sounds lonely," I said, and then regretted it. "Isn't there some kind of intake system? Maybe an orientation session? 'Dead 101,' or something like that?"

"No angels," Nick said, with somber amusement. "No harps. Definitely no 'Dead 101.' It took a while to figure it out, actually—that I'd croaked, I mean."

"I thought you said you saw your corpse at the morgue, then attended your own funeral. I don't want to be crass or anything, but either of those things could be called a clue."

Another grin, this one rueful. "At the time, I thought I was dreaming. People who die suddenly, or violently, usually react that way."

I felt a stab of something. Maybe it was sympathy. "And if I forgive you, you can get on one of the trains and go—where? Real estate heaven? Are they replacing the streets of gold with asphalt these days, and slapping up little stucco houses that all look alike?"

"You could be nicer to me, you know," Nick said. "After all, I *am* dead."

I sat up straight. Chester gave me a look of reproach for almost dumping him to the floor. "Wait a second—"

"No," Nick told me quietly. "I haven't seen your parents."

"Can you ask around a little?"

He shook his head. "It's not as if there's an information booth," he said.

"You're not a lot of help, Nick."

"And you're deliberately being a bitch."

I smiled. "Sorry."

"That's okay," Nick said graciously. "I forgive you."

"Gee, thanks."

A ruckus broke out downstairs, in Bad-Ass Bert's. Sounded as if somebody had upended a pool table, but I wasn't alarmed. It was Friday night, and a good brawl was always on the weekend schedule.

"How do you stand this place?" Nick asked.

I remembered that I'd promised to take care of Russell so Bert and Sheila could go camping at Oak Creek Canyon. I hoped the dog wasn't caught in the cross fire of flying fists, steel-toed boots and swinging pool cues.

"I don't have a choice, thanks to you and your mother," I answered sweetly. "Besides, it's not so bad. I guess you could say home is where the heart is."

"How would you know?" Nick fired back. "You don't *have* a heart, as far as I can tell."

I remembered the nights I'd called all over town looking for my missing husband. The nights I'd cried myself to sleep. The day I finally figured out that Nick was never going to change, no matter how hard I tried to be the wife he wanted.

And I didn't give a damn if he could see those memories. Let him take a good look.

"What about Chester?" I asked, when a little of the silent angst had receded. "You never told me how you found him."

"He found me," Nick said.

"How did you know he was my cat?"

"I looked into his head, and he took a peek into mine. We discovered we had you in common." Another smile, this one wan. I squinted, looking for the telltale glow. Were his batteries petering out?

"I forgive you," I said.

"You have to mean it," Nick answered.

"I *do* mean it."

"I can read your mind, remember?" The noise downstairs reached a wicked crescendo. Nick frowned.

I got a little quiver in the pit of my stomach. "What is it?"

"You'd better call the cops," Nick said. "Your friend Bert-the-bartender is in big trouble."

Chester disappeared.

Nick evaporated.

I bolted for the outside door.

CHAPTER

Cars and bikes peeled out, in noisy contrast to the ominous silence from within the building, as I sprinted for the open doorway at the side.

I rushed in. "Bertrand! Russell!"

I heard a groan, from the direction of the pool tables, and ran toward it. Bert lay sprawled on his back underneath the one on the left, bleeding copiously into the sawdust on the floor.

I dropped to my knees and crab-scrambled to his side.

"Bert!"

He looked at me for a long, terrible moment, and then his eyes rolled back into his head. I shoved up his muscle shirt, swabbed the hairy skin with one palm, and saw the knife wound.

Nick's words of advice came back to me. *You'd better call the cops.*

I shimmied backward, out from under the pool table,

soaked. It brought back some elemental memories, all of them sensory rather than specific, but I didn't have time for introspection.

I hurried to the wall phone behind the bar, grabbed the receiver, and punched the pertinent digits, leaving crimson fingerprints on the buttons.

"Help," I said, when the dispatcher answered.

I looked down. Russell huddled between two boxes, gazing up at me with huge, despairing eyes.

I crouched to run a hand over his broad back.

"I'm at Bad-Ass Bert's Biker Saloon in Cave Creek," I told the operator. "A man's been hurt."

"Your name?"

I knew this was standard procedure, but it still set my teeth on edge. While we were chatting about vital statistics, Bert was probably bleeding to death. "Mojo Sheepshanks," I answered. "I live upstairs, above the bar. Get somebody here, *please*—"

"There are police and ambulance units on the way," the woman answered calmly. "Are you injured in any way, Ms. Sheepshanks?"

"No," I said. "I'm not sure about the dog, though."

Russell whimpered, and I gave him a quick once-over with my free hand and both eyeballs. Except for delayed-stress syndrome, he seemed to be all right.

A siren screamed in the distance.

"Stay on the line, please," the operator said.

"I'm here," I answered. "But I'd like to go back to Bert. He's under the pool table, and I don't want him to think he's alone."

"Is there anyone else on the premises?"

Also standard procedure. Can't have the cops and the EMTs rushing into a potentially dangerous situation.

"Just Bert and the dog and me," I answered. By then, I was queasy. The smell and feel of all that blood made me shift to my knees. I leaned forward and rested my forehead between Russell's soft, floppy ears.

The siren was getting closer, and I heard other sirens kick in behind it, farther away, a shrill, weaving braid of sound.

"I need to find out if Bert's still holding on," I said. There was a cord on the phone, and it wouldn't reach to the pool table. I was effectively pinned.

"Render aid if necessary," the dispatcher instructed. "But please do not break the connection."

I nodded, being in shock, and left the receiver to bounce back to the wall and then dangle.

"It's okay, boy," I told Russell. "The cops are on their way. Just hang out right here, and everything will be all right."

Russell probably didn't believe me. Hell, I didn't even believe myself.

I left him, grabbed a bar towel, and went back to Bert.

I wadded the towel and pressed it to the wound in his chest, hoping to staunch the flow of blood.

The nearest siren gave a blipping shriek, and blue-and-red lights flashed across the interior of the bar.

They're here, I thought. *Thank God, they're here.*

"This way—under the pool table!" I yelled.

More sirens. More lights. Lots of flying gravel. Emergency vehicles, I thought, must go through tires like there's no tomorrow.

Maybe, for Bert, there wouldn't be.

Two guys in blue shirts dropped to their knees and joined the party. I backed out from under and held on to the edge of the table to hoist myself up.

Cops and more medics streamed in through the door.

Russell howled.

I searched the arriving faces for Tucker's, but he wasn't there.

"Freeze," one of the cops ordered, when I started around the bar.

I put my hands out from my sides and froze, trying to see things from his perspective. For all the cops knew, I was the one who'd stabbed Bert, and I could have been going for a gun.

"The dog," I said pitifully.

Russell low-crawled from behind the bar, his gaze fixed on me, imploring, as if he'd fallen out of a boat into white water, and I was his only lifeline.

I went to him, knelt, wrapped him in my arms.

A gray-haired detective dropped to his haunches, on the other side of Russell, and he seemed kind. His eyes were gentle as he took us both in.

"What happened here?" he asked quietly.

"I don't know," I answered. "I live upstairs. I—heard something, and came down to see what was going on." I nodded in the direction of the pool table. The EMTs had lifted Bert onto a stretcher, and they were sliding him out from under. "I found Bert—all bloody—"

"Take it easy," the detective said. "Did you see anyone else?"

I did some deep breathing before I answered. Shook my head. "No."

"The place was empty? Was it closed for business?"

I shook my head again, told him about the cars and bikes flinging gravel as I came down the back stairs.

The EMTs snapped the ends of the gurney down and rolled by with Bert.

Russell yelped and tried to follow.

I held him, and cried.

"Somebody should call Sheila," I said. Words tumbled out of my mouth, and I was literally terrified that I'd never be able to stop talking. "Can I take the dog upstairs? He's pretty shook up."

The detective brought me to a merciful halt by touching my shoulder, considered my request, then nodded. "In a minute." Translation: as soon as the ambulance pulls away.

Russell barked and struggled furiously to get free. He'd have scrambled into that ambulance with Bert if he'd been allowed to, stayed with him through whatever came.

I cried harder, because there was no way to explain so the dog could understand.

"Does he have a leash?" the detective asked quietly.

I searched the old memory banks, neatly avoiding the ones marked No Admittance. I'd never seen Russell on a leash; he'd always arrived at the bar in the sidecar of Bert's Harley. But he was wearing a collar.

"Look behind the bar," I said. "There's a junk drawer, under the hot dog machine."

The cop nodded, got to his feet and left Russell and I to watch the milling uniforms and plainclothesmen. It made me dizzy, and I finally had to look away.

The detective returned with a leash. Hooked it through the link on Russell's collar. "Let's go, fella," he told Russell.

The guy must have been in charge, because nobody questioned us when we left the scene of the crime, though he did pause briefly, just outside, to speak with a young woman pulling on rubber gloves. Upstairs, my door gaped open; I hadn't taken the time to close it. Russell trundled inside, sniffing the air, and I wondered, momentarily distracted from the horror we'd just left, if he'd caught Chester's scent.

"I'd like to take a shower," I said. I hadn't planned on saying that, but it sounded reasonable, given that every stitch I was wearing was saturated.

"Not yet," replied my official escort. "Your clothes will have to be taken into evidence. A crime scene tech will be up here as soon as they can spare one downstairs."

I nodded glumly. "Am I a suspect?"

The detective smiled. "A person of interest," he clarified, as though there might be a difference. I'd read *The Damn Fool's Guide to Criminal Investigation,* and I knew the drill. The next step after "Person of Interest" was "You have the right to remain silent."

He took out a pad, uncapped a pen. "Let's start with your name, Miss—?"

"Sheepshanks," I said. "Mary Jo."

Mary Jo? Where the hell had *that* come from?

"Everybody calls me Mojo," I added.

"Andy Crowley." He handed me a card. I guess we were past the flash-the-badge stage.

My landline jingled.

I looked at Crowley, eyebrows raised.

He nodded his permission. He also followed me into the kitchen.

"Thank God you're there," a woman blurted.

"Sheila?"

Bert's girlfriend gave a blubbery sob. "I'm in Phoenix," she said. "Somebody just called on my cell and said the parking lot at Bert's is swarming with cop cars, and they saw an ambulance, too. Mojo, is Bert all right?"

I bit my lower lip, glanced down at Russell, who, like Crowley, had tailed me from the living room. The dog's coat was smudged with blood where I'd touched him.

"No," I said gently. "Bert's not okay, Sheila. Somebody stabbed him. He's been taken to the hospital." I looked questioningly at Crowley, wanting to tell her which hospital, where.

"Either Scottsdale Healthcare or Paradise Valley General," Crowley supplied.

I raised my voice to repeat the information to Sheila, who was almost wailing by then.

"God *damn* it!" she ranted. "I knew something like this was going to happen—"

"Sheila," I broke in, "is somebody with you? You shouldn't drive when you're this upset."

Crowley nodded with somber approval.

Oh, yeah. I was on top of the vehicular safety issue.

Too bad I was also a person of interest in a case of criminal assault that might just turn into murder any minute.

"Russell!" Sheila cried. *"What about Russell?"*

"He's with me," I said. "He's safe."

Crowley strolled over to the coffeemaker, filled the carafe at the sink.

"Bert's been hurt," I heard Sheila say, apparently addressing a companion. "Mojo's got Russell. She says he'll be taken to either Scottsdale Healthcare or Paradise Valley—will you call and find out?"

There was a murmured reply, then Sheila addressed me again. "Ellie's calling the hospitals," she said. Ellie was her best friend; I'd met her at holiday gatherings in the bar. "She'll drive me there as soon as we find out for sure where he is."

I nodded, tried not to think about the way my T-shirt was clinging to my upper body, stiffening as it dried. I broke out in gooseflesh, and wished I could strip to the bare essentials, right there in the kitchen. Anything to escape the feel of that bloody fabric against my skin. "Okay," I replied. "Let me know how Bert is when you get a chance, will you?"

Crowley found the coffee in the cupboard next to the sink, measured some into the basket and pushed the button. He wasn't staring at me anymore, but I knew he was taking in everything I said, and how I said it.

"Sure," Sheila answered moistly. "Thanks for keeping Russell."

"No problem, Sheila. Try not to panic, okay?"

"Okay," she said, without much hope of succeeding.

We disconnected.

"What's your relationship to the victim?" Crowley asked, pulling back a chair for me at the table.

I collapsed into it.

"He's my landlord," I said. I looked down at Russell, lying in mournful silence at my feet. "And my friend."

"And you knew there was trouble because—"

Because my dead husband told me.

"There was a lot of noise."

"That's unusual?" Crowley snooped through cupboards until he found the mugs, and set two on the counter, in front of the laboring coffeemaker. It was an ancient machine, and of roughly the same quality as my luggage.

"No," I said. "There was just something—"

Crowley nodded encouragement, leaning against the counter now, arms folded. There were leather patches on the elbows of his lightweight tweed jacket.

"Weird," I finished.

"No disputes over the rent, the air conditioning, anything like that?"

I'd been in shock at first. Now, I was beginning to get pissed off. "I didn't stab Bert," I said, linking the words together like boxcars, each one with an inaudible *clank*.

"How do you know he was stabbed?"

My cheeks burned, and I felt sick at the memory, and the smell of blood rising from my sodden T-shirt. "I guess it was the three-inch slit in his chest," I said tautly.

The coffeemaker made a *chuppa-whuppa* sound, like a helicopter circling in for a landing.

Crowley poured java for both of us, and joined me at the table.

I considered adding a dollop of Christian Brothers to

mine, but it didn't seem like a good idea, given that I was trying to present myself as a solid citizen.

"These questions are routine, Ms. Sheepshanks," he said mildly, once he was settled. I kept the sugar and the powdered creamer in the middle of the table, along with a plastic spoon, so we doctored and stirred, in our turns. Crowley was a gentleman; he let me go first.

"What's next?" I was a little foggy on the details, but I didn't want to jump up and consult a *DF Guide*. It might be considered suspicious behavior and, anyway, I was too dizzy.

"A crime scene tech will collect your clothes. With your permission, she'll take a few photographs, too. Then we'll leave and you can take your shower."

I felt my eyes go wide. "What kind of photographs?"

"Routine ones," Crowley said.

A rap sounded at the outside door.

Russell lifted his head and gave a grunting woof, but he didn't get up to investigate.

"Come in," Crowley called.

The same woman I'd seen downstairs appeared in the kitchen doorway, with the handle of a backpack in one hand and a folded paper bag in the other.

The promised crime scene tech had arrived.

I signed a release, agreeing to let her take pictures. Legally, they couldn't force me to pose, not without a lot of paperwork anyway, and it would take time, but I wanted to cooperate.

"I'm Jennifer," the tech said, snapping on a fresh pair of gloves.

"That's nice," I replied.

Jennifer and I trekked to the bathroom and, once inside, she watched clinically as I peeled off my clothes, dropping each garment into her evidence bag as I handed it to her. After that, she took pictures of my naked, blood-smudged body, from every possible angle. It was all very businesslike, but I still felt like a white rat on a lab table.

When the ordeal ended, Jennifer excused herself and stepped out, and I tucked the shower curtain inside the tub, turned on the taps, and dived under the spray. I scrubbed and scoured, and when I got out, I dried hastily and shrugged into my bathrobe, tying the belt tightly at my waist.

As expected, Crowley was still in the kitchen, drinking coffee.

Jennifer was long gone.

"Am I being watched?" I asked, emptying my mug in the sink and then refilling it from the carafe.

Crowley pushed back his chair and stood. "Not anymore," he said.

He'd been keeping an eye on the suspect until the evidence could be collected, I realized.

"Don't leave the area without checking with me," he told me, inclining his head toward the table, where his business card lay, face up. He'd had the good grace to replace the bloodstained one, at least. Or maybe he'd just wanted my fingerprints.

I nodded.

Crowley paused on the threshold between the kitchen and living room. "Is there somebody you can stay with? The guys will be downstairs for a while, but it might be safer to spend the night elsewhere."

A chill shivered up my spine. With all that had happened, it hadn't crossed my mind that whoever knifed Bert might come back, when the coast was clear, and do the same thing to me, just in case I'd seen something and remembered it later.

I could call Greer, I supposed. She'd take me in, but she'd probably make Russell sleep in the garage. Tucker was either waiting in line in the celestial train depot or tunneling through the underworld of users and dealers.

I needed to get out more. Make friends with people who would let me crash on their couches in an emergency.

"I'll be fine here," I said, hoping it was true.

I saw Crowley to the door, locked it behind him and turned around to find Russell standing at my heels. His expression was baleful, but then, he always looked that way.

I fired up the computer, figuring I might as well do some billing and coding, since I probably wouldn't sleep. While the program was loading, I went back to the kitchen and searched the shelves until I came up with a can of beef stew, stuck behind the roasting pan in the rear of my tiny pantry. Russell might have been traumatized, but there was nothing wrong with his appetite.

He snarfed up the stew, and I headed for the computer, only to think of Jolie and retrace my steps. My cell needed charging, so I reached for the wall phone, after wiping it off with a paper towel and some antiseptic spray cleaner. I tapped into the voice mail, intending to use the breather to work out what I could say to Jolie beyond "I'm sorry."

Only there wasn't a breather.

The first message was from Greer, and she sounded as though she'd been crying. "Mojo, I really need to talk to you. Call me."

I took a deep breath. Now I had *two* conversations to rehearse.

The second caller was Jolie. "You've got some fancy explaining to do, girl. Walking out on me like that. I'd better hear from you *pronto*. Like, I mean, *tonight*."

I let out a long sigh. I was in for it with Jolie, and my account of finding Bert under a pool table, stabbed in the chest, probably wouldn't prompt any sympathy. At least, none for me. Bert would get all of it.

The droning voice was distorted, probably by one of those spy devices they sell on the Internet, and it jolted me out of my reflections about talking to Greer and Jolie. "Did you get my text message? I meant what I said. You *will* die." Pause. "The question is, when? And how badly will it hurt?"

I dropped into a chair at the kitchen table, staring at Andy Crowley's cop card. I was ninety percent certain the call came from Geoff, and I knew I needed to report it, since I had a strong desire to stay alive. That was reason one. Reason two: there might be a connection, however remote the chances seemed, between the phone threat and what had happened to Bert. The information could help the police identify and find his attackers.

I was so stunned that the fourth message ended without my hearing a word. I had to suffer through the whole sequence again, because I couldn't take the chance that someone at Sunset Villa had called with urgent news about Lillian.

It turned out to be from a food-delivery service; a perky unisex voice promised a free Chinese dinner if I called before Monday.

I was on the national no-call list, supposedly off-limits to telemarketers. Fat lot of good it did me.

Disgusted, I punched in Greer's number. Triage, Mojo style. Jolie was pissed, but something big had to be up with Greer. I'd heard tears in her voice, and since I'd seen her cry exactly once since I'd known her—when we met at the hospital after Lillian had her stroke—I switched her to priority one.

She answered on the second ring, with a breathless, "Hello?"

"It's Mojo," I said.

Greer sniffled. "About time."

I closed my eyes. Waited.

Russell had finished his stew. He snuggled against the side of my chair, laid his muzzle on my right thigh and passed gas.

"Are you there?" Greer demanded testily.

I didn't want to breathe. I jumped up, found some matches in a drawer, and struck one.

"I'm here," I sputtered.

"I need your help."

I leaned down to pat Russell's head, so he'd know I wasn't holding the toxic fumes against him. His expression was sadly adoring.

"No more stew for you," I said.

"I beg your pardon?" Greer put in.

"Talking to the dog," I explained. "Why do you need my help, Greer?"

"I can't talk about it over the *telephone*!"

I looked at the clock. After eleven. It was dark outside, I'd just listened to a robotic death threat, and that was the *high point* of my evening. For all I knew, there was some maniac waiting right outside the door with an ax, cops or no cops.

"It can't be that bad, Greer." She wasn't sobbing. She wasn't screaming.

"That's what *you* think!"

"In the morning," I said patiently.

"Mojo, I'm desperate!"

"Then you'd better tell me what's going on, because I'm not driving out there unless you're bleeding." I grimaced, remembering poor Bert. *Let him be alive,* I prayed.

Greer started to cry.

I almost gave in. As I said, my sister wasn't a weeper.

"Listen, Greer, I've had a really bad night, and the day wasn't so great, either. So maybe we could do this tomorrow—"

"I'll come over there, then," Greer broke in, sounding peevish. "This is *serious*, Mojo."

I really wished she'd stop italicizing every third word. "Okay," I said cautiously, "but there's a crime scene downstairs, and the cops might not even let you into the parking lot."

Now we were talking *serious*.

For a moment, the old Greer was back. "No shit? What happened?"

I explained, taking care to include Bert's wound, my clothes being taken for evidence, the nude photo shoot and the fact that I had temporary custody of a flatulent basset hound.

"See you in twenty," Greer said, when I'd finished.

All righty, then.

"Bring kibble," I put in quickly, before she could hang up.

"Kibble?"

"I mean it, Greer. I gave this dog canned stew and, given his digestive system, we could be on the threshold of an environmental disaster."

She said a hasty goodbye and rang off.

With luck, I could get through the long-distance confrontation with Jolie before Greer arrived. The threatened ETA was twenty minutes, but that was without the stop for dog food.

I steeled myself and dialed Jolie's number.

She must have been sitting on the phone, and she definitely had caller ID. She jumped straight onto my back. "Mojo Sheepshanks, you did a rotten, lousy thing, storming out of here like that!"

"You're right," I said. I couldn't quite get to "meek," but I did "regretful" credibly.

The admission stunned her to silence, but I knew it was temporary.

"I'm sorry," I added. It was the equivalent of sitting on top of the refrigerator and throwing frozen pot roasts to Sweetie. And I really did feel terrible about bailing on her.

If I hadn't, though, Bert would probably be dead by now.

Assuming he wasn't.

"Me, too," Jolie said.

I caught my breath. "What did you say?"

"I said I'm sorry, Mojo. I should have kept my opinions to myself. About your job, I mean."

I was beyond relieved.

"You still there?" Jolie asked. "Or did you sky on me again?"

"I'm here."

"I was thinking I could come up to Cave Creek, bunk at your place. I'd like to see Lillian anyway, and it would be like old times, you and me and Greer talkin' trash."

"God, Jolie," I said, almost whispering. "That would be great." I glanced at Russell. He'd been through enough, without coming face-to-face with Sweetie. "Are you planning to bring the dog?" I put the question carefully, because I didn't want Jolie to get mad and change her mind about the visit.

"Sweetie can stay with some friends of mine, out in the country. They're always inviting him for play dates with their dogs."

Play dates? Any breed smaller than a bull mastiff might end up as a snack.

"The sooner you can get here," I said, "the better."

"I should roll in sometime tomorrow afternoon. I'll stop at Sunset Villa and then drive up from there."

Russell broke wind again.

I lit another match, half-expecting a methane explosion, and wished I'd asked Greer to pick up industrial-strength air freshener as well as kibble.

"Sounds good," I said, waving my free hand.

"We're going to have company," I told Russell, after Jolie and I hung up. I crouched to ruffle his ears gently. "All we gotta do is hold on, buddy. Things are bound to get better."

Russell craned his almost nonexistent neck to lap at my cheek. I probably tasted of tears.

We communed for a while, the basset and me, and then I

gave him a bath with paper towels and sink water. That done, I rounded up some extra blankets and made him a bed in the kitchen. Once Russell was settled, I stood on tiptoe to look out the window, peering down at the parking lot. There were still six squad cars, parked at urgent angles, and plenty of uniforms and suits moving in and out of the bar.

I saw Greer's car pull in, splashed in the glow of a streetlight, come to a sleek stop next to a policeman.

I could just imagine how she was charming his regulation socks off. If she was still tearful, he wouldn't have a chance against her.

Russell began to snore, and stunk up the place with another poot before I sneaked out and headed for the exit. I waited on the landing as the cop waved Greer in, following the car on foot.

She popped the trunk from inside, and Officer Friendly leaned into it, came up with a huge bag. She'd remembered the kibble, then.

Smiling, the cop carried the thing up the stairs, looking very young and very earnest, with Greer mincing along behind him in high heels, murmuring something appreciative and admiring.

The guy looked as though he'd just rescued a baby from a burning house.

Sucker, I thought, but kindly.

I stepped back, so he could get by, and he lugged that bag all the way to the kitchen, after I pointed the way.

Russell opened his eyes, lying on his bed of blankets, but he didn't make a sound.

Greer thanked the policeman sweetly, and he returned to parking lot duty.

"Thanks," I said to Greer, with some amazement, taking in the bag. It was gourmet stuff, with a snooty-looking poodle preening on the front—one hundred percent organic and human grade.

In other words, if money got tight, Russell and I could share rations.

Greer smiled, pleased by my obvious gratitude, but her eyes were puffy, and her nostrils seemed chapped. She stood there in my kitchen, looking like a butterfly with one bent wing.

"How much do I owe you?" I asked. My purse was sitting on the counter, and I reached for it.

"Don't be silly," Greer scolded. "You can't begin to afford it."

I grinned. This was the Greer I knew. Plus, she hadn't italicized anything.

Russell stretched, yawning, and got off the blanket pile to sniff at the kibble bag, then Greer's ankles.

"Sit down," I told my sister, taking charge. "I'll make you some tea."

Something shifted in Greer. She nodded in acquiescence, looking as delicate and uncertain as she'd sounded on the phone, and plunked herself into the nearest chair.

I put the kettle on to boil, scrounged up a couple of tea bags and dished up some fancy grub for Russell, setting a bowl of water down alongside it. All that time, Greer said nothing. She merely looked on, as if she'd never seen a dog crunching kibble before.

"Okay," I said, when the tea was ready and I'd taken the chair across from Greer's. "What brings you to Bad-Ass Bert's in the middle of the night?"

Greer fidgeted, licked her lips and looked me straight in the eye.

I waited, uneasy again.

"I'll pay you ten thousand dollars," my sister said, "if you can prove my husband is fooling around."

I blinked, peering at Greer. "Did you just say you were willing to pay me *ten grand* to prove the doc is cheating on you?"

Greer bit her lower lip and nodded.

"For that much money," I said, still recovering, "I'd set him up myself."

"I'm *hoping* he's *not* being unfaithful to our wedding vows," Greer said tersely. "And my trust in you had *better* not be misplaced."

There she went, italicizing again. "Right," I said.

Russell farted, unabashed.

"*Good God*!" Greer bolted from her chair, cheeks bulging with a thwarted exhalation, and hoisted the kitchen window open. Cop voices murmured below, but I couldn't make out what they were saying.

"Why me?" I asked, of a largely disinterested universe.

Greer gave Russell an accusatory look and stayed close to the open window to let out her breath and suck in more air. "Why you?"

I brought her gently back to the point of her visit. "Yes. Why would you hire me to check up on Alex, instead of some big detective agency?"

"Don't you want the money?" Greer challenged.

Hell, yes, I wanted the money, and she damn well knew it. I just looked at her, hoping she hadn't changed her mind.

"You're a born snoop," my sister said. "You've got a lot of free time, and I *trust* you would be discreet—*and* be completely fair to Alex in the process."

"Any top-flight agency would be discreet," I pointed out. "Plus, they would have experience and resources."

Damn it. Whose side was I on, anyway? I could do a lot with an influx of cash like that, and since Geoff had put me off the casinos for a while, this was the only chance I was likely to get.

Greer gave Russell another wary glance, then sat down, all very serious. "Alex belongs to every civic organization in Arizona," she told me. "I'm afraid any agency I called would tip him off, as a professional courtesy—or just out of spite."

"Okay," I said uncertainly.

She opened her shoulder bag—one of those rhinestone studded numbers with a real gold buckle—and took out a sheaf of papers and her checkbook.

"I don't have a private investigator's license, you know," I felt compelled to say. I do have standards. And I wouldn't *really* have framed Alex as a cheater just to collect the ten grand.

Which is not to say I wouldn't be tempted. I just wouldn't actually do it.

Greer ignored my statement and handed me the papers. Turned out they were printouts from a computer-generated address book. "I've highlighted the suspicious names and numbers," she said. While I studied them, she produced a fountain pen and opened her checkbook. "I think the one with the star beside it is with him at the medical conference, even as we speak. You'll need a good camera, and there are bound to be expenses, so I'm giving you a retainer."

It required all the discipline I had not to lean across the table and get a look at the numbers on that check.

"Right," I said. That was always safe with Greer. She liked to be right.

"What makes you so sure Alex is running around?"

"All the little signs are there."

Yeah, I thought, *probably the same stuff that made his first wife suspicious when the two of you were scorching the sheets.*

"Like what?" I asked reasonably.

"The usual. Suspicious phone calls. Having his mail forwarded to his office. Late hours, even for a doctor." Something bruised flickered in Greer's eyes. "I'll die if she's pregnant."

"Whoa," I said. "Pregnant?"

"What better way to snag somebody else's husband?"

I didn't argue with that. If Alex was stepping out, the other woman was probably in her twenties, since Greer herself was only thirty-two. It was a common enough scenario with men in his age and income brackets, meaning fiftyish and rich, to trade in the used model for something sporty, long-legged and preferably blond. I see these victims of midlife crisis in public places all the time, sitting with some sharp number young enough to be their daughter. Kids, too, a lot of the time—and anybody but a skeptic would take them for grandchildren, given the age gap.

Do these guys actually believe it's their virility, not their wallets, that puts a sweet young thing on their arm?

They really should get a clue. It's the Beamer, stupid, and the bank account and the big house. It's *so* not the other thing.

And you're not fooling anybody.

Greer brought me back from my ramblings by ripping out the check, slapping it down on the tabletop and shoving it toward me.

Five thousand dollars.

My eyes must have bulged.

"Greer," I said, "this is really a lot of money. I could—"

"I want you to have it," Greer said.

I took the check. Logic demanded that I get on a plane, fly to wherever the medical conference was being held and peek at Alex and the chickie from behind a few potted palms, but I wasn't free to do that. Detective Crowley had told me not to leave town, and Jolie was arriving the next day for a visit.

I explained.

Greer was undaunted. "Do what you can," she said. Then she stood to leave. Business completed. No comment on the events of the evening or Jolie's impending descent upon Cave Creek.

I studied her. "I'm grateful for the chance and for the check, Greer," I said, "and I truly hope whatever I find out is good news to you. But are you really just going to waltz out of here without responding to any of the things I just told you?"

Greer looked confused for a moment, then horrified. She dropped back into her chair, and her eyes glistened with moisture. "You're right," she said miserably. "When did I become so self-absorbed?"

I offered no comment.

Greer untangled her arm from the strap of her purse, propped her elbows on the tabletop and rubbed her temples so hard her forehead squenched together from the sides. "It must have been terrible for you, finding your friend hurt and bleeding like that, especially after—after—"

"Take a breath, Greer. It's okay."

"And *of course* it will be wonderful to see Jolie again." She stopped, bit her lip. "If she wants to see me, that is."

"Why wouldn't she want to see you?"

"You know how she feels about Alex, Mojo."

I nodded. "Yes," I agreed. "But she's not expecting to see Alex. Just you."

Greer squirmed a little. Dried her eyes with the back of one hand, smearing mascara across both cheekbones in the process.

"Better check your makeup," I said. Letting Greer go out like that would be an unforgivable sin, from her point of view, like allowing a friend to walk into a job interview with parsley in her teeth.

She got out her gold compact, snapped it open, consulted the mirror and groaned. "I look awful. No wonder my husband is messing around with other women."

"If your husband is 'messing around with other women,' Greer, it's because he's a selfish asshole, not because your mascara is smudged."

"You don't like him, either," she said, like it was news. "Do you have any baby wipes?"

After I'd made the leap over the gap where the segue should have been, I pushed back my chair. "Come on. We'll see what's in the medicine cabinet."

"You keep your makeup in the medicine cabinet?"

I chuckled. "Yes, Greer. I own one tube of mascara, one bottle of foundation and one tube of lipstick. I can't see investing in a train case."

"You should have a makeover," Greer prattled, as she followed me through the living room to the bathroom. She didn't know what to say to me anymore, it seemed, but I didn't take offense. Most likely, she saw my entire life as a restoration project, and not without reason. Letting somebody slather high-priced goop on my face in some department store probably seemed like the second best place to start, the first being that whopping check she'd just written.

As it happened, the only smeared-mascara solutions I had to offer were a new bar of soap and a jar of Vaseline. She chose the soap, and I left her to the repair job.

Glancing out the kitchen window, I saw that the cop cars were gone, and Greer's SUV sat alone in the parking lot, except for my Volvo.

We met in the living room, which was the middle ground between the bathroom and kitchen.

"Maybe you should spend the night," I said.

"I was thinking the same thing about you," Greer replied. "Why don't you pack a few things and come home with me?"

I was touched that she'd ask. "I can't leave Russell."

"Who's Russell?"

"The *dog,* Greer." I cocked a thumb in his direction.

"He stinks," she said matter-of-factly, and without apparent rancor.

There was no denying that Russell was aromatically challenged, and now that I thought about it, I recalled that Bert had warned me about the fart tendency when he asked me to look after Russell while he and Sheila went camping.

I wondered why Sheila hadn't called. I'd been taking surreptitious glances at the clock all evening, and anxiety thrummed in my nerve endings. I caught a flash of white out of the corner of one eye and realized, with rising spirits, that Chester was back.

Greer didn't notice, of course, but Russell waddled in from the kitchen, sniffing the air.

"I'll walk you to your car," I told Greer, because I didn't want her in the parking lot alone. I didn't want myself in the parking lot alone, for that matter, but what was I going to do? If anything happened to my sister, I'd never forgive myself.

"Nonsense," she said. "Just stand on the landing and watch until I'm inside. As soon as I start the engine, the door will relock."

I accompanied her as far as the top of the stairs, stood guard while she descended, key fob in hand. Behind me, inside the apartment, I heard Russell growl tentatively.

Greer got into her SUV, fired up the engine, flashed her lights and drove away.

Russell gave another growl, and I turned and went inside, careful to turn the dead bolt and put on the chain. When I stepped into the living room, I was startled to see the basset hound and the cat sitting face-to-face in the middle of the floor, smelling each other's noses.

It took a moment for the implications to register. After all, I'd had a long and difficult day.

Russell could see Chester.

I wasn't hallucinating.

I wasn't losing it.

Chester raised a paw and batted playfully at Russell's long nose. Russell backed up a few inches, without lifting his butt off the floor.

I did a little victory dance.

I was sane!

And the phone rang.

I raced for the kitchen extension, my heart thudding. It was after midnight and, let's face it, the good news ratio goes way down by then.

I squinted at the caller ID panel; the reading was 'no number available.'

"This is Mojo."

Silence.

Oh, God. It was my brother again. Or Heather.

"I'm sorry to call so late," Sheila apologized, sounding flustered and weary, both at once, "but you said—"

I was relieved, then worried again. "How's Bert?"

Russell ambled in, with Chester traveling practically in lock-step beside him. They both sat down, like a pair of churchgoers wedged into a crowded pew, and watched me with consuming interest.

Sheila began to cry.

I closed my eyes, standing rigid in my bathrobe and bare feet, and waited for the ax to fall. Bert hadn't made it. The knife had hit some vital organ. My palm sweated where I gripped the receiver. "Tell me, Sheila. Is Bert—?"

"He's been in surgery all this time," Sheila wept.

My knees almost gave out. "He's alive?"

"Yes!" Sheila wailed. "He's in recovery now, and the doctor thinks he'll be okay, but I can't leave him and I don't know when I can come and get Russell and the first thing he's going to ask me about is that dog—"

"Sheila," I interrupted gently. "Don't worry about Russell. I'll take care of him as long as necessary."

Russell growled again, and when I glanced in his direction, I saw Nick standing in the doorway, one shoulder braced casually against the jamb. He gave a jaunty little salute.

Russell crossed the room, sniffed at Nick's pant leg and wagged his tail.

"He can see you," I mouthed.

"I'd better go," Sheila finished, and I realized she'd been talking right along. "I want to sit with Bert, be there when he wakes up. Thank you so much, Mojo. I don't know how I will ever repay you."

"Thank you so much, Mojo," Nick repeated. "I don't know how I will ever repay you."

I made a face at him, said goodbye to Sheila and hung up.

By then, he'd wandered over to the table, with no interference from Russell. Greer's check lay faceup, and Nick whistled when he read the figure.

"You probably saved Bert's life," I said. "So I forgive you for every lousy thing you've ever done to me." I smiled and spread my hands. "Now, you can leave."

Nick eyed me skeptically. Shook his head.

I sighed. "Listen. I am really tired and I want to go to bed, and I don't need a ghost watching me sleep. So if you wouldn't mind—"

"I *do* mind. I heard what that cop told you. You shouldn't be alone tonight. So Chester and I are going to burn a little extra ectoplasm and stick around till morning."

"You're a ghost. What could you do if somebody broke in?"

"You'd be surprised," Nick said.

I narrowed my eyes.

"Mojo, go crash before you collapse."

"You've got to promise—swear—that you won't climb into bed with me again. That *really* freaked me out."

"I promise," he said, raising one hand and setting the other on an imaginary Bible.

"Like your word means anything," I challenged. But I *was* tired.

Nick rolled his eyes. "You said it yourself—I saved your friend's life. Now, you're practically calling me a rapist."

"I did *not* call you a rapist."

"That's about the only thing you haven't called me."

"Go away. *I forgive you.* Now, zip on back to the train station and get your ticket punched."

"Not," he said.

I looked down at Russell. "If this man so much as moves toward my bedroom door, bite him."

Russell whimpered.

"Well, then, at least bark!"

Chester took another friendly swat at Russell's nose.

Russell walked over to Nick and licked his left shoe.

So much for canine loyalty.

"*Good night,* Mojo," Nick said. He leaned to pat Russell on the head, then dropped into my chair at the computer. Tapped a few keys.

I was intrigued—since when did ghosts use computers?—but too tired to investigate. I retreated as far as the bathroom, washed my face and brushed my teeth.

A few minutes later, I tumbled into bed.

I'd closed the door and considered putting a chair under the knob, since it didn't lock, but I knew that wouldn't stop Nick if he wanted to get in. As if to prove the point, Chester sprang through the wood and hopped onto the mattress to join me.

A thump sounded from the other side, along with a dog whine.

Poor Russell. He'd tried to follow Chester's lead, with the inevitable result.

I sighed, got out of bed and went to let Russell in. He made several pathetic attempts to jump onto the mattress, but his legs were too short.

I gave him a hoist.

"Too many frankfurters, buddy," I told him, huffing a little from the exertion. "And there will be absolutely *no* farting."

Russell curled up on the pillow opposite mine, sighed as eloquently as I had and closed his eyes.

I crawled back into bed. Turned onto my stomach.

Chester planted himself in the middle of my back.

I smiled. He weighed a ton, but it felt good, just knowing he was there.

I closed my eyes, and when I opened them again, it was morning.

I smelled coffee brewing.

Russell was snoring on the pillow, and Chester was gone.

I used the bathroom, washed up, pulled on sweat pants and a tank top and headed for the kitchen.

"Nick?" I called. I was about to thank him for making coffee and not jumping my bones during the night when my breath caught in my throat.

Tucker turned from the counter, where he was opening a bakery box.

There were deep shadows under his eyes. He hadn't shaved, his clothes were rumpled and he needed a shower.

I would have been glad to give him one personally.

"Who the hell is Nick?" he demanded.

Who was Nick?

How was I supposed to explain *that*, to a cop, no less, without ending up under psychiatric evaluation?

Before I could think of an answer, a horrible thought streaked through my sleep-befuddled mind like a comet trailing fire.

"You're not dead or anything, are you?"

Tucker stared at me. "What kind of question is that? Do I *look* dead to you?"

"If you are, just tell me, okay? Don't beat around the bush, because my nerves can't take it."

He laid both hands on my shoulders and pressed me into a chair. Leaned down to search my eyes. "Mojo, are you on something?"

My heart beat a little faster. His fingers felt warm, even through the fabric of my bathrobe. His breath tingled against my lips. I reached up, laid my palm on his chest.

A heartbeat.

"You're alive!"

He reached back, awkwardly, groping for a chair. Dragged it close and sat down hard. "Moje," he said, "I *told* you not to believe the news—"

I planted a smacking kiss in the center of his forehead. Slipped my arms around his neck.

He removed them. "Who's Nick?"

I bit my lip. My eyes burned. "You're not going to believe a word I say."

"Try me," he said.

Might as well just spit it out, so he could have me committed and be done with it. "Nick's my dead ex-husband."

"Do you want me to levitate something?" Nick asked, from just behind my right shoulder. "It might convince him."

I didn't look back or answer. Nick could read my thoughts. All right, then, I'd give him the full benefit of my Anglo-Saxon vocabulary.

Tucker plunged his fingers into my hair, dragged the sides of his thumbs lightly over my cheekbones. "Moje, what's going on here?"

I wished Nick would get out. Maybe Tucker and I could share a shower before he called for the wagon and had me hauled away.

"My ex," I repeated lamely. "He's been haunting me."

Everything in Tucker's face went absolutely still. "You were talking to a dead guy?"

I nodded, patently miserable and wildly happy, at the

same time, because Tucker hadn't blown up in his car. He wasn't on leave from the train station.

"I told you, you wouldn't believe it."

"He believes you," Nick supplied helpfully. Now, he was standing directly behind Tucker. "But he's a logical kind of fella. Ask him about his cousin Jessica. She was hit by a car when she was four and he was seven, and he saw her every night for six months after it happened."

"*Will* you not help?"

Tucker cupped my chin, turned my head so we were eye to eye again. From his perspective, I'd been talking to empty space, and I expected some comment on that. "When I was seven," he said instead, "a bunch of us were playing baseball in a park. My cousin—" He stopped, and his jaw worked.

I was too shaken to speak.

"Her name was Jessica, and she was a tomboy. She wanted to get into the game, but she was only four and she wasn't supposed to leave our grandparents' yard. She ran into the street—"

I closed my eyes, made myself open them again. Swallowed hard.

"She called my name," Tucker went on. "I turned around, and I was about to yell at her to go home. Instead, I was just in time to see an old pickup come around the corner on two wheels and—"

I touched his hair.

"Practically every night for the next six months, I woke up and found her standing at the foot of my bed."

"See?" Nick said. "What did I tell you?"

Get out, I told him mentally, without looking away from Tucker's face, *or I'll never forgive you. Not ever.*

"I thought I was dreaming," Tucker finished hoarsely. "But I've always wondered, because she looked so real. I used to get up, turn on the light, go downstairs for a drink of water—whatever I could think of, and when I got back, she'd still be there."

"Did she ever speak to you?"

Tucker shook his head. "She'd just watch me. After five minutes or so, she'd vanish. Then we moved—my dad got a job in Flagstaff—and I never saw her again."

"Know what?" I asked gently.

"What?"

"I believe you, Tucker."

"'I believe you, Tucker,'" Nick mimicked.

WILL you get out?

"Thanks," Tucker said gruffly, and rested his forehead against mine.

"You just want to get him naked," Nick accused.

You're damn right I do, I answered. *Thanks for sticking around all night, and goodbye.*

Nick sighed. I felt him leave.

"What you need," I purred to Tucker, "is somebody to wash your back."

Tucker kissed the tip of my nose. Then he kissed my mouth.

His tongue tasted of mint mouthwash.

One thing about Tucker. Even when he was working undercover, he practiced good oral hygiene.

The harsh buzzing of my ancient doorbell interrupted, chewing its way between us, pushing us apart.

"You'd better get that," Tucker said, sounding a little breathless. His lips were almost touching mine; I felt a subtle vibration coming from them.

"If we ignore them," I reasoned, "they'll go away."

"Not if it's the cops," Tucker said.

I sighed. Mental note: I am a person of interest in a felony assault.

I hate it when that happens.

The bell rasped through the air again, more insistent this time.

Tucker grinned. "I'll grab a shower. You deal with whoever's out there." He kissed me again, just before shoving off his chair and rising to his feet. He waggled his eyebrows at me. "Get rid of them."

I waited until he was behind the bathroom door before I answered the bell. I kept the chain on and peered around it.

An acne victim of indeterminate gender stood on the landing, holding a striped box in both hands and looking irritated.

"I didn't order anything," I said, none too patiently.

"It's your free Chinese dinner," the delivery person insisted, sounding testy, and probably male. "We called and left a voice mail. You won it."

"I don't want—"

"It's free," he said.

"Oh, for Pete's sake," I replied, "just leave it on the mat."

"People are starving in Africa, you know."

Ah, a philosopher. I have never understood that line of

reasoning. How would my eating something help the hungry in other lands?

"If you're angling for a tip, you're wasting your time," I said. I have a rule. I don't tip rude people, especially when they interfere with my love life.

"Look, lady, it's my job to deliver this chow mein or whatever it is. A quarter from you is not going to change my life. Just take the freakin' box, will you?"

I made up my mind to call the food-delivery service, at some point in the near future, and complain about their personnel. So what if the food was free? I hadn't ordered it, or the attitude.

I took the chain off and grabbed the stupid box.

By now, Tucker was in the shower, naked and lathered and sleek.

"Thanks for nothing," I told the kid, "and tell your boss to take me off the phone list."

"Whatever," the kid snapped.

I slammed the door.

I didn't bother to carry the free chow mein as far as the kitchen. I set the box on the coffee table with a thump and headed for the bathroom.

I'd promised myself I wouldn't succumb to Tucker's charms, and there were all kinds of reasons to support that decision—his ex-wife, his crazy job, my own history of poor taste in men—but this was elemental. Until I'd walked into the kitchen that morning and found him standing there with a box of doughnuts, and even for a few minutes after that, I'd half believed he was dead.

Bert had nearly died the night before, and life seemed terribly tenuous.

I needed to celebrate, even though I knew I would probably regret the decision later.

When I burst through the bathroom door Tucker was out of the shower, clean and gloriously male. He gave me a devilish grin and held out his arms.

"Wait," I said.

He cocked an eyebrow. "What?"

"I have to brush my teeth."

Tucker stood close behind me while I dabbed paste onto the old bristles, scrubbed and foamed. He lifted my T-shirt, laid his hands on either side of my waist, and slid them down into my sweatpants, over my hipbones.

I nearly choked on my toothpaste.

I bent to spit and rinse, and when I did, I came into direct contact with Tucker's erection. I straightened again, with a gasp.

He chuckled and eased me back against him. At the same time, he slipped a finger into the moist curls between my legs and teased me until I groaned, my head resting against his shoulder.

"We—shouldn't—do—this," I said, knowing all the while that we would.

Tucker nibbled at my earlobe. "Umm-hmmm," he agreed.

I turned to face him, wrapped my arms around his neck, looked up into his eyes. "I thought you were dead," I told him. His hands were up under my T-shirt now; his thumbs grazed my bare nipples.

"So you said," he murmured, and nibbled at my mouth.

"No, I mean *really* dead—"

Tucker hoisted me off my feet, and if I'd been the kind of woman who worries about such things, I might have been embarrassed at the way I automatically wrapped both legs around his hips.

"You're about to find out how really *not dead* I am," he said.

Fortunately, the bed wasn't far away; Tucker made the trek with me entwined around him, and we fell to the mattress together. The bedsprings creaked so loudly that I was glad Bad-Ass Bert's was closed until further notice; I wasn't tracking at the moment, or I would have been ashamed of such a thought, given what had happened.

Tucker was lying on top of me, and this was one of those times where there wasn't going to be any foreplay. He felt so good, everywhere we were touching, and the way he kept kissing me almost brought on the big O well before the fact.

He sampled my breasts, simultaneously tugging down my sweatpants, and I was beyond ready for him when he suddenly lifted his head and looked into my eyes. "I didn't bring—"

"I don't care," I said.

Tucker came into me with a long, hard thrust of his hips.

My eyes rolled back; damn it, I was coming. Already. My entire body seized around him, buckling with a release so sudden and so ferocious that I couldn't even cry out. I was too busy falling apart.

Forget the long, slow build—I'd been working on that ever since the *last* time we'd made love, more than three weeks before.

Tucker was a man focused on the job at hand; his body moved rhythmically on and within mine. I was already starting another climb, and when I could focus again, I noticed the half smile quirking his mouth. He was taking his time, shifting his hips slightly, from side to side.

The friction was delicious.

I clawed at his back. "Oh, damn, Tuck—"

"Slow and easy, babe," he rasped.

I exploded again three seconds later, and when I came out of the daze, breathless and slick with perspiration, he was still setting his own pace.

We climaxed together the next time, and it was so intense, so powerful, that I yelled. Tucker went deep, and closed his eyes, and I saw the muscles tighten in his face.

I don't know how long we lay there, when it was over, cross-wise on the bed, our arms and legs entangled, our bodies still joined. Presently, Tucker rolled to one side and fell asleep. I forgave him, since he'd been working undercover for days and he'd just given me the ride of my life.

I kissed him on the forehead, covered him by doubling the bedspread back, and got up. I didn't sleep after sex; it always energized me.

I took a quick shower, put on jeans and a tank top and started for my computer, intending do a little Googling on the list of names Greer had given me the night before.

The first thing I saw was the chow mein box, lying open on the floor. Before I could get mad about the mess, I spotted Russell. He was full out on his right side, and he was way too still.

Alarm—the instinctive kind—clenched at my insides like a fist made of cold steel, and for a second or so, I couldn't move at all. "Russell?" I whispered, and that broke my inertia; I dropped to my knees beside him, much the way I'd done with his master the night before, under the pool table. "Russell!"

He didn't lift his head, but he did raise one eyelid.

"Tucker!" I shrieked. "Tucker, come quick, there's something wrong with Russell!"

Tucker appeared in less than a minute, jeans fastened, tugging on his shirt. "What happened?"

"I don't know!" I cried. "I just came out here and found him like this—"

Tucker went back to the bedroom, returned in a flash with a blanket. He dropped to one knee, wrapped Russell, and got to his feet again. "Come on, Mojo," he said. "We've got to get him to the vet."

I nodded, grabbed my purse, pulled out my car keys.

"You'd better drive," Tucker told me.

I couldn't think. Which vet? Where? I was beside myself. I did the only sensible thing, and that was panic.

We got downstairs to the Volvo, somehow, and I took the wheel.

Quietly, Tucker directed me to turn left out of the parking lot. We passed several restaurants.

"Right at the light," Tucker said.

"Where are we going?" I asked, none too calmly.

"Just keep driving," he answered, cradling the blanket-bundled Russell as gently as he would a feverish child.

We'd probably traveled three miles when Tucker indicated the next turn, through a gate and up a long driveway toward a large Territorial-style house.

"Go around back," Tucker instructed.

I did what he said.

"Okay, you can stop," he told me. He got out of the car, still carrying Russell, and strode toward a long, low building of white stucco.

I caught up with him just as a long-legged woman in boots, jeans and a fitted western shirt came through a screened door to meet us. She had lush brown hair, piled on top of her head, and a stethoscope dangled from her neck.

"Allison," Tucker said, "this dog is sick as hell. I think he might have been poisoned."

Allison.

Our gazes collided, and mine glanced off first, to land on a neatly lettered wooden sign hanging beside the door she had just stepped through.

Allison Darroch, DVM.

"Bring him inside," she said. She gave me another glance, then let Tucker move past her, into the clinic. She entered next, and I was right behind her.

Tucker laid Russell gently on a shining steel examining table.

Allison unwrapped the dog from the blanket, clicked on a penlight plucked from her shirt pocket, lifted one of his eyelids, and peered in. "Do you know what he ingested?" she asked, just as if it weren't perfectly obvious, from his clothes and mussed up hair, that Tucker and I had crawled out of the same bed within the last half hour.

Tucker glanced questioningly at me.

"Chow mein, I think," I said.

Allison popped Russell's mouth open, stuck her nose in, and sniffed.

"I'm going to induce vomiting," she decided. "You might want to step outside."

Tears stung the backs of my eyes. I sniffled. "I can't leave him."

Allison turned to Tucker, and something passed between them. Their faces were grim and still.

Tucker turned, crossed the room to me, caught me firmly by one elbow, and ushered me outside.

I tried to get back in.

He restrained me.

"Allison is a good vet, Mojo," he told me. "If anything can be done for the dog, she'll do it."

"Dad!" Two voices called, at the same time, mingling and yet clearly separate.

I turned and saw the twins barreling across the yard. The little boy, Danny, wore jeans and a T-shirt, the little girl, Daisy, had on a pink leotard, tights, and a tutu. They launched themselves at Tucker, and he crouched and caught them with the ease of long practice, one in each arm.

I bit down hard on my lower lip.

I felt like a home wrecker, watching that scene.

A home wrecker and a lousy dog-sitter, too.

"Who's that lady?" Daisy asked, looking up at me. "And why is she crying?"

Tucker stood, slipped an arm loosely around my shoulders. "This is Mojo," he said. "She's a very good friend of mine, and she's crying because her dog is real sick."

Shyly, Daisy took my hand. "Don't worry," she told me. "Mom is the best vet in Arizona. She'll make him better."

My heart turned over. "Thanks," I said.

"Mojo is a weird name," Danny observed, squinting as he checked me out. "What kind of name is Mojo?"

"A weird one," I answered.

"I might be late for dance class," Daisy announced. "There's a birthday party afterward, and I have a present."

I looked desperately to Tucker.

"You'll make it," he told his daughter.

"Mom was going to drive me over as soon as she finished checking on the sleepover patients," Daisy went on. Her aspect was sunny, without a trace of petulance. "Are you finished with the job where you had to be dead, Dad?"

Tucker adjusted the beaded tiara atop her head. The gesture was so gentle that it made my throat ache. "I'm finished with the job where I had to be dead," he confirmed.

Danny huffed out a sigh. "It was hard not to tell," he said manfully. "But Mom said we had to zip our lips or else."

Tucker grinned wanly. "I appreciate that," he said.

The screen door creaked, and Allison appeared in the opening, wiping her hands on a white towel.

"You can see the big fella now," she told me. "He ought to stay overnight, though. So my assistant and I can keep an eye on him."

I nodded. "Thank you," I said, and I meant it.

She stepped back to let me pass, and I hurried inside. Russell was still on the steel table, but now he had an IV going, and a young girl in jeans and a pink scrub shirt stood beside him, stroking his quivering side.

She smiled at me. "He'll be all right," she said. "What's his name?"

"Russell," I answered.

I moved around the table, so I could look Russell in the face. His hound-dog eyes looked bleary, but I'd swear he tried to smile at me.

"He was a pretty sick guy," the girl said. "You sure brought him to the right vet, though. Dr. Allison is the best."

I nodded, stroking Russell's silky ear. The other one stuck out under his head, like a jaunty wing, pink and tender. "You're going to be okay, buddy," I told him. "But you've gotta do a sleepover."

"We'll take good care of Russell," Allison's assistant promised. I looked for a nametag, and didn't see one.

She smiled. "I'm Bethany," she said.

"Mojo," I answered.

If Bethany thought my name was weird, she didn't say so. She just smiled again. "I'll put Russell into a kennel, make sure he's comfortable, and then I'll get your phone number, so we can call when he's ready to come home."

I leaned down and kissed the dog on top of the head.

Bethany maneuvered Russell easily onto a gurney, managing his IV line and the rolling pole without a hitch, and wheeled him into a back room.

I stayed where I was, not wanting to go outside, because I knew Allison and Tucker were talking—I could hear the low murmur of their voices. There was no yelling, but the sounds had a parrying quality. I expected the clink of sword blades at any moment.

Bethany reappeared, with a clipboard in hand. I gave her my contact information, realized I'd left my purse in the car.

"I'll just get my checkbook—" I said, but the sentence fell apart, because I did not want to walk out there and get caught in the middle of whatever was going on between Tucker and Allison.

"We'll bill you," Bethany said cheerfully. "Or you can pay tomorrow, when you come to pick Russell up."

"Okay," I said.

The screen door opened, and Allison stepped in. She'd just saved my friend's dog and I was grateful, but I knew I was about as welcome on her property as a rabid bat.

She skewered me with a glance, then shifted her attention to Bethany, smiling like a sitcom mom. "I'm taking Daisy to dance class, and then to Gillian Pellway's birthday party," she said. "Danny's coming with us. Call my cell if there's a problem."

"I will," Bethany promised. Her smile faltered a little as her eyes moved from Allison to me and back again.

"Thank you for looking after Russell," I told Allison. I didn't put out my hand, because I knew she wouldn't take it.

Allison nodded, but she didn't speak.

She turned and went outside, and the screen door slammed smartly behind her.

Bethany gave me a thoughtful look. "I'll call about Russell," she said.

I thanked her, for probably the fortieth time and, hearing an engine start up outside, followed by the crunch of wheels on gravel, I took my leave.

Allison and the kids were heading down the driveway in a late-model truck, built for off-road travel, leaving a plume of dust behind. Tucker stood in the yard, hands on his hips, watching them go.

I couldn't speak, looking at him. There was real despair in the way he stood, even though his shoulders were squared and his spine was straight.

He finally turned his head, saw me standing there in the stay-at-home clothes I'd pulled on after he'd made love to me. My hair was frizzed from the shower, I was wearing my Sponge-Bob slippers, and I hadn't bothered with a bra.

"Hey," he said, and smiled a little, but it was a sad smile. The kind that makes you feel worse, not better.

"Hey," I replied weakly.

Tucker thrust out a sigh, ran one hand through his hair. He'd never combed it, after his shower, and then we'd gone to bed. The kids were too young to know, but Allison must have put the pieces together at the first glance. "I left my cell phone here," he said, starting toward the back door of the house. "Want to come in?"

I shook my head, feeling numb. I didn't belong in that house, where Tucker and Allison and the kids had lived together, a regular family. Where they'd decorated Christmas trees and celebrated birthdays and laughed at each other's jokes.

When, I wondered, had the laughter stopped?

I felt homeless in that moment, as though I didn't belong

anywhere, as though I were a stranger in the universe, or someone who had sneaked in from a lesser dimension without buying a ticket.

Tucker stood watching me for a few seconds, and I knew he wanted to say something, and that he wouldn't.

He went inside. I headed for the Volvo and slipped into the driver's seat. Waited there until he turned up.

I started the car.

"Moje," Tucker began.

"It's okay, Tucker."

"No," he said. "It isn't. I should have warned you that we were coming here, prepared you to meet Allison, but you were so upset about the dog—"

"I'm grateful—to you and to Allison. Please, Tucker—just let it go at that, all right?"

"Moje—"

"Please?"

"Okay."

We turned back onto the main road, toward Cave Creek. Neither of us spoke until we pulled into Bert's parking lot, and I stopped the Volvo within a few yards of Tucker's Harley.

He was looking at the sign painted on the side of the weathered, rustic building. "Welcome to Bad-Ass Bert's," he read aloud. Then he sighed heavily. "Guess he's not such a bad-ass, after all."

"It would have killed me to tell Bert his dog was dead," I said. "He trusted me."

Tucker didn't speak. His jaw was set in a hard line, though, and I knew his mind was working.

I couldn't stand the silence. "Maybe you should go home."

Tucker met my gaze. "The chow mein," he said. "Where did you get it?"

I drew in a sharp breath. Some P.I. *I* was going to make— I didn't put the pieces together until that moment. Tucker, on the other hand, was a professional, and he'd probably been processing the information from the moment he'd noticed the food on the floor—as he surely had, being a keen-eyed detective type—and the dog lying almost comatose.

I was just now catching up. Russell must have knocked the box off the coffee table, in his never-ending search for pepperoni and frankfurters, and then scarfed down some of the chow mein. I didn't need the cast of *CSI* to tell me the grub had been poisoned, and Russell wasn't the intended target.

I was the one meant to bite the dirt, not the basset hound.

"Moje?" Tucker prompted. I guess he must have been tired of waiting for me to hook up all the links.

"Somebody tried to kill me," I said, stunned.

"It was the Chinese gunk," Tucker ascertained. He didn't make a move to get out of the car, and neither did I. "Somebody laced it. Who could have done it, Moje? Where'd you get the stuff?"

"A kid brought it to the door. There was a sales pitch on my voice mail when I checked my messages last night. Some food-delivery service, offering a free meal as a come-on. I didn't call them back, and never thought about it again."

Tucker nodded once, shoved open his door. "Let's have a look at the box. There might be a company name, though I doubt it."

We piled out of the Volvo and double-timed it up the steps, Tucker in the lead.

"Did you delete the message?" Tucker asked, on the landing.

That was when I remembered the other message. The death threat.

"No," I said. "But there was a call from somebody who wanted to kill me."

Tucker paused in the act of opening the door—which we hadn't taken the time to lock on the way out—and glared at me. "And you're just mentioning that *now*?"

I bristled. "It's not as if I've been sitting around twiddling my thumbs."

No, indeed. I was an honorary suspect in a criminal investigation, with all the attendant responsibilities. Then, of course, there was the distraction of screwing Tucker's brains out. Followed by the Russell crisis.

Tucker shook his head. I guess he thought I should have worked the crank call into the conversation somewhere, and maybe he had a point.

That didn't mean I had to actually *admit* to anything.

I would have followed him into the apartment, but he barred my way with one arm, and the unspoken "Wait here" was evident in his body language.

After a few moments, he called me inside.

He was sitting on his haunches on the living room floor, holding the food box gingerly and examining it. "No name, of course," he said. "But there might be fingerprints."

"Mine," I said. "The kid's."

Tucker stood, headed for the kitchen. There, he grabbed the phone and keyed into the messages.

He all but rolled his eyes, listening to Greer and then Jolie.

The sales call came next. He frowned as he listened, then saved it.

I watched his face intently as he took in the last message. He saved that, too, then did what I would have done, if I hadn't been so rattled. He star-69ed the call, gesturing for something to write with.

I gave him a pen and the envelope from my light bill.

"Who is this?" he demanded, into the receiver.

He listened.

I listened.

The whole world seemed to pause on one big indrawn breath.

"Right. Thanks. What's the address?"

He scribbled.

"Thanks again," he said, and hung up.

"Well?" I asked, when he didn't immediately volunteer the details.

"Convenience store in north Phoenix," he answered briskly. "I'll have it checked out." He got back on the phone, waded through Greer and Jolie again, and did the same with the food-service message.

"A cell phone," he told me, scribbling down another note. "Probably a throwaway, but I'll see if I can have it traced."

Scared as I was, I felt a certain admiration for Tucker's competence.

He placed a call, reeled off the information he had concerning the two voice-mail messages, gave out my number and rang off.

"Now what?" I asked.

Tucker thrust the phone at me. "Call whoever's in charge of the investigation into Bert's assault," he said.

I took the receiver, rummaged through the stuff on the table for Andy Crowley's card, and dialed the number. I got voice mail, and left my name and contact information.

"How did you know what happened to Bert?" I asked. Things were limping into my mind, overdue. Tucker and I hadn't talked about much of anything, after he told me about his cousin Jessica's death, and how he'd seen her ghost.

"I'm a cop, Moje. I'm in the loop."

"Even when you're undercover and the whole world thinks you're dead?"

"Even then," he said.

"Sit down," I said, drawing back a chair and taking my own advice.

Tucker sat.

Another bus hobbled into my mental depot. "Allison knew the truth," I said. "About your undercover assignment, I mean."

"Yeah," Tucker answered carefully. "I couldn't have Danny and Daisy thinking I'd been blown to pieces, Moje. They're cop's kids, and they're used to keeping secrets, as young as they are." He paused, looking sad. "It isn't fair to put a burden like that on a pair of seven-year-olds."

"Just how close are you and Allison?" I'd been wanting to ask Tucker that question from the day we met, and though we'd danced around it numerous times, we'd never gotten to the crunch.

No time like the present. A lot of other things were going down, but that was important, and I was tired of guessing.

"I'm out of the marriage," Tucker said. "But Allison and I have the kids, and that means there will be regular contact."

"You left your cell phone at her place," I ventured, picking my way. Whatever Tucker and I had together, it had the potential of becoming something very good. I didn't want to blow our chances. "I called you back, after that call about your going undercover in the first place, and I got Allison. She wasn't exactly thrilled to make the connection."

Tucker sighed. "I left the phone with Daisy," he said. I could see in his eyes that he wanted me to believe him, and wasn't sure I would. "Allison must have found it."

It scared me, how much I longed for Tucker's words to be true. I also knew how easy it would be to buy into the scenario because I wanted it to be that way.

"Allison didn't want the divorce," I said. Dangerous ground, but it had to be crossed.

"Allison *instigated* the divorce. She hated my job. Wanted me to go to law school."

"Is that the whole story?"

"Of course not," Tucker replied bluntly. "There are human beings involved. It's complicated."

"You're trying to win full custody of the twins?"

"Partial custody," Tucker clarified. "Right now, I can only see Danny and Daisy when Allison agrees."

"Why?"

Tucker widened his eyes impatiently. "Because of my job," he said. "Allison claimed the kids would be in deadly peril at my place, and the judge agreed."

"So the solution is—?"

"I have to quit what I'm doing," Tucker said quietly.

"Then you could go back to Allison. Sign up for law school. From the looks of that house, she can afford to pay the bills while you hit the books."

"I don't *want* to go to law school," he replied, "and it's over between Allison and me. Too much water under the bridge."

"What kind of water, Tucker?"

The telephone rang before he could answer, and he looked relieved.

I snapped out a "Hello."

"This is Crowley. You called?"

I told the detective about the chow mein incident.

He surprised me with, "And you're sure the dog will be okay?"

I liked him a little better than I had before. "The vet said he'd recover. I can probably pick him up tomorrow."

"That's good. Now, for the official cop-speak. Don't touch the chow mein or the box. I'll be over as soon as possible, with an appropriate crew. I take it you're up to speed on Mr. Bad-Ass's current condition?"

I watched as Tucker opened the pastry box, thought twice about it, and chucked the whole works into the trash. "I talked to his girlfriend, Sheila, late last night. She was hopeful."

"He was upgraded this morning from critical to stable," Crowley said.

Relief hit me swiftly, and hard, like a punch to the belly. "Thank God."

"We'll be taking his statement as soon as the doctor clears it. Unless he fingers you, you'll be off the hook."

"That's comforting," I said, "since I didn't do it."

"Remains to be seen," Crowley answered. "Sit tight. We'll be there in an hour or two."

"Guess it's a good thing nobody has a knife to my throat," I told him.

He chuckled. "Touché, Ms. Sheepshanks," he said, and hung up in my ear.

"Why did you toss the doughnuts?" I asked, when I'd replaced the receiver on the wall hook. By then, Tucker was sniffing the coffee canister. Maybe he expected to get a whiff of cyanide or something.

"I'm paranoid," he said. "We didn't lock the door when we left, and whoever tried to nail you with the chow mein could have gotten in and done more damage."

We weren't through hashing out what Tucker meant to do about the job-custody situation, and I wasn't ready to let it go.

"What would you do if you couldn't be a cop anymore?"

Tucker decided to risk agonizing death and started a pot of coffee. *I* decided I wouldn't have any until he'd downed a cup without foaming at the mouth.

"I've been thinking about starting an agency," he said. "Private investigation."

I brightened. While I didn't go so far as to take it as a sign from the universe that I was finally on the right career track, it did seem like synchronicity. "I'm in the same business myself," I said, somewhat proudly. "My sister, Greer, gave me five grand as a retainer. I get another five if I can either prove or disprove that her husband is a sneaking, skinny-dicked son of a bitch."

Tucker stopped, stared at me.

"You're hanging out a P.I. shingle?"

"I guess it depends on how successful I am with this first job."

"Do you have any training?" The set of Tucker's face said the question was rhetorical, since he already knew the answer.

"I've read *The Damn Fool's Guide to Private Investigation*," I said. "A little review, and I'm golden."

Tucker looked as if he might either yell or laugh. He sort of hovered in the middle while the coffeemaker did its groan-and-steam routine.

"Do you have a *Damn Fool's Guide* to everything?" he finally asked.

I grinned. "I wish they'd publish one on how to pick emotionally available men," I said.

Tucker made a face. Poured himself a cup of coffee before the machine was done, so the drippings sizzled on the little hot plate at the bottom. A strong java scent filled the air.

He sipped.

I waited.

He didn't keel over, so I had a cup, too.

Crowley and his evidence crew arrived an hour later, by which time Tucker and I had made love again, and he'd been home to get fresh clothes. While he was gone, I did some repair work on myself. By the time we all gathered for the collection of the spilled chow mein, I looked fresh and virginal in a cotton sundress, with my hair tamed and caught up in a squeeze clip.

Crowley listened to both the voice-mail messages, took some notes and called the station to have both of them tapped by some Big Brother computer program. That done, he asked me about a hundred questions, and oversaw the removal of the toxic evidence.

While he was overseeing the process, his cell phone blipped. He answered with a crisp, "Crowley." Listened intently. His gaze swung to me, landed and warmed. "Okay. Yeah. That's good news for some people, and bad news for others. Thanks."

He clicked the end button.

"Mr. Bad-Ass," he said, "says you weren't involved."

I let out my breath, and my shoulders went limp with the release of tension. "That's the good news?"

Crowley nodded. "The bad news is, he can't remember what *did* happen. One minute, the place was full of customers and he was tending bar, as usual. The next, the crowd had thinned, and somebody stabbed him. After that, it's the proverbial blur."

I could identify.

Crowley's gaze still contained a disturbing tinge of speculation. "Of course, I plan to question him myself."

"Of course," I agreed, wondering if I was still a person of interest after all.

The cop answered my unspoken question. He'd probably

had a lot of experience, doing that. "Meanwhile, Ms. Sheep-shanks, you're free to go on about your business."

Whatever that was, I thought.

"Thanks," I said. "Did your contact happen to mention whether or not Bert could have visitors?"

"I'm thinking no," Crowley answered. "Give it a few days."

I nodded.

"If you remember anything else about the chow mein delivery, or if you happen to see the kid again someplace, be sure and let me know. Same thing if you hear from the mystery caller again."

I'd told Crowley earlier that I suspected my half brother, Geoff, aka Steve Roberts, R.N. and health guru, might have been the perp. Ditto Heather, the stalker queen. I reminded him.

"I'd change the locks if I were you," he said, "and don't accept anything edible from strangers."

Was he kidding? From then on, I wouldn't take so much as a morsel from one of those sample ladies in the grocery store.

Crowley left, and Tucker and I went back to bed.

I woke to a dark apartment, an expanse of empty sheets and somebody hammering on the door.

I got up, fumbled my way through the dimly lit rooms and down the hallway. I didn't have a peephole, so I had to hope mimicry didn't number among my enemy's many skills.

"Who's there?"

"Jolie," my sister answered. "Let me in. I need to pee like a racehorse."

I opened the door. An attacker might have been able to do Jolie's voice, but the urination metaphor was a throwback to when we were kids, and I doubted that my almost-Ph.D. sister used it in a public context.

Fortunately, I was right.

Jolie and I hugged on the threshold, and she came in, carrying a name-brand suitcase.

"The place is dark as a tomb, I don't smell food and you look like you've been rolling around in the sack with a man all afternoon," she observed.

"Good to see you, too," I replied.

Jolie made for the bathroom, while I set her bag in my room. I was smoothing the covers when she appeared in the doorway.

"Lillian looks bad," she said. "She didn't even recognize me."

I'd forgotten, with all that was going on, that Jolie had planned to stop off at Sunset Villa on her way to my place. I'd also forgotten, I realized with a start, that she and I were expected at Greer's for supper.

I nodded sadly. "It kills me, seeing Lillian like this. She was always so—*Lillian*."

Tears stood in Jolie's eyes. "I think she's dying, Moje."

My throat constricted. "Probably," I managed to say. The word came out sounding like a croak.

"I called Greer from the car," Jolie said, deftly turning the conversation in a direction both of us could deal with. "She's under the weather, and wants to get together tomorrow night."

I frowned. "Is it serious?"

"It sounded like a bad case of too much vodka to me," Jolie said. "Greer's really unhappy, isn't she?"

"Miserably," I agreed. I was hungry, and I knew Jolie was,

too. No way I was having anything delivered after the chow mein experience, so I suggested we head for the nearest IHOP.

On the way there, in Jolie's Pathfinder, I told her about the attack on Bert, Russell's near-miss with the chow mein and the recorded phone message from Distorto-voice.

She took it all in, in her thoughtful way, then asked, "So what about the sex?"

"I beg your pardon?"

"Don't go into your tap-dance routine, Moje. I saw the tangled covers on your bed, and you've got a certain glow about you. With all that's been going on, there can only be one explanation, and that's multiple orgasms in the very recent past."

I blushed. "Did you learn that in your forensics classes?" I dodged.

Jolie chuckled. "No. I learned it having good times with bad men. Was it the cop?"

"Yes," I admitted. Jolie had a nose for the truth, and she was as persistent as a bloodhound.

"So it's back on with you two?"

"I don't know," I said. "He has kids, an ex-wife. And he's thinking of changing jobs. There's a pretty good chance Tucker's rebounding, and I'm the trampoline."

Jolie winced. "Not good," she said.

"Not good at all," I agreed.

"And then there's the sex."

I sighed again. "And then there's the sex."

"Good?"

"Beyond good. Beyond excellent."

"Aaak," Jolie said.

That about summed it up.

At the IHOP, over breakfast suppers swimming in syrup, we switched subjects.

"You still thinking of becoming a crime scene tech?" I asked.

"I've got an interview with Phoenix PD," she said. "Tomorrow afternoon, one o'clock." She smiled softly, holding a crisp slice of bacon between two fingers. "Remember how we used to love it when Lillian served breakfast food for supper?"

I felt a pang. Nodded. "It was always a treat," I said. "Looking back, I figure it really meant she and Ham had run out of money before they ran out of month."

Jolie grinned. "Probably."

"Did you get Sweetie all squared away with the friends in the country?"

"Yes," Jolie said. "And it's okay to say you're relieved I didn't bring him with me. He gave you a pretty hard time the other day."

I shuddered slightly at the reminder of being trapped on top of Jolie's refrigerator for several hours with nothing to do but memorize the instruction book for the microwave. If I ever ran into a French person with thawing problems, though, I'd be ready.

"I don't think Sweetie likes me," I said.

"He likes you fine," Jolie replied, chomping into her bacon.

"Maybe with salt and pepper and a side of fries."

Jolie laughed. "He wouldn't have eaten you."

"It wasn't the eating part I was worried about," I told her. "It was the gnawing."

She smiled.

"It would be great to have you living in Phoenix," I said. "I miss you, big-time."

"If you miss me so much," Jolie reasoned, "why did you boogie like that the other night? Why didn't you stay and talk it through?"

"I don't know." It seemed I'd been saying that a lot lately.

"I'm on *your* side, Moje. You were rattled because some of your memories were coming back, and you panicked. I could have listened, maybe helped you sort things out, if you'd given me a chance."

"A part of me doesn't want to remember," I confessed.

"Ya think?" Jolie chimed. She sounded smart-ass, but I saw the concern in her eyes.

"Maybe it's better not to start digging things up," I mused. "After all, it's been twenty-three years. It's old news."

Jolie put down her fork, pushed her plate to one side for the waitress to remove. "Lillian must have thought you were in danger, to kidnap you like that," she said. "She'd have gone to prison, maybe for life, if they'd caught her. She blew off her whole life—her home, her friends, everything, to get you out of Dodge. Has she ever told you why?"

I shook my head. "I've asked, but she always said it was better to leave the past alone. She was a great mom. She was also a master at stonewalling. The more questions I put to her, the less she was willing to say."

"I've often wondered how much she told my dad," Jolie reflected.

"Me, too."

Jolie signaled for the check.

I'd left my ATM card at home, and I didn't have any cash. I hadn't deposited Greer's check, either, since I'd been a little busy. I snatched the bill, just the same, since Jolie had paid the time before, at the Italian place in Tucson, and handed the waitress my credit card. I offered a silent prayer and hoped for the best.

The waitress returned, and the apologetic look on her face was a clear indication that my prayer was stuck in some heavenly cyber-queue.

"I'm sorry," she said, "but the credit card company declined payment."

Jolie was ready with a twenty-dollar bill.

The waitress took it and hurried away gratefully.

"It bites, being poor," I said, my face hot with embarrassment.

"You really got burned in that divorce," Jolie said. "I thought you'd paid all that stuff off."

"That's the last one," I said. "I cut up the other cards a long time ago." I thought of Nick, and his mother, and seethed. I'd rarely used plastic, but Nick had flashed them everywhere he went. Most likely, I'd taken the fall for a lot of hotel rooms, romantic dinners and sexy lingerie. Nick DeLuca was going to be a while getting out of the train station up yonder if he needed *my* forgiveness to buy a ticket.

"Better take the whackers to that one, too," Jolie suggested.

"You can bet on it," I said.

On the way back to my place, Jolie pulled into a supermarket parking lot and loaded up on groceries. Maybe she'd looked in my fridge between going to the bathroom and catching me at smoothing the bed. Maybe—and this was worse—she just felt sorry for me because I was a schmuck with a piecework job and bad credit.

We carried the bags up to my apartment, and Jolie went off to take a shower and put on her pajamas while I put the stuff away.

Nick popped in just as I was turning away from the refrigerator.

"Creep," I said, in a whisper, because I didn't want Jolie to hear and demand an explanation. It was enough that I'd had to tell Tucker I saw ghosts, and if it hadn't been for the Jessica story, I would have been up against it in the credibility department.

Nick looked offended. He was holding Chester, or I'd have smacked him with something.

I grabbed my purse, dug out the credit card, and shoved it in his face. "This *bounced* tonight, thanks to you and Mommy Dearest, and I was humiliated. Again."

Nick frowned, put the cat down on the floor. "There was life insurance," he said. "A lot of it."

"Fat lot of good it did me," I said. I yanked open the junk drawer, got out the scissors and snipped the card into pieces. Okay, I should have checked the available credit before I tried to use the thing, but I'd been making minimum payments for about a hundred years, and I figured there was room for two pancake specials at IHOP.

Nick backpedaled. Maybe because I still had the scissors in my hand. I couldn't kill him, but ectoplasmic puncture could conceivably be a problem. In that moment, I *really* wanted to test the theory.

"Where's the dog?" he asked.

I choked on a sob I hadn't known was coming. "Russell was almost murdered," I answered, still keeping my voice down. I could hear Jolie rattling around in the other end of the apartment, though, so I figured I was safe. "I had to leave him with the vet."

"Murdered?" Nick repeated.

"Yeah," I snapped. *"Murdered."* I took a deep breath, but it didn't help. So much for *The Damn Fool's Guide to Self-Control*. I'd have demanded my $14.95 back if I hadn't highlighted so many pages. "I don't think this forgiveness thing is going to fly," I added. "You may need to take another approach to boarding your train."

"There *isn't* another approach," Nick said quietly.

"Maybe your mother could work something out for you. Stick it to whoever's in charge up there, the way she stuck it to me."

Nick closed his eyes. Opened them again.

"I'm sorry," he said.

"You know," I whispered back, "you look like you mean that. You even sound like you mean it. But since you probably never told me the truth in your selfish life, I'm having a hard time believing you."

"Mojo—"

Jolie stepped into the doorway, wearing cotton pajamas that made her look about eleven years old. Her gaze glided right past Nick without catching. "I thought you were on the phone," she said.

I smiled. "I was," I told her. "It was just a telemarketer."

"Liar," Nick said, close to my ear.

My smile turned to a grimace.

"They're hiring people in India and places like that," Jolie said. "To make sales calls, I mean. That's how they get past the no-call list." She grinned. "Next time, just tell them you'd love to buy everything they're selling, but a waitress at IHOP chopped up your last credit card."

"Ouch," Nick said.

My face was beginning to hurt. I wanted to tell him to shut up, and a few other choice things, too, but I didn't dare.

I'd forgotten how perceptive my sister could be.

"Is that ghost here?" she asked. "Is that why you look as if rigor mortis set in while you were watching Comedy Central?"

"Yes!" I said, relieved, gesturing toward Nick. "He's right here."

"She can't see me, Mojo," Nick said.

"Where?" Jolie asked, squinting.

I sighed. "Never mind." Turned to Nick. "Get out," I said. "Go rattle chains at the foot of your mother's bed or something."

Jolie was wide-eyed. After all, from her viewpoint, I was talking to an empty kitchen.

Nick blinked out. Chester, however, remained, curling around my ankles and purring.

"No wonder you didn't want me to bring Sweetie," Jolie said.

I was stumped.

She looked down. "The cat?"

I gasped. "You can see him?"

"Of *course* I can see him. He's right there, circling your shoes."

I scooped Chester up and sank into a chair at the table.

"What's wrong?" Jolie demanded.

"He's dead," I said.

"*Who's* dead?" My sister took a seat of her own.

"This cat."

"Nonsense," Jolie said. She put out a hand to pet him, and before she could make contact, he disappeared.

My arms ached, suddenly empty. I felt the echo of an old loss in my heart.

Jolie's eyes were enormous. "What just happened here?"

"Do you believe me now?"

"No," Jolie said. "I still think you're full of shit. How did you do that?" She turned in her chair, scanning the kitchen. "With a projector, right? Some kind of hologram?"

"Sure," I said. "My credit card was denied at IHOP, but I can afford all *kinds* of sophisticated video equipment. Disneyworld has nothing on me."

Jolie's rich mahogany complexion paled. I'm not sure how that was possible, but I saw it with my own eyes. "I am *losing* it," she said, with a gulp, and I instantly felt sorry for her.

Nobody knew better than I did what a jolt it was to see a ghost.

"You're perfectly sane, Jolie."

"That was the cat—"

"The one Geoff killed, when I was four," I said.

Jolie wrapped her arms around her middle and rocked a couple of times. I got up and got her a bottle of water, from the dwindling store in the fridge, and handed it over—after checking to make sure the seal hadn't been broken.

The encounter would have been hard on anybody, but Jolie was a scientist. She'd be a long time getting the situation straight in her head, especially since her brain was heavily weighted to the left side.

"What—what does it mean?" she asked.

"I don't have the slightest idea," I answered.

Jolie tested my forehead for fever, then her own.

The phone rang, and I was so concerned about Jolie that I didn't check caller ID. If I had, I wouldn't have taken the call.

CHAPTER

12

"This is Margery DeLuca," said Nick's mother. She sounded uncertain, as though she were as surprised to find herself calling me as I was to hear from her. "Maybe you remember me?"

I also remembered Attila the Hun, Genghis Khan and Jack the Ripper. "How could I forget?" I countered sweetly.

"I was just awakened, from a sound sleep, by the strangest dream—"

Jolie peered at me curiously.

I put the phone on speaker.

"O-kayyy," I said, drawing the word out.

"I would have sworn Nick came to me." Saying this, Attila DeLuca sounded so small and so sad that I almost felt sorry for her. And I stress *almost*.

I didn't speak. I'd rehearsed what I would say to the monster-in-law a million times, if I ever got the chance. Now, here it was, and not a damn thing came to mind.

"I suppose you're wondering why I called you, dear."

Dear.

Jolie grimaced.

"I guess I am," I said.

"I feel an urgent need to meet with you in person," Margery said.

Jolie shook her head wildly from side to side, made a throat-slashing motion with one hand.

Like I needed clarification.

"I don't see the point," I said. God, I was proud of my self-restraint. Plus, the way my life had been going lately, I could find myself in some train depot at any moment. I didn't want any guff at the ticket booth.

"I was in such a state after Nick's death," Margery went on. "I might have overlooked some things."

Yes, I thought. My jugular. My vital organs. And maybe there was a dime somewhere, in the bottom of an old purse in the back of my closet, that should have been hers.

"It's okay, Mrs. DeLuca," I heard myself say. "Nick was your only son, and it was terrible, the way he died. But it's all in the past, and I really can't imagine what we have to say to each other now."

"Please—just let me buy you lunch. Tomorrow, perhaps?"

"All booked up," I said, looking to Jolie as exhibit A. Of course, Margery couldn't see her, but it gave me the illusion that I was telling the truth.

Attila started to cry. I was not prepared for that.

"We *must* talk," she said.

"Mrs. DeLuca, I'm very busy."

For the first time since our conversation began, she showed some steel. "Too busy," she replied, "to discuss my son's life insurance policy? It seems you were the beneficiary."

Nick loomed behind Jolie, and he looked smug as hell.

Jolie followed my gaze and whirled.

"She still can't see me," Nick said.

"Nick and I were divorced two years before he died," I reminded Margery calmly. *As if* she didn't remember dancing naked around a bonfire the day the decree came through. "If I was still listed as the beneficiary, I'm sure it was an oversight."

Nick shook his head.

Jolie looked behind her again.

"It is a sizable amount of money," Margery said.

I swallowed. Jolie made a bring-it-on motion with both hands.

"I'm really not—"

Nick morphed over to the trash bin, fished out several pieces of the cut-up credit card, and held them under my nose.

Jolie fainted.

"I have to go," I told Margery, and thumbed the button.

Nick stepped out of my way, and Jolie was already coming around by the time I got to her.

"Are you okay?"

"No," Jolie said. "I'm seeing things."

I helped her to her feet, settled her in a chair, and handed her the water bottle I'd gotten out earlier.

"Vanishing cats," Jolie murmured. "Garbage, floating in midair."

I gave Nick a look.

He shrugged and spread his hands.

"You need a good night's sleep," I told Jolie.

"I need a shrink," Jolie argued.

"If you do, so do I," I said, trying to console her.

"Is that supposed to be reassuring?" Jolie countered.

"I can't believe you're sisters," Nick said. "You bicker a lot, and there's no family resemblance to speak of." I guess he thought he was being droll. "Maybe a little around the eyes."

"I've had about enough of you for one night," I told him.

Jolie looked hurt.

I laid a hand on her shoulder. "I'm not talking to you," I said. When I was sure she wouldn't faint again, I went into the living room, folded down the couch and made a bed for her.

She crashed without so much as a whimper of protest.

I was a lot longer getting to sleep, and when I woke the next morning, it was to the buzz of my doorbell.

I kept the chain on and peered around the edge of the door to see a uniformed messenger on the landing, holding an oversized envelope.

"Ms. Sheepshanks?"

"Yes," I said suspiciously. I had reason to mistrust unexpected deliveries.

What was in the envelope? Anthrax spores?

"I'm not expecting anything," I told the messenger.

"Sign here," he said, and shoved a clipboard through the crack in the door.

Oh, what the hell?

I signed, took the envelope, and shut the door hard.

No return address.

I like to live dangerously. I pulled the little tab and peered inside.

No spores, unless they were invisible.

Just a piece of paper.

I fished it out, read it, and yelled.

"What's that?" Jolie asked, jolted from sleep. Seconds later, she stood blinking at the end of the short hallway.

"It's a check," I answered, waving it. Doing a little dance. "Jolie, *it's a check!* Get your clothes on. We're going out for breakfast, and *I'm* paying!"

THE YOUTHFUL TELLER at my bank deposited Greer's check without a quiver, but when he saw the numbers on the second one, signed by Margery DeLuca, he gulped, examined me speculatively and summoned a manager.

The pair of them disappeared into a back room, and Jolie and I waited, she tapping her foot nervously, me smiling from ear to ear. My former mother-in-law was every kind of awful—at least in context with me—but she wasn't likely to pass bad checks. She had a position to maintain.

"Three hundred and fifty thousand dollars," Jolie kept whispering, under her breath, like a mantra. "What will you do with that kind of money, Mojo?"

"Breathe," I said. Of course, I wanted to set a chunk aside for security. I'd pay off that last credit card balance, too. And then I would set myself up in business as a P.I.

I already had one case, didn't I? Okay, so the client was

my sister, and it was a low-danger job. But Greer had been right when she said I'd make a good detective.

The manager returned, smiling ingratiatingly, the DeLuca check in hand. "We'd like to talk to you about some of our more elite investment programs," he said.

"I'm sure you would," I replied. I sounded really business-like. Seemed like a good idea to start practicing that. "For now, just put the money in my regular checking account, please."

"Certainly," the manager said. I could tell he'd been build-ing up a spiel about bank stock and certificates of deposit, and he looked disappointed at having to swallow a speech he'd spent a whole five minutes composing in his head.

"It's time to get serious," I told Jolie, as we walked out of the bank. My branch was in a supermarket, alongside a Starbucks, and I'd sprung for double-mocha supreme frap-pacinos on the way out.

It was also time to pick up Russell—Bethany had left a message on my cell phone that he was good to go—and I was glad Jolie was with me, because despite my sudden riches, I wasn't real thrilled about facing Allison Darroch again.

We did the drive-through thing for breakfast, since we were in a hurry, and juggled our sausage biscuits and de-signer coffees as we drove out of town. I followed the same route Tucker had taken the day before; another reason to be-lieve I could make the detective thing work.

I'm good with directions. That would come in handy on stake-outs and in high-speed chases.

"So you take Russell to the vet, and the doc turns out to be Tucker's wife," Jolie recapped what I'd told her earlier, while we were both peering into the mirror over my bathroom sink, doing a sort of Siamese-twin makeup thing.

"Not his wife," I stressed, sucking up some frappacino. "His *ex*-wife."

"From what you said before, I'm not convinced she's made the shift."

I sighed. "You can say that again. The way she looked at me, I might have had a neon sign over my head, flashing 'Other Woman, Other Woman.' But Allison's a good vet, and she's professional. She probably saved Russell's life."

"We need to be done in time for me to make that job interview," Jolie said. She was a detail person. Always keeping little checklists in her head.

"No problem," I told her.

When we arrived at the Darroch place, I pulled around behind, took a deep breath and jammed my frappacino into the cup holder between the front seats.

"Here goes," I said.

As it turned out, my lucky streak, for which I was long overdue, I'd like to say, held. Allison was nowhere around. Maybe she was out helping a cow give birth or something. Bethany greeted us with a smile and a whopping bill, and I could hear Russell barking exuberantly in the back at the sound of my voice.

I wrote a check, and Bethany sprang the basset hound from his kennel.

He trotted toward me, tail a blur, tongue lolling. A lot of people say dogs don't smile, but I know differently. Russell was beaming.

I crouched to ruffle his ears. "Hey, buddy," I said.

He licked my face.

Jolie, the dog and I piled back into the Volvo, Russell sitting in the middle of the backseat, ready to take on the world.

I glanced at Jolie as we started down the long driveway, back to the road. I knew she was disappointed that we hadn't encountered Allison. I was relieved enough for both of us.

"What now?" Jolie asked.

"I need to do some investigating," I said. "You can get ready for your interview while I'm Googling all Alex Pennington's possible girlfriends."

"Right," Jolie said, but she sounded uncertain. "Do you think the dead cat will be around when we get back to your place?"

A lump rose in my throat. Whenever I thought of Chester, I was reminded that his presence in my life was temporary. Once he'd accomplished his mission, whatever it was, he'd be getting onto one of those trains Nick talked about, and that would be the last goodbye.

"I hope so," I said softly.

Bad-Ass Bert's was still closed, of course, and it looked lonely. I wondered if Bert would give in to pressure from Sheila and sell the place. It wouldn't be the same with a new owner.

"Everything changes," I mused, as I parked the Volvo.

"You just figuring that out?" Jolie asked.

"It's a process," I replied. "An unfolding."

"Where do you get this stuff?" Jolie teased. "Is there a *Damn Fool's Guide to Psychobabble?*"

"Shut up," I told her, but I meant it in the kindest possible way.

We hiked up the stairs, Jolie, Russell and I, and I unlocked the door. Scoped the place out, detective style, scanning for unexpected food deliveries and other signs of intrusion.

Zip.

With routine reconnaissance out of the way, I proceeded to the kitchen, filled Russell's water dish and checked the voice mail.

Glory hallelujah.

No death threats.

No special offers from my personal Lucretia Borgia.

Jolie disappeared into the bedroom, to get ready for the big interview.

The phone rang, just as I was logging on to the computer, and I had the cordless receiver on the desk beside me.

I picked up. "Sheepshanks, Sheepshanks and Sheepshanks," I said confidently. Sure, there was only one Sheepshanks in my new agency, but adding two more gave the business substance.

Tucker laughed. "Whatever you say, Moje," he said. "Sorry to indulge in hot sex and run, but I got a call."

I was in a good mood, so I let him off the hook. "It's not as if I just sit around here waiting for you to give me an orgasm," I said loftily. "I'm starting a business. People are trying to kill me. I don't have a lot of free time."

"You're really serious about this private dick thing?"

"Serious as a flat tire on a lonely road," I replied. "And I think I can do it without a dick."

He laughed again. "True enough," he said. "But it takes money to start an agency. Even a shoestring operation like the one you're probably planning."

"It just so happens that I *have* money."

"What Greer gave you won't—"

"I have *more* than that."

"Have you been playing slot machines again?"

I thought with regret of the credits I'd left behind on the last visit, and the shock of Geoff appearing beside me, at the Sizzling Sevens. Remembering made my nape tingle. Geoff was still out there someplace, and he might have been the one to send the poisoned chow mein. He was almost certainly the mystery caller, too.

I decided not to get so happy about the windfall from Margery DeLuca that I relaxed my guard.

Later that day, I would buy myself a gun.

A private detective needs a gun, right?

For a fraction of a second, my clothes felt heavy and wet. Blood-soaked. I saw a black pistol with a long barrel, lying on avocado-green shag carpeting.

I warped out of the memory without missing a beat in the conversation with Tucker, but it left me a little dizzy.

"No," I said stiffly. "I have not been playing the slot machines. And even if I had, it's not illegal."

Tucker sighed. "No, babe, it's not illegal. And I didn't call to talk about your gambling habit."

"I don't *have* a gambling habit."

"I'll concede that, too," he said quietly. "Did you pick up Bert's dog?"

"Yes," I said, with relief. "Better still, I didn't run into Allison."

"She's got a parent-teacher meeting today," Tucker said.

"And you weren't invited?"

"I could go, but Allison would make me out to be some kind of renegade, super-psycho robo-cop. I don't need that, and the kids don't, either. Besides, I'm on a case."

"What kind of case?"

"An *undercover* case, Moje. That means it's a secret."

"I just thought you might be able to fill me in a little," I said. "You know, one professional to another."

"Right. One professional to another. What's with you, anyway? Is there a coupon in the back of one of those books you read? Send this in and you get a free decoder badge?"

"I could do without your sarcasm. And if you didn't call me to talk about slot machines, what *was* your purpose?"

Tucker sighed again. "Sorry," he said. "You get into enough trouble as it is without putting your name, address and phone number in the yellow pages for every nut in Maricopa County to see, but right now, that's beside the point. The tox report came back on the chow mein, Moje. Rat poison. You would have tasted it with the first bite, which means the perp is either an amateur, or somebody who wants to be perceived as one."

"Well, that doesn't exactly narrow the field, does it? Heather Dillard might have done it. She'd definitely qualify as an amateur. Then there's Geoff."

"Your whacko brother may not have been involved."

"How do you know that?"

"Fingerprints, Sherlock. On the delivery box. They ruled him out first thing—he's been in the system, so he's on file. No matches on the others, except, of course, for mine."

"Fast work," I said. "I thought it took longer to run prints."

"It's all in who you know," Tucker replied. "Of course, psycho-sib could have done the original doctoring. He just didn't handle the box."

I put Geoff on a mental shelf and glanced at Russell, who was snoozing as close to my feet as he could get. "What's the official word on Bert's condition? I've called the hospital a couple of times, and they claimed they didn't have a patient by that name."

"They're telling the truth. He's been moved."

"Where?"

"I can't tell you that, Moje. Your line could be tapped. You're a *detective*—look it up in *The Damn Fool's Guide to Witness Protection*."

"*Witness Protection?*"

"Who's in Witness Protection?" Jolie demanded, from directly behind me.

I almost had a heart attack. I gave her a don't-sneak-up-on-me-like-that kind of glare.

"See you in a few days, Moje," Tucker said.

"Wait—"

He hung up.

"Shit," I said, and shut off the phone.

"What? The check from Big Mama bounced? They cancelled your *Damn Fool's* book club membership? *What?*"

I took in my sister's sleek beige suit, high heels and taste-fully contained braids. "You really look good," I said.

"Thanks for sounding so surprised," Jolie grinned, but then she did a little twirl. "Do I look like the perfect candi-date for the job with Phoenix P.D.?"

"Do crime scene techs dress like that? I'd peg you for what you are—an almost Ph.D. with a fancy job in a well-funded lab." I frowned. I still wasn't clear on why Jolie wanted to throw over a high paying position in a prestigious field of science to pick hairs and fibers out of carpets and the trunks of cars.

Jolie checked her watch. It was old-fashioned, with fake diamonds around the face. Once, it had been her mother's, which was why she treasured it. "I'm out of here," she said. "If you hear from Greer, tell her we're coming to her place tonight for supper and we'll bring the food."

I nodded. "Good luck, Jolie."

She snatched up her purse, which matched her shoes, and breezed out. I heard her Pathfinder start up, and went back to my detective work. I really wonder what P.I.'s did before Google. An hour at the computer, and I knew practically ev-erything there was to know about every woman on Greer's suspect list.

Of course I'd have to do some legwork, but I had three solid candidates for Alex's extracurricular love-muffin activ-ities. One of them was attending the same medical confer-ence, but that only meant it would be easier to snoop through her residence and place of business.

At the time, I actually thought I was going to get to that.

I left the computer, put on some lipstick and switched my sweatpants for a good pair of jeans, my sneakers for boots and my T-shirt for a silk blouse that changed my eyes from green to blue.

I was ready to go detecting, but it bothered me to leave Russell alone. He was vulnerable and, after all, he'd just gotten out of Dog General Hospital.

"Nick?"

No answer.

No sudden appearance.

No Chester.

I addressed the empty room. "Listen, Nick, if you're here, thanks for whatever you did to make your mother pay up. Maybe you're low on ectoplasm or something, so you can't pop in, but if you can hear me, would you mind looking after Russell for me for a few hours?"

Nothing.

I patted Russell's head, told him to be a good boy and filled a second bowl with Greer's gourmet kibble before slipping out of the apartment. I might have had some qualms if the dog had whimpered, or even looked lonely, but he just thumped his tail on the floor once and went back to dreamland.

I left with a clear conscience and some low-grade anxiety.

The first candidate for Alex's squeeze-on-the-side ran a gallery in Old Town Scottsdale. Her name was Gina Marchand, she was thirty-five, three times divorced and struggling to keep the store open. All that, I'd learned by Googling. Now, it was time to get a firsthand look at her. Size her up.

I stopped off at Wal-Mart on the way and bought a digital camera and a pretzel the size of a Frisbee.

Proper nutrition is fundamental to the achievement of any goal—*The Damn Fool's Guide to Success,* page 72.

Gina was in the shop when I walked in, explaining the virtues of a twelve-foot bronze statue of a bear eating a fish to a middle-aged woman who'd apparently thrown in her lot with the I-shall-wear-purple movement. No red hat, though, so maybe she was on the fence.

Ms. Marchand resembled the publicity picture on her Web site. She looked up at me briefly, as I entered, and dismissed me in the next moment. I checked the front of my blouse for pretzel crumbs.

"We can certainly ship the piece to Cincinnati with no problem," she told the woman in purple.

I wandered over to examine an oil painting on the eastern wall. It was gigantic, roughly the size of the area rug in Greer's dining room, and showed four dead outlaws, of the Old West persuasion, strapped to boards and leaning against the facade of a vintage saloon. The title was, "Wages of Sin," and I could have bought an Escalade, fully loaded, for what it cost, according to the discreet little card tucked into the lower right hand corner of the frame.

"You probably can't afford it," Gina Marchand said, stepping up beside me.

Maybe she smelled the Wal-Mart pretzel on my breath.

"You might be surprised," I countered. I *could* have bought that painting, but it would have been a crazy thing to do. It wouldn't fit on any of the walls in my apartment and, besides, I had enough ghosts hanging around without adding a band of outlaws to the mix.

"Somehow," Gina said, "I just don't think you're here to buy art."

I smiled winningly. "You're right," I said. "I'm really here to find out if you're sleeping with Dr. Alex Pennington. If you are, I'll get the goods on you."

She paled. "Alex is a customer," she said. "A *collector*."

He was probably a collector, all right. Greer was expecting him to be involved with one woman, and still hoping she was wrong on the count. I figured there was a harem.

"You know, of course, that he's married." I was deliberately goading her, just to see what she'd do. She'd either kick me out of the place, or admit something.

Gina glanced nervously at her customer, who was busy filling out forms at the counter. The bear and the fish were as good as on their way to Cincinnati. "As I said, Alex—Dr. Pennington—is a client of the gallery. And I resent your coming in here and accusing me—"

"I didn't accuse you of anything, Ms. Marchand." Up close and personal, I could see that she probably wasn't in the running for any trophy wife upgrade Alex might be planning. Her makeup was impeccable, but there were fine lines around her eyes and mouth, and she was, after all, three years older than Greer. "If you're boinking Dr. Pennington, however, I would advise you to stop. You could be named as a correspondent in the divorce, if there is one, and the publicity would not be good for business."

"This is outrageous! I have half a mind to complain to Alex—"

"You do that," I said, though I was bluffing. If she described me to Alex, my cover would be blown. Entry #1 for my P.I. log-book: Don't give yourself away by running off at the mouth.

"What's your name?" she demanded.

"Greer Pennington," I said. "Alex is my husband."

Gina's mouth dropped open, and she took a step back. I figured she'd been in her share of catfights, with the scars to prove it, and she wasn't willing to tangle.

"Can you give me a break on the shipping?" the woman in purple called.

Gina was distracted, and I took that opportunity to duck out.

I had a few things to learn about being a P.I., but I was pretty sure Greer's worst suspicions were right on target. Hospital rounds weren't the only ones Alex was making.

I really wished it wasn't true.

"YOU ACTUALLY *investigated* someone?" Jolie asked, two hours later, when we were both back in the apartment. She'd gotten there first, let herself in with the spare key I'd given her earlier and exchanged her power suit and heels for jeans and a tank top that showed off her toned arms. She was clearly relieved when I came in; it probably freaked her out being alone in the place.

"Yes," I said, disgusted, "and I did a lousy job. Greer will probably fire my ass and demand her retainer back." I rifled the bookcase for my copy of *The Damn Fool's Guide to*

Private Investigation. Time to bone up a little. "How was the interview?"

Jolie beamed. "I'm hired. I start on the first of June."

"I guess that's good news," I said warily.

Jolie put her hands on her hips. "You don't seem all that happy," she said. A mischievous light danced in her eyes. "What's the matter, Moje? Ain't this town big enough for both of us?"

"Spare me the western movie clichés," I said. "Of course it is. It's just weird that you'd give up your lab job, that's all. You must be down for a major cut in pay, for one thing. You have a nice condo in Tucson, friends—"

"I need a change," she said. "I have plenty of money saved, so I won't feel the pinch for a long time, if ever." She paused. "And I want to be closer to Lillian."

"I still think there's more to it," I insisted, but I understood about Lillian. From the looks of things, she didn't have a lot of time left and, like Jolie, I wanted to be there for her.

"Like what?" Jolie challenged.

"Like a man," I said. "If somebody done you wrong, you can tell me. It's not as if I've got any room to judge."

"No man," Jolie said, and then she looked away, so I knew she was lying.

Before I could think of what to say next, she picked up a copy of the newspaper, lying on the coffee table and handed it to me.

"Isn't that your uncle's wife?" she asked.

I focused in on the picture. Sure enough, it was Barbara Larimer, presiding over some charity event. She was rich and influential, so there was nothing unusual about that. What struck me like the heel of somebody's palm to my larynx was that she was standing up.

"Where's the wheelchair?" I muttered, scanning the article. I'd thought the photo might have been pulled from some file, and thus from an earlier and more mobile time in Babs's life, but it was current.

"What wheelchair?" Jolie asked.

"She was in a wheelchair when I met her." I tapped the picture. Mrs. Senator-and-Maybe-Governor was smiling, her blond hair gleaming, and she looked strong enough to kick off her ritzy shoes, hike up her Vera Wang and run a 5K without sweating through her makeup. "What the hell?"

Jolie shrugged. "I just thought you'd want to see it because she's—you know—family."

"You and Greer are family," I said. "Uncle Clive might even turn out to be family. But Barbara Larimer—well—let's just say she and I won't be posing for shots for anybody's scrapbook."

"You don't like her?"

"I didn't say that." I read the article again, slowly and carefully this time. Barbara and the other senators' wives had raised a slug of money for charity. If she'd had a miraculous recovery since I'd encountered her a few days before, the reporter hadn't seen fit to include an account of it.

I was bugged.

I dug out Uncle Clive's card and called his office number.

I got Joseph. I knew who he was even before he introduced himself, by the freeze in his voice when I gave my name.

"I'm sorry," he said. "The senator is in a meeting and can't be disturbed."

"I just have one question," I replied. "When did Mrs. Larimer shout hallelujah and rise out of her wheelchair?"

"It's really none of your business," Joseph retorted, "but if it will get you off the phone, I'll tell you." He waited.

I waited.

I had to pee, so I finally gave in.

"All right," I said. "Tell me and I won't call again." *Unless, of course, I damn well feel like it.*

"Mrs. Larimer suffers from MS, and in this case, that is not an abbreviation for Mojo Sheepshanks," Joseph said. What a smart ass, but I gave him points for a quick wit. "She has periods of remission, and only needs a wheelchair when she's very tired."

"I see."

"Good," Joseph said. Then he hung up on me.

"Arrogant bastard," I said to the receiver.

"If I didn't know about Tucker," Jolie interjected, with a smile, "I'd say it was love."

I snorted. "The man is a pig. He practically called me trailer trash the first time we met, and if he didn't live so far away, I'd put him on the list of suspects for the chow mein caper."

"Is he cute?"

"He's a troll." I slammed the paper down. Okay, a *cute* troll, but he probably gets his mail under some bridge.

"Why is this important to you?" Jolie asked reasonably.

"Damned if I know," I admitted, but it *was* important.

I made a visit to the bathroom, then proceeded to the kitchen to check messages.

No mad killers.

No telemarketers.

Just Greer, wanting to know if we'd pick up some pasta salad at A.J.'s before we came over for dinner that night.

I hit 88 and called her back.

"Is Alex still out of town?" I asked.

"Hello to you, too," Greer replied sunnily.

I wondered if I ought to tell her that I'd muffed my first real attempt at investigating her case. I definitely *didn't* plan to confess that I'd assumed her identity. She'd be mortified, if only because of my wardrobe.

"Hello, Greer," I said patiently.

"Hello, Mojo," Greer answered, with a laugh in her voice. At least she didn't sound crazy, or depressed. That cheered me up a little.

Presently, she went on. "Alex won't be home until tomorrow night," she said. "I just talked to him on the phone. He sent me two dozen pink roses and said I ought to expect a package at any minute."

Oh, shit, I thought. She was going to cancel the job and ask for her money back. "So everything is all sweetness and light?" I asked carefully.

She laughed. "Hell, no," she said. "The bastard is just trying to cover his tracks. Have you got anything on him yet?"

I felt guilty as hell because I was *glad* Greer wasn't going to pull my first case out from under me. What kind of sick attitude was that? I was cheering for the wrong side—I should have been hoping Alex would turn out to be innocent.

But I wasn't.

What did that mean? What did it say about me, as a person?

Was I a heartless, money-grubbing bitch?

Or did I simply hope that, if Greer lost Alex Pennington, she might find herself again?

"Not yet," I said. "I paid a call on one of the suspects today. Gina Marchand. She runs a gallery in Old Town."

"Do you think they're doing it?"

I swallowed, glanced uncomfortably at Jolie, who looked pensive as she listened shamelessly to my end of the conversation. "If I had to make a bet, I'd say they've done a tango or two."

Greer let out an audible breath. "Is she pretty?"

"You put her in the shade," I said, and I meant it. Okay, I might have been a little prejudiced, but Greer was a beauty by anybody's standards. Except maybe her cheating rat of a husband's.

"Does she have potential?"

"As what?"

"The mother of a second family." Greer sounded wistful. Alex's *first* family lived on alimony and child support, somewhere in Scottsdale. The wife was active in local politics, and I'd run into her once, at Fashion Square Mall. The original Penningtons weren't hurting financially, but there are a lot of other ways to hurt.

Just ask me. I'd been through a similar thing with Nick,

and the check from his mother wasn't going to change that. We didn't have kids, and we weren't married very long, but it still felt as though somebody had punched me in the stomach whenever I thought of it. While I was dreaming of picket fences and backyard swing sets and Christmas cards that said, "From the Three of Us," Nick was making a lie out of every promise he'd ever made to me.

And believe me, there were plenty of promises.

I loved Greer. I really and truly did. But I couldn't help empathizing with the wronged wife.

"Her eggs would have to be rehydrated," I said, shaking it off. "Alex might have banged her a few times, but she's no long-term threat."

Greer was silent for a long, uncomfortable moment. "I know what you're thinking," she finally said, softly and with no rancor. "What goes around, comes around."

"I'm not thinking anything of the kind, Greer," I replied. "I'm on your side."

She wasn't listening. "I broke up a home, and now someone else is about to take a sledgehammer to mine. What am I going to do, Mojo?"

"You might be able to work things out."

Another silence. I wondered if Greer was crying.

"Get here as soon as you can, okay?" she finally said.

"You got it," I told her gently.

"And you can bring the dog."

I said goodbye, hung up the phone and turned to Jolie.

"What's wrong?" she asked.

"She said we could bring Russell."

Jolie's eyes widened with sisterly concern. "Get out," she said.

An hour later, Jolie and I arrived at Greer's in Jolie's Pathfinder, with three bags from A.J.'s, a basset hound and a whole lot of questions.

Even with all that was going on in our separate lives, there was something soothing and almost tribal about the three of us—Greer, Jolie and me—sitting around the same table again, there on the Pennington patio. A candle burned in the center of our little circle, like a campfire at the mouth of some primitive cave. Twilight fell softly, with a smattering of stars overhead, and the water-fall at one end of Greer's pool burbled cheerfully in the background, providing a subtle "do-wah" to our sister-song.

While Jolie told Greer about the new job and recounted her visit to Lillian the day before, we nibbled pasta salad from the deli at A.J.'s. Greer served cold chicken breasts laced with rosemary and gallons of San Pellegrino. I was relieved at the absence of wine, since I suspected big sister had been hitting the sauce in lonely moments.

"I think you're crazy," Greer said, apropos of Jolie's career change, but she looked wistful at the same time.

"Why?" Jolie challenged gently. "Because I'm taking a cut in salary? Sorry to be trite, but money isn't everything."

"Great," Greer sighed, looking from Jolie to me and back again, as though she were searching for some secret we were keeping from her, one that would make her life all right again. "You sound like Mojo. Take it as it comes. Skim the surface and never get in too deep."

Jolie straightened slightly in her chair, and I tensed. It would be easy to call Greer on the glaring disparity between her talk and her walk, but it wouldn't be kind, and Greer needed kindness at the moment. We could deal with the bullshit later, when she was strong again, and capable of fighting back.

"Do you ever regret closing the design business?" Jolie asked quietly.

I let out my figurative breath.

Tears stood in Greer's eyes. "Yes," she said, after a long, uncomfortable pause. "Does that make you happy?"

"Pull your head out of your butt, Greer," Jolie said, in her singular Jolie way. "Mojo and I are on *your* side. I know all about the cheating husband, and how you hired Mojo to prove or disprove the theory. But something else is going on here—something you're not telling. If you fess up, we might be able to help you."

Greer became fascinated with the waterfall in the pool.

Under the table, Russell shifted, in some doggy dream, and thumped his tail against the patio stones.

Jolie and I waited. I was nervous, but Jolie looked like a woman with her teeth in something and meaning to chew.

"I'm being blackmailed," Greer said, after three or four changes in the partisan balance of Congress.

"Blackmailed?" I echoed, no longer slumping in my chair. "By whom?"

"Well, if I knew that," Greer told me tersely, "I could put a stop to it, couldn't I?"

"Details," Jolie demanded. "How did they contact you? Letters? E-mail? Have you told you the police?"

"Of course I haven't told the police," Greer answered, in a peevish tone. She was huddling inside herself again, holding herself together with both arms. "I don't want this to become public knowledge. That, after all, is the whole *point* of giving in to blackmail, isn't it?"

"Why didn't you say something before?" I asked, more hurt than angry. In the years since Lillian and I had rescued Greer from the bus station, I'd never discovered anything real about her background. It was as if her life started that day in Boise, and the trail she'd followed to get there had dissolved, or never existed in the first place. I'd had to go on guesswork and suppositions.

Greer said nothing. She just looked at me.

"Shit," I said, as revelation struck. "You were *testing* me. If I could nail Alex for adultery, then you would consider siccing me on the blackmailer."

"Maybe," she said.

"Are you going to tell us exactly what's been happening or not?" Jolie asked.

"No," Greer answered, and I knew she meant it. Her tone was flat and cold, with no give at all.

"We're your sisters," I pointed out.

"You," Greer told me, with the same lack of inflection as before, "are somebody I met in a bus station in Boise." While I was reeling from that, she turned to Jolie. "And you are Lillian's stepdaughter."

"That's all we mean to you?" Jolie asked sharply. I was too stricken to speak. I wanted to load Russell up and boogie, and I deserve some credit for not doing exactly that. Sticking around showed I'd experienced some personal growth. Plus, of course, we'd come in Jolie's rig, not mine, and she had the keys.

"That's all I can afford to *let* you mean to me," Greer said. "Lillian Travers is the only person in the world I know for sure wouldn't betray me, and she's practically comatose."

"This sucks," I said. "It totally sucks."

Jolie plucked her elegant linen napkin off her lap and threw it down on the table. "Who the hell are you?" she barked, glaring at Greer. "And what have you done with *my sister?*"

So much for tribal spirit.

I scrabbled for my purse, rooted out my checkbook. I could afford to give back Greer's retainer, thanks to Margery DeLuca's apparent fit of conscience, and that was what I intended to do. I wouldn't miss the money.

I *would* miss the job. And I would miss Greer even more.

"Jolie," Greer said, with cool intensity, "sit down. Mojo, put away the checkbook. I'm not cutting either of you out of my life. I'm just saying that this is big, and knowing you can trust somebody and doing it are two different things. I need some time."

"You might not *have* time," Jolie pointed out fiercely, but she looked as though she'd stopped hyperventilating, even if she still refused to sit back down at Greer's table. "Blackmail is serious stuff. Whoever's behind it could turn violent at any time. Have you ever thought of that?"

"Of course I've thought of it," Greer said. "*Sit down,* Jolie."

Jolie sat.

"Let us help you, Greer," I said, once I'd swallowed the lump of hurt sticking in my throat like a burr. After all we'd been through together, after all the laughter and all the fights and all the girl-secrets we'd shared, lying in twin beds in some motel room, or in sleeping bags in the back of whatever car Lillian happened to own at the time, Greer was afraid to trust me?

"I want to," Greer said.

"Then tell us the truth," Jolie insisted, in an angry whisper.

"I can't," Greer answered. "Not yet."

After that, the party was over, and leaving felt like limping, wounded, away from a losing battle.

"I am *so* pissed!" Jolie blurted a few minutes later, when she was behind the wheel of her Pathfinder and I was buckled into the passenger seat. Russell barely missed a beat in his nap—he was already snoring in the cargo hold, nestled on a blanket I'd brought from the apartment.

I was biting my lip. "Did Greer ever tell you anything about her past? Before she hooked up with Lillian and me, I mean?"

"No," Jolie said. She tossed me a concerned look before shifting her gaze to the rearview mirror to back out of Greer's driveway. "Look, Mojo, I know she hurt your feelings, but try not to take this too personally, okay?"

"I thought we were a family," I said. "It never occurred to me that Greer didn't feel that way, too."

"She does, though," Jolie replied. "She's just scared. And if she won't tell us who's blackmailing her, and why, we'd better try to find out on our own."

"How?" I asked. "Greer isn't her real name any more than Mojo Sheepshanks is mine. Lillian got her a new Social Security number, so we can't run a trace on that."

"You're the private detective," Jolie said, tossing me a grin. "Look it up in a *Damn Fool's Guide*. Check out some old lost kid/runaway sites on the Web. Most of all, chill. Greer's being a bitch because she's terrified."

"Pretty lofty speech," I observed dryly, "for somebody who made a scene at the table."

"I'm human," Jolie said. "Where to, Sherlock?"

I felt something intangible dance up my spine. Turned in the seat to look back at the headlights behind us.

"I think we're being followed," I said.

Jolie sighed, glanced at the rearview. "You're taking this private eye thing a little too seriously," she said.

"Somebody tried to poison me, I've been getting death threats and Greer's being blackmailed. Excuse me, but concern does not equal paranoia in this case."

The car zoomed up behind us, lights on bright. Whipped alongside.

Jolie swerved to keep from being run off the road.

"Convinced?" I asked calmly.

"Probably just road rage," Jolie said, but she sounded shaken.

The tail sped past, laying rubber on the blacktop. A black Mercedes sedan, late model.

"Follow them," I said.

"Are you out of your mind? Whoever's driving that car could have a gun!"

"Just do it, Jolie!"

"Why?"

Yeesh. "Because I think that was Alex Pennington's car. So either he's not away at the medical conference, like he told Greer, or he left the car with a girlfriend."

Jolie gave the Pathfinder a little gas, but not enough to suit me.

Up ahead, at a four-way stop, the Mercedes hung a right and shot down the highway.

"We can't be too obvious," Jolie said, in reply to my unspoken question.

"Keep up, Jolie."

Once in a while, the traffic gods smile. Just as we made the right hand turn, I saw a squad car whip out of a side-road up ahead, lights whirling.

The Mercedes pulled over.

The squad car drew up behind it.

"Whoop-de-do!" I yelled.

"You really need to get a life," Jolie said, but she slowed so we could rubberneck.

The cop waved us on.

"Pull over," I told Jolie.

"Yeah, right."

"I mean it. Pretend you have car trouble. I want to see who's driving that Mercedes."

"I just accepted a job with Phoenix PD," Jolie argued. "I'm not getting fired for interfering with the duties of an officer of the law."

"Then just go around the block."

"What block? This is a private road."

"Turn around, then. If we get stopped, we'll say we forgot something at Greer's."

"Damn," Jolie said, but she turned around at the base of somebody's gated driveway and cruised slowly back past the Mercedes.

The cop ignored us. He was busy giving Alex Pennington a sobriety test on the side of the road.

"Hot damn," I said.

Alex glared at us as we passed. He might not have recognized Jolie's ride, but he'd known we were at Greer's. And he hadn't liked the idea.

If I'd been driving, I would have given a few cheery toots on the horn, but I wasn't.

"I thought he was away at some conference," Jolie said.

"So did Greer." I felt smug. I was getting the hang of this detective thing.

"Why would he want to scare us, Moje? For all he knows, we were just hanging out with Greer. Come to think of it, he could have joined the party back at the house."

"He doesn't want Greer to know he's in town," I said. "And Gina Marchand probably told him I was in her shop today, asking embarrassing questions. I said I was Greer, but if the squeeze described me to him, he'd know it was me."

"So why try to run us off the road? Now he's blown his cover." We'd reached Greer's driveway again. Jolie pulled off on the opposite side. "Is there another way into town?"

I gave her directions, but I was almost backward in my seat, watching as the squad car pulled back onto the road, headed the other way. Alex's Mercedes followed, at a much slower pace.

"We could go back the way we came," I suggested.

"Not a chance," Jolie said. "Alex looked really pissed. I wouldn't put it past him to wait for us up there somewhere and cut us off. Then what would we do?"

"Ask him why he was following us, for one thing."

"Oh, that's brilliant," Jolie replied. "Did you see the look on his face when we went by the second time?"

I smiled. "Yeah," I said. "We've got him on the run."

"You're nuts, Mojo Sheepshanks, or whatever the hell your name is."

She kept right on going in the direction we were heading. "What is your name, anyway?"

"You know damn well who I am."

"After talking to Greer, I'm not so sure I know who anybody is."

"I was born Mary Josephine Mayhugh," I said. "I told you that years ago, Jolie, when I found the accounts of my parents' murders on that computer at the library."

"There are still a lot of secrets in this family," Jolie said. We were on the outskirts of Scottsdale proper by then.

I settled into my seat, thinking. "Maybe *Alex* is the one blackmailing Greer," I speculated. "If he wants a divorce, he might be trying to scare her into hitting the road. You know, so he could keep the house and all the money and move the next wife in without a hitch."

"Has anyone ever told you that you have issues? All we know for sure is that Alex lied about being out of town and he's got a bent toward road rage."

"If I'm going to be a detective," I said, "I need to consider all the angles."

"Yeah, well, not every man is like Nick DeLuca. And you're *not* a detective, Moje. You're a billing clerk."

A silence descended. Scottsdale flashed by on either side as we headed north, toward Cave Creek.

"Not that there's anything wrong with being a billing clerk," Jolie said, after a long time.

I sat with my arms folded. "Well, it's not the same as being, say, a *forensic scientist.*"

"I am not going to let you pick a fight with me, Mojo. And this time, you can't just hop in your car and go home, because you *are* home."

"I didn't start this," I pointed out, taking the high road. "You did."

"You're pissed because I called you a billing clerk. Moje, you *are* a billing clerk. If you don't like it, be something else."

"I'm trying to be a detective, but you won't let me."

"Oh, frick, Mojo, you're a damn *detective* then!"

I grinned. "Thanks."

"Bitch," Jolie said.

"I love you, too," I replied lightly.

When we got home, Russell did the poop thing in the parking lot, lifted his leg against the corner of the building and trotted hopefully over to the side door, where he and Bert always entered the bar.

My heart ached. According to Tucker, Bert was in Witness Protection, which probably meant the separation between him and Russell was permanent.

"Come on, buddy," I called to him. "Time to go upstairs."

Russell whimpered and scratched at the door.

"Damn," I whispered, and walked toward him.

That was when I noticed that the padlock wasn't fastened.

My heartbeat quickened. I gestured for Jolie.

"Don't you dare," she whispered, from a few feet away. Evidently, she'd noticed the open padlock, too. I briefly considered taking her on as a partner in Sheepshanks, Sheepshanks and Sheepshanks, then decided the fact that I couldn't pay her a salary would probably get in the way.

Russell let out a yelp and stood on his hind legs, scrabbling at the door with his forepaws.

I put my hand on the knob.

"Mojo!" Jolie rasped.

I turned the knob.

Russell, the canine ramrod, forced the door open with his body weight and galloped in. The whole matter was decided, I figured, since I couldn't let the dog face whoever was inside all by himself.

One green-shaded lamp was lit, over the pool tables.

The bar had been tipped over.

The jukebox was smashed.

Russell darted under the pool table, where I'd found Bert, and sniffed frantically.

"It's okay, boy," I said nervously, looking from side to side. "Anybody here?" I felt Jolie hovering behind me.

"I'm calling 911," she said. I heard the corresponding beep-beep-beep as she dialed.

Russell came back to me, wagging his tail, then darted away again, heading for the storage closet.

The pool cues were scattered like pickup-sticks on the sawdust floor. I armed myself with one and followed.

"Who's there?" I asked, sounding a shitload braver than I felt.

I heard a muffled, moaning sound. Russell did his door-scratching number again.

I got him by the collar and gently pulled him back.

"Mojo," Jolie called, probably from the doorway, "don't open that door. The police are on their way!"

I drew a deep breath, tightened my sweaty grasp on the pool cue, turned the handle on the door and pulled.

Sheila was inside, lying on her side on the floor. There was duct tape around her mouth and also binding her wrists and ankles together. Her eyes were blackened, and the front of her T-shirt was soaked with blood.

Russell went wild.

I dropped the pool cue. "Jolie, hold the dog!" I called.

She used both hands to grip Russell's collar, but it was still all she could do to restrain him.

"It's okay, Sheila," I said. "It's me, Mojo. Nobody's going to hurt you—"

Sheila tried to wriggle away, disappear into the back wall of the storage closet.

Sirens shrieked in the distance.

I ran behind the bar, found a pair of scissors and rushed back to Sheila. Russell yelped hysterically, still fighting Jolie, who hung on grimly, her eyes huge.

"It's me," I told Sheila, bending to cut away the tape between her ankles and her hands. "It's Mojo."

She made a trapped animal sound behind the tape and kicked at me. She was way past scared, deep into pure terror. Her bruised, swollen eyes glinted when they fixed on the scissors in my hand.

I cut the tape at the back of her head and scrambled backward when she launched herself out of the closet, snarling like something rabid. I tossed the scissors as far as I could, so she wouldn't get hold of them, and braced myself to sustain a few defense wounds.

Sheila landed on me.

We rolled.

Jolie screamed.

I had serious concerns about her future in law enforcement.

Brown uniforms surged around us, hands dragged us apart.

Russell barked his brains out.

Somebody righted an overturned chair and sat me down in it. I realized, with some relief, that it was Jolie.

The room swam.

Jolie forced my head down between my knees.

EMTs arrived, sedated Sheila and took her away.

"Well, Ms. Sheepshanks," a familiar voice said, "we meet again."

I blinked.

Andy Crowley came into focus, went out again.

"I think she's hurt," Jolie fretted, from somewhere off to my left.

"Are you hurt, Ms. Sheepshanks?" Crowley inquired mildly. He was sitting, facing me, our knees almost touching.

"No," I said. "No, I'm okay."

"Then maybe you wouldn't mind telling me what the hell happened here."

I fumbled my way through the events of the evening, starting with Russell heading for the door of the saloon when we got home from Greer's, my noticing the broken padlock when I went to pull him back, right through to finding Sheila hog-tied on the floor of the storage closet.

"And the victim attacked you because—?"

Everything came into clear focus. "I guess she was scared. She thought whoever beat her up had come back."

Crowley nodded, but his face was impassive, and I wondered if he believed me. In the next moment, he cleared that right up. "Two violent incidents," he said, "in the same place. And you're there both times. That's quite a coincidence, wouldn't you say?"

"Not really," I reasoned. "I live upstairs. And I'd say it's a damn good thing I came in to investigate when Russell raised a fuss, because Sheila might have lain in that closet for a long time if I hadn't."

He looked around at the wreckage. "Quite a toss job," he said. He ran his eyes over me with dispatch. "As you said, you live upstairs. The *first* time there was a problem in this bar, you heard noises. So I'm wondering why you didn't hear anything this time. That woman has been worked over pretty thoroughly. She must have screamed. And smashing a place up like this is loud business."

"I wasn't home," I said, not for the first time. Maybe he was checking to see if my story changed.

"That's right," Jolie put in bravely. "We were out all evening."

"And besides," I told Crowley, "Sheila's mouth was covered with duct tape when I found her. Nobody would have heard her if she screamed."

The implications of that sent a cold shudder through me.

"She's the owner's girlfriend?" Crowley asked.

I knew he was fishing. "Yes," I said.

"And you and he weren't involved." He took in the scene again, slowly. "This looks like the kind of thing a woman might do in a jealous rage."

"That is so sexist," Jolie said.

"Shut up," I told her.

Crowley arched an eyebrow and waited. His attention was all mine, lucky me.

"Bert was—is—my friend. My landlord. There was never anything romantic between us."

Crowley didn't speak.

"Am I under arrest or what?" I asked.

"No," Crowley answered, "but you're a person of interest again."

"Don't leave town?"

"Bingo."

"Just exactly what constitutes not leaving town?" I was going to have a hell of a time corralling Alex Pennington's harem if I couldn't leave Cave Creek, and then there was Lillian. "My job entails some traveling, and my foster mother is in a nursing home in Phoenix."

"You're free to visit your mother," Crowley said. He leaned in a little.

I knew what he was doing—turning up the heat, trying to get me to crack. I'd seen the tactic on TV and read about it in at least one *Damn Fool's Guide*. Actually, I kind of admired his technique, and if I ever had to grill somebody, I'd be ready.

"Since when does your job involve traveling?"

I reddened. Of course he'd know all about my job. He'd probably run a background check when I was a person of interest the first time around. "I have to pick up printouts from the doctor's offices and clinics I bill for," I said.

I could scratch Alex off the list, after tonight.

"I thought that was all done over the Internet these days," Crowley remarked easily. "Age of technology, and all that."

"Can I go now?"

Crowley nodded, pushed back his chair and stood.

"Next time you hear noises, or see a broken lock, Ms. Sheepshanks," he said, "call us before you barge in, will you?"

"Right," I said.

"And Ms. Sheepshanks?"

"What?"

"Bad-Ass Bert's is a crime scene. Stay out of it."

I swallowed. "Okay."

Jolie took me by the arm and helped me to my feet. She and Russell and I went out, weaving our way between cops. Russell, so fierce before, seemed worn out now. Downright disheartened.

Upstairs, in the apartment, Jolie turned on every light in the place.

"You really need to move," she said.

I gave Russell some fresh kibble and refilled his water dish. "Where would you suggest I go?" I asked reasonably. "As a person of interest, my options are limited."

"Maybe you and I could get a place together."

"I'm not living with Sweetie. Go figure, but I don't like the idea of spending half my life on top of a refrigerator, waiting for you to come home from work. Besides, he'd probably rip Russell limb from limb."

"Sweetie is a very nice dog," Jolie said, insulted.

"I think we shouldn't talk for a while," I replied.

"Fine," Jolie snapped. She always wanted the last word.

"Fine," I said.

She swept out of the kitchen.

Russell lumbered over to his food bowl and crunched kibble.

I patted him on the head, full of sympathy. Did Witness

Protection allow dogs? For that matter, why was *Bert* a candidate? Sure, he ran a biker bar and had road maps tattooed on both arms and probably the rest of his body, too, but other than that, he was an ordinary guy.

I glanced at the phone.

My cell hadn't rung all evening, but that didn't mean somebody wasn't trying to get in touch with me. Say, to set up another poison delivery, or threaten me with a painful death.

I sighed.

Picking up the receiver, I heard the familiar signal, punched in my voice-mail code.

First message: "Mojo, this is Margery DeLuca. I hope the check I sent over convinced you that I'm sincere. I'd still like to meet with you in person—please call me back as soon as possible so we can set something up."

Delete. Call me ungrateful—the woman had given me three hundred and fifty thousand dollars. She'd also made my life miserable before, during and after my marriage to her son.

Second message: "Hello, Mojo. Alex Pennington here. I just wanted to tell you that you're fired, and if you know what's good for you, you will stop poking around in my private life."

Save. If he killed me, the recording would be evidence.

Third message: "Ms. Sheepshanks, this is Dr. Alice Bilbin at Sunset Villa Nursing Home. I tried calling your cell, but I must have the wrong number. No one answers at Mrs. Pennington's residence, or at Miss Travers's, either.

Your mother is in crisis, and I think you should come as quickly as possible. I do hope you're not out of town or anything." She left a number. I scribbled the digits on the heel of my palm, hung up the phone, and yelled.

"*Jolie!*"

CHAPTER

14

I called Sunset Villa on my cell phone from Jolie's Pathfinder, as we raced down the 101. The receptionist was not helpful; she informed me tersely that:

1 - Dr. Bilbin was gone for the night, and could not be disturbed at home.

2 - No information about Mrs. Travers's condition would be released over the telephone, because, well, Jolie and I could be *anybody*, couldn't we?

3 - We should turn around and go home because we would not be admitted to the patient's room outside of visiting hours, and it was now after midnight.

I informed *her,* just as tersely, thank you very much, that we would be there within forty minutes and we *were* going to see Lillian. Not the next day at 2:00 p.m., but *now*.

The receptionist hung up with a bang. The phone was on Speaker, and Jolie had heard the whole thing.

"That woman is probably calling security at this moment," my sister observed practically. "Hanging around with you, I'll be lucky if I don't get fired from the department before I set foot on my first crime scene."

I would have rubbed my hands together in anticipation of a knock-down-drag-out confrontation if I hadn't already been dialing Greer's number. "Security? Please. I've seen the day guy, and he's at least a hundred and fourteen years old. We can take him easy."

Jolie smiled at the prospect. "I should have brought my makeup. Now I'm going to look bad in my first-ever mug shot."

Greer didn't pick up on her landline, so I tried her cell.

She answered with a blurted, "Mojo! Lillian is—"

"I know," I broke in quietly. "Jolie and I are on our way to Sunset Villa now. ETA, about thirty-five minutes."

"I just pulled into the nursing home parking lot," Greer answered.

I raised an eyebrow. "It would have been dandy if you'd called us," I said evenly.

Jolie, concentrating on the relatively light traffic, slanted me a sidelong look. The message was clear enough: *Not now.*

"Well, I assumed you knew," Greer said, with a sort of impatient desperation. I heard her car door slam, the sound bouncing, night-muffled, from her phone to the satellite to my cell. "I'll meet you in Lillian's room."

"Look out for security," I said.

"Security," Greer countered, sounding breathless now,

as though she'd run part of the way from Scottsdale, "had better look out for *me*."

I clicked off. "I wonder if they do group mug shots. You, me and Greer, booked and fingerprinted, holding up our little letter-boards. We could scan the picture and use it for a Christmas card."

"I would appreciate it," Jolie said evenly, "if you would not make jokes." A tear slid down her cheek, glittering in the freeway lights. "Lillian could die. She might *already* be—"

"Sorry," I said, for the sake of the peace. I loved Lillian as much as Greer and Jolie did, and I was only trying to cope. Sometimes my methods leave something to be desired, though, when it comes to sensitivity.

Jolie dashed at her cheek with the back of one hand. "I didn't mean to snap, Moje," she said. "I'm just scared."

"Me, too," I replied.

Jolie put the pedal to the metal, and we streaked south. In the Sunset Villa lot, we screeched to a crooked stop next to Greer's luxury vehicle, popped our seat belts and bolted.

The reception area was completely empty, which could be either a very good sign or a very bad one. We didn't stop to deliberate.

Three women in too-cheerful print scrubs hovered in the corridor outside Lillian's room, murmuring to each other. Jolie and I zipped past them and came upon one of those scenes that stick in a person's memory forever.

Greer stood next to Lillian's bed, a metal pitcher in one upraised hand, ready to swing. She looked unbalanced, her eyes glittering with ferocious purpose. An octogenarian security guard faced her, his back to us.

It was a standoff, but that wasn't the most interesting thing.

Lillian was sitting up in bed, her eyes bright, a crooked but cognizant smile on her mouth.

"My—daughters—" she said, laboriously but with proud clarity.

Greer slowly lowered the pitcher and turned to stare. Jolie and I brushed past the befuddled guard on either side, like water flowing around a rock in a rushing stream.

"Lillian!" I gasped. "You can talk—"

She shook her head. "Too—hard—" she said, gargling the words like mouthwash. "Soon—though." With that, she raised both her arms, and Greer and Jolie and I all scrambled to do the huddle thing.

Lillian clung to us, managed somehow to plant awkward kisses on each of our faces. I felt tears against my cheek, and couldn't have said who they belonged to, because we were all crying.

"This is highly irregular," one of the nurse's aides protested.

"Get lost," Greer sniffled.

Lillian waited until we all receded. Then, eyes shining, she cupped our faces in her withered hands, each in our turn.

I came last, and by then she looked serious again.

"Be—careful—" Lillian said fiercely. "Queen. Page. Death."

I knew she was referring to the Tarot cards she'd given me during that earlier visit. "I don't understand," I whispered, frustrated to the point of desperation.

Her hands tightened on either side of my skull. She kissed my forehead, closed her eyes and sighed.

For a moment, I was electrified with fear. I thought she'd died.

"She's sleeping, Moje," Jolie reasoned gently, pulling me away. "She's just sleeping."

Greer remained close to Lillian's bedside, took one of her hands, held it tightly in both her own. She looked terrified, as though she thought she would sink into some abyss if she let go.

Jolie tugged me out into the corridor.

The trio of nurse's aides and the security guard receded a few steps, like a sluggish tide, wide-eyed with alarm.

"How long has my stepmother been awake?" Jolie demanded.

One of the women took a half step forward, a reluctant volunteer. Her eyes were huge, and her chin wobbled a little. "She just woke up a few minutes ago, far as we know, right while you was in there. Till then, she was in a coma. That's why Dr. Bilbin called you all."

I put a hand to my heart; it was pounding so hard it made my head swim, and I couldn't seem to catch my breath. I must have looked pretty bad, because the prehistoric security guard shuffled over, took my arm and steered me to one of the plastic chairs along the hallway wall.

"Lillian was *comatose?*" I swayed from the effort of speaking.

"Drink this water," ordered the ancient one, shoving a flimsy cone-shaped paper cup under my nose.

I grabbed it so hard that the contents spilled over my hand, splashed onto the floor.

"Oh, dear," said the rent-a-cop. He looked so upset that I was afraid he'd end up as a patient at Sunset Villa, instead of an employee.

"It's okay," I told him.

He sank into the chair next to mine, breathing audibly.

"Now look what you've done," one of the nurse's aides scolded. "Fred, are you all right? Rotika, get me some smelling salts."

Rotika hurried off, returned with a small bottle, unscrewed the lid and waved it under the old man's nose. The stuff was so strong that it revived me, as well the intended victim, and after a shared whiff, both Fred and I were good to go.

Greer meandered out of Lillian's room, looking dazed and, to be frank, slightly peculiar. "She's going to be all right," she murmured. *"Lillian is going to be all right."*

"You need to go home now, the lot of you," Rotika said. She'd put the cap back on the stink bottle, but traces of genie b.o. still lingered. "You come see Mrs. Travers in the morning. She got to rest now."

I must have looked rebellious as I came to my feet, and Greer was still smiling that odd, befuddled smile. Jolie took each of us by the arm and said, "Rotika's right. We'll come back tomorrow."

"I don't want to leave," I said.

"Too bad," Jolie replied, marching Greer and me down the corridor, past the reception desk and out into the warm Phoenix night. "You're not driving," she told Greer, and hustled her into the back seat of the Pathfinder. Jolie's gaze swung to me. "Get in, Mojo."

"But, Lillian—"

"Get in," Jolie repeated.

I glared at her.

She glared at me.

A person has to choose her battles in this life. I got into the passenger seat, though I did slam the door.

"My car," Greer said, from the back. And then she burst into tears.

"Your car will be fine," Jolie told her, tossing back a box of tissues as she spoke. "You can pick it up tomorrow. In the meantime, I'm taking you home. Mojo and I will spend the night with you."

I thought of the two break-ins at Bert's, the text message, the death threat and the poisoned chow mein. "I can't leave Russell alone all night," I said.

"Russell," Greer rallied enough to say, "is a *dog*."

I had an uneasy feeling, not only about Lillian, but about Russell, too. Part of the magic that is Mojo, I guess. "You can both stay at my place."

"Right," Greer said snippily. "Jolie and I will just share your *couch*."

Under other circumstances, I might have reminded Greer that she'd slept on bus-station benches—among other unsavory places—in her time, and my *couch* would probably compare favorably with any of them. The problem was that Greer was obviously on the ragged edge and she needed some slack, whether I felt like cutting it or not.

"Drop me off at the apartment, then," I said quietly.

"It's nice to know where your loyalties lie," Greer retorted.

"Greer," Jolie said, "put a sock in it."

Everybody fell silent, and that's how we left it.

The trip back to Cave Creek was a long one.

Back at Bert's, Greer waited in the car, and Jolie came up-stairs with me to collect a nightgown, her toiletries and a change of clothes.

Russell greeted me with sleepy gratitude. If Nick and Chester were around, they weren't showing themselves. God only knew where Tucker was and what he was doing. The apartment felt overwhelmingly empty.

Jolie paused, coming out of my bedroom with her things. "You'll be okay here?"

I nodded, bit my lower lip. I wasn't usually fragile, but, hey, I'd been through a lot in the past week. I felt like some-body who'd just been flung off some hyped-up merry-go-round, and my equilibrium was disturbed.

Jolie approached, touched my shoulder with her free hand. She balanced her stuff in the curve of her arm, deo-dorant, toothpaste and brush resting on top of the pile. "Greer's not herself, Moje," she said softly. "I'm trying to be more patient with her. Are you in?"

I grinned wanly. Nodded again. "I'm in," I said.

"Be sure to lock up behind me," Jolie said.

I followed her to the door, Russell at my heels, and stood on the landing until she was safe in the Pathfinder again. As Jolie and Greer drove away, I put on the chain and turned the dead bolt.

I was almost relieved when I turned around and found myself practically standing on Nick's toes.

"How long have you been here?" I asked.

"Long enough," he said. He studied my face, his eyes thoughtful, and I knew he was getting a virtual tour of the inside of my brain. "I thought you'd be happier, once I scared my mother into forking over the life insurance money."

I laughed, sounding a little raw, and shoved my hair back from my face with one hand. "I need tea," I said. "Feel free to join me and sniff a few Oreos."

He followed me into the kitchen, Russell trotting at our heels. "Your head is a real jumble. Lillian's awake. Greer's acting weird. And you wish you knew where the cop is, and whether or not he's sleeping with his ex-wife."

I thought hard about Lillian, since I didn't want Nick viewing anything *else* that might pop into my head, especially where Tucker was concerned.

He sighed. "I've accepted it," he said. "You're boinking the cop."

I whirled on him, in the kitchen doorway. "You didn't—?"

"Watch?" Nick grinned. I was blushing like mad, and he clearly enjoyed my discomfiture. "Nope. Too much male ego for that. And give me credit for a *little* class, will you?"

"I forgive you. Go away." I wrenched open a cupboard door, tossed him the bag of stale Oreos.

He caught them easily and chuckled, but his eyes were sad. "You really don't want me to leave. You're lonely and you're upset and you figure I'm better than nothing. Admit it. I'm right."

"You're right," I said. I snagged the tea kettle off the stove, filled it at the sink and slapped it back down on the burner. I glanced around, almost afraid to ask the question. "Where's Chester?"

"No idea," Nick said, sticking his nose into the Oreo package and inhaling deeply. The exhalation came out as a long sigh. He looked down at Russell, who was sniffing his shoes, with an expression of speculative regret. "I hope you're not counting on him as a watchdog," he remarked.

"Why shouldn't I?" I countered, getting out the tea bags and plopping one into a mug. I was still thinking mostly about Lillian; I should have been thrilled that she was awake, and even regaining her powers of speech, but something about the whole situation troubled me.

"Mainly because there's a woman hiding behind your shower curtain," Nick said.

Good thing I wasn't holding the tea kettle. It was already beginning to steam at the spout, and Russell and I would both have been scalded when I dropped it. "*What?*" I started for the bathroom.

Nick sprang up in front of me like one of those ducks in an old-fashioned shooting gallery. "Wait a second," he said. "She could be dangerous. Even armed. Better to call the cops, don't you think?"

"It would take them half an hour to get here," I replied, and kept walking.

I strode into the bathroom, threw back the curtain and found Heather there, a pair of nail scissors clasped in one hand.

I guess I was too outraged to be scared.

"How did you get in here?" I demanded.

"I have my ways," she said.

"I'm calling the cops," I told her. "If you get out before they arrive, so much the better, because I *totally* intend to press charges."

"Don't turn your back on her," Nick warned quietly, from the doorway.

I *had* forgotten the nail scissors.

"Stay out of this," I said, but I kept my eyes on Heather as I backed out of the bathroom.

Heather stepped daintily over the side of the tub. She was dressed for stealth—black jeans and turtleneck, black shoes. She even had the stretchy stocking cap. "How did you know I was in here?" she asked conversationally, as though she and I were friends and this was just some harmless practical joke.

"A ghost told me," I said.

"I don't believe in ghosts," she replied.

"There you go," I replied, backing down the hallway toward the living room. "I answered your question. You answer mine. How did you get into my apartment?"

"A man let me in," Heather replied.

My blood froze. I glanced at Nick, but he shook his head.

"What man, Heather?"

"Just a man," she said.

"Describe him."

"He was just a man," Heather insisted, as though put upon. "He said if I killed you, he wouldn't have to get his hands all bloody."

My stomach turned over.

Geoff?

Where would he have gotten a key to my apartment, assuming that was how he'd opened the door?

Actually, there were several disturbing possibilities. Bert, being my landlord, probably kept a set in the bar. Geoff could have stolen them—he might even have been the one to attack Sheila the night before. The building was old, and so were the locks. It was certainly conceivable that there was a skeleton key out there somewhere, or he could have used a burglar's tool of some sort, and Heather, obviously a few votes short of a majority, had mistaken it for a key.

I eased toward the telephone.

Russell crawled under the coffee table and whimpered.

Nick was right. He'd never make a watchdog.

Heather sat down on the couch, and I actually felt a flash of pity, because she seemed oddly limp and jangly at the same time. She still held the scissors in a white-knuckled grasp, though, so I gave her a wide berth.

"I'm so tired," she said.

"Poor baby," said Nick.

I ignored him and nipped into the kitchen. The tea kettle was boiling over, making a screaming sound, and I shoved it off the burner as I passed, headed for the phone.

"I have a prowler," I told the 911 operator. I was establishing a relationship with those people; pretty soon, I'd be able to call and say, "The usual."

I went back to the living room, still on the line with the dispatcher.

Heather was nowhere in sight, but Russell still cowered under the coffee table, and Nick stood with his arms folded.

"Behind the couch," he said.

I'd barely registered that when Heather suddenly sprang up from her hiding place, vaulted over the sofa back and came at me. She touched down once on top of the coffee table and flew through the air like some screeching hawk snagging a mouse.

I yelped and dropped the receiver, prepared to defend myself. Everything shifted into a weird cinematic sequence, slow-mo. The background music was the blood thudding in my ears.

Smaller than I was, Heather nonetheless had momentum going for her. She hit me like a locomotive, and both of us went down. I struck the floor so hard that the wind rushed out of my lungs, and I couldn't seem to take in even a shallow breath.

Heather straddled me.

We grappled. I made distracted plans to order *The Damn Fool's Guide to Physical Fitness,* since *Self-Defense for Women* didn't seem to be packing it.

She raised the scissors high; I saw light catch on the tips and tried to roll out of the way, but shock had turned every muscle in my body rigid. The brain gave orders, but the body didn't respond.

"Nick," I gasped out, *"do something!"*

The scissors began to descend.

I screamed.

Russell yowled.

And a blur of shrieking, hissing cat shot into my limited

range of vision like a white meteor plunging to earth. Chester landed on the back of Heather's neck, claws bared, fur standing out all over his body, eyes feral.

Heather screamed and flailed, dropping the scissors. Chester hung on, like some kind of feline demon.

I threw Heather off, rolled free, scrambled to my feet.

I could hear the 911 operator calling something from the discarded phone receiver.

"Chester," I rasped, when I caught my breath. "Sit."

"Sit?" Nick asked.

I picked the scissors up off the floor, threw them across the room, and pried my ghost cat off Heather's back.

Chester was bristly as a porcupine, and he still had a lot of fight left in him.

Heather, who had fallen to her knees under the attack, got to her feet and fled. I stroked Chester's back until he mellowed out. When I went to set him down, I saw that his coat was bloody.

I screamed.

Memories surged out of every dark closet, cupboard and cubbyhole in my mind. I must have passed out, or just put my brain on standby, and when I came to, Nick was gone. Chester was gone. And two cops were crouching on either side of my prone body, looking concerned.

Russell growled uncertainly from his post beneath the coffee table.

"Lie still, miss," the younger cop said. "You've been stabbed. There's an ambulance on the way."

Stabbed? I didn't remember being stabbed. I hadn't felt

anything, during the whole tussle with Heather, besides stark, undiluted fear.

"It was only a pair of nail scissors," I said, in what I thought was a sensible tone.

"Well, you're bleeding a lot," said the second cop.

"I'm not going to the hospital."

"Excuse me?" asked the first cop. I focused on his name tag. Rodriguez.

"I will not leave the dog," I said. "He's been traumatized."

Rodriguez and his partner exchanged looks.

"I mean it," I insisted, trying to sit up. I was woozy.

"We'll see," said Rodriguez, pushing me gently back down. "Just lie still."

The EMTs arrived.

I was examined, disinfected, bandaged and propped on the couch for questioning by Andy Crowley, who arrived late. I think he liked to make an entrance.

He spared me a concerned smile. "*Now* what?" he asked.

I filled him in, but grudgingly. I thought he could have been a little more sympathetic, given that the whole universe seemed to be out to get me.

"Have the nutcase picked up," he told Rodriguez and the partner. I'd tried to get a look at the other cop's name tag, but the light always blanked it out.

Twenty minutes later, Crowley took a call on his cell phone. Heather was in police custody.

I breathed a little easier, except now that I knew my stab wounds were *stab wounds,* I was hurting.

"You really ought to check in at the emergency room,"

Crowley said. "You probably need antibiotics, not to mention something for the pain."

I shook my head. "I'll be okay until tomorrow," I said, wondering if I would. I planned on heading for Sunset Villa at first light, with or without Greer and Jolie. I wanted to see for myself that Lillian was really on the mend. Stopping off at my HMO for a long stint in the waiting room and a handful of drug samples was not my primary objective.

It was the middle of the night when the cops trailed out, and by that time I was so tired I couldn't sleep.

Plus, I kept remembering what Heather had said, about a man letting her into my apartment and essentially telling her that if she killed me, she'd save *him* the trouble.

He wouldn't have to get his hands bloody.

I coaxed Russell out from under the coffee table with a piece of lunch meat, only a little curled on the edges, and took him downstairs for a poop tour of the parking lot. Back in the apartment, I wedged a chair under the knob on the outside door, double-checked that all the windows were locked and fired up my computer.

I did billings until just before sunrise, then made coffee.

While I was waiting for the machine to chug its way through the usual cycle, I took a shower with the curtain most of the way open, taking care not to get the bandages on my right shoulder wet. A little floor-swabbing after the fact seemed a small price to pay for a non-*Psycho* experience.

I found Chester lying across the foot of my bed. I'd searched the apartment for him after the police left the night before, but to no avail. He'd vanished, along with Nick.

The bloodstains on his coat had disappeared, but he looked less substantial somehow, and I knew he'd undergone some kind of severe energy drain, attacking Heather the way he had.

My heart ached, and tears were imminent.

Seeing me standing there in my after-shower underpants and T-shirt, complete with bandage-bulge, Chester lifted his head and gave a soft, almost apologetic meow.

I blinked a couple of times, trying to compose myself, and stretched out beside him on the mattress, shimmying as close as I could get. I stroked him lightly, and he purred, content.

"Cat Avenger," I said, with a sniffle. "That was some kind of last hurrah, wasn't it, pal?"

"Meow," Chester replied sadly, and butted my chin a couple of times with the top of his head.

My vision blurred. "God, Chester, I am going to miss you so much."

"It's not as if he's dying," Nick put in.

By then, I was so used to my ex's sudden appearances that I didn't even start. I saw him out of the corner of my eye, a watery image leaning against the dresser in front of the bedroom window. Sunlight rimmed his lean frame and cast his features into shadow.

"But he's going away," I murmured.

"Inevitable," Nick said, not unkindly but with a quiet matter-of-factness that I didn't even try to understand. I think a person would have to *be* dead to follow ghost logic, and I wasn't ready to empathize quite that much.

"Will I see him again, Nick?"

"I don't know, sweetheart."

I looked up at Nick. He could have taken the easy way out, said Chester would be waiting to wrap himself around my ankles when I croaked and stepped out of the tunnel, into the Light, and I wouldn't have known the difference. But he hadn't.

"Don't call me 'sweetheart,' you coward," I said. The fur at the back of Chester's neck was matted with my tears. "Chester saved me. You just stood there, like a big lump. Never send a man to do a cat's work."

Nick chuckled. "I told you about the maniac hiding behind your shower curtain," he pointed out. "Not that she could have killed you with those manicure scissors. I see you sustained a few puncture wounds, but that's probably as bad as it would have gotten."

Chester was beginning to fade. It was all I could do not to hold on with a death grip, crush his little body to me in the futile hope that he could stay.

It was all too much.

I sobbed.

Chester turned his head, nuzzled my cheek and blinked out. It was as if someone had flipped a switch. Cat here, cat gone.

Nick's hand rested lightly on my hair. "I'm a bastard," he said, "but I wish you'd cry like that for me when I take the last bow."

I sat up, rubbed my wet cheeks with a swiping motion of both hands. "Is that on the schedule?"

"Don't be so eager," Nick scolded, but he was smiling. "I'll be a long time gone."

"Listen to me," I said. "I need to get my life back to normal, and for a start that means no ghosts."

Nick rocked on his heels, hands caught behind his back. "In that case," he said, "your life will *never* get back to normal."

I stiffened. "What the hell do you mean by that?"

"I've told a few people about you. Back at the train station, I mean."

"You've told—"

"They need help, Moje." Nick actually looked as if he gave a rat's ass if anybody else was in trouble. Amazing.

"Why me?"

"Why *not* you?"

"I'm not psychic. I don't commonly see dead people—"

"Don't worry," Nick said. "You'll only have to deal with murder victims."

I was speechless.

No, really.

Nick reached out, cupped my chin, and gave it a hoist, ostensibly to close my dangling mouth.

He leaned down, kissed the top of my head lightly.

I finally found my voice again. "What did you do, write 'For a good time, call Mojo' on some celestial men's room wall?"

There was no answer, of course.

I had plenty of reasons to forgive Nick, I realized. I could think of three hundred and fifty thousand good ones, right off the top of my head. But if I forgave him, he would vanish forever, the way Chester had.

So what if he did? I asked myself. I was falling for Tucker Darroch, in a big way. Maybe I was even a little in love with him. He was a flesh-and-blood man. He could hold me, make love to me and, on top of all that, he cooked.

Nick, on the other hand, was a ghost, if not a hallucination. He morphed in at disconcerting times and had a way of getting on my very last twitching nerve.

I *wanted* him to disappear, once and for all.

Forever.

Didn't I?

CHAPTER

15

Sticking to the plan, I left for Sunset Villa at daybreak, with Russell riding shotgun. The puncture wounds in my shoulder ached, still stinging from the mouthwash I'd applied before replacing the EMT bandages with little round stick-ons. I was going to have to bite the proverbial bullet and check in with my HMO, since there might be some muscular damage, not to mention potential infection, but that was priority number 2. Number 1 was seeing Lillian.

I felt a little guilty about not calling Greer and Jolie before I left, or even in transit, but I rationalized that it was too early to call. My foster sisters were grown women, they had access to reliable transportation and they knew something big was going on with Lillian. Besides, if it had been up to me, we wouldn't have left her in the first place.

Hunger struck, midway down the 101, so Russell and I

took an exit, whipped through a drive-through and breakfasted on sausage biscuits, with cheese and eggs.

When we arrived at the nursing home, there was an ambulance parked in the side-bay, lights whirling, motor running, back doors open and waiting, like a giant mouth, to swallow somebody.

An instant and elemental panic seized me.

I buzzed a window partway down for Russell's breathing convenience, slopped a bottle of water into the bowl I'd brought along for the purpose, locked the Volvo and bolted for the main entrance.

I'm not psychic, regular ghost interactions and slot machine mojo aside, but somehow I knew the bell was tolling, and it tolled for Lillian.

I ran past the reception desk and along the corridor, repeating a frantic litany under my breath.

No, no, please, no…

Every nurse in the place must have been in Lillian's room, along with two EMTs who'd arrived with the ambulance. The stillness was terrible; nobody was moving. It was an underwater scene, everything blurred.

My cry was like a stone, shattering fragile glass.

"Lillian!"

I rushed toward her bed, where she lay with her eyes closed, mummylike, ready to crumble at the slightest touch. Rotika, looking some the worse for wear, caught me in a two-arm body hold.

"She's gone," she said.

I struggled, but I was no match for Rotika. *"No!"* I screamed.

"I'm sorry," Rotika said, without slackening her grip. The woman could have been a bouncer at Bad-Ass Bert's, she was that strong.

The room came into sharp focus, with an abruptness that made me queasy. The colors were brighter, the lines knife sharp. One of the EMTs was still holding a pair of defibulator paddles. He set them back in their holders with a sigh of resignation.

Rotika shuffled me out of the room. I didn't struggle; by then, I was counting on her to hold me up. All the starch had gone out of my knees, and my backbone had melted like beeswax left in the Arizona sun.

She sat me down in the same chair Fred had pressed me into the night before. "You gotta stop breathin' so shallow and so quick," she said. "You'll hyperventilate."

I nodded.

About that time, Felicia came in through the main door, carrying a brown-bag lunch in one hand and wearing a glare of indignation, along with pink-and-white striped scrubs that made her look like a neon zebra. "Somebody done left a dog locked in a car out there in the parking lot. That's inhumane, and I'm callin' the cops."

It's strange, the things people think and say when they've just lost a loved one. "Please," I whispered, "don't have Russell arrested."

"Bring the dog inside," Rotika said quietly to Felicia. Her big hand landed lightly on my shoulder. "You give Felicia the keys to your car now, honey. We'll look after your pet until you pull yourself together."

I managed to find the keys and hand them over to Felicia, whose eyes had gone big and round. "That ambulance—" She stretched the word out, into three distinct syllables. *Am-bu-lance*. "Don't tell me it's Mrs. Travers they've come to fetch. Not when she was doin' so good."

Rotika didn't say a word, and neither did I. We watched as the realization that she'd been right dawned in Felicia's face. She fumbled, took a firmer grip on the keys and rushed back out to collect Russell.

"I'm so sorry," Rotika told me.

"What happened?" I asked miserably. One of the EMTs must have slipped out the side door; he returned shortly pushing a gurney. A body bag lay folded on top. Out of the corner of my eye, I saw Felicia bring Russell through the front door and shut him up in a room.

He yowled in protest.

Rotika gave a heavy sigh as she dropped into the chair next to mine. "I don't *know* what happened," she said wearily. "The rotation nurse came in to make rounds, maybe an hour ago. Everything was all right then. He left, and the next thing I knew, Mrs. Travers's heart monitor took to beeping like crazy. I called for an ambulance—that's in the policy manual—and I tried to help her. I really tried."

Even through the fog of grief, the word 'he' struck me like a bus. Knocked the breath out of me.

My intuition screamed *Geoff*.

"What was his name? Is he still here?"

"I don't know his name," Rotika said, hoisting herself to her feet. By that time, the other nursing home employees had trailed out of Lillian's room. "We get whoever the health department sends over, and he came and went, like they all do. Must have signed in and out, though. You gotta sign in and out. That's the rule."

I got to my feet. "I want to see the record—*now*."

"I can't just go showin' you records," Rotika told me patiently. "It wouldn't be ethical."

Geoff, my brain chugged along the same track, faster and faster. *Geoff, Geoff, Geoff!*

"Murder isn't ethical either," I argued, headed for the nurses' station. I'd watched *ER*. I knew sign-in sheets were kept on clipboards, and the clipboards were either on or behind the desk.

"You stop," Rotika said, with firm hopelessness.

I found the clipboard, scanned the entries.

Geoff hadn't signed his real name, of course, or even the alias, Steve Roberts. I wouldn't have recognized his handwriting, after all those years, but the line might as well have been written in blood, the way it stood out from the other entries. He'd scrawled, *U.R. Dead,* on the signature line, and drawn a tiny smiley face after it.

I clutched the clipboard to my chest.

Rotika tried to wrest it away.

The EMTs rolled Lillian's body out of her room, zipped up in that black vinyl bag I'd seen earlier.

Everything stopped again, with a lurch, as surely as if the

hand of God had reached out and grabbed the planet in a death grip.

I collapsed.

The clipboard clattered to the floor.

The EMTs left Lillian and rushed to me, kneeling on either side, the way Rodriguez and his partner had done the night before, after Heather stabbed me with the manicure scissors.

"Shock," one of them said.

"Call—the—police—" I pleaded.

I heard the front doors whoosh open, and for a crazy, disconnected moment, I thought the gurney had rolled outside on its own.

Then I saw Jolie's face peering down at me, over the shoulders of the crouching paramedics, shining with tears.

"Lillian?" she said.

I nodded, tried to sit up. Failed.

"Take it easy," one of the EMTs said, taking my pulse, while his partner pressed a stethoscope to my chest.

"It was murder, Jolie," I said. "They're going to say it was natural causes, but *it was murder*—"

A blood pressure cuff squeezed my upper arm.

"Through the roof," one EMT told the other.

"Let me up!" I protested.

"Take her to the emergency room," Jolie said.

"No!" I choked out.

"I'm her sister," Jolie insisted, "and I want her checked over."

Everyone looked up at her in disbelief. My mind took a

bumpy little side road, bouncing over the ruts. I wondered where Greer was.

"You're black," Rotika told Jolie.

"Yes," Jolie said tartly. "I know." She swept everybody up in a fierce glance, including me. *My sister needs medical attention.*

That was how Lillian and I ended up sharing an ambulance ride.

I learned later that Jolie and Greer followed, with Russell in the back of Jolie's rig.

In the E.R., I was examined and sedated, and when I woke up, hours later, I found myself in a hospital room, hooked up to an IV and a couple of monitors.

At first, I didn't remember that Lillian was gone, and Geoff had killed her.

When I did, I let out a howl and tried to pull out the IV needle, so I could go after him. So I could tell somebody, anybody, what had happened.

A nurse rushed in and knocked me out again with some mega-drug, sent me spiraling into a twilight world where my eyes wouldn't focus.

I saw Jolie and Greer leaning over me.

Then I saw Lillian.

The pharmaceutical miracle sucked me under again, and I flailed my way back to the surface.

It was dark in the room.

A shadow moved beside my bed, and I felt a cold rush of fear.

"Shhh, little sister," Geoff said, smiling down at me, fiddling with the IV bag suspended above my head. "It'll be over soon."

I shrieked and jerked the needle out of my arm, scrambled out of bed, trying to escape. Was it a nightmare?

Please, God, let it be a bad dream!

I heard running feet, felt Geoff rush past me, like an icy breeze.

Arms gathered me up, held me tightly.

Tucker.

I knew his scent, knew the feel of him, the hard substance of his chest.

Words spilled out of my mouth in a frantic rush, and I clung to him. "Tucker—it was Geoff—he killed Lillian—he was here—"

"Shhh," Tucker said.

"The bag," I said. "He put—something in the IV bag—"

"Stay back," I heard Tucker say. I saw no one, but I was aware of others crowding the room. Lights went on, dazzling me to a temporary blindness, and I felt myself rising in his arms.

"The IV bag," I pleaded. Geoff might still be in the room, innocuous in his hospital garb, waiting for his chance to finish me off. "Don't let them—"

"It's okay, Moje," Tucker told me. "Nobody's going to hook you up to anything."

Great, shuddering sobs rolled up inside me, tore their way out of my throat. I clawed at Tucker's arms and shoulders—anywhere I could get a grip—as he laid me on the bed.

"He killed her—he killed Lillian—"

"Babe," Tucker said. "I'm here. Everything's all right. Nobody's going to hurt you."

I believed him.

I gave in to the darkness rising up around me, and when I woke up, the room was full of light so bright that, for a second, I thought I'd died after all.

Then I saw Tucker grinning down at me. He needed a shave.

"Russell," I said, remembering.

"He's at Allison's," Tucker told me. "Safe and sound."

"How did he get...?" Once again, I tried to sit up.

Tucker held me gently but firmly to the pillows. "Bethany came and picked him up, after Jolie called the clinic to make arrangements. He's all right, Moje. The question is, are *you* all right?"

"No," I said. I was sure of that much, at least. "Lillian—"

He smoothed my hair. "I know," he said. "I'm sorry."

"It was murder, Tuck."

"The report says natural causes," Tucker told me carefully.

"Look at the sign-in sheet, at Sunset Villa—Geoff was there—he wrote—"

"Easy," Tucker said.

I settled back, tried to breathe normally. Tried to get a grip. I wanted to stay conscious. I was also desperate to convince Tucker to get hold of the paperwork from the nursing home.

Tucker ran the backs of his fingers down my cheek. Somehow, that centered me.

"How did you know I was here?" I asked, after what seemed like a very long time.

"Scanner," he said. "I'm a cop, remember?"

"Jolie and Greer?"

He smiled. "In the cafeteria, swilling bad coffee. They're quite a pair, your sisters. Made me show a badge, and Jolie called in the number for verification."

I strained for a smile, though I couldn't quite reach.

"Did I dream it? That Geoff was in my room last night? That he tampered with my IV bag?"

Tucker's eyes never left mine. "I don't know, babe," he said. "The bag's been taken to the lab, so we'll find out soon enough."

"What lab? Tucker, if it's here in this hospital, he could have access—"

"Phoenix PD has it," Tucker insisted quietly.

"I need to get out of here. Lillian—"

"One thing at a time, Moje," Tucker broke in. "Your sisters are taking care of the funeral arrangements. Allison's got the dog. And for the time being, I'm in charge of Project Mojo. When they let you out of here, you're coming to my place."

"Tuck, he's a nurse. He'll try—"

"Listen, Moje, I can't put an APB out on the guy for showing up in a nightmare. What I *can* do is make sure you're protected—from yourself, if necessary. Meanwhile, the official wheels are turning, and you're going to have to be patient."

I began to get my bearings. "You must have things to do. You were on an assignment…"

"I'm off the assignment." He grinned fetchingly. "In fact, I'm unemployed. Will that change our relationship?"

"We don't *have* a relationship." I paused, sifting through a lot of mental sludge. "Do we?"

"I'm not sure," Tucker said. "But we're going to find out."

I WAS RELEASED from the hospital at four that afternoon.

Greer wanted me to stay at her house, and I refused. The last thing I wanted was to be under the same roof with Alex Pennington, especially in a vulnerable state. I couldn't face going back to the apartment, either, at least not until I was myself again. Too much had happened there, both downstairs and up.

I didn't want Nick to be there.

I didn't want Nick *not* to be there.

It was a lose-lose situation.

Tucker's place was a rented condo in north Scottsdale. Bethany met us there, with Russell, and immediately went out again, for groceries, with Tucker's list and a wad of bills in hand.

"Sorry about the mess," Tucker said, gathering scattered newspapers, empty chip bags and a few stray socks as he spoke. His furniture was worse than mine, and that's saying something.

I was settled on the couch, numb with sorrow over Lillian. Underneath that was an urgent, revving sensation. I needed to find Geoff before he found me.

A little of the fog cleared. "Is Bert really in Witness Protection?" I asked. "And how's Sheila?"

Tucker stopped moving, studied me intently for a long

moment. I knew he was wondering how much more I could take, and I braced myself.

"Officially," he said, finally, "Bert is dead. Sheila's with him."

"They're *dead?*"

"Officially," Tucker reiterated.

I hoped that meant not-dead. As in, new identities, in new places. I also knew Tucker was never going to tell me the straight-up truth. He couldn't, unless—

Unless.

"You quit your job?" I asked carefully. Russell climbed up onto the couch and stretched out beside me, resting his big head on my ankles. "You said you were unemployed—"

"Yes," Tucker said, standing very still. "The custody thing."

"Right," I agreed. "So if you're not a cop anymore, you could tell me the truth about Bert and Sheila."

"I told you all I could, Moje. Leave it at that, okay?"

I sighed, stroking Russell's head. Missing Lillian. Missing Chester. Missing the parents I barely remembered. There were so many empty places in my life where loved ones should have been.

"Okay," I said, and noticed that Tucker's gaze was resting somberly on Russell.

I tensed. "What?"

"Dogs can be in Witness Protection," Tucker said.

I felt a mingling of hope and sorrow. Hope because in cop-lingo, "officially dead" doesn't always mean "*really* dead," sorrow because Russell was probably going away.

"Soon?" I asked, and the word came out squeaky-hoarse.

"Yeah," Tucker said. He leaned down, kissed the top of my head, and vanished into the kitchen.

I ruffled Russell's ears. "I'm happy for you, bud," I told him, "but you're going to leave a big hole when you go."

Tucker was banging around, probably making tea. There was a certain comfort in his knowing what I needed when things got stressful.

Besides that.

"So I think I could make a place for you in Sheepshanks, Sheepshanks and Sheepshanks," I said, when Tucker came back with a steaming mug of tea and set it on the ugly coffee table in front of me.

"So long as I don't have to change my name," Tucker replied, with a slight grin. "Are there benefits? Health insurance? Paid vacation? 401K? Double-time for holidays?"

"Get real," I said.

"Half the profits?"

"I offered you a job, not a partnership."

"Yeah, but you didn't mention a wage."

"Half of whatever business you bring in."

"Gee, Moje, what a deal."

"Take it or leave it."

He grinned again, but he looked tired as he sank into a recliner patched here and there with ragged scraps of duct tape. "Can't we call the company Sheepshanks and Darroch?"

"That would make you a partner."

"Well, hell, at least I'm real, which is more than I can say for the other two Sheepshankses."

I straightened my back, which made my scissors wounds hurt again. "Take it or leave it," I repeated.

"You drive a hard bargain."

"So do you," I said, very softly. With all that had been going on, I could have used a little distraction.

It wasn't to be.

Bethany chose that moment to come back with the groceries. She said a few muffled words to Tucker, patted Russell on the head and departed.

Tucker made grilled cheese sandwiches and stood over me until I took my pills, one for pain, one an antibiotic.

I fell asleep on the couch, and when I woke up, it was dark in the room, and someone was pushing at my left shoulder. I thought I was back in the hospital, with Geoff looming over me, and came up swinging.

Tucker caught my wrists together. "Moje," he said. *"It's me."*

I blinked, looked around. Something was different.

Off, somehow.

Well, *yeah.* There were two Tommy Lee Jones types standing in the middle of the room, men-in-black. Their eyes didn't flicker, their haircuts were military and their jaws might have been chiseled from bedrock. Between them, they couldn't have come up with any part of a sense of humor.

I was terrified, for Tucker, for myself.

"Moje," Tucker reasoned. "They're feds."

"Russell—" I groped frantically for the dog, but he was gone. My stomach went into a freefall. "Tucker, *where's Russell?*"

"Come with me," Tucker said, helping me to my feet.

The men-in-black didn't move or react.

Tucker led me into the kitchen.

Bert was kneeling on the floor, jostling Russell's ears while the dog licked his face in a whole-body effort.

"Bert," I whispered.

He smiled. "Thanks for taking care of the mutt, Moje," he said.

My eyes burned, and my throat closed tight.

Tucker helped Bert to his feet—he was still awkward from the stabbing and there were bruises on his face—and the feds wafted in from the living room. The inside door leading to Tucker's garage stood open.

"I left you Bad-Ass Bert's in my will," Bert told me. He pushed up one sleeve of his sweatshirt. "Look. No tattoos."

Sure enough, the road map was gone. The skin looked inflamed, as though the body-art had been scrubbed away with a wire brush, but nothing remained of Route 66.

It made me feel sad.

"What am I going to do with a biker bar?" I asked. Okay, it was a stupid question, and a little insensitive, but the circumstances weren't exactly normal.

Bert grinned. "You can sell it," he said. "You can burn it to the ground. You can run it and make a decent living. It doesn't matter to me, because I'm going to be in—" His gaze flicked to the agents, and back to my face again. "Another place," he finished.

"Why me? You must have someone—"

"You'll do fine," he said, and touched the tip of my nose with an index finger.

I blinked hard and kissed his cheek. Squinted at the even little rows of hair sprouting on his previously shaved head. Another of the wonders of the federal witness protection program, I guessed. Shaved head today, flowing tresses tomorrow.

"Goodbye, Bert," I said. I couldn't even look at Russell, because some goodbyes are just too hard to say.

Bert nodded.

One of the agents hooked a leash onto Russell's collar. Handed it to Bert.

"I guess we're leaving now," Bert said.

I watched as Bert, Russell and the two feds went out through the garage door. Russell didn't even look back, which both stung and made me feel like whooping for joy.

I turned into Tucker's arms.

He held me.

"It'll be okay, Moje," he said.

I would have loved to believe him.

CHAPTER

16

It seemed ironic to bury Lillian in the cemetery at Cactus Bend. After all, she'd fled the place, nearly a quarter of a century before, and steered clear of it ever since. Now, a week after her death, by the terms of her own will, she was back to stay.

Jolie, Greer and I stood together, in our tasteful black dresses, surrounded by people who remembered Lillian as the woman who snatched little Mary Josephine Mayhugh, and subsequently eluded the police, the FBI and watchful citizens all over the United States, for more than twenty years.

Senator Larimer attended the simple graveside memorial, as did his wife, Barbara, once again enthroned on her wheelchair, with Joseph standing protectively behind her, clasping the handles in a white-knuckled grip.

A warm breeze whispered in the cottonwood trees.

I was moving in a bubble composed of shock and grief,

but some awareness began to leak through. I felt people's eyes on me; word had obviously gotten around—thanks, no doubt, to Boomer and a few others—that I was Mary Jo Mayhugh, daughter of Ron and Evie, all grown up. I felt their unspoken but still intrusive questions, too, like thrusting elbows in a crowd.

I wanted to escape, fly away, forget there was ever such a place as Cactus Bend, Arizona, and feel my way through the rest of my life.

I would piece it together, bit by bit, task by task. Move out of Tucker's place, where I'd been staying for the last week. Dig up dirt on Alex Pennington. Help Jolie with the move from Tucson to the little brick house she'd rented in Phoenix. Decide what to do with Bad-Ass Bert's Biker Saloon.

I hadn't been back to my apartment at all since the day I was released from the hospital; early on, Jolie and Tucker had picked up some of my clothes. Tucker's condo had been a refuge, and he'd done all he could to make me feel welcome—but being there was like wearing unmatched shoes, neither one fitting. I'd checked my voice-mail messages periodically, nervously expectant.

There were no more death threats.

Just one call—from Brian Dillard, Heather's former husband. She was in the hospital, under psychiatric observation, with an arraignment pending, he'd said sheepishly, and the kids were with his mother. Somehow, he'd saved the ticket for the slot machine credits I'd left behind at the casino, the night Geoff scared me off, and I could pick it up any time.

It wasn't high on my priority list.

I shifted my attention back to the sad matter at hand.

Lillian's coffin gleamed in the sunlight. Greer, Jolie and I each laid a white rose on top and whispered our goodbyes. The funeral home people would lower her into the ground later, I presumed, to spare our sensibilities.

I wanted to fling myself on that casket, like some frenzied gothic heroine, but I was afraid someone would sedate me if I did. I was in enough of a stupor without medical intervention to make it worse.

So I waited it out, standing there in the dress Greer had scrounged from the back of her closet, my eyes so dry they hurt, my throat pulled into such a raw knot that, once or twice, I thought I tasted blood.

Clive Larimer approached as my sisters and I were making our way back to the mortuary's limousine.

"Barbara and I are having a few people in," my uncle said quietly. "We were hoping the three of you would join us."

I stared at the senator, unsure how I felt. It seemed an odd time for an invitation.

"Now?" I asked.

Greer nudged me. Her eyes were red-rimmed from crying, but she wasn't too stricken to overlook a social opportunity. This was her chance to add a state senator and his very prominent wife to the guest list for her next party. Not to be missed.

"How kind," she said. "Of course we'll come."

I planted my feet. Barbara had zipped up alongside her husband, in the motorized chair, with Joseph keeping a proprietary watch. I looked at her, then Joseph, then the senator.

They'd attended the services to show support for me, I supposed, but it seemed to me that an after-funeral party for a woman they'd seen as a kidnapper was a little over the top. If Lillian had been caught at any point during the runaway years, the Larimers probably would have lobbied for life in prison.

The question I wanted to ask, but couldn't find the words for, must have shown clearly in my face.

My uncle cleared his throat diplomatically and spoke in a low voice. "The press is waiting to close in," he told me. "Do you feel like dealing with them? They'll have a million questions, all of them pretty personal."

I looked around. Sure enough, there were people with microphones and cameras among the blatant gossips and curiosity seekers. Some members of the fourth estate were already interviewing the locals who'd attended the service, but I knew Clive was right. They were ready to pounce. And they wouldn't stop with inquiries into my years on the run with Lillian. They'd want to know about the murders, too.

About the blood, and the fear.

How did it feel, hiding in a clothes dryer, after witnessing a double homicide?

"No," I said, with a slow, dazed shake of my head. *"No."*

My uncle took my arm. Several of his aides materialized out of the crowd and walked in casual but practiced formation around us until we reached the limo. Joseph leaned in on the front passenger side, spoke quietly to the driver.

Clive, meanwhile, held the back door for us.

Greer blushed prettily, fetching even in a whiter shade of pale, and slid in. Jolie followed, though not so readily. I stood warily before the opening.

"You would have sent her to prison," I said, looking up into Clive's face. "Back then, I mean. When she took me."

"Yes," he answered.

For a moment, we just stared at each other, in measuring silence.

Then I got into the car.

A few minutes later, we glided into the driveway at the Larimers' place, the press effectively stopped at the heavy steel gates behind us.

Peculiar, I thought, that I hadn't even noticed those gates on my previous visit. They must have been open before. Now, they made the estate seem as impenetrable as a fortress with the drawbridge up.

I felt a paradoxical combination of claustrophobia and relief, like a baby struggling to be born, then summarily sucked back up into the womb by some incomprehensible force.

"Nice place," Greer said, in a reverent whisper. Up ahead, the Larimers, chauffeured by the ever-present Joseph, got out of a black Jag. Joseph hurried to open the trunk, where Barbara's wheelchair was stowed, but she shook her head and entered the house on her husband's arm. "Just think," Greer said. "If Lillian hadn't abducted you, you might have grown up here."

A surge of defensiveness seared its way along every vein, like the unseen impact of a blast. Before I could speak, though, Jolie squeezed my hand.

"Let's get this over with," she said.

The driver opened the door on my side, and I got out.

Rested one hand on the roof of the limo to steady myself a little. Joseph sprinted down to the gates, and they swung open to admit another car.

Barbara and I are having a few people in, my uncle had said, back at the cemetery. I wondered who they were, these "few people," but in the final analysis, I didn't really care. As long as they didn't ask any questions, we'd get along fine.

The gathering was held on the large patio behind the main house. In daylight, the Larimer swimming hole looked roughly the size of the reflecting pool at the base of the Washington Monument. A variety of cold cuts, crackers and cheeses had been set out on a long table set in the shade of the extended roof.

I was suddenly starved. At the same time, I knew if I tried to swallow so much as a nibble, my throat would clamp shut or I would retch.

I waited for a cue from Senator Larimer, but it was Joseph who came to my side.

"Good thing they didn't put out the heirloom silver," I told him, sotto voce, indicating the elegantly casual picnic spread. "Plastic flatware is a lot less risky, with me around."

"Truce," he said, with the semblance of a smile. "Can I get you something?"

I wasn't ready to sign a peace treaty and, anyway, anger felt a smidgeon better than the incessant, throbbing sorrow of losing Lillian. "Cyanide?" I suggested. A wild thought landed, and I examined him narrowly. "Or maybe chow mein with a dash of rat poisoning for flavor?"

Either Joseph was genuinely puzzled, or he had a SAG card tucked away somewhere. "Maybe you should sit down," he said, frowning. "You're really not making much sense."

Barbara passed by, elegant in the kind of black knit suit they sell out of vaults, greeting perhaps a dozen guests. I didn't recognize any of them, but that didn't mean anything. I was used to strangers; I saw one looking back at me out of the mirror every morning.

"She must be having one of her good days," I said, of the splendid Mrs. Larimer.

Joseph thrust out a sigh. He didn't like me, I didn't like him. But, of the two of us, he was the one trying to be polite. "Most likely," he said, "she'll overdo it and take to her bed for a week."

Barbara looked strong to me, even confident. She was in her element, playing the hostess, and I felt a faint flicker of resentment. A fragmented memory flashed at the back of my mind, and for a millisecond, I knew I was seeing Barbara through my mother's eyes.

I felt the faintest echo of envy.

Barbara worked her way around to me. The good political wife. Her china-blue eyes were clear as she looked steadily into my face.

"Perhaps you and your…sisters…would like to spend the night in the guesthouse," she said. "Avoid the press a little longer."

Something jammed up inside me at the brief hesitation before the word "sisters." My mother's helpless jealousy of this woman, I supposed—the contrast between Barbara Larimer's life and hers must have been hard to take—along with an emotion singularly my own, though I couldn't quite identify it.

"Thank you," I said. "But we all have things we need to do back home."

Jolie was in the process of moving. She was eager to be reunited with Sweetie and start her new job.

Greer was walking on eggshells with Alex, either waiting for the marriage to collapse or still hoping against hope that it wouldn't really happen.

And I was going back to an empty apartment, over the biker bar I had just inherited. I'd been at Tucker's long enough, and even though we'd had some serious medicinal sex, I'd merely been marking time. I was ready to get off the treadmill and face up to the rest of my life.

For a moment, Barbara looked as though she might say something more, try to persuade me to stay after all. In the end, though, she simply nodded, exchanged glances with Joseph and walked away.

I scanned the small, quiet crowd. Greer was hobnobbing with Clive and a well-dressed couple, a glass of champagne in hand. She looked elegant and fragile, and even though I knew her mourning was real, I also knew she was deliberately using it to grease the social wheels.

I definitely loved my sister, but there were times when I didn't like her much, and that was one of them. Jolie appeared at my side. "We're only putting off the inevitable, you know," she said. "The reporters will follow us back to the mortuary when we go to pick up my car. If they can't get answers there, they'll probably follow us all the way home."

I nodded, swallowed. "I know," I said. "I just wanted a few minutes to get a grip. Maybe I should go ahead and talk to them. Get it over with."

Jolie touched my arm. "Not now, Moje," she counseled. "You're not ready for that. Anyway, what would you say? There's so much you don't remember."

Some part of my brain had been closed for business for twenty-three years, and yet there *was* a stirring. At Tucker's, on two different nights, I'd dreamed, the images so vivid, so in-my-face, that forgetting them should have been impossible, waking or sleeping. Both times I'd rocketed into half-consciousness, trembling and drenched in cold sweat, only to find that the memories had submerged themselves again.

Tucker had held me, but I had been afraid to close my eyes.

"God, Moje," Jolie whispered, "what *is* it? You look as though you're going to pass out again."

I felt a prickly sensation on the back of my neck, automatically turned my head and caught Barbara Larimer staring at me. I looked at Jolie again. "I'm *not* some fragile flower," I told my sister tersely, "and I'm getting really tired of everybody watching me as though I might come unwrapped at any moment!"

"Time to go," Jolie said, almost singing the words under her breath. "I know you're tough, Moje, but you're only human, and your life has been a horror show lately. I'll snag Greer and convey our thanks to the Larimers, then we're leaving."

"Okay," I said. I'd used up all my firepower protesting the

current and obviously widespread perception that I was on the verge of emotional collapse, and now I was practically in crawl mode again. I almost smiled at the irony.

When Jolie returned, she had Greer in tow, and Uncle Clive came along with them. He'd removed his suit coat and rolled up his sleeves. It was warm, but he might have been trying to look like a man of the people, too. When I'm faced with a choice between suspicion and benefit-of-the-doubt, I usually go with suspicion.

"Is this wise?" he asked. "Leaving now, I mean?"

I didn't care if it was wise or not. I just wanted to be home, so I could cry and miss Lillian, and if that meant running a gauntlet of barking newshounds, that was what I would do. The point was to get from here to there.

I repeated my things-to-do speech.

Clive listened, nodded and leaned down to kiss my cheek. "Barbara and I want you to consider this your home," he said. "Say the word any time you need a place to come to, and we'll welcome you with open arms."

I nodded.

Jolie, a reluctant Greer and I all got into the mortuary limo again. The gates whispered open at the bottom of the drive-way, and three vans and a couple of cars, parked alongside the road, pulled out behind us.

"Good Lord," Greer said, practically kneeling on the seat to stare out the tinted rear window. "One of those vans is from CNN!"

I ignored her.

"Greer," Jolie said.

Greer sagged in the plush seat, kicked off her shoes and sighed.

We reached the mortuary and piled into Jolie's Pathfinder before the vans could come to a full stop. One reporter actually ran to my side of the car and tapped on the window with a microphone. Jolie nearly ran over his toes, backing out of visitors' parking.

The caravan followed us all the way to Greer's place just outside Scottsdale, and hemmed us in from behind.

I was trapped between the reporters and Alex, who came out of the house to glare holes into me from beneath the portico.

I chose the reporters.

"Miss Mayhugh," one of the women cried, leaping out of a van and rushing me like a quarterback. "May I call you Mary Jo?"

"My name," I said, "is Mojo Sheepshanks."

"You mean, that's your *assumed* name."

I wasn't going to argue.

"Mojo," a man asked, pushing past the woman who wanted to call me Mary Jo. "What is your relationship to Senator Larimer?"

"He's my uncle," I said.

"Mary Jo," the woman persisted, elbowing to stay at the front of the pack, now that the slower ones were catching up.

I didn't speak.

The CNN crew spoke up next. They had the cameras rolling, and I shielded my eyes from the brightness of the sun and their portable lights. "Ms. Sheepshanks," the lead reporter began, "tell us what it was like to be on the run all those years. Were you afraid? Did you ever try to escape? Did Ms.…Travers abuse you in any way?"

"No one abused me," I said.

Had I been scared? Hell, yes. But not of Lillian.

"You were a witness to your parents' brutal homicides, weren't you?" someone else inquired.

"I was," I answered, "but I don't remember what happened."

"Are you aware that there is some speculation that *you* might have been the one to fire the fatal shots?"

Acid stung the back of my throat.

"She was five years old, you ninny," Jolie put in, all but pushing up her sleeves in preparation for a fight. "How could she have killed anyone? Even if she'd gotten hold of a gun, she wouldn't have known how to fire it!"

"My half brother, Geoff Waters, confessed to the murders and spent time in a correction facility in California," I said carefully. I hoped I sounded calm; inside, I was churning like an off balance washing machine on spin.

"You don't remember *anything*?" The young male reporter who asked that question looked so disappointed that I was tempted to make something up. Maybe this was his first job, and getting information out of me could put him on the map.

"I recall hiding in the dryer," I said, instead. "My clothes were covered with blood. That's about it, except—" I paused. Everyone waited expectantly, including Jolie and Greer. "Except that sometimes I feel as though I'm on the verge of remembering."

Alex had apparently had enough of the paparazzi. He came striding down the driveway, still handsome, with his gym-fit physique and full head of steel-gray hair. His eyes were Mel Gibson-blue, and they practically took the skin off me.

"This," he said, taking a possessive hold on Greer's arm, "is private property. Harass Ms. Sheepshanks all you like, but get out of here before I have you removed!"

"Dude," said the young reporter.

"Who are you?" asked a woman on the CNN crew.

"My name is Dr. Alexander Pennington, and *you are trespassing*. Clear out!"

Greer looked up at her husband in alarm, but she didn't try to pull free of his grasp, and that bothered me. It looked as though he was squeezing her arm hard enough to leave bruises.

I took a step toward him.

"Can you comment on Ms. Sheepshanks's case, Dr. Pennington?" asked some intrepid soul.

Alex's gaze sliced to me, and it was so viciously angry that I stopped, between one step and the next, as abruptly as if I'd just run into an invisible wall.

"Yes," Alex spat. "She's a liar and a cheat. I wouldn't be surprised if she'd gunned her parents down and blamed her brother!"

"*Alex*," Greer whispered.

He released her with such force that she almost fell. Stormed back up the driveway, got into his Mercedes and roared toward us at top speed. Everyone scrambled to get out of the way.

The reporters recovered first.

They thrust cards at me, from every direction.

"Call if you remember anything."

"We'd like an exclusive."

I didn't take the cards, but Jolie did. She shoved them into the side flap on my purse.

"Please go," Greer said, watching as Alex's Mercedes raced along the road below, practically fishtailing on the dry pavement. I think she was talking to the reporters, but she might have meant all of us.

"Stay here with Greer and me," Jolie pleaded, catching hold of my hand.

"Not a chance," I said. "I need a ride back to Tucker's place, so I can pick up my car. Then I'm going home to the apartment."

"You shouldn't be alone," Jolie protested, but I could see in her eyes that she knew I wouldn't give in.

Greer, a beat or two behind, nodded agreement with what Jolie had said. She looked shaken and gray.

"I *need* to be alone," I said.

Greer turned, without a word, and trudged slowly toward the house. Jolie got into the Pathfinder, fired up the engine and waited, her face set.

"Did you see the way Alex grabbed Greer's arm?" I asked, when I was buckled in on the passenger side. "Jolie, do you think...?"

"I don't know what to think," Jolie said. "About *either* of you."

That was pretty much the extent of our conversation.

She took me to Tucker's place, and came in with me while I gathered up my stuff.

"Hey," she said, looking around, "where's the dog?"

I bit my lower lip. "Some relative of Bert's claimed him," I answered. I didn't like lying to her, but I couldn't put Bert and Sheila at risk by telling her what I knew, either. Jolie wasn't a gossip, but people can't accidentally reveal things they don't know.

"You really liked him, though," Jolie murmured sympathetically.

"I really liked him," I agreed.

"If you won't go to Greer's with me, then I'll come and stay at your place." She shuddered. "Spooky hotbed of crime that it is."

I shook my head, went into the kitchen. "I meant it when I said I needed some alone-time," I told her. There was a dry-erase board hanging on the front of the fridge, and I smiled a little at the lone notation scrawled across the top. *Daisy's dance recital, Friday, 7:00.*

Uncorking the marker dangling from the board by a string, I added, *Gone home. Thanks for everything. Mojo.*

"You're nuts not to stay here," Jolie said. "Tucker's a cop. He can protect you."

"He's not around," I retorted, "and I can protect myself."

"Oh, right. Says what *Damn Fool's Guide?*"

I backtracked to the front door, picked up my garbage-bag weekender and stepped outside. Jolie had no choice but to follow, and she stood glowering while I locked up.

"You won't change your mind?" she urged, sounding as anxious as she looked.

"I won't change my mind," I confirmed.

We parted on the street; she got into her Pathfinder, and I got into my Volvo.

I stopped for groceries, since I planned on holing up for a while, but within an hour of leaving Tucker's, I pulled into the lot at Bert's and sat there, looking at my inheritance. Rusted-out beer signs adorned the weathered wood walls, and the air conditioner perched on the roof looked like it might fall straight through my place and land on one of the pool tables in the bar.

I got out of the car, gathered my groceries and tramped up the outside stairs.

"Nick?" I called, as I entered.

My voice echoed back to me, hollow-sounding.

I decided to scope the place out before I put the chain on and turned the dead bolt, and before I did that, I needed to put my purchases away, since some of them were frozen. Once the foodstuffs were safe in the cupboards, fridge and freezer, I did a quick but thorough search.

I looked in the back of the closet, under the bed and, heart hammering, behind the shower curtain.

I was well and truly alone.

All clear on the maniac front.

I made coffee, grabbed the phone and sat down at the table to check for voice mail.

Alex had called to say he was going to sue me for harassment if I didn't stop prying into his affairs. I thought that was an interesting choice of words, since his *affairs* were precisely the point.

Two other doctors—both friends of Alex's, of course—called to say my coding and billing services were no longer required.

Good thing I was going into the P.I. business.

The last call made me sit up and take notice.

"Mojo, this is Allison Darroch. I'm calling because there's something I think you need to know about Tucker. He's not a cop."

Was she drunk?

"Ask him what he *really* does for a living," Allison finished. A long pause followed, then she said, "Oh, *hell*. I can't believe I'm doing this. Forget it. Forget I ever made this stupid call. I'm—I'm sorry."

Click.

I sat staring at the receiver.

He's not a cop.

Ask him what he really does for a living.

"Well, I'd love to, Allison," I said out loud.

I played through her message again and pressed 88 at the end, for a call back.

"Dr. Darroch," Allison answered crisply.

"Mojo Sheepshanks," I said.

Uncomfortable silence. Allison broke it, finally. "Look, about that phone call. I don't—I was upset—"

"What does Tucker 'really' do for a living, Allison?"

"Please let this go. He'll be furious—"

"You opened this can of worms," I reminded her. "Not me."

"Ask *him*."

"I can't. I don't know where he is, or when I'll see him again. Case of the disappearing—what?"

"Cop."

"Not buying, Allison."

"I really can't tell you."

"You wanted me to know he wasn't telling me the truth," I said. "That's why you called in the first place, isn't it?"

"I know you must think I'm some kind of jealous, co-dependent idiot—"

"I can't imagine why you'd care what I think," I said, and hung up.

For a while, I just sat there, staring at the wall.

Tucker had lied to me about his work?

How could that be? I'd seen the write-up in the news-paper, when he'd supposedly been killed in an explosion. Academy graduation photo, cops-in-mourning, the whole bit.

Still, Allison's statement resonated.

Something *was* off, and I'd sensed it all along. That was one of several reasons I'd been so reluctant to let things get too serious, too soon.

I'd known, on some level, that Tucker wasn't telling me the truth.

What *else* had he lied about?

I'm not sleeping with my ex-wife.

Well, that one was up for grabs.

You won't get pregnant. I had a vasectomy two years ago.

Yikes. I got up and checked the calendar on the wall. Heaved a sigh of relief.

The phone rang again. I checked the caller ID, and it said, Number Unavailable. Probably Tucker, on a borrowed cell, calling to feed me some other line of b.s.

"Hello," I snapped.

It was Distorto again. "There's a way into your place you don't know about," he said, in that weird electronic warble. "I don't need a key."

If I hadn't been so pissed off, I would have been terrified. "Geoff? Look, I know you killed Lillian. I *know* you did."

He laughed. "Whoever Geoff is," he said.

At least, I *thought* it was a he. Because of the distortion device, I couldn't tell.

I don't need a key.

"Heather?" She was in the hospital, wasn't she? I couldn't keep the quaver out of my voice, and that pissed me off even more.

Another robotic laugh. "You have a lot of enemies, don't you? I'll have to hurry if I'm going to kill you before somebody else beats me to it."

I decided to brazen it out. "The police know you killed Lillian," I said. "They know you *tried* to kill me, while I was in the hospital. They're going to pick you up any minute now. It's all over, you goddamned mother-murderer! You freaking cat-killer!"

Yeah, taunted a little voice in my head. *He's going to be arrested. As soon as they get the analysis back on that IV bag, if it ever went to the police lab in the first place. Tucker lied about being a cop, so he must have lied about the inves-*

tigation, too. Maybe he was just humoring me, all along. Maybe he never followed up.

"I saw you at the funeral today," Distorto went on. "I see almost everything you do."

I made a mental note to pick up a new telephone, the kind with a recorder. At least if he called again, I could play the call back for Detective Crowley. "Did you put flowers on Mom and Dad's graves while you were there, *Geoff?*"

Silence.

Finally, he said, "You killed them, you know."

I knew he was jerking my chain, but a chill of dread went through me just the same. What if it was true? How the hell would I live with the knowledge that I was the shooter?

"You killed them," the caller went on, "and your brother took the rap."

"Right. I was five years old, and my *brother* loved me so much that he put an arrow through my cat in honor of my fourth birthday. I'm sure he would have done the noble thing and gone to prison to save me."

"You did it. You did the murders. Don't you remember the blood?"

I *did* remember the blood.

I just didn't remember the events that led up to the spilling of it.

Had I shot my parents? Gotten hold of a gun somehow, and pulled the trigger? It happened all time.

One victim? That could be an accident. But two? Possible, but not very likely.

My stomach roiled.

"Don't call me again," I said evenly, "and don't come near me. I didn't shoot Mom and Dad, but I won't hesitate to shoot you if you come near me again."

"Sweet dreams, Mary Josephine. And remember what I said. There's a way into your apartment. I'll prove it."

The line went dead.

I set the receiver down with a thunk.

Call Detective Crowley.

I thought Nick was back, until I realized the voice had come from within my own head.

I dug out Crowley's card.

Stared at it.

I couldn't do it.

Scared as I was, I couldn't do it.

Not yet, anyway.

Crowley and I had been spending way too much time together lately. First, the incident with Bert. Then Sheila. *Then* Heather stabbing me.

I had to be losing credibility with the guy, if I'd ever had any in the first place.

Tell him about Lillian, the voice insisted, *and Geoff's note on the sign-in sheet at the nursing home. Tell him how Geoff tried to tamper with your IV bag that night in your room.*

I'd told *Tucker* those things, believing he was a cop. That he'd make a report. For all I knew, the police were still completely in the dark.

Tell him.

I dialed Detective Crowley's number.

"Guess who," I said, when he answered.

"I just saw you on TV," Crowley drawled in response. "You're that little girl who was abducted down in Cactus Bend, a month or so after the Mayhugh murders."

I bit my lower lip, closed my eyes. "Yes."

Long, pensive silence. "What can I do for you, Mojo? Or is it Mary Jo?"

"It's Mojo."

"Well, then, *Mojo*, what is it this time? Please tell me you haven't stumbled across yet another crime victim, because that would make me feel real suspicious."

So much for the wisdom of the still, small voice.

"My foster mother—Lillian Travers—was murdered."

"I see," Crowley said. "She was buried today, wasn't she? Saw that on the news, too."

"Yes, but—"

"And you believe she was murdered."

"I *know* she was murdered. And I know who did it. Furthermore, the same person tried to kill me, too, while I was in the hospital."

"I'm listening," Crowley said.

I told him the whole spiel, and all the while, I knew he thought I was crazy as the proverbial tick.

CHAPTER

17

After the phone conversation with Crowley, I was restless.

He'd promised to "look into" everything I'd told him, but I wasn't going to hang by my thumbs in the meantime, waiting for justice to be served. Lillian had already been buried, and unless the autopsy report showed something out of the ordinary, her body would have to be exhumed. That required a court order, at the very least; digging up bodies was drastic business. No judge would sign off on the heavy equipment without proof.

I paced.

Distorto's words flowed ominously through my brain.

There's a way into your apartment.

I don't need a key.

I imagined waking up in the middle of the night to find Geoff standing over my bed, and my heebie-jeebies came to a full boil.

I reminded myself that I had some options.

I could swallow my pride, brave Alex's antipathy and take refuge at Greer's place.

I could rent a room in some motel.

I could drive back down to Cactus Bend and bunk in with the Larimers.

None of those things had much appeal. I was a private detective, I had money in the bank, I owned a biker bar. Time I started acting more like a Bad-Ass.

I grabbed my purse.

The first thing I was going to do was make a run to Sunset Villa and beg, borrow or steal that sign-in sheet, the one with the *U.R. Dead* signature and the smiley face. Maybe Geoff's fingerprints were on the paper, or even some smidgeon of DNA.

I considered giving the home a jingle first, but only briefly. A telephone call would give Rotika and the floral-scrubs bunch time to dispose of the sheet, recruit better security or simply have the cops waiting when I got there.

Better to take them by surprise.

I locked up, ran down the stairs and sprinted for the Volvo.

Forty-five minutes later, I pulled into the lot at Sunset Villa, looked around to make sure Geoff hadn't followed me and walked purposefully toward the entrance.

Rotika was on duty at the reception desk, and her eyes went wide when she saw me.

"You were on TV," she said, sounding almost accusatory.

I nodded. "I need that sign-in sheet, Rotika. You know the one I'm talking about."

"I chucked that out," she said. Her face fell a little. "Looked like Mrs. Travers had herself a nice service. Wish I could have gone, instead of just catching it on the news. Lots of people there."

Was I the only person in the world who hadn't seen the segment?

"Yes," I said. "It was—nice." I paused, steered the conversation back in the original direction. "You wouldn't lie to me, would you, Rotika? Say you threw out the sign-in sheet when you didn't?"

"'Course not," Rotika said. Something quickened in her round, earnest face. "Might as well give you Mrs. Travers's stuff while you're here, though."

I imagined Lillian's blue chenille bathrobe, a Tarot deck with three of the seventy-eight cards missing, maybe her bridge-work. And suddenly I felt a longing to wrap myself in the robe, breathe in the scent of the only mother I'd really known.

I'd thought I was keeping it together pretty well, but tears came instantly.

"We boxed everything up yesterday," Rotika said sympathetically, hoisting her sizable backside out of the reception-ist's chair. "Let me just get it for you right now. You'll have to sign for the stuff, of course."

"Sure," I said.

Rotika disappeared through a door behind the desk, and I heard her rummaging and muttering.

I leaned over the desk, snatched the clipboard and flipped through.

There were pages for each of the last three days, but nothing before that.

Rotika came out of the backroom lugging two boxes, one on top of the other. Her eyes narrowed when she caught me with the clipboard in my hands.

"I done *told* you—"

"I'm a private detective," I said. "I have to be sneaky."

Rotika heaved the boxes onto the countertop; she looked at me, intrigued. Shoved a piece of paper at me, along with a pen. "You're a *private detective?* I thought you worked in the medical field."

"It's a front," I whispered, scanning the form and signing off on Lillian's things.

She studied me. "Now that's an interestin' job," she declared, tearing off a copy of the receipt and handing it to me.

I nodded solemnly. So far, except for the botched visit to the art gallery in Scottsdale, my P.I. experience consisted entirely of Googling bimbos on the computer in my living room, but Rotika didn't need to know that.

"I guess it means you gotta do stuff like dig through Dumpsters," she said speculatively. "Lookin' for incriminating evidence and all like that. You ever been in a fight?"

I thought of Heather, launching herself off my coffee table with manicure scissors in her upraised hand. "I was stabbed," I said.

Rotika goggled. "That's why you was bleedin' the other day, and they had to take you to the hospital," she recalled breathlessly.

"That's why," I confirmed.

"Let me help you with them boxes," she said.

We loaded Lillian's things into the trunk of the Volvo.

I thanked Rotika, and we shook hands.

She trundled back into the building.

I went around back to do a little Dumpster diving.

Private investigation is not as glamorous as it looks on TV. Suffice it to say, some of the things nursing homes throw away spike right into the red zone on the gross-o-meter.

I made up my mind to die before I got old enough to be admitted as a permanent resident.

And I didn't find the sign-in sheet.

I drove back home in a daze of thought and headed for the shower without even checking the place for maniacs first.

I came out of the bathroom, wrapped in a towel, and found Nick sitting cross-legged in the middle of my bed, like a yogi perched on a panel of spikes.

"Your shoes better not have grave dirt on them," I said. I looked around hopefully, but there was no sign of Chester.

"Sorry about your mom," Nick told me.

I sort of slithered to the dresser, careful not to turn my back on him, and plucked a nightshirt out of the top drawer, one-handed and without looking. I used the other hand to keep the towel in place.

"Maybe you saw her—Lillian, I mean—in the train station?"

He shrugged. "Lots of people come and go," he said. "If she passed through, I didn't see her."

I felt the walls of my heart teeter a little. "Oh."

"Good news about the cat, though," Nick told me. "He's living in a mansion with a sweet old lady who calls him 'Baby' and hand-feeds him sardines."

"How do you know all that?"

Nick grinned. "Word gets around."

"What are you doing on my bed?"

"I was meditating. You should try it. Very centering."

"Thank you, Sahib-Rosneesh-Whatever," I said, scooting back toward the bathroom door.

When I came out a minute later, wearing the nightshirt *and* a bathrobe, Nick was off the bed, gazing pensively out the window over the dresser.

"You really need to move," he said, without turning around. "The energy here is lousy."

"I own the place now," I told him. "That puts a whole new light on the situation."

He turned, wearing an expression of amused disbelief. "You have got to be kidding."

"I inherited it from Bert."

"Bert's not dead," he said, sobering.

"Maybe he got his ticket and boarded a train while you weren't looking."

"He's *not dead*," Nick reiterated. He looked intense, and more than a little rattled. "I saved his life by telling you he was in trouble. It was part of my—"

I'd been moving toward the hallway door, but at Nick's words, I stopped. "Part of your *what*?"

"I guess you could call it penance," Nick said.

"I thought getting me to forgive you was all you had to do."

"I asked for an extra assignment, since the main one wasn't going all that well. They gave me Bert."

I started for the kitchen. I needed coffee with a splash of Jack Daniel's.

Or maybe just the Jack Daniel's.

"So now you're off the hook?" I tossed the question over my shoulder.

Nick practically stepped on my heels. "Not if Bert's really dead, I'm not."

"Good news," I whispered, in case the place was bugged. After all that had happened, nothing would have surprised me. Sometimes, paranoia is justified. "He's a new man."

Nick gave a sigh of obvious relief. "Well," he said, "that takes care of the tax issues."

I stopped again. In my mind's eye, I saw my three-hun-dred-and-fifty-thousand smackers flying out the window. "What tax issues?"

"Not to worry," Nick said quickly, and with the flash of a grin. "It happened after we were divorced. Just a little figure-juggling. The IRS never caught me, but, wouldn't you know, they have a branch office in the train station."

"I don't believe you."

Nick's eyes twinkled. "Never cheat on your taxes," he said.

"I wouldn't dream of it. What else do they have in this train station?"

"Well," Nick said, warming to the subject, "there's a Bureau of Unreturned Library Books."

I laughed.

"You'd better take back that copy of *Catcher in the Rye,*" he added, with a shake of his finger. "The one you swiped off the 'forbidden' shelf that time?"

Shit.

I *had* snitched the book when I was fourteen, and Lillian, Greer and I had hit the road before I could put it back where it belonged. I didn't even remember what state we'd been in at the time, let alone the town or the name of the library.

"What happens if I don't?"

"You don't want to know," Nick said, with a slight shudder.

"Hell," I muttered, trying to remember what I'd done with the slim volume.

"Well, it's not quite *that* serious."

"Thanks a lot," I said, and got the coffee started. "Now, to what do I owe the pleasure of yet another visit?"

"Where's the boyfriend?" Nick countered. He stood behind one of the chairs at the kitchen table, gripping the back tightly.

"No idea," I said. The reminder of Tucker touched some sore spots inside me. I'd kept thoughts of him at bay while I was busy digging through the Dumpster behind Sunset Villa, but now, thanks to Nick, he was right back in the forefront of my mind.

"He's not a cop." Nick said this ponderously.

"Have you been listening in on my voice mail again?"

"No. I'm reading your mind."

"Well, stop. My brain is private. No trespassing."

Nick raised both hands, palms out. "Okay, sorry."

"*Stay out of my head,*" I said, in case he didn't get it the first time.

"It's a pretty scary place, your head. Especially when you're dreaming."

I stopped everything. Set down the coffee mug I'd just taken from the cupboard and turned to stare. Suddenly, the library book was not an issue. "You see *my dreams?*"

A muscle bunched in Nick's jaw. "Sometimes," he said.

"When I was—when I was away, I had these nightmares—"

Nick's eyes seemed to glisten, and he looked infinitely sad.

"I was terrified in those dreams, Nick," I said carefully, "and when I woke up, I couldn't remember them. I know they were about the murders, though, and if you saw anything—anything at all—you really need to tell me."

Nick murmured a word that would probably earn him another fifty years cooling his heels in the depot. "Moje," he said, "maybe there's a reason you're blocking the memories. Maybe it's better not to know."

"Tell. Me. What. You. Saw."

"You," he said hoarsely. "I saw you, Mojo."

I closed my eyes. Forced myself to open them again.

"Doing—*what?*"

No answer. Nick stood as still as if he'd been carved out of wood and painted to look like a man.

"Nick."

"You were little. And you were holding a gun."

For the next few moments, all I heard was the sound of

my own blood, pounding in my ears, a steady, relentless, *thud-thud-thud*. Then I *saw* blood, smelled it, felt it, slippery and warm. Suddenly, I was five, and so scared that I'd wet my pants. I was going to get in trouble, I thought, for wetting my pants.

I struggled to keep my grasp on the heavy gun, but it slithered out of my small hands, struck the floor and went off with a roar that made me shriek with renewed terror.

I was still screaming when I morphed back to the grown-up me.

Nick was gripping my shoulders.

"It's true," I whispered, in agony. "It's true—I *killed* them. I killed my mom and dad—"

"Maybe not," Nick said. "That was all I saw, Mojo. Just you, with the gun in your hands. You dropped it, and it went off. Maybe you only picked the thing up after someone else threw it down—"

"And maybe," I said, sick to the center of my soul, "I found a pistol lying around somewhere, and I—and I—"

"I shouldn't have told you," Nick lamented. His hands suddenly felt stone-cold where they rested on my shoulders. I knew, even in the frenzy of remembering the weight of that gun, and the blood, that he was about to do another fade-out.

"Don't leave—"

He was gone.

"Me," I finished forlornly.

Alone again.

Naturally.

I know I should have stayed put.

I should have called Jolie or even Andy Crowley.

But I didn't.

I found my purse, banged out of the house, jumped into the Volvo, drove to the 101, followed it south to the 10 East.

I didn't know I was headed for Cactus Bend until I took the exit, after an hour and a half on autopilot. A glance at the dashboard clock told me it was after 10:00 p.m. That jolted me, because up until then, I couldn't have said whether it was night or day.

The big gates were shut tight at Casa Larimer.

I leaned on the horn.

Lights came on in the big house.

I honked again.

A figure sprinted down the sloping driveway, and I recognized Joseph.

He looked annoyed, when I caught a flash of his face in the headlights, but he opened the gates. I rolled down the window.

"I need to see the senator," I said. I don't know exactly what I intended to do at that point. Turn myself in, maybe. Or just ask for advice.

Joseph's annoyance gave way to concern. "My God, Mojo—what's the matter with you? You look—"

"I want to see my uncle."

"He's not here," Joseph said quietly. He opened the car door. "Move over," he said. "I'm driving."

I was clearly not myself. If I had been, I would have told him he wasn't doing anything of the kind. Instead, I moved to release my seat belt, discovered I'd never fastened it in the first place and scrambled inelegantly over the console into the passenger seat. It was only then that I realized I was still wearing my nightshirt and bathrobe. I was barefoot, too—I must have walked over the gravel in the parking lot at Bert's without even feeling it. Not good, since there were usually broken beer bottles mixed in with the tiny, sharp rocks.

"Where are you taking me?" I asked. I could have had a career playing the dumb victim in B horror movies.

"I *should* take you to the nearest hospital," Joseph said. "What the hell are you on, anyway?"

"I'm not 'on' anything," I protested.

"You couldn't prove it by me, lady." Joseph shoved the Volvo back in gear and streaked up the driveway and around to the guesthouse, behind the manor.

"I'll scream if you touch me," I warned.

"Go ahead and scream," Joseph said. "The senator's away and Mrs. Larimer is upstairs, blitzed out on pills."

He stopped the car, shut off the engine, got out and stalked around to my side. Pulled open my door.

I tried to hold onto the seat, but he grabbed me by the knees and cranked me around sideways. I was just about to make good on my decision to let out a real howler when he crouched and took hold of one of my ankles.

"Your feet are bleeding," he said. "What the—?"

I started to cry.

"I killed my parents," I said.

He lifted his head, looked full into my face. "You are certifiably nuts," he told me, but there was a new gentleness in the way he spoke. "Come on, Ms. Sheepshanks." He got to his feet, leaned in and lifted me off the seat and into his arms.

"Let's get you inside before you bring shame and degradation on the family name."

I laid my head on his shoulder.

Like I said, I was not myself.

"I killed my own parents," I said.

"Crazy as you are," Joseph answered, "I seriously doubt it."

"I remembered—"

"Joseph! What in the world is going on out there?"

Joseph stopped cold. We both looked up and saw Barbara Larimer staring down on us from what was probably the balcony of the master suite.

So much for the blitzed-on-pills theory.

"Mojo's hurt herself," Joseph said. "She's upset. I was just taking her into the guesthouse."

"Bring her in here instead," Barbara ordered. "If she's hurt, we ought to call a doctor."

"It's pretty minor," Joseph told her.

"I might get blood on the carpets," I added, trying to be helpful.

"Shut up," Joseph rasped.

"I'm coming down there," Barbara decided. "I'll need my chair."

Joseph swore softly. Then he said, "Right away, Mrs. Larimer!"

"Suck-up," I said.

"Are you drunk?"

"I really, really wish I were."

Joseph opened the front door of the guesthouse, carried me through it and set me on the swanky leather couch. That done, he flipped on a couple of lamps, took a better look at the bottoms of my feet and swore again.

"Stay here," he said. "*Right* here." He pulled my car keys from his pants pocket and jingled them for emphasis. "Read my lips. You do not have transportation."

"Gotya," I replied.

When he returned, Barbara was with him, motorized and very, very concerned.

Unfortunately, between the time of Joseph's departure and their return, I'd dropped onto my side and fallen into a drooling sleep. I sat bolt upright when the sound of their entering jolted me awake, and wiped ineffectually at the spit stain on the leather couch.

"It looks like a nervous breakdown to me," Joseph told his employer, who whizzed around the end of the coffee table to give me the once-over, up close and personal. "She's been muttering some nonsense about killing her parents."

"Go and call Dr. Henderson," Barbara said to Joseph.

"Please, don't," I said. I'd driven for an hour and a half in my nightgown and bathrobe. I'd confessed to murdering my mother and father. Talk about a blight on the family name. I wasn't up to the questions a doctor would ask.

"You're not well, dear," Barbara assured me. For a moment, I thought she was going to pat me on the head. "You need medical attention."

I had planned—insofar as I'd done any planning at all—to tell my uncle what I'd remembered, leaving out the part Nick played in the revelation, of course, and ask him what to do next. In my confused mental state, I'd never figured

Barbara into the equation at all. And I was not anxious to be alone with her.

"I'm really—just—drunk," I said.

Joseph left the room. I heard the low murmur of his voice and knew he was summoning the medicos. If they brought a net, I'd make a run for it, sore feet or none.

"Drunk?" Barbara asked, sniffing delicately. "I don't smell alcohol."

I started to cry. Why hadn't I called Jolie? Now I'd painted myself into a corner, and I might never get out. I would probably go to jail, even if I had been only five when I committed the crime. Uncle Clive would advise me to turn myself in, I was sure. And plead insanity.

Joseph came back. He carried a first aid kit in one hand.

"What did the doctor say?" Barbara wanted to know.

"He's out of town," Joseph answered, pushing back the coffee table, forcing Barbara to wheel back out of the way. "It's a judgment call. We can look after her ourselves, or take her to the emergency room."

"I'm not going to any hospital," I said.

Prison, maybe. But no more hospitals.

"Well, I'd like to keep this out of the news if possible," Barbara said practically. She tilted a lamp shade so Joseph could get a better view of my feet, which were now in his lap. He sloshed them with alcohol, and I winced and tried to pull away.

"Good luck," Joseph said.

I wasn't sure whether he was talking to me or Barbara.

"Everything will look better in the morning," she said.

I heard the words like an odd, muffled echo, coming from the long ago and far away.

Everything will look better in the morning.

Scented hands, tucking me into a strange bed. I was small and scared. Earlier, a maid had scrubbed me clean in a bathtub big enough to swim in, and before that, men in uniforms had asked me a lot of questions I couldn't answer.

I wanted my mother, and the hopelessness of the longing was a giant, pulsing bruise inside me.

Everything will look better in the morning.

Back in the present moment, I covered my face with both hands.

"Are you all right?" Joseph asked.

I felt a peculiar tension in the air, looked up. It was coming from Barbara.

I knew what she was thinking.

Her husband was a state senator. A cinch for governor.

And now this crazy relative had turned up, just in time to ruin everything.

"I want to go home," I said. "I can drive, really."

"You're not going anywhere," Joseph replied flatly.

Where, I wondered, had he put my car keys?

He disappeared into the bedroom where I'd slept on my previous visit.

Barbara studied me intently. "I saw you on the evening news," she said. "The interview in your sister's driveway."

"Sorry about that," I answered. I'd mentioned that the senator was my uncle, I remembered that much. Chances were, I wouldn't be invited along on any vote-gathering junkets.

Joseph came back. Lifted me off the couch and carried me out of the room.

"She hates me," I confided, in a whisper. I hadn't had anything to eat or drink since I'd arrived, but I felt rummy, as though I'd been drugged.

We reached the bedroom. The covers had been turned back, and Joseph laid me on the cool sheets.

"I'll get you some water," he said.

"I don't want to ruin these sheets," I told him, remembering my cut feet and swinging them over the side of the bed.

Joseph put me right back where I'd been before, and covered me up. "Forget the damn sheets," he said. "You've got much bigger problems."

"Are you going to call the police?"

"No," Joseph said. "That's for the senator to decide."

"Do you think I could have some aspirin?"

"You probably shouldn't take anything." There was an "else" hanging on the end of that sentence, though Joseph didn't actually say it.

I closed my eyes.

Opened them.

Barbara was sitting beside the bed.

Wheelchairs should make more noise. I was so startled that my heart shinnied into my throat, clawing like a kitten trying to get out of a sack.

"Good night, dear," she said.

I managed a smile. "Good night," I replied.

Barbara went out.

Joseph brought the water. Left again.

I heard the front door close in the distance.

I tried to sleep.

I couldn't.

Where were my car keys? In Joseph's pocket?

Or had he hung them on a hook inside the main house, possibly in the kitchen? If I went after them, I'd probably set off an alarm.

I couldn't face that.

Desperate for something to do, I fiddled with the built-in remote on the bedside stand and switched on the plasma TV.

The news was on.

"A fugitive was laid to rest today in Cactus Bend," a woman said, as the camera panned across the gathering at Lillian's graveside. I saw Greer and Jolie and myself. The senator and Barbara, and a lot of strangers.

And there, leaning against the trunk of a cottonwood tree, almost out of camera range, was Geoff.

CHAPTER

I stared numbly at the TV, watched with half my brain as the graveyard segment filmed that morning during Lillian's memorial service melted into a driveway shot of me, standing in front of Greer's place. I caught only snatches of the things I'd said—*He's my uncle…except that sometimes I feel as though I'm on the verge of remembering…*

I couldn't seem to connect. It was like watching and listening to another person, who looked like me but wasn't.

I shut off the set, with a motion of my thumb, and just as I did so, my cell phone chimed, from the separate and largely unexplored cosmos inside my purse.

Contact with the outside world!

I dived for it. Didn't even take the time to check the caller ID first.

"I came home," Tucker said, without bothering with a

hello, "and you were gone. According to your note, you went back to your place. I've been there. You, on the other hand, are definitely *not*."

Something odd flashed into my mind.

There's a way into your apartment.

I don't need a key.

Tucker didn't have a key; he'd given it back, albeit reluctantly, a month before, when we decided to give each other some space. We hadn't actually stuck to our guns on that score. I had a key to his place, because I'd been staying there—I'd used it to lock up when I went back with Jolie to get my things. But as far as I knew, it had been a one-sided exchange.

Which didn't mean Tucker couldn't have made a copy before the breakup.

Even more disturbing.

How had he gotten in, that morning when I found him in my kitchen, after he'd come back from the dead?

"Moje, are you there?"

"I'm here," I said, letting out my breath.

There were a great many things I didn't know about Tucker, like what he did for a living, for instance. The idea wasn't easy to face, but it was within the realm of possibility that *he* was the one who'd made those mechanically distorted phone calls. He might even have arranged for the delivery of that almost-fatal chow mein.

But why? What motive could he have had for doing those things?

If he'd laced the chow mein with rat poison, why had he turned right around and helped me save Russell?

Maybe because he was after you, not the dog.

"How did you get into my apartment?"

"I'm not in your apartment. I'm on the road."

"I mean that morning, when I thought you were—someone else?"

"When you called me Nick," Tucker said. "Bert let me in. Mojo, what's going on? Where are you?"

"I'll ask the questions, if you don't mind."

He sighed. "All right. Shoot."

Unfortunate choice of words, an instant reminder that I'd come to Cactus Bend to tell my uncle that I'd gunned down both my parents. Nausea swept through me.

"You're not a cop. Allison told me, and I believe her, because she might be a jealous ex-wife, but she's also a competent professional. So don't deny it. You lied to me, Tucker, and that raises serious trust issues."

"We're not going to discuss this over the phone. Where are you, Moje?"

"Never mind where I am. We're not going to discuss it in person, either. E-mail me, or something. Send me a fax."

Not that I had a fax machine.

"Have you completely lost your mind?"

I was facing an uncertain future, to say the least. Either I'd be tried and sent to prison for the murder of my parents, or I'd be locked up in some hospital for the rest of my natural life.

Maybe Heather and I could room together.

Yeah, the odds seemed very good that I *had* lost my mind.

"Probably," I said, limping around the room as I talked, getting used to the pain in the bottom of my feet.

I'd watch for the senator to come home, I decided, and when I saw him pull in, maybe I could find a way to slip into the house behind him. Locate my keys and get out again without setting off the alarm.

Cute trick. What I needed was *The Damn Fool's Guide to Burglary*.

"Look, Moje," Tucker said, "you're really starting to scare me."

"Back at you, buddy. I thought I knew you, and now I find out you're not who you said you were."

"Does this mean I don't get to join the ranks of Sheepshanks, Sheepshanks and Sheepshanks?" The timbre of his voice was darkly amused.

I felt a pang at the reminder of all the things I wasn't going to get to do, now that I knew I was a murderer. Sheepshanks, Sheepshanks and Sheepshanks was one of those things.

My promising career as a P.I. was over before it began.

I'd never get to spend the windfall from Nick's mother, adopt a dog or a cat from the pound or figure out what to do with Bad-Ass Bert's Biker Saloon.

Worse, I'd never go to bed with Tucker again.

"That's what it means," I said miserably. By then, I was in the living room, peering out the front window. I hung up the phone with a press of my thumb, set it down and watched as Joseph went through my car like a customs agent at the border.

The cell rang again, and I didn't pick up.

Joseph locked the Volvo, tossed the keys in the air and caught them.

Headed for the house.

He stopped, near one of the tables lining the swimming pool, set the keys down and raised his cell phone to his ear.

I held my breath.

I couldn't hear what he was saying, but the way he was gesturing indicated that the call represented some kind of unpleasant surprise.

I waited and watched.

Sure enough, he went into the house, evidently forgetting that he'd left the keys outside, on the table. I stared at them, glinting in the lights surrounding the pool, my heart skittering unevenly.

After about thirty seconds, I shut off my cell phone, dropped it into my bathrobe pocket, eased open the guesthouse door and dashed for the poolside table. Snatched up the keys.

I barely noticed the sting in the bottoms of my feet as I ran to the Volvo, zapped the locks from the fob and jumped inside.

I left the headlights off and drove slowly around to the main driveway. About the thousandth thing I needed was for Joseph to see or hear me and thwart my escape.

The gates presented a major problem.

They were closed.

I could crash through them, of course, but I suspected that technique worked better in the movies than it would in real life. I was sitting there, like a lump, wondering what to do, when I saw headlights swing off the main road, coming in my direction.

I backed through a flowerbed, hoping the Volvo and I were hidden from view in the shrubbery.

The senator's Jaguar purred to a stop on the other side of the gates. By electronic magic, they swung open.

I gunned the engine the instant I thought there was enough space to pass through and shot past the Jag, flipping on my headlights as I streaked toward the road.

Glancing into the rearview mirror, I saw the taillights of the Jag, still sitting in front of the open gates.

After that, I didn't look back again.

If I had, I might have seen something important, but I wasn't exactly in the zone when it came to taking sensible precautions. I just knew I needed to get out of there, fast.

I headed straight for the cemetery. I'm not sure why—just some instinctive need to be close to Lillian, I guess. I wished she'd appear to me, the way Nick had, and answer all the questions she'd never been willing to deal with in life. All the while, I knew she wouldn't. I wasn't going to get that lucky.

There were no gates at the graveyard. At the time, fresh from my break from Casa Larimer, I saw that as a good thing.

I drove past my parents' graves and pulled over a stone's throw from Lillian's. I shut off my headlights, and realized for the first time that the moon was nearly full. The cemetery was bathed in an eerie light, shot through with shadows of tombstones and the occasional cottonwood.

I got out of the car, picked my way gingerly over the rocks at the side of the one-lane road, welcomed the cool softness of the grass.

A mound of raw dirt marked Lillian's final resting place. Greer had ordered an elaborate Italian marble headstone off the Internet, but it would have to be carved and then shipped all the way from Carerra. Maybe by the time it arrived, the grass would have grown in like a green blanket over Lillian. Her grave wouldn't seem so anonymous then, so new and exposed.

"Why didn't you tell me I killed them?" I asked.

A night breeze played in the treetops, and I thought I heard the call of a mourning dove. Something else, too—maybe traffic out on the main highway.

I knelt next to the grave, sat on my haunches.

"You wanted to protect me. I understand that. But it didn't work, because the one person I can't run away from is myself."

Another sound came then, so faint that I wasn't sure I'd heard it at all.

I turned to look behind me, and saw nothing.

"Boomer?" I asked hopefully. Maybe he lived on the premises. That was it. He'd seen me drive in and, being the caretaker, come to investigate. Kids liked to party in cemeteries, and vandalism was probably a factor, too.

I turned back to the grave, and that was when I saw the figure standing on the other side.

Definitely not Boomer.

Moonlight caught on the barrel of a pistol.

"Geoff?"

Laughter. *Female* laughter, low and throaty.

I wondered crazily if my brother had turned transvestite during his years in the joint, but the shape wasn't right. It *was* familiar, though.

Everything will look better in the morning.

"*Barbara?*"

She'd been wearing a dark scarf or a hat. Now, she pulled it off with her free hand, letting her blond hair show in the moonlight.

"You remembered," she said. "I knew it for sure when I saw you on television today. *You remembered.*"

The truth was, I *hadn't* remembered what happened the night my parents were killed, but now, facing what I knew would be my own death, the floodgates opened in a rush of crimson and black images, like a video tape on fast-forward.

I was five again.

It was an ordinary summer night.

I was lying on the floor, on my stomach, coloring in a mermaid's tail in a book full of pictures.

Dad sat at his computer. He was so proud of that bulky, mysterious machine, and his big fingers made a comforting clicking sound as they tapped the keys.

Somebody knocked at the front door of the trailer.

"Get that, will you, kid?" Dad said, without looking away from the flickering blue words on the screen of his TRS-80.

I laid down my crayon, got to my feet, and hurried to unlock the screen door. Aunt Barbara came in, put a gloved finger to her lips.

I was a kid. I was delighted that there was a surprise afoot.

I barely noticed when Geoff slipped in behind her.

Dad didn't turn around. "Who is it?" he asked.

Aunt Barbara put her finger to her lips again. Reached into her black shoulder bag.

Everything happened quickly after that.

Barbara pulled a pistol out of the bag, walked over to my dad and shot him point-blank in the back of the head.

Blood splattered everywhere.

Droplets of crimson gleamed on the pages of my coloring book.

Before I could scream, Mom rushed in, eyes wide with horrified alarm. She was wearing a green bathrobe, and her freshly washed hair was wrapped in a towel. She was on the nightshift at the truck stop that week. She liked working those hours, because the tips were better.

Barbara turned, fired the gun again.

A bright red wound opened in my mother's throat. Her eyes, vibrant with fear only a moment before, widened in disbelief. She landed hard on the floor.

Geoff moved Dad's inert, bloody body and plucked the floppy disk from a slot in the side of the computer. He didn't seem to mind the gore covering him, soaking his clothes.

Barbara dropped the gun. She went to stand over Mom, put her foot on the body, gave it a cruel little shake.

I tried to scream again, but no sound came out.

"Where's the kid?" she asked.

I'd taken refuge behind Dad's easy chair, without being aware of moving at all, but I knew they'd find me soon.

"She probably ran out the door when you shot Ron-the-Moron," Geoff said lightly. "Don't sweat it. She's five years old, and scared shitless. Nobody will believe a word she says anyway."

I heard a siren shrieking in the distance.

I couldn't tell where it was coming from.

Was it inside the memory?

Or was it on the road leading to the cemetery, where I was looking up the barrel of Barbara's gun?

It was a strange, schizophrenic sensation. My mind had literally split in two; I was in both the past and the present at the same time.

"*Why?*" I croaked, and the word popped me back to my adult self.

Barbara stood rigid on the other side of Lillian's grave.

"Why?" I repeated. I'd gone past elemental fear now, into a rage black enough to kill from. "*Why did you kill my parents?*"

"Because they were going to ruin everything," Barbara said tersely. "Your father had come across some incriminating paperwork and made copies of it." The night lay silent and weighted around us. I guessed I'd heard the siren in the other place, the long-gone trailer where Barbara Larimer had murdered my mother and father.

I lunged at her. The gun went off.

If I'd been shot, I didn't feel it.

We struggled.

I heard the siren again, closer now.

Barbara was strong for a woman who used a wheelchair most of the time, but I was stronger. I was straddling Barbara, and my hands were around her throat. I let go long enough to retrieve the pistol with my right hand. I pressed it into her forehead.

"Tell. Me. Why."

Barbara swallowed. Maybe she was hoping the cops were on the way. And when they got there, *I'd* be the one arrested.

It would be her word against mine, and it was no great leap to predict the winner.

I cocked the pistol, which was a gamble, because I didn't know enough about guns to be sure it wouldn't go off. At the time, I didn't give a damn.

"Trash," she choked out, "all of you. Money, money, money—that was all any of you cared about! And now that *criminal* is blackmailing me—"

"Geoff," I said. My ears were ringing, and my vision blurred. My voice seemed to come from somewhere other than my own throat. "You must have paid him to take the blame for the killings. Then he wanted more. They always want more, don't they, Auntie Barbara? Those nasty poor people?"

I don't know why, but suddenly, I snapped again. Just like that, I was back in the trailer.

Geoff and Barbara were gone.

I crept out from behind the easy chair, knelt beside my mother, tried to wake her up. When that failed, I threw myself on her, sobbing soundlessly. I came away bloody.

I heard a noise. They were coming back, my brother and my aunt.

They'd remembered the gun.

They'd remembered me.

They would shoot me, the same way they'd shot Mommy and Daddy.

I half crawled, half scrambled to the middle of the floor, where the gun lay.

Picked it up. I didn't know how it worked.

"Hello?" a man's voice, coming from the front door.

I dropped the gun for the second time, fled along a dark corridor, through the kitchen, onto the covered back porch. I opened the dryer and curled up inside it.

My back slammed hard into the ground, and I was in the graveyard again, only this time, Barbara was on top, and the barrel of the pistol dug hard into the base of my throat.

"I should have killed you then, you little bitch," she said. "I should have killed you then!"

"Barbara." Again, a man's voice. I fought not to slip back into the past, where another part of my psyche was huddled, mute with terror, in that dryer.

But this was a different voice. A familiar one.

"Barbara, put down the gun."

I struggled.

Barbara pulled the trigger.

A click. A roar.

The two sounds intermingled.

I waited to swallow a bullet. To die the way my mother probably had, full of a frenzied desire to live, strangling on her own blood.

Barbara toppled to one side.

I lay still, gasping.

I could be alive. I could be dead.

I wasn't sure which.

Joseph loomed over me. "Are you all right?"

I couldn't speak.

He retrieved Barbara's gun, tossed it away. Crouched to check her pulse.

"Mojo," Joseph said. "Say something."

"Is—is she dead?"

"Yes," he answered. "Are you hurt?"

I ran a mental scan. The results were encouraging. "I don't think so," I said. "Did I just hear a siren?"

"No," he answered.

I sat up. I was instantly dizzy, and rested my forehead on my knees, struggling to stay conscious.

"Barbara Larimer killed my parents." That weird, disjointed sensation came over me again. I wondered if there had been physical evidence to link her to the crime. Maybe, in some dusty box, forgotten in some evidence room, there were fibers, or hair samples. Back in 1983, forensic science as we know it was pretty new, and DNA analysis was considered speculative, and therefore inadmissible in court.

I heard a crackling sound, realized it was a radio. "Backup," Joseph said.

"Roger that," someone replied. "We're rolling."

"Are you going to shoot me?"

"I'd love to," Joseph replied, "but I can't think of an excuse right now. Being stupid and impulsive, alas, does not constitute just cause." He flipped open a wallet, and a federal-looking badge gleamed golden in the moonlight. "DEA," he said.

My mouth dropped open. "Drug Enforcement?"

"Yeah. We've been after the senator for years. You damn near blew about a decade of hard work tonight."

I stared at him. "You've been investigating Clive? But it was Barbara who—"

"Your uncle ran a big-time cocaine operation, between

Mexico and the U.S., back in his salad days. My predecessors suspected him, even then, but they couldn't come up with any proof. When he married Barbara, she thought he was a prosperous businessman. Needless to say, she was not happy when she found out the real source of his money. Scourge on the family name, you know." He looked down at Barbara's dead body, and he seemed so detached that I got scared all over again. I was alone in a cemetery with this man, and he'd just shot a woman. So what if he'd flashed a badge? They're easy to get. "Your dad evidently got the bright idea to tap Clive for enough to buy his own tire store," he went on. "Barbara didn't want the scandal, let alone the expense, so she offed him."

I fought back a swell of nausea. "Isn't there a statute of limitations on drug running?" I asked. I was in shock, and having a hard time tracking. No choice but to play catch-up.

Joseph nodded. "Yes, but some people connected with the operation turned up dead from very unnatural causes, and that kept the case viable."

I grappled with that for a few seconds. Then my attention shifted back to Barbara. "Don't people like her usually hire hit men?"

"That would have been an even bigger risk, for somebody like Mrs. Larimer. Cactus Bend is a small town, and people talk. After we found some random notes and cancelled checks—some of which were your uncle's—the theory emerged that she'd hired your brother to take the rap. Most likely, once he'd spent what she gave him, he wanted more."

I heard cars racing up the cemetery road. Blinked in the

glare of the oncoming headlights. It was my turn to nod. "She told me Geoff was blackmailing her," I said. My breath caught as the implications of what Joseph had just said sank in. Clive had written some of the checks. "Are you saying my uncle *knew* Barbara had killed my parents? He knew it all the time, and covered it up?"

Joseph gave me a pitying look. "We matched several of the blackmail payments to some of Larimer's private accounts."

I absorbed that. Shifted emotional gears again. "He's a *senator*. Why didn't the opposition ever dig up any of this stuff?"

"Until he decided to run for governor, Larimer was just another member of just another state legislature. Governors have a habit of running for the presidency, though, so the heat would have been on sooner or later."

"It's been twenty-three years since the murders," I said bitterly. "You sure took your sweet time wrapping this up."

"We didn't have a lot to go on at first," Joseph answered easily. "It took a while to get the official ball rolling, and even longer for me to be hired by the senator, then win his trust so he'd let me work as his bodyguard and personal assistant. When you showed up, I thought you were going to screw it all up for sure."

"That explains the rude remarks."

"Sorry," Joseph said.

Two cars screeched to a stop on the road, parking at angles behind the Volvo and a compact SUV. Imagine my surprise when Tucker got out of one of them, and made a beeline for us.

"What are *you* doing here?" I demanded.

"I was going to ask you the same question," Tucker answered. "Since I've got a badge and you don't, I win."

Joseph and the other man conferred over Barbara's body. A police car swept in, lights whirling.

Tucker looked strange, standing in the red-and-blue flash.

"Are you hurt?" he asked.

"No," I said. "And you *don't* have a badge, you damn liar."

He grinned, squatted beside me, pulled something from the pocket of his shirt. I saw my second fed shield of the evening.

I squinted at it. Very convincing, but I was still wary.

"Tucker Darroch," Tucker said. "DEA."

I glanced at Joseph, who was busy with crime-scene stuff. Shifted my gaze back to Tucker. I probably looked skeptical.

"Right," I said.

Tucker helped me to my feet. Unfortunately, my legs had gone to sleep, and I folded like a rag doll. He caught me.

"You lied to me," I said.

"I told you I worked Narcotics," Tucker said, lifting me into his arms. "Close enough. And I really was with Scottsdale P.D.—once."

More cop cars screamed up the road.

Tucker sat me sideways in the front seat of the Volvo.

"You're going to have to tell this story a lot of times," he said, squatting to look up at me, "so if you don't want to explain what you're doing here, barefoot and wearing a bathrobe, I'll understand."

I sighed. Where to begin?

I started with the night Barbara Larimer shot my parents.

Tucker listened without interruption, never looking away from my face.

Cops came and went.

Federal agents came and went.

"Aren't they going to remove the body?" I finally asked, when it was almost dawn and I was exhausted from giving my long, involved account. By then, Tucker had transferred me to a government car and wrapped me in a blanket. Boomer had arrived on the scene, and he brought us each a cup of coffee.

"It's a crime scene, Moje," Tucker said quietly. "Pictures have to be taken, and somebody from the M.E.'s office will need to sign off before anything can be disturbed."

"Barbara would have shot me," I said, though Tucker and I had been over that ground before. "She pulled the trigger. She *actually pulled the trigger.* The thing must have jammed."

Tucker stroked my hair. "It's all over, babe."

"Why didn't you tell me you were DEA?" I swallowed, and answered my own question. *"Because you were investigating Bert."*

Tucker looked away, looked back, said nothing.

"That's why you spent so much time hanging out at the bar."

Still nothing.

I pressed on. "Why would Bert have trusted you in the first place? It doesn't make sense. I can't see him as a drug dealer, and even if he was, he thought you were in Narcotics. He'd have been stupid to open up to you."

"I wasn't investigating Bert. I was after the people who stabbed him, and beat the hell out of Sheila."

"But—"

"We made it look like I was on the take," Tucker said reluctantly. "That's why they trusted me. They operated out of the bar. Bert suspected it for a long time, but he wasn't sure what to do. Things finally got too hot, and he called us."

"Did you get them? The guys who hurt Bert and Sheila, I mean?"

He was silent for a long time before he said, "Yes."

"And Bert and Sheila had to go into the witness protection program because they're going to testify?"

"Yes."

"You're not really quitting the DEA, are you?"

"I'll probably take a desk job. Allison won't share custody unless I do."

I sighed. "I guess all that talk about your joining Sheepshanks, Sheepshanks and Sheepshanks was just that—talk."

He grinned. "I wouldn't mind helping out with the more interesting cases. That way, maybe I can keep you from getting yourself killed."

I bit my lower lip. Geoff was still at large. Keeping me from getting killed might turn out to be a major challenge.

"My brother murdered Lillian."

"I know," Tucker said.

I blinked. "You *know?* How?"

"The autopsy report came back. He gave her enough morphine to stop her heart, and his prints were on the bag. He was grandstanding."

"What about *my* IV bag?"

Tucker paled, or at least seemed to, in that early morning light, still dim and thready. "Drain cleaner," he said. "He wanted it to hurt. Chances are, the rat poison in the chow mein was his doing, too. He probably made the pitch-call himself, then paid some kid to carry the box."

A prickly shiver went through me. "He wasn't trying to cover his tracks in the nursing home or the hospital. Geoff's a nurse. He would have known about drugs that wouldn't leave a trace, and he'd have had access to them."

Tucker nodded slowly. His eyes burned into my face. "Have you seen him since that night at the casino, Moje?"

I glanced toward Lillian's grave. "He was at the funeral. I caught a glimpse of him in the news clip."

"You're still in a lot of danger," Tucker said, at some length. "I can arrange for you to disappear." He must have seen the objection brewing in my face. "Just until we nail your brother," he finished.

"You may never get him, Tuck. He's a psychopath, and psychopaths are—"

"I'll get him," Tucker said grimly. He paused. "You're not going to cooperate, are you? By hiding out, I mean."

I shook my head. "I've spent my whole life running from things. I can't do it anymore."

"Then I guess I'll have to let you help," Tucker said.

"Guess so," I replied.

CHAPTER 19

The wheels of justice, as they say, grind slowly. I was questioned endlessly, in the tiny Cactus Bend police station, before finally being released into Tucker's custody, like some errant teenager after a joyride. My Volvo waited in the lot behind the cop shop, blissfully reporter-free. By midday, Senator Clive Larimer had been arrested on federal drug charges, along with some related killings, and every journalist in Arizona was probably camped either outside his office in Phoenix or at the gates of Casa Larimer.

I was starved, but I was also still wearing my nightshirt and bathrobe, so my dining choices were limited. We settled for drive-through.

My cell was kaput, since I hadn't charged it recently, and given the fact that news travels fast, especially when it's bad, I figured Jolie and Greer were probably pretty worried by now.

I borrowed Tucker's phone.

Jolie answered on the first ring, with a breathless, "Hello?"

"It's Mojo," I said.

"It's Mojo," Jolie repeated, in a muffled voice, probably talking to Greer.

I glanced at Tucker, who was driving with one hand and holding a hamburger-with-everything in the other. "I guess the story about Barbara Larimer's shooting has probably broken by now," I began.

"Nothing's been said about that," Jolie answered, "but your uncle is all over the news. No wonder he looks like a walking dead man—he's under arrest for drugs and murder *and* his wife is—"

"Dead," I finished, when Jolie's voice fell away.

"*Tell* me you weren't involved," she said, after a moment or two of recovery. "Greer and I have been trying to get in touch with you since last night. Your cell phone is shut off or broken or something, and we went to your apartment, but—" She stopped, drew an audible breath. "Do you have any idea how petrified we've been?"

I swallowed a mouthful of double-deluxe all-beef with cheese. "What do you want first? Whether I was involved, or whether or not I caught the clue train and figured out that you might be stressing a little over my general well-being?"

"Involved," Jolie said tersely.

"Affirmative on that," I answered.

"Holy shit," Jolie said. "I was afraid of that. Greer, she was *involved*."

Muttered exclamations from Greer.

Jolie cut back to the chase. "Are you hurt?"

"No," I said. "I'm fine." I looked down at my bathrobe. "Jolie, I remembered. I remembered everything—about that night, I mean."

"Tell me, damn it!"

Another sidelong glance at Tucker. I told my sister about the night my parents were murdered, sparing no details. After all, she was a forensic biologist and soon-to-be crime scene tech. She could deal.

"Lillian must have thought you did it," Jolie said bleakly, when I'd finished the grisly tale. "*That* was why she snatched you and ran. And why she refused to tell you whatever she knew."

"That's my guess. We'll probably never know for sure."

"So why do I feel that this isn't over?"

I sighed. "Geoff is still on the loose. He was Barbara's accomplice, Jolie. He took the fall for her because she paid him to do it. I was right—he killed Lillian, and he tried to do me in, too."

A call-waiting blip sounded on the cell phone. "Gotta go, Jolie," I said quickly. "There's a call coming through for su-peragent, and it might be important. I'll be home in a little under two hours." I clicked the pertinent button and an-swered, to give Tucker time to put down what remained of his hamburger.

"Tucker Darroch's phone," I said.

A chill bounced up to the satellite and back down, hitting me square in the solar plexus and radiating out from there. I knew exactly who was calling before she said a word.

"This is *Allison* Darroch. Is My Husband Around?"

It is not good when people capitalize an entire sentence. I winced and handed Tucker the cell, miming Allison's name as I did.

A muscle bunched under Tucker's right temple. "Hello," he said. A spattering of anxious words reached my ears as, roughly, yada-yada-yada. I watched the color drain from his face as he listened. "I'll be there as soon as I can. Keep the kids where you can see them, and for God's sake, try to stay calm. If you panic, they will, too."

He rang off, dropped the cell phone onto the console and hit the gas so hard that my cheeks almost blew back to my earlobes.

"What is it, Tucker?" I asked, when he didn't volunteer anything.

He didn't look at me, and when he did answer, there was no inflection at all in his voice. "There's no school today, so Daisy's dance class held a dress rehearsal for their recital on Friday night. One of the other kids—Daisy's best friend, Gillian—went missing. Nobody saw anything. Nobody heard anything. Gillian's just—gone."

"Maybe she only wandered off?"

"They've searched the whole area. No sign of her." He was silent for at least a mile. "She's only seven, Moje. And it could have been Daisy."

I moved to lay a hand on his thigh, then thought better of it. "But it wasn't, Tucker."

We zoomed on, zipped through Phoenix, up the 101, taking the Tatum Boulevard exit and continuing north. Tucker was in no mood to talk, at least, not to me. He had me dial a couple of different numbers on his cell phone, and he had plenty to say to the law enforcement agencies on the other end.

"I need to borrow your car," he told me, whipping into the otherwise empty parking lot at Bad-Ass Bert's. Tucker had left his own rig at the cemetery in Cactus Bend, so I wouldn't have to drive home, and another agent had agreed to bring it as far as Scottsdale later.

Both of us had forgotten about Geoff by then.

Tucker was scared sick for little Gillian, and so was I.

I tried to concentrate on some kind of normal order of business. I needed a shower and clothing suitable for daytime, and so I focused on that, as much as I could. As I got out of the car, I recalled that Rotika had given me two boxes full of Lillian's things.

"It's yours as long as you need it," I said, hopping a little because my bare feet were stinging as they made contact with the gravel. "But there's some stuff in the trunk—"

Tucker popped the trunk and started to get out.

"I can do it," I said.

"You're not even wearing shoes," he answered.

Tucker carried me piggyback to the stairs leading up to my apartment, then schlepped the boxes that far. His harried glance strayed once, up to the door. "Maybe you should come with me," he said.

"You know that won't fly," I replied. "I'd only complicate matters between you and Allison and, besides, I'm not dressed for search-and-rescue. Guess I'd better get my house key before you leave, though."

Tucker gave a reluctant nod of agreement and started past me, headed up the stairs.

I grabbed his arm. "Just give me the key, Tuck," I said quietly. "You don't have time for this."

He stopped, looked up at the door again, sighed and pulled out the Volvo keys, which he'd automatically stuffed into the pocket of his jeans.

"The leopard skin one," I told him.

"Figures," he said, with a grin so faint and so full of despair that it twisted my heart. He worked the key off the ring, handed it over and kissed me quickly on the mouth. "Call your sisters," he ordered. "Have them come and get you."

Jolie and Greer knew my ETA. They'd be arriving any minute, and I told Tucker so.

Reassured, he sprinted back to the Volvo and sped off.

I watched him go, said a little prayer that Gillian would be kept safe and found quickly and went upstairs.

The place was stone silent.

I stood on the threshold for a moment, trying to sense whether anyone was there or not. There's usually the slightest quiver in the air, when there's another person present.

No vibes.

I put on my Sponge Bobs and carried the boxes upstairs, one at a time. When Jolie and Greer arrived, we'd go through Lillian's belongings together, laugh a little and probably cry a lot. It would be a sort of informal, just-us tribute to her memory.

I set the cartons in the middle of the living room, started a pot of coffee brewing and grabbed a shower. Afterward, dressed in shorts and a tank top, I felt presentable again.

Poured myself a coffee, doctored it and wondered what was keeping my sisters.

I dug my cell out of my purse, remembered the battery was D.O.A. and plugged the thing in to recharge.

Speculating that Jolie or Greer might have left a message on my voice mail, I picked up the landline, heard the tone indicating I'd missed some calls and keyed in the access code.

There were three hang-ups, then Jolie's voice came on. "Moje, it's me," she said. "Listen, there's been sort of an incident and—well—we'll be a little late. Just don't worry, okay?"

Sort of an incident?

Just don't worry?

Jolie brought it home. "See you soon."

Click.

I stared at the receiver for a few seconds, wondering if this was some kind of passive-aggressive payback for running off to Cactus Bend the night before in my pj's and giving my sisters some anxious moments.

I punched in Jolie's number hard enough to make some of the buttons stick.

"Hi," chimed a recorded voice, when I opened my mouth to demand an explanation, "this is Jolie Travers. I'm not available right now, but please leave your name, number, and a brief message. If it's appropriate, I'll call you back."

"Mojo Sheepshanks," I said irritably, "480-555-4956. What the hell do you mean by 'sort of an incident'? That could be anything from a flat tire to a gunshot wound, and you damn well know it!"

I crashed the phone down hard.

That's when I remembered that I hadn't slept in over twenty-four hours. What I needed was a jolt of caffeine. That would rocket me back into the world of relatively civil people.

Coffee always wakes me up.

This time, it made all the muscles in my body go limp.

I studied my cup, frowning. Had I brewed decaf by accident? Not very likely, since I'd never bought the stuff in my life. I'd read those forwards on the Web about how they used embalming fluid to take the pizzazz out of the java.

No way, Juan. I was only planning to be embalmed *once*, and not in the immediate future, either.

A fog rolled in, clouding my brain. I seemed to be wandering in a dream sequence, only I was awake. Wasn't I?

I rubbed my temples with the fingertips of both hands.

Sniffed the coffee.

What did caffeine smell like?

Wooziness overtook me.

Disjointed thoughts queued in my head and kept changing places. The intracranial version of the maypole dance.

Then I felt a sudden rush of relief.

Of course.

I was simply tired.

I'd lived a lifetime in the last twenty-four hours, without sleeping, and now it was catching up to me. I'd just lie down—yes—and grab a few winks. When I woke up, Jolie and Greer would be there.

Or Tucker, bearing good news. Daisy's little friend— Gillian, wasn't it—had been found safe and sound. It was all just a big mistake. Little girls didn't *really* disappear from dance rehearsals in the middle of the day, surrounded by dedicated parents.

Of course they didn't.

I yawned, smiled and padded out of the kitchen, through the living room, and into my bedroom. I tossed back the covers and sank into the soft, soft mattress.

I would have sworn somebody tucked me in.

Lillian?

It would be nice to think that, I reflected. I tried to open my eyes and find out, but the lids felt heavy as manhole covers.

I slept, deeply and dreamlessly.

If the phone rang, I didn't hear it.

If anybody knocked at the door, ditto.

I was completely out of it.

Still, the faintest sound awakened me.

The room was in twilight, but I had no idea what time it was.

I stretched.

Sat up.

Swung my legs over the side to stand.

And hands grasped my ankles, from underneath the bed, as soon as my feet touched the floor.

In the first instant, I couldn't believe it was actually happening.

I used to scare myself with that scenario, when I was a very little kid. Before the murders. I'd always thought I'd scream, and someone would rush to my rescue, but now, even though I opened my mouth, all that came out was a garbled squeak.

I struggled.

The hands were strong—they gave a powerful wrench and I plunged to the floor, banging my right shoulder, still healing from the scissors wounds. Hyper-pain spiraled through me.

I still couldn't scream.

The hands released me, and the monster crawled out from under the bed, grinning.

Geoff.

I kicked violently, rolled onto my side, my knees—*get away, get away*—but he threw me down again.

"Bad dream, little sister?" he drawled.

"Help!" I whispered.

"All alone," Geoff singsonged. "All, all alone."

"Damn you," I croaked, fighting again. "Let me go— what are you—?"

"I told you there was a way into your apartment," Geoff said, in that same crazy, nursery-rhyme meter. "I *told* you." He smiled vacuously. The lights were on, the dogs were barking and nobody was home. He put a finger to his lips, and I was reminded of Barbara, pretending there was some nice surprise in the offing when what she really planned was to pump bullets into the two people in the world I loved and needed most. "It's *under the bed,*" Geoff went on, almost conspiratorially. "A sort of crawl space. All you have to do is stand on the bar downstairs and push the vent grating out of the way, and there it is. The secret passage."

I tried to squirm away, but he took another grip on my ankles, harder this time, his fingers biting deep into my flesh.

"I happened to be in the bar one night," he droned on.

"Right downstairs from you, Mary Jo—so close—so very close—and I noticed the vent."

"Wh-why are you doing this?" I gasped. "What have I ever done to you?"

Geoff's blankly handsome face assumed an expression of perverse indulgence. "You were *born*," he crooned. "My mother slept with that baboon—I heard them sometimes, in the night, and I wished they'd both die. Then I pretended it was only a bad dream. It worked—I could pretend she wasn't letting him touch her. Until you came along, that is. Mary Jo, the living proof."

I started to tell him he was nuts, but since that was clearly established, it would have been redundant. If I was going to survive—and even though my chances weren't great, I fully intended to come out of the experience alive—I couldn't afford to waste my breath stating the obvious.

"Married people sleep together," I said carefully. "They have babies."

I tried to sit up and, to my surprise, he let me.

Geoff got out to his feet, covered in dust bunnies. He reached down, caught me by my sore arm, and yanked me upright.

"Not my mother," he said, spitting the words into my face.

I decided to push him a little. It was an instinctual thing, not even a distant cousin to common sense. "You were there that night, in the trailer. The night of the murders. You didn't try to stop Barbara—you were in on the whole thing."

Geoff smiled at the memory. From his expression, he might have been recalling a family picnic, or an especially good Christmas, instead of the savage slaying of his mother and stepfather.

"You didn't do it just for money—did you?"

His face changed, in an instant, to that of a hard-eyed, soulless predator, closing in on its prey. "Mom was going to send me away to some school," he said. "She *called* it a school, but it was really a hospital. A place where they could help 'boys like me.' That's what she said. 'Boys like you.' Like I was some kind of freak."

He'd shot a four-year-old's cat with a bow and arrow, and God knew what else he'd done, before and since. *Mom* had known, though. She'd probably had a list of atrocities running mercilessly through her head, things she'd tried to ignore, or explain away, and finally had to face. She'd thought the situation was serious enough that her son needed help.

"The hospital would have been better than prison, Geoff."

"Prison," Geoff rasped. "Do you know what Barbara paid me for going to that hellhole? Twenty-five thousand dollars. I was a kid. It sounded like *so much money*."

"Why didn't you tell the police—or someone—what really happened?"

He grabbed my hair, on either side, and gave my hair a hard pull. The pain made my sinuses burn. "I told a counselor once, on the inside. I told him what they were doing to me in that place. And he laughed at me, Mary Jo. *He laughed.* After that, I didn't tell anybody anything!"

I closed my eyes, took a breath, girded myself to look into his face again. It was like being nose-to-nose with the devil.

"You look like her, you know. Mom, I mean," Geoff mused.

I swallowed. "But I'm not Mom, Geoff," I said, very quietly and very carefully. "I'm Mary Jo Mayhugh. I'm your half sister. And I never did anything to you."

Geoff raised one eyebrow. "How shall I kill you?" he asked, in a tone more suited to someone reading a menu, deciding what to have for dinner. Red wine, or white? Fries, or mashed potatoes?

Bludgeoning, or strangling?

Decisions, decisions.

"First tell me why you killed Lillian," I said.

He smiled again, and it was more terrible than I would ever have believed a smile could be. "Because she was old and sick and ugly. Because I *could*."

"How many others have there been?" I pressed.

He shrugged, spreading his hands. "Who knows?" he asked merrily. "It's a rush, killing somebody. I like it."

It's a rush.

I like it.

"Especially when it hurts a lot," he added. "I like that best of all."

I must have paled. The truth is, I wasn't all that scared of death itself, because I knew there was something beyond it. Nick and Chester were proof of that. On the other hand, I was *really* scared of the *way* I might die.

Trapped in a burning car, for instance.

The victim of some painful, incurable disease.

I stopped there, because I knew I was standing on the precipice of something a lot worse than either of those things.

"How many times did you visit Lillian before you killed her?"

"Once, twice, three times. I wanted her to be scared."

Suddenly, in one flashing instant, I understood the three Tarot cards Lillian had given me that day in the nursing home. I gave myself a mental slap on the forehead; everything I'd read in *The Damn Fools Guide to Tarot* suddenly jelled.

The Queen of Pentacles. Pentacles meant money, and worldly success, among other things, and of course the queen indicated a woman in midlife or later.

Barbara Larimer.

Lillian had been afraid of my uncle, too. I remembered her reaction that day, when he showed up at the nursing home.

Hope stirred in me. Maybe Lillian *hadn't* believed I was guilty.

Maybe she'd been trying to protect me from deadly relatives.

It was possible that Mom had confided in her, way back when, about Clive's drug-running operation.

Then there was the Page of Cups. A young man, standing on the shore, pondering a chalice with a fish flopped inside. Cups usually deal with human emotion—in this case, the distorted emotions of a maniac. Geoff had gone to prison in California—Lillian had loved the beaches there—and she would have remembered him as a sixteen-year-old.

She'd been trying to warn me about Geoff. And trying to save herself, because by the time she gave me those cards, he'd visited her at least once.

As for the third card, Death—well, that was a no-brainer.

Lillian had wanted me to know that both our lives were in danger.

"Oh, Lillian," I said softly. "Lillian."

"Shut up!" Geoff shouted, and backhanded me so suddenly and with such force that I crashed into the wall next to the bathroom door. I tasted blood on my lower lip.

I watched, sick with dread, as my brother pulled a roll of duct tape from the pocket of his dusty coat. Next came a brand-new box cutter, still in the blister pack.

I began to get some idea of his specific plans for me, and I bolted for the door, screaming. I made it as far as the living room.

Geoff was right behind me, and he caught me hard by the back of my hair and hurled me down again, all the way to the floor. This time, I fell so hard, I couldn't catch my breath.

I knew when I did, I'd have no problem screaming again.

No problem at all.

But who was going to hear me?

Bad-Ass Bert's was closed until further notice, and therefore empty.

My sisters were dealing with an "incident."

Tucker was busy searching for his daughter's lost classmate.

I was totally screwed.

I got to my hands and knees, tried to scramble away, launch myself onto my feet.

But Geoff slammed me back to the floor again, even harder than before, and I struck my head. Saw stars. The drive-through hamburger I'd eaten on the way out of

Cactus Bend hit the back of my throat in a glob. I was on my stomach now, and Geoff pulled my wrists together behind my back. I heard the sound of tape peeling off the roll.

My heart hammered.

And then I saw shoes.

Nick's shoes.

Like he was going to be of any help, I thought. I was the only one who could see him.

I turned my head, looked up at my ex-husband's ghost.

"Not to worry," he said.

Not to worry?

I was alone with a psychopath who intended to swathe me in duct tape and cut me up—slowly—with a box cutter. And I wasn't supposed to worry?

Geoff shoved me onto my side.

I stared up at Nick. He'd probably come to escort me to the train station, but the time before my ticket got punched could be a real bitch to get through. At the moment, I was a candidate for a segment on *Forensic Files*. I'd be the one with the chalk outline drawn around her mutilated body.

The rest of the room receded. All I saw was Nick, standing there in his dapper burial suit, raising both hands like claws and making a face.

Geoff must have seen something entirely different, because he let out a bloodcurdling shriek and dropped to his knees.

I screamed too—I guess it was pent-up fear, or maybe I was just getting into the spirit of the thing.

Nick stepped over me, still doing the Frankenstein bit.

If it hadn't been for the predicament I was in, I would have thought it was funny. I mean, it was the kind of thing you do when you're a kid, playing monster in the backyard.

Geoff screamed again, from some primal, subhuman place inside himself, and rocked on his knees, covering his head with both hands.

"This is ridiculous," I said.

"Don't break my concentration," Nick replied.

The outside door crashed against the wall.

Geoff didn't even seem to hear it. He was still screaming.

"The boyfriend's here," Nick said, with a little sigh.

Tucker boiled into the room like muddy floodwaters taking out a levee. He slammed Geoff's face to the floor, jammed a knee in the middle of his back and handcuffed him, all in one long, fluid motion.

I gotta say, I was impressed.

You didn't learn stuff like *that* in a *Damn Fool's Guide.*

"How did you know?" I asked.

Tucker pulled the duct tape off my wrists. It stung, but it was the kind of pain that calls for celebration. It was *I-am-alive* pain. "I heard you scream," he said.

"Your hero," said Nick, folding his arms.

"You're a hero, too," I told him, and I meant it.

"Is he here again?" Tucker wanted to know. "Your dead ex-husband?"

He still had his knee in Geoff's back, and my brother the serial killer was sobbing now, like a terrified kid.

"Yes," I said. Apparently, I had seen one Nick, but Geoff had seen entirely another. And just as Chester had used up his vital forces to save me from Heather, Nick had spent some serious ghost-juice putting on enough of a horror show to scare a homicidal maniac into blithering submission. "He's here." I paused, and my voice got small. "But not for long, right, Nick?"

"Right," he said softly.

Tears filled my eyes. "Thanks," I said.

He gave a little salute. I thought he'd say something corny, like, "I've got a train to catch," but he didn't.

He simply disappeared.

And I knew I would never see him again.

"I forgive you," I whispered.

Tucker was on his cell phone, calling the cops, but he rubbed my back with one hand while he spoke. Geoff turned his head and lay there, staring at me with a blank focus that froze my blood.

"Mess with me," I said, "and see where it gets you."

CHAPTER 20

J olie and Greer arrived at the apartment at the same time as Andy Crowley and the usual crew of uniforms and crime scene techs. Greer had a fresh cast on her left arm, and deep shadows lay like swipes of soot under her haunted eyes.

I gasped. Forgot, for the moment, how close I'd come to being dissected on my living room floor.

"Did Alex do that?" I demanded, pointing at Greer's cast.

She bit her lower lip, shook her head and stared at Geoff, lying inert on the floor, handcuffed. Her mouth moved, but she seemed to have lost the use of her vocal chords.

I could identify.

"Christ," Jolie whispered.

"Far from it," I replied.

"What happened this time?" Crowley wanted to know.

I glanced at Tucker, hoping he'd explain, but it wasn't his story to tell, it was mine.

I started with the coffee, and how I got sleepy after drinking it.

Crowley dispatched one of the crime scene techs to collect my java supply, along with the things I'd stirred in.

I told the gathering how I'd awakened, put my feet on the floor and been grabbed around the ankles.

A tic moved under Crowley's right eye. He'd been a kid once, unlikely as it seemed, and probably remembered his own version of the old monster-hiding-under-the-bed routine. Or maybe he was just impatient, wanting me to get on with it.

I related the rest of the tale, leaving out the part about Nick.

Two officers hoisted Geoff to his feet and ushered him out of my apartment, none too soon as far as I was concerned.

Everyone watched him go but Tucker and me; we were looking at each other.

"There's a hole under your bed?" Jolie said, breaking the difficult silence.

For a moment, I was confused. How had she known that?

I'd included the detail in my horror story, of course.

I nodded numbly.

We all trooped into the bedroom, and Tucker and a couple of the cops pushed the bed to one side. Sure enough, the vent I'd never known was there, gaped in the floor. It was two feet square, obviously big enough for a full-grown man to climb through, a straight shot to Bert's prized Tombstone bar.

There's a way into your apartment.

I don't need a key.

"You'll want to plug that right up," one of the younger cops said, sagely chipper.

"No shit, Sherlock," Jolie replied.

I gave her a look. *The police are our friends.*

Her eyes were round with residual fear as the gravity of what I'd so narrowly escaped dawned on her.

"You have *definitely* gotta move," she said. "Soon."

I made one of those decisions that just pop into a person's brain and right out of their mouth, unpremeditated and fully formed. "I'm going to use this place as an office," I announced, "and reopen the bar as soon as I can score a liquor license."

"You're going to run a bar?" Greer asked.

"An office for what?" Jolie said, at the same time.

I sorted the jumble of words into two sensible sentences.

A look passed between Tucker and me.

"Yes, Greer," I said, "I'm going to open a bar. I'll call it 'Mojo's.' And I'll need an office for Sheepshanks, Sheepshanks and Sheepshanks."

"Sheepshanks—?" Crowley began.

"Don't ask," Tucker counseled.

"I like it," Jolie beamed.

"You're both nuts," Greer said. "Mojo, you're coming to live with me. You can stay in the guesthouse until you find something decent."

"Alex would love that," I pointed out.

I was hoping Tucker would jump in and invite me to shack up, which was crazy, because if he had, I'd have refused. It was too early for that, and things were still too complicated between us.

He didn't offer, so it was a moot point.

And it only hurt a little.

"Alex is gone," Greer said woodenly. "He took his things and left."

The guesthouse began to seem like a possibility.

"ANY LUCK finding Gillian?" I asked Tucker, an hour later, when he and I were standing in my kitchen. The cops were gone by then, Crowley included, and Jolie and Greer were in the living room, poking through the boxes Rotika had given me a century before, at Sunset Villa.

Tucker shook his head, leaning against the kitchen counter. "It doesn't look good, babe. Somebody found a ballet slipper a mile from the dance school, in a vacant lot. Gillian's name's written inside."

I moved close, slid my arms around his waist. "Don't give up, Tucker. Maybe she's still—"

Tucker's jaw tightened, but he rested his hands on my hips. "I've got to get back," he said.

I nodded, rested my forehead against his chin for a moment. "Thanks for saving me from the bad guy," I murmured.

"I think I had a little help," he said. He curved an index finger under my chin and lifted, and I looked up at him. Nodded.

"Nick came through in the crunch," I told him.

"You miss him?" Tucker asked gently.

I thought for a moment. "Yeah," I answered.

He kissed the tip of my nose. "That's okay," he said. "You

are going to tell me what really happened, aren't you? When things settle down and we have time to talk?"

I nodded again.

"You'll go home with your sisters? I want you to promise me you will, Mojo, because I'm not going to be able to concentrate if you don't."

"I promise," I said. "But it's only temporary, Tuck. I need my own place."

"Fair enough," he replied. He kissed me again, this time on the lips, and I felt the familiar stir. "Gotta go," he said.

I walked him through the living room, past Jolie and Greer, who were kneeling on the floor, absorbed in what was left of Lillian's life and history. When I came back, sans Tucker, Greer looked up at me and smiled sadly.

"I could really use a cup of tea," she said. "Too bad the police took all your groceries away, in case that maniac poisoned them with something."

I plunked down on the couch. "What happened to your arm, Greer?" I asked. "And when did Alex leave?"

Greer and Jolie exchanged looks.

"Spill it," I said.

"We stopped to buy gas on our way over here," Jolie explained. "I was inside, getting us some coffee, and Greer was at the gas pump. This guy screeches up in an old van and grabs her—tries to throw her into the back of his rig."

I was sitting up straight by then. "Can you describe him, Greer? Did you get a license plate number?"

"I've been over all that with the police," Greer said, her voice thin with remembered fear. "They met Jolie and me at the emergency room. That's why it took us so long to get here." She paused, bit her lower lip. "I've never seen the man before, and the license plate was covered."

"Thank God you got away," I breathed.

"I had some help from Jolie," Greer answered. "She came running out of the convenience store and poured hot coffee down his back. He yelped and let me go. The police are checking hospitals and walk-in clinics for patients with scalds."

"He let her go," Jolie clarified, "but not before he snapped her arm like a chicken bone."

I winced.

"Do you have any idea what the attack was about?" I asked gently. Greer was clearly fragile, and I didn't want to push her too hard. "Was it random?"

Greer shook her head. "I think Alex paid him to kill me," she said. A tear slipped, unnoticed, down her right cheek. "God, Mojo, you can't imagine how scared I was."

"I think she can," Jolie told her quietly. "Her psycho brother was going to filet her like a side of beef, right here in this living room."

Greer's gaze found its way to me, unsteady and a little blank. "Oh," she said. "Yeah."

"We know what happened with Geoff," Jolie said, watching me. "Tell us about last night."

I described my graveyard adventure.

"Why would you go to the cemetery in your bathrobe?" Greer asked, when I'd shared every heart-stopping detail.

"She really does need tea," I told Jolie.

"She needs *whiskey*," Jolie replied.

"I want to go home," Greer said.

Jolie and I nodded. I packed a trash bag, and Jolie and I loaded Lillian's boxes into the back of her Pathfinder while Greer sat in docile silence in the front passenger seat.

"I am really worried about her," Jolie confided, after I'd locked the apartment and joined her in the parking lot. "And not just because of the broken arm."

I nodded. "Do you think the guy with the van was really working for Alex? He's three kinds of a bastard, but I can't imagine him siccing somebody like that on Greer."

"I don't know," Jolie said. "Maybe it was connected to the blackmail."

"Did she tell you anything more about that?"

Jolie shook her head. Looked up at the apartment, and shuddered visibly. "Let's get out of here," she said. "This place gives me the creeps."

"Tell me about it," I replied.

We stopped off at a supermarket on the way back to Greer's and made her go inside with us, so we could run interference if another sicko came out of the woodwork and tried to nab her.

The three of us stocked up on wine, French bread, various cheeses and every other decadent thing we could think of, and then went on to Pennington Palace.

As promised, Alex had vacated the premises.

His car was gone.

Most of his clothes were gone.

His Rolex was gone.

Fine by me.

I stashed my trash bag in the guesthouse, which was half the size of the one at Clive and Barbara Larimer's place, but still equipped with a plasma TV and all the modern kitchen appliances. There was even an alarm system, and I made a mental note to change the code and check under the bed for a hole in the floor.

"We forgot to get coffee," Jolie told me when I entered the kitchen via the patio. Greer was at the table in the breakfast nook, bathed in sunlight. She looked so alone, even with Jolie and me right there.

"I cannot function," I said, "without coffee. I'll go get some, and you look after Greer."

Jolie nodded and handed over her car keys. "Drive carefully," she said. "I'm still making payments."

I grinned. "Careful," I said, "is my middle name."

"Like hell," Jolie retorted, but she was grinning.

I'd picked up two cans of java and all the stuff that makes it palatable, and I was headed back to Greer's when suddenly I got that tingly feeling, and the little hairs stood up on my arms and legs.

Somebody was in the car.

Besides me.

Impossible. Like any good paranoid, I'd checked for stowaways when I put the coffee in the backseat. Thanks to Heather, Geoff and Barbara Larimer, I was in a semipermanent state of mistrust.

Still, the air felt almost electrified.

I risked a glance into the rearview mirror, gasped and bumped off the road, onto the shoulder, coming to a jostling stop. The driver of a blue Escalade honked furiously as he/she/it roared by, narrowly missing my back bumper.

I turned in the seat, my heart pounding.

My passenger was about seven years old.

She wore a tutu, leotard, tights, all pink, and one ballet slipper.

"Gillian?" I asked.

Her gaze sought mine, landed.

Ice formed in my veins.

She nodded.

"Please tell me you're not—"

A tear trickled through the grime smudging her face. I noticed the grass stains on the knees of her tights, the rip in one side of her tutu.

"Can you talk?" I scrabbled for my cell phone, remembered I'd left it at the apartment, plugged into the charger.

Gillian said nothing, but her eyes were round and eloquent, and their message was clear.

Help me.

She was dead.

Tucker and the others hadn't found her in time.

How *could* I help her?

I wanted to climb into the backseat and gather her into my arms, tell her everything would be all right, but I sensed that she didn't want to be touched.

"Nick?" I asked hopefully, looking around the interior of Jolie's Pathfinder.

Nothing. By now, Nick had his ticket. He was onboard the glory train.

I swallowed painfully.

"Honey, can you tell me what you want?"

Her eyes pleaded with me, but she didn't make a sound.

I watched as she faded slowly away.

And then I sat there, beside the road, shaking.

When I felt I could drive again, I drove to the nearest phone.

It was outside a convenience store, and I wondered distractedly if this was the place where Greer had almost been forced into a madman's van.

I fumbled for change, dropped it, gathered it and tried again.

Tucker answered on the second ring. "Darroch," he said.

I started to cry.

"Mojo?"

I sniffled. Got control of myself. "Tucker," I said, "Gillian's dead."

"I know," he answered, his voice hard with anguish and disbelief. "We just found her body half an hour ago. In a ditch alongside a desert road." Pause. "Which begs the question—how did *you* know?"

"I saw her."

"The way you 'saw' your ex-husband?"

I sobbed. "Yes." If he didn't believe me, I didn't know what I was going to do. The burden was too big to carry by myself, and the image of that poor, frightened child, in her ruined ballet clothes and missing a slipper, was seared into my brain, probably for all time and eternity.

"Her stepfather was arrested twenty minutes ago," Tucker said, his voice toneless.

I felt a tug at my arm and looked down.

Gillian stood beside me, a tiny ghost ballerina, her eyes huge with sorrow.

"Did your stepfather do this to you?" I asked.

Slowly, somberly, she shook her head from side to side.

A woman walked by, staring at me. I could understand her horrified interest; she couldn't see Gillian, so from her perspective, I was talking to nobody.

"Tucker," I squeaked.

"What?"

"You've got the wrong man. Gillian says her stepfather wasn't the one to—to hurt her." I swallowed hard. I hadn't chosen this new path or talent or curse or whatever the hell it was; *it* had chosen *me*. And whether I liked it or not, whether *Tucker* liked it or not, I was involved. I knew I couldn't turn my back on a child who needed me, dead or alive.

I had a visual of Tucker running splayed fingers through his hair. "She's actually *there*? Right now?"

"Right here, right now," I said.

Gillian's eyes filled with tears.

Tucker thrust out a sigh. "Listen, Moje, I know you mean well, but you can't be part of this. You're not—official. You don't have a badge *or* a P.I.'s license."

I held out a hand, and Gillian took it. Her grasp felt small and solid and stone-cold. "No," I said, "but I have a heart."

He swore under his breath. "You're not going to back down, are you?"

I squeezed Gillian's hand. "No," I repeated.

I'd just stumbled into my next case.

* * * * *

In December 2006, look for SIERRA'S HOMECOMING, *the first of two* McKETTRICK WOMEN *books from Silhouette Special Edition. And now turn the page for a sneak preview of* McKETTRICK'S LUCK, *the first title in the* McKETTRICK MEN *contemporary romance series available in February 2007 from Harlequin Books*

"Can't this wait until tomorrow?" her mother had asked after coffee at the kitchen table, Cheyenne announced her intention to track down Jesse McKettrick.

With a shake of her head, Cheyenne had said no, gathered her wits, smoothed her skirt and straightened her jacket, and made for the rental car.

McKettrickCo seemed to be the logical place to start her search—she'd already discovered, via her cell phone, that Jesse's number was unlisted.

Cheyenne knew, having grown up in Indian Rock, that the home offices were in San Antonio. The new building housed a branch of the operation, which meant the outfit was in expansion mode. According to her research, McKettrickCo was a diverse corporation, with interests in cutting-edge technology and global investment.

Jesse's name wasn't on the reader board in the sleekly

contemporary reception area, a fact that didn't surprise Cheyenne very much. When she'd known him, he was the original trust-fund bad boy, wild as a mustang and committed to one thing: having a good time.

She approached the desk, relieved that she didn't recognize the woman tapping away at the keyboard of a supercomputer with three large, flat-screen monitors.

"May I help you?" the woman asked pleasantly. She was middle-aged, with a warm smile, a lacquered blond hairdo and elegant posture.

Cheyenne introduced herself, hoping her last name wouldn't ring any bells, and asked how to locate Jesse McKettrick. With luck—and she was due for some of that—she wouldn't have to drive all the way out to his house and confront him on his own turf.

Not that any part of Indian Rock was neutral ground, when it came to the McKettricks.

The receptionist assessed Cheyenne with mild interest. "Jesse could be anywhere," she said, at some length, "but if I had to make a guess, I'd say he's probably in the back room over at Lucky's, playing poker."

Cheyenne sniffed. Of course he'd be at Lucky's—fate wouldn't have it any other way. How many times, as a child, had she sneaked through the back door of that place from the alley and tried to will her father away from a game of five-card stud?

She produced a business card, bearing her name, affiliation with Meerland Real Estate Ventures, Ltd., and her cell number. "Thanks," she said. "Just in case you see Mr.

McKettrick before I do, will you give him my card and ask him to please call me as soon as possible?"

The woman studied Cheyenne's information, frowned and then nodded politely. "He doesn't come in too often," she said.

Of course he didn't.

Still Jesse, after all these years.

Cheyenne left McKettrickCo, got back in her car and drove resolutely to Lucky's Main Street Bar and Grill. The gravel parking lot beside the old brick building was full, with the dinner hour fast approaching, so she parked in the alley, next to a mud-splattered truck with both windows rolled down.

For a moment, she was a kid again, sent by her misguided mother to fetch Daddy home from the bar. She remembered propping her bike against the wall, next to the overflowing trash bin, rehearsing what she'd say once she got inside, forcing herself up the two unpainted steps and through the screened door, which always groaned on its hinges.

When the door suddenly creaked open, Cheyenne was startled. She wrenched herself out of the time warp and actually considered crouching behind the Dumpster until whoever it was had gone.

Jesse stepped out, stretched like a lazy tomcat at home in an alley and fixing to go on the prowl, and adjusted his cowboy hat. He wore old jeans, a western shirt unbuttoned to his collarbone, and even mud and manure couldn't disguise the fact that his boots were expensive, probably custom-made.

When Cheyenne's gaze trailed back up to Jesse's face, she realized that he was looking at her. Grinning that lethal grin.

She blushed.

Someone flipped the porch light on from inside, and moths immediately gravitated to it, out of nowhere. Drawing an immediate parallel between Jesse and the bulb, she took half a step back.

He took in her suit and high-heeled shoes in a lazy sweep of his eyes. He clearly didn't recognize her, which was at once galling and a relief.

He tugged at the brim of his battered hat. "You lost?" he asked.

Cheyenne was a moment catching her breath. "No," she answered, fishing in her hobo bag for another card. "My name is Cheyenne Bridges, and I was hoping to talk to you about a business proposition."

She instantly regretted using the word "proposition," because it made Jesse's mouth quirk with amusement, but she was past the point of no return.

He descended the steps, with that loose-limbed walk she remembered so well, and approached her. Put out his hand. "Jesse McKettrick," he said.

There was nothing to say but "I know." She'd given herself away with the first words she'd spoken.

"Bridges," he said, reflecting.

Cheyenne braced herself inwardly. Glanced toward the screen door Jesse had come through a few moments before.

"Any relation to—?" He paused, stooped slightly to look into her face. Recollection dawned. "Wait a second. *Cheyenne Bridges*." He grinned. "I remember you—Cash's daughter. We went to the movies a couple of times."

She swallowed, nodded, hiked her chin up a notch. "That's right," she said carefully. Cash's daughter, that's who she was to him. A shy teenager he'd dated twice, and then lost interest in. He didn't know, she reminded herself silently, that she'd pinned every picture of him she could get to the wall of her bedroom in that shack out beyond the railroad tracks, the way most girls displayed photos of rock starts and film idols. He didn't know she'd loved him with the kind of desperate, hopeless adoration only a sixteen-year-old can feel.

He didn't know she'd prayed that he'd fall madly in love with her. That she'd imagined their wedding, their honeymoon and the birth of their four children so often that sometimes it felt like a memory of something that had really happened.

Thank God he didn't know any of those things. She wouldn't have been able to face him if he had, even with Mitch and her mom and Nigel all depending on her to persuade him to sell five hundred unspoiled acres of land to her company.

"I heard about your brother's accident," he said. "I'm sorry."

Shaken out of her reverie, Cheyenne nodded again. "Thanks."

"Your dad, too."

Her eyes stung. She tried to speak, swallowed instead.

Jesse smiled, took a loose grip on her elbow. "Do you always do business in alleys?" he teased.

For a moment, she was affronted. Then she realized it was a perfectly reasonable question. "No," she said.

"I was just heading for the Roadhouse to grab some supper. Want to come along?" He gestured toward the muddy truck.

The Roadhouse, also known as Road*kill,* was an institution in Indian Rock, a haven for truck drivers, bikers, cowboys and state patrolmen. Ironically, families dined at Lucky's, probably pretending that the card room behind it didn't exist.

"I'll meet you there," Cheyenne said. She'd have been safe enough with Jesse, but no way she was climbing into that truck in a straight skirt. She had *some* dignity, after all, even if she did feel like the scrawny ten-year-old who'd parked her bike in this alley and gone inside to beg her father, with a stellar lack of success, to come home for supper.

"Okay," Jesse said easily. He walked her to the rental car, which looked nondescript beside his truck. Like his boots, the vehicle had seen its share of action. Like his boots, it was top-of-the-line, with dual tires and an extended cab. Probably leather seats, too, and a CD changer made by Swiss elves.

Once she was behind the wheel of the rental, with the window rolled down, Jesse leaned easily against the door and looked in at her.

"It's good to see you again, Cheyenne," he said.

"You, too," she replied. But a lump rose in her throat. *Don't go there,* she told herself sternly. *This is business. You'll buy the land. You'll help Nigel get the construction project rolling. You'll collect your bonus and take care of*

Mitch and your mother. And then you'll go back to San Diego and forget Jesse McKettrick ever existed.

"As if," she muttered aloud.

Jesse, in the process of turning away to head for his truck, turned back. "Did you say something?"

She gave him her best smile. "See you there," she said.

He waved.

Hoisted himself into the truck and fired up the engine.

Cheyenne waited until he pulled out, and then followed.

If she'd been as smart as other people thought she was, she reflected, she'd have kept on going. Sped right out of Indian Rock, past the Roadhouse, past Jesse and all the other memories and impossible dreams, and never looked back.